The Blue Door

ALSO BY DAVID FULMER

The Dying Crapshooter's Blues

Rampart Street

Jass

Chasing the Devil's Tail

THE BLUE DOOR

DAVID FULMER

HARCOURT, INC.
ORLANDO AUSTIN NEW YORK SAN DIEGO LONDON

www.HarcourtBooks.com

Library of Congress Cataloging-in-Publication Data
Fulmer, David.
The blue door/David Fulmer.
p. cm.
1. Private investigators—Fiction. 2. Singers—Crimes against—Fiction.
3. Philadelphia (Pa.)—Fiction. 4. Musical fiction. I. Title.
PS3606.U56B57 2008
813'.6—dc22 2007019423
ISBN 978-0-15-101181-0

Text set in Sabon
Designed by Cathy Riggs

Printed in the United States of America

First edition

A C E G I K J H F D B

For the true members of the Giambroni and Prizzi families, larger heroes than I could ever create.

And in particular to my mother, Flora Prizzi Fulmer; my father, Thurston Fulmer, who long ago earned an honorary vowel on the end of his name; and my sister, Karen Mertz, who is the bravest of us all.

It is my honor to be the blood of their blood.

I want to hit him, step away,
and watch him hurt. I want his heart.

—Joe Frazier

The Blue Door

ONE

At ten thirty on the night of March 21, 1962, Eddie Cero walked out the back door of the Southside Boxing Club in Philadelphia with a bloody bandage over his eyebrow and forty dollars cash in his pocket.

The cut hadn't hurt when it opened. Now it was throbbing, and all he wanted was to go somewhere and have a drink to kill the pain and another one to toast what looked like the end of his life as a welterweight.

He didn't want to see anybody and he didn't want anyone seeing him, so he cut down the alley behind the club, zipping his jacket against the night's chill. Fifty feet away from the East Allen traffic, he heard someone grunt and another voice curse, and he glanced into a doorway to see two punks roughing up a third man, who looked to be getting the better of it. He walked by with no intention of meddling in their business. Then one of the punks turned around and said, "What the fuck are you lookin' at?" in the wrong tone. Eddie stopped.

A face as thin and pitted as a crescent moon glared from the shadows. "I said, motherfucker, what the *fuck* are you lookin' at?"

The partner, a chubby greaseball in a motorcycle jacket that was two sizes too small, turned like a fat lizard to put his two cents in. "Take a hike, asshole."

The poor chump in the middle let out a strangled gasp. Eddie stayed where he was.

"Whaddya, fuckin' deaf?" The moon-faced punk came stalking out in a rude ballet set to the click and flash of a blade. He had taken three steps when it dawned on him that the interloper hadn't cut and run. By then it was too late, because Eddie had one coming, a quick right to the jaw. The punk went down as if a trapdoor had opened under his shoes. The switchblade skittered across the bricks.

"Whoa, fuckin' A," said the fat boy.

Staring up at the night sky with glazed eyes, the pimpled punk moaned and twitched a couple times.

Eddie rubbed his knuckles. "You better get him out of here."

The fat boy let go of their prey and edged into the alley. He bent down, wrestled his partner under the arms, and dragged him off in the direction of Ninth Street. Once he got a little distance, he looked back over his shoulder and said, "We'll see ya 'round, Sal."

The guy named Sal slumped against the doorframe. "Yeah, yeah, same to ya." His voice was a weary croak.

Eddie walked over to have a look at the victim, a middle-aged guy, Italian. His lower lip was swollen, his left eye was puffing up all purple, and there was fresh blood dribbling out of one nostril. He looked like an empty sack of nothing, as if the beating in an alley was just the last insult in what had been a bad day all around. He weaved on his feet, trying to straighten his tie with one hand and brush the dirt from his sport coat with the other.

"Jesus Christ," he said. "That was a hell of a smack you gave him." He peered at Eddie with his good eye, then pointed a stubby finger. "Hey, I know you. You're a fighter, right?"

"Yeah, that's right," Eddie said shortly. "You going to be okay?" He started moving away.

"Hey, wait a minute." Sal ambled woozily after him. "Hey, let me buy you a drink. How about it?"

"That's all right."

"C'mon, you saved my ass here."

Eddie said, "It was nothin'. You were doing okay."

"I wanna buy you a drink, goddamnit!"

Eddie sighed. He didn't feel up to arguing. "All right. One drink. But you don't owe me, okay?"

"Yeah, yeah, okay," Sal said. "I don't owe you. God forbid. So what's that name again, tough guy?"

"Eddie Cero."

"That's right. I remember. Like zero with a C, right?"

"Yeah, that's right."

"Salvatore Giambroni." He offered a thick meatball of a hand. "Sal."

On a good night, Eddie would have gone to Barney's on Frankford Avenue, but he didn't want to meet up with that crowd, so he headed two blocks up to the Corner Bar & Grill on Richmond, where hardly anyone knew him. Plus they had a better jukebox. Sal shuffled along, one hand dabbing his bloody nose with a handkerchief, while he probed his battered eye with the fingers of the other and muttered under his breath.

Eddie held the door for him, and they stepped into a long, narrow room of black and gray shadows punctuated by rainbow-colored beer signs and, at the far end, the amber glow of the jukebox. Shapes huddled against the bar and around the tables. The few people who were talking kept their voices low. It was that kind of joint.

Eddie headed directly for the booth in the far corner. Sal stopped at the bar and ordered two shots and two bottles of

Schmidt's. He brought the drinks to the table, sat down, and let out a noisy sigh.

"Here's to ya, kid." He clinked Eddie's glass and downed his whiskey in one gulp. Piece by piece, he pulled himself together. His back straightened, his good eye widened, and he flexed his sore jaw.

"Yeah, that's more like it." He grinned. "Hey, how about me and you? You got a bad eye; I got a bad eye—how about it, eh?"

In the dim, dirty light, Eddie got his first good look at Sal and saw a dago who had obviously been around the block and then some. They were about the same height, but Sal had at least forty pounds on him. His round face was pockmarked bronze and boasted an angled hunk of a Calabrese nose, all under a mat of dark brown hair that swept this way and that in Brylcreemed waves. The eyes—actually, the eye Eddie could see—was as black as an olive and had a merry glint to it, despite the condition of the rest of the face. All in all, Eddie thought he looked like Louis Prima minus a couple inches and plus a couple pounds.

"So what happened to you?" Sal Giambroni asked, as if he had a right to know. "You have a fight tonight?"

"Yeah."

"Who won?"

"The other guy."

"What other guy?"

"T-Bone Mieux."

"Oh, yeah, I've seen him," Sal said. "He's decent."

"He's a fucking cheap-shot punk," Eddie said.

Sal gave him a quizzical look and leaned over the table as if divulging a secret. "So, you wanna know what that was about? I mean in the alley there."

Eddie said, "It's none of—"

"I poked my nose into the wrong hole."

Eddie took a tiny sip of his whiskey, then a small sip of his beer. He was going to hear about it whether he wanted to or not.

"I'm a private detective," Sal said. "An investigator. Of private matters, all right? This one particular party doesn't care for my modus operandi and sent those punks to teach me a lesson."

"Did they?"

Sal sat back. "Nah, that was nothing. Once I had this *cafone* try to run me over with his car. Another time a guy tried to push me out a window. Twelfth floor. I saw the gates of heaven, it was that close." He spread his hands, palms upward. "These things happen. What you call your occupational hazards."

"Maybe you should get another occupation."

"Yeah, look who's talkin'," Sal retorted. Eddie shot him a hard glance, and Sal said, "Hey, that'll heal, right? So when's your next fight? Maybe I'll come, y'know, see you in action."

"I don't have one."

Sal gestured at the bandage. " 'Cause of that?"

Eddie drummed absent fingers. "I think I might stop for a little while. Do something else."

"Yeah? Like what?"

"Like, I don't know right now."

The older man drank off his beer and placed the empty bottle on the table, along with a five-dollar bill. "Hey, how about you go get us another round," he said. "I got something I want to talk to you about."

Though Eddie couldn't imagine what Sal Giambroni wanted to talk to him about and was sure he didn't care, he got up to fetch the drinks. He asked the bartender to wrap some ice, too. While he waited, he stepped over to the jukebox, dropped in a quarter, and picked out five plays. An oily Dean Martin gave way to a gritty Irma Thomas. It never failed; right away he felt better.

Sal accepted the balled towel with a grateful nod, planted it over his swollen eye, and waited for Eddie to get settled. Then he said, "The deal is I need somebody to help out with some things."

"What things?" Eddie said.

"Cases and so forth," Sal said. "Mostly surveillance, occasionally somebody to be a physical presence, et cetera, et cetera. Nothin' you couldn't handle. I wouldn't pay you a salary. It would be on a case-by-case basis. Which means cash in your hand pretty much every day."

Eddie sat back. "I wouldn't be interested in anything like that. Thanks for the offer, though."

The brow over Sal's unswollen eye arched. "Oh, no? You ain't going to fight, so what are you going to do?" He drew himself up, trying to look dignified. "You work for me, you don't have to break your ass, and once in a while something interesting happens."

"What, like getting run over by a car? Or pushed out a window? Or worked over in an alley?"

Sal made a shooing motion. "These things occur now and then. Don't worry about it. Hey, c'mon, who's going to fuck with you?" He grinned and hunched over in a fighter's crouch, his fists bobbing like meaty pistons. "Middleweight, right?"

"Welter," Eddie said.

Sal kept talking and he kept shaking his head, and they both kept drinking. The party moved to a club on Seventh Street called the Blue Door. They walked in just in time to catch the last heartfelt throbs of a blues song and then see a slip of motion as the singer turned and left the stage to a round of applause.

The house music came up amid a swirl of curling smoke, painted lips, and the blush of cleavages, as glass tinked and women laughed all sultry and wicked, a kind of jagged jazz all on its own.

In the backstage closet that served as a dressing room, the singer dabbed the sweat from her brow with a ragged towel and studied her reflection in the cracked mirror. Her throat was aching just a little, the way it always did by the middle of the evening. Once she got her second wind, she could go all night. She could keep on singing as if there was no tomorrow and wash everything away: the smoke, the faces, the rude chatter, and the hard memories of what had brought her to this place.

She picked up the cigarette that was burning in the ashtray, stood up, and made her way to the side of the stage, where she could watch the room without being seen.

It was late and the crowd was thinning, mostly stragglers and those few kind souls who had come just to listen to her. Then she saw an odd pair, a thickset man who flailed his arms as he was talking and a younger partner who was listening to him, or pretending to. The younger one stood still amid the noise and motion, cutting a figure in his poise and silence that was just a little dangerous. His eyes shifted and for a moment seemed to fix on her, causing her to take a step away, even though she knew he couldn't see her in the shadows.

She scanned the rest of the crowd, saw no one to draw her interest, and slipped back to the dressing room to rest. Late as it was, she still had two shows to go.

They went on swilling drinks, Sal kept yakking, and somewhere along the line, Eddie heard himself agreeing to report on Monday to "SG Confidential Investigations," as it said on the card. That's how it started.

TWO

Eddie lived in a dingy brick boardinghouse on Eleventh Street just off Catherine in South Philadelphia. His room was a box at the end of the hall on the second floor that contained an iron bed frame with a mattress that sagged on one side and was full of lumps on the other, a night table, chest of drawers, and lone chair, all standard hotel issue. A grimy window looked out on a narrow side alley, where old cars sat rusting and dirty kids sometimes played. The radiator clanked with feeble heat in the winter, and in the summertime the place was an oven. His private joke was he liked it because it reminded him of home.

He woke up Sunday morning to an icy drizzle, a last angry gasp of winter that had veiled everything beyond the windowpanes in a cold gray mist. He lay still for a long time, thinking about the fight, then rolled out from under the blanket. As soon as he sat up, he realized that along with the cut he was going to be nursing a hangover. After the Blue Door, he had wandered out onto Seventh Street and back to the Corner Bar & Grill, where he sat alone, drinking shots, washing them down with beer, and getting up to put more quarters in the jukebox. He hadn't done anything like that in a long time, and now he was paying for it.

He pulled on his sweats and a pair of heavy socks and went looking for some aspirin. As he dug through his pants pockets, he came across a business card, now bent and frayed, and recalled that he had agreed to go work for Sal Giambroni, a private detective. In the light of day it sounded dumber than it had the first time, and he tried to remember why he'd gone along with it. Whatever the reason, he decided that as soon as he felt half human, he'd use the phone in the foyer to call the gumshoe and explain that he'd made a mistake. Except it was Sunday, so it would have to wait until tomorrow. Fine; he would travel to the address on Sansom Street and deliver the news face-to-face. It was the least he could do; the guy had offered him a job.

And he was thinking that maybe his fight career wasn't over. The cut would heal; they always did. A couple weeks, a month at the most, then two or three club bouts, and he'd be back at it. So what if that prick Benny didn't want to work with him? There were other trainers, and if not in Philly, then in Baltimore, Newark, even New York. A guy who was willing to give or take a pounding could always make a buck. He might even find someone who gave a shit enough to help him hone his skills and work around his weaknesses, so that he could take some decent bouts and make some decent dough for once. When he thought about it that way, things didn't seem so bad.

He put his jacket on over his sweats and walked through the cold rain to the corner store on Tenth, where he picked up the Sunday *Inquirer* and a coffee to go. When he got back to his room, he sat on the bed and studied the Sports section until he found the write-ups of the previous night's fights. About halfway down the column, he was informed that Thibodeaux "T-Bone" Mieux (10-6-1) had been "impressive" in stopping "Fast Eddie" Cero (18-8-2) in four rounds.

Eddie felt a twist in his gut. The reporter probably hadn't even been there, or he would have seen Fast Eddie playing out his fight plan, which was to let his opponent potshot him for two or three rounds, long enough for the guy to get brave, then lower the boom. It had been working. Mieux had come in with his head because, after three rounds of having his way, he was suddenly eating jabs and hard hooks, and he knew it was the only way he'd get out of there on his feet. The Creole wasn't about to let the same guinea pug beat him a third time. Nobody was paying attention, so no one saw the butt, and Mieux got himself an "impressive" win.

It didn't matter that it was intentional. It didn't matter that every fighter in Philly knew Mieux was a cheap-shot artist. What mattered was that it had opened the scar tissue over Eddie's left eye in a bloody spout that no amount of styptic could stanch. What mattered was that the ref called it as a punch and gave Mieux a TKO. What mattered was that it was the fourth time he had been stopped on a cut, and when they got to the dressing room, Benny announced that he wasn't going to hang around until he caught the one that blinded him. And that was that.

Eddie thought for a moment about throwing the newspaper in the trash. Then he saw the item from New York about Benny "Kid" Paret being carried out of the ring at Madison Square Garden on a stretcher, beaten unconscious by Emile Griffith after twelve terrible rounds. It gave him a spooky feeling and brought a memory of the night he fought Willie Allred. He folded the section carefully, got off the bed, and stuck it in the bottom drawer of the dresser, under the shoe box where he kept his clippings.

He went down the hall to the bathroom, where he pulled the string on the bare bulb and surveyed the damage.

Nobody'd ever call Eddie Cero a movie star, though it wasn't a bad face, either. Especially for one that had weathered twenty-eight fights. Your standard-issue southern Italian, oval and olive, full around the mouth, with black, hooded eyes. His brown hair was cut short, because it went wild if he let it grow. So far nothing had been broken. The only thing off was the way his nose was pushed in on the one side, about halfway up. That and the mangled flesh over his left eye.

He reached up and peeled away the bandage with his fingertips. It didn't look good, a thin, angry gash that started on the edge of his brow and curved down around his eye socket, the raw red startling against his olive skin. Fucking Benny should have sent him for stitches, but it was too late now. So he'd have a scar on the scar. He could live with that. No more than a month to heal, and he could get back at it. Except for the cut, Mieux hadn't done any damage. He wasn't even sore. He left the bandage off to give the wound some air.

He turned out the light and went back down the hall to his room. The house was quiet, the other tenants either at church or sleeping off their Saturday-night drunks. He boiled water for more coffee and carried his cup to the window. Looking out at the freezing rain, he wondered if he was kidding himself about getting back in the ring. Though he was fairly quick for a white guy, he couldn't bang with the real knockout artists; and he had an annoying tendency to bleed like a stuck pig whenever he took a shot (or a butt) from a certain angle. And there wasn't a trainer on earth who could fix that.

Even if he was done, it didn't mean he had to take up with some snoop for hire. There was something creepy about it, following people around, pushing your nose into private business, listening in on secrets. Creepy and definitely not for Eddie Cero. It brought to mind the cheesy advertisements in the back of comic books: BE A PRIVATE DETECTIVE!!! They always came with a coupon to be clipped and sent off to an address in Chicago.

He didn't know what he was going to do, and he didn't want to think about it anymore, so he busied himself making his bed. He could worry about all of it tomorrow.

It was his habit to spend his Sundays quietly, especially the morning after a fight. First he'd read the paper. Then he'd go across the street for a breakfast with two cups of coffee. After which he'd come back to his room and spend the better part of the day shuffling through the collection of 45s he kept in boxes under his bed, placing his selections one by one on the spindle of his Airline record player. After that he'd get some dinner and go to sleep early.

The record collection was the only thing of value that he owned. Starting when he was fourteen, he had gathered the discs with the fussy care of a curator and now owned some impossibly rare items, doo-wop and jump blues and rockabilly by artists who were long gone or forgotten. The records were even a treat for the eye, sporting a rainbow of labels from Apt, Rayna, Red Boy, Specialty, Excello, and dozens of others. He had four Elvis Presleys, all on Sun, and a much rarer John D. Loudermilk on that same label. Three versions of "Gloria," including the hit by the Cadillacs, and the no less turgid rendition by Vito and the Salutations. He also had two versions of "Eddie My Love," and in his studied opinion, the Teen Queens' surpassed the Chantels'. Though the latter group's "Look in My Eyes" made him think of a choir singing.

He also owned most of the 45s from Cameo-Parkway, Philadelphia's hometown label, each one of them recorded in a little building on Locust Street, a mile and some change from his door. He'd been over that way and thought about knocking on the door. The building looked so ordinary that he was sure it was the wrong place and never got around to going in.

When he was a kid, he had daydreamed about being a musician, but it didn't happen. Now there was no way. He was too old to start, and his knuckles were swollen all the time and too banged up to handle an instrument. He really loved his music, though, and the record store was one of the few places he spent money, when he had any to spend.

There was a time when he went to the rock-and-roll jamborees that shook the walls at the Regal and the Paramount and the revues on Steel Pier and saw wild men in luminous suits gyrate across the stage, screaming like banshees, doing splits and spins, their processed pompadours slashing the air, as the drums, guitars, and pianos and the screams of the girls ripped and roared and soared around them. He'd seen some great shows. He finally stopped going because he felt like the oldest person in the room.

It was just as well. Things had changed. Most of the bright lights were missing in action or dead, and the airwaves were filled with fluff sung by pretty boys and cute girls chosen for their dimples, hit today and gone tomorrow. Soon, he guessed, there'd be nothing but the kind of mush anyone's parents would enjoy. Unless someone came along to save it, rock and roll would be dead.

Still, Eddie could find decent jukeboxes all up and down South Street, he had long ago located the best record store in the city, and knew where on the dial to find the holdout radio stations.

He never turned the volume up loud enough for anyone else to hear and instead sat with his head bent to the tinny speaker of the record player or the radio, drinking in every note, feeling an anguished lyric float up like smoke or a driving rhythm jump-start his heart. No matter what, it always made him feel better.

For some reason on this cold, gray day, he wasn't up to it, and instead of dragging the boxes from under the bed, he leaned over the night table, turned on the radio, and twiddled the knob until he found WTDF, the little station out of North Philly.

Early one Sunday morning a year after he had moved to the city, he turned on the radio and thought he'd discovered some new rock-and-roll station. Listening closer, he realized they were shouting wild praises to Jesus, with the help of rollicking piano, drums, and guitar. The station played impassioned gospel on Sunday mornings and then switched over to the devil's music for the rest of the day. It was a lesson in music history, and definitely his kind of fare.

He went down the hall to refill his pan with water, then spent what was left of the morning drinking coffee, listening to the radio, reading the newspaper, and watching the cold rain. Late in the afternoon he opened a can of soup, warmed it on the hot plate, and ate out of the pan. And that was Sunday.

THREE

He was up Monday morning in time to catch the buses that would get him to Sansom Street. He didn't want the guy to think he was passing on the job because he was a bum or, worse, a dumb pug, so instead of his usual blue jeans and T-shirt, he wore one of his two long-sleeved sport shirts and a pair of khakis. Though the rain was gone, it was still chilly, so he pulled on the brown suede jacket he'd owned since high school.

On his way over to Lombard, he stopped at the corner of South Street to gaze down the waking thoroughfare and muse about packing up and heading somewhere new. He had made up his mind to leave before, more than once, but never quite got around to it. The truth was he loved the place.

He didn't know it the way the old-timers did, of course; South Philly was a city unto itself, a community with roots that were as deep as Philadelphia proper. It had always been a different place, an interesting, sometimes volatile mix of people and geography. It had its own odd history.

South Street was the main drag, a narrow avenue that because of its vibrant life registered as a broad boulevard, especially at night. It ran from the Delaware to the Schuylkill like an electric backbone of stores, restaurants, and clubs.

Deeper into the streets of South Philly, the row houses and the storefronts, whether bright and tidy or shabby and rundown, seemed to be connected under one dirty city sky. Sometimes the sidewalks fairly vibrated with kids playing shrieking games, old people shouting back and forth as if everyone was deaf, and the more general din of the workday.

South Philly still kept a foot planted in the Old World, wherever that happened to be, with voodoo charms, black Madonnas, and Italian women who gravely cast the *malocchio*.

It was also true that a long-running current of crime trickled in the background. There were winks and whispers about gambling, dope, hookers, and heists as hoods strutted in olive oil operettas. Every now and then, a bullet-riddled body would turn up in the trunk of a car. More often a certain party would simply not be around anymore. It was part of the larger drama.

Along with these sights, Eddie enjoyed the smell of the place, the aromas of meats and baked goods and special dishes cooking, cheesesteaks, kugel, manicotti and fatback gravy, and all the other primitive scents of different tribes thrown together in one small place.

More than anything else, he reveled in the disjointed symphony of the streets. At the bottom was the grind of cars, buses, and trucks, and the rude noise of jackhammers and steam shovels at work. Then came the voices: people laughing, fighting, and praying out loud, in a dozen tongues. On top, as a joyous crown, was the music. From one street to the next, it was rock and roll and rhythm and blues, polkas and waltzes, nightclub croons and gospel, an Italian block to an Irish block to a Negro block, and on and on, each contributing to the grand work.

Eddie always felt that the heart of the city beat the loudest in South Philly, and he couldn't imagine leaving it behind. The question was what he would do if he stayed, other than working for a run-down sack of a private snoop.

He found the old brick building a couple blocks past Rittenhouse Square and climbed narrow steps over a store with a yellowed window that displayed a dusty arrangement of crutches, wheelchairs, and other medical supplies. The office displayed SG CONFIDENTIAL INVESTIGATIONS in paint-chipped letters on the door. Eddie was ready with a short speech he had prepared while he shaved and then practiced on the bus: *Thanks, but no thanks. Not my cup of tea. Good luck to you.*

He never got a chance to deliver it. As soon as he stepped into the tiny reception area, Sal yelled: "Cero! There you are!" and appeared in the doorway to the office in back, waving a photograph, a folded sheet of paper, and a set of car keys, all of which he shoved into Eddie's hands.

"I need you to sit on this clown. Name's Stollman. He's the boss at this plant down off Passyunk. Keystone Valve. Take my car—it's in the lot around back. Blue '56 Chevy four-door. He probably won't go anywhere before lunch, but I still need you there. Just follow him, don't let him see you, and call me when he gets back to his office."

Eddie opened his mouth to protest as Sal shooed him out the door. "Go, all right? It's twenty bucks for sitting on your ass. *Go!*"

The mention of the money did it. Eddie went.

The car was parked around back, a battered, baby-blue four-door Bel Air. He took Passyunk south to the address on an industrial side street off Eastwick Avenue. Keystone Valve seemed to be a decent place, a two-story building with a brick facade, a tidy paved parking lot in front, and a larger gravel lot around the side. The real work got done in a machine shop that was attached to the back and took up a good part of a quarter block. Eddie wondered if they needed help on the dock.

He parked across the street and spent a few minutes recollecting how he had landed there. Presently, the scene in the Blue Door came back to him. Along with the drinks he'd been caught up in the moment, the shadows and echoes in the room, the glimpse of a lovely singer disappearing into the offstage darkness, like a page out of a mystery novel.

In the light of day, he understood that it was the twenty bucks that changed his mind, at least for the moment. It was half what he pulled down for an eight-rounder, and he could always use that kind of money. Telling Sal Giambroni that he wasn't interested in a job could wait.

To pass the time, he studied the photograph and listened to the radio. He didn't like sitting still and wanted to get out, but he thought a guy wandering around the street might look strange. And what if the man he was supposed to be watching—this Stollman character—looked out the window and saw him? He did get out one time, though, and cut down a narrow space between two storage buildings to take a leak, making sure to count the cars in the parking lot first. They were all there when he got back.

He gave Stollman's photo a closer look. Though the subject had tried the pose of a man who knew what he was about, a real in-charge business executive, everything about his face betrayed him: the small, close-set, startled eyes; the phony smile; and the weak cut of the chin reminded Eddie of nothing so much as a frightened bird. Or a guilty one. Laying the photograph aside, he stared out the window, bored.

At least he wouldn't have to bleed for the twenty dollars, and he wouldn't have to stand at the toilet pissing red from his battered kidneys afterward. He would not spend the night tossing and turning, unable to find a position that wouldn't make him groan with pain, and trying to make his brain stop rehashing the fight and all the things he should have done and didn't. All he had to do was dog some total stranger.

A little before noon, the photograph lying on the seat came to life when William Stollman—tall, thin, and all gawky angles—walked out the front doors of the plant and got into a year-old

Chrysler 300, a shiny red yacht of a car. Eddie let him get a head start before pulling out.

The Chrysler headed south on Lindbergh Boulevard then cut over to Woodland and pulled into the parking lot of a branch of the Delaware Bank & Trust. Stollman hurried in and out in less than ten minutes. He drove another two blocks onto Baltimore Avenue, parked at a little steak house, and went inside. Forty minutes later he reappeared, slid into the Chrysler, and drove back to the plant. Eddie watched him disappear once more. A less-than-average man going through an average day. It didn't seem to amount to much of anything.

At the gas station on the corner, Eddie dropped a nickel and told Sal what he had seen.

"Okay, fine, you're done. I'll send Bink out. You had lunch?"

Eddie said no. And who was "Bink"?

Sal said, "Come on in. I'll get sandwiches," and hung up.

Eddie stepped into the back office to find Sal sitting behind a gray metal desk that was covered with a mess of file folders, papers, and photographs. The walls were bare except for a bulletin board with some notes tacked up and a calendar featuring covered bridges. In one corner was a file cabinet, also gray metal, and a GI footlocker was shoved against the side wall. A single, dusty window faced Sansom Street. It looked kind of worn-out, not unlike its proprietor. Though the marks of the beating the detective had taken on Saturday night were starting to fade.

Sal pushed a bottle of Dr Pepper and a hoagie wrapped in waxed paper across the desk. "Siddown, have a bite and something to drink," he said.

Eddie cleared his throat. "I wanted to tell you that the situation you offered here ain't right for me."

"Oh, yeah?" Sal put down his sandwich and picked up a napkin to wipe his fingers. "And what situation would be right for you? I mean, other than getting punched in the face?"

Eddie was trying to remember his speech when the detective said, "You told me you were done fighting, my friend."

Eddie shifted his feet and crossed his arms. "I said I was stopping for a while."

Sal's brow furrowed comically. "Okay, so let's see. You ain't fighting. I guess you could spar, but then you'd probably end up with scrambled eggs for brains. Or maybe you wanna go down to the waterfront and hump cargo with the rest of the guineas. Or drive a cab until you can't walk or until some hophead jungle bunny puts a bullet in your ear." He drew himself up with as much dignity as his pummeled face could muster. "Hey, c'mon, what's it going to hurt for you to help me out with a few things here? It ain't like I'm asking for a lifetime of loyal service."

Eddie said, "I gotta think about it."

"Fine, you do that." Sal pointed to the chair. "In the meantime, siddown, eat your hoagie. G'head, *mang'*."

They ate their sandwiches and drank their sodas, and Sal let Eddie in on a little bit of his story. He was the son of immigrants from the south of Italy, Calabrese to be exact, a shoemaker and his wife who had settled in Philadelphia right off the boat. Like most of the city's immigrant children, young Salvatore lasted only until the eighth grade. He worked jobs around the neighborhood and got involved in some petty thievery from the docks. The takes were decent, and he briefly considered a career in crime. He knew all about the Black Hand, had noticed the flashy-looking hoodlums around the neighborhood, with their long black sedans, fine suits, bejeweled fingers, and blond dames. Then one morning he saw one of the gentlemen sprawled halfway into a gutter, a broken mannequin, his fine suit full of ragged, bloody holes, his mouth and eyes gaping at the gray sky, and his ring-encrusted fingers crabbed in a death grip. Sal decided to take the other path.

He joined the Philadelphia police force and worked his way up to detective, then went to the war and served as a Marine MP captain in the Pacific. Afterward he went back on the force and stayed another seven years. By then he'd had enough of the Philly PD. So he set himself up in a little office where he didn't have to look at dead bodies and he didn't have to look away when the pad money got spread around, while "confessions" were beaten out of hapless suspects, and good cops turned into bad cops who thought abusing the badge was part of the job. Along with some retired patrolmen to help out now and then, a neighborhood guy named Bink came around, but he was slow in the head. The detective had an ex-wife who lived on Thirty-first Street and a son and two daughters living outside the city. He was fifty-four years old.

When he finished, he settled back in the creaking chair, as if waiting for Eddie to take his turn. Eddie drank off his Dr Pepper and set the bottle aside. Sal shrugged and went into one of his drawers. He opened a cash box, took out a twenty-dollar bill, and pushed it across the desk.

"So, you coming back tomorrow?" he said.

Eddie picked up the bill. "Yeah, okay. But just so we got it straight here. One thing I ain't going to do: I ain't going to hurt anybody. I ain't going to beat people up for you."

Sal nodded and said, "All right. Tell you what. If I want someone to beat people up, I'll call whatshisname, T-Bone Mieux."

Eddie glared at him for a second. Then he let out a short laugh, his hard eyes crinkling almost merrily.

Sal was astonished. "Well, sonofabitch," he said. "Look at that. The tough guy's got a sense of humor. I'll be damned."

FOUR

Eddie figured it would be a couple days and then he'd find something else. But a week went by and a second one came around, and it kept slipping his mind that he was supposed to be looking for another job until he could get back in the ring.

Though it was tedious work, he started to learn things here and there. Sal taught him how to use the little Leica camera that he kept in the Chevy's glove box. The detective opened the footlocker and showed him a tape recorder, a selection of microphones, an 8 mm movie camera, and other surveillance equipment. He dropped basic bits of advice on tailing people without being noticed, picking up information on the sly, and that sort of thing.

The second day on the job, Sal handed him a clipboard with a pad attached. He was to have it on hand at all times, because nothing worked as well for a cover. Give a bum a clipboard and he instantly became an official with important business at hand. It never failed, the detective said, as long as you remembered to write something down. Anything would do, he added, as long as it wasn't doodles of people fucking. Eddie thought he caught a hint of rueful experience in the detective's snicker.

Sal insisted that Eddie, who hadn't scribbled more than a few lines on a postcard since high school, write reports. So he found himself having to labor over detailed recountings of his days, dull as they were. Sal claimed that he had closed cases from what seemed a worthless detail jotted in a margin. Though Eddie hated it, at the end of each day he sat down and wrote.

He met Bink that first week, a little man with a round, crew-cut head, bulbous blue eyes, and a pug nose. He could have been one of the Seven Dwarfs. He grinned at everything and stuttered when he talked. Eddie liked Bink right away; he reminded him of the guys who helped out at the gym, not at all bright, but tough and loyal.

Speaking of which, Eddie was stunned that no one seemed to notice that he hadn't been back since the Mieux fight. Nobody came around to ask after him. He had been a daily fixture around the place for almost six years, and he didn't even rate that.

The day he went in to collect his gear, he found the big room stone quiet. One of the cornermen whispered that the news had just come from New York that Kid Paret had died after being carried out of the ring in a coma. Everyone knew Paret; he had fought in Philly and had sparred in that very gym. And they all knew Griffith was a class fighter who didn't deserve to be on the other end of the bleak story. But a referee had permitted a slaughter to go on, and they would be burying Kid Paret in the morning.

The cornerman saw the look on Eddie's face and said, "You okay, kid?" Eddie nodded.

Benny wasn't around, so he told the gym manager that he was laying off for a while. The response was a vacant "Sure, okay, whatever you say."

Two days later he exchanged the bandage for flesh-colored Band-Aids, then nothing. The scar wasn't as bad as he thought it would be; it was mostly covered by his eyebrow, with just the end curving down a quarter inch from his eye socket in a red tail. It was there for him to see every time he passed a mirror.

Though he still couldn't muster much interest in the work, during a lunch break he decided to buy some ballpoint pens and a notebook like the one Sal carried. The detective didn't comment when he noticed, but Eddie could tell he was pleased. A couple days later, Sal handed him a small stack of business cards, printed up simple, just SG CONFIDENTIAL INVESTIGATIONS and the phone number. He said, "Any cops bother you, show them one of those."

His days went pretty much the same. He showed up in the morning, and Sal sent him out on a tail. Most days it was William Stollman. Once or twice it was a furniture-store owner named Taylor who wasn't doing anything wrong that Eddie could detect. He did a lot of sitting on his ass and staring out the window. He drank too much coffee. Sometimes Bink would show up to replace Eddie, sometimes a guy who looked as though he'd just been tossed out the back door of some gin mill. In the late afternoon he would drive back to the office, write his report, pick up his day's pay—ten or twenty dollars, depending on the job—and go home.

Sal figured out ways to keep him around. On the Friday afternoon of his second week, as he was getting ready to leave, the detective said, "You can't be driving the Chevy all the time. I need it."

Eddie said, "Yeah, well, I can't afford to buy anything."

"I know, I know," Sal said brusquely. "I got you one."

Eddie was stunned. "You bought me a car?"

"No, I didn't buy it, ya dumbass. What do you think I am? It so happens I have an arrangement with a guy who has a lot. My friend Dominic."

"What arrangement?" Apparently, Sal had a deal for just about every occasion, and every one of them had a story attached.

"I saved his ass in a big way," the detective explained. "He was screwing some young girl, this piece that had come in to buy a car. He basically gave her one for free, but of course it wasn't free, because he got to bang her a couple times a week. Somehow his wife got wind of it, and she was getting ready to divorce him and hang him up by his balls with alimony and all that. He called me and I did some checking and found out that his poor, betrayed little missus was having regular afternoon parties of her own. I think it was the fucking paperboy or the kid that cut the grass or some such shit. So in the end they got a nice, tidy divorce and that was that. Dom thinks I saved his life. So anytime I need wheels, he provides." He wrote down an address. "Go see him."

By five o'clock Eddie was tooling down Broad Street in a 1949 Ford two-door. It was an ugly rust brown piece of crap, he had to muscle the gearshift into low to get it to move, and it smoked like a chimney, but it ran and that was plenty. His last car was a decrepit bathtub Hudson that had blown up two years before, and since then he had been riding the bus, taking cabs, or walking. He wondered if Sal had any connections for decent rooming houses.

Eddie was grateful and out of consideration tidied up the mess in the office. One morning while Sal was out, he found some ammonia in the broom closet down the hall and cleaned the window. He also tried to dress a little better, to look more professional. Even though the man he was working for seemed to buy his suits rumpled.

At first he didn't ask questions about the investigation game. Then the boredom and his curiosity got the better of him. Plus, he thought it was dumb to be toting a notebook with nothing written in it.

Over coffee one morning, he stood around mumbling for a couple minutes until Sal realized that he was asking about work. The detective raised an eyebrow, then took the opening to give him the big picture. He explained that his cases were pretty much split between business and pleasure, or money and sex, meaning somebody was screwing the books or screwing the *boss*. In both cases, the injured party—a business partner or spouse—hired guys like him to get the goods on the erring half. The subject might be up to embezzling while banging his secretary. Sometimes, Sal said, the schmuck was stealing the money so he could *keep* banging his secretary.

It so happened that William Stollman was a case in point. Eddie had been on the subject three days during his second week, and all three days Stollman visited a bank, though a different one each time.

"Yeah, the greedy fuck is stealing with both hands," Sal told him. "God knows what he's covering it with, but my guess is he's writing himself checks, cashing them, and then squirreling the dough away in safe-deposit boxes."

He told Eddie that the aggrieved party was the wife, who was also the daughter of the founder of Keystone Valve. Stollman was making off with the in-laws' fortune even as he humped someone who was not his spouse, and right there in the family plant to boot.

"He goes home at night like a good boy, so he's doing her on the premises, probably bending her over his walnut desk." He paused. "It'd be nice to have a shot of them in the act. That'd be tough, though. His office is up on the third floor." He shrugged. "It don't matter. We got everything but on them."

"Who's the girl?" Eddie inquired.

Sal smirked. "This young thing works in Shipping and Receiving. Her name's Mary McQueen. A mick from West Philly. Nineteen years old. Kinda homely in the face, but"—he cupped his hands a foot from his chest—"she's got certain virtues. And nineteen is nineteen. I'm sure she fucks like a mink. Mr. Stollman is in his forties. You get the picture."

"How do you know?" Eddie asked.

"How do I know what?"

"About this girl."

"Oh. Right, I didn't tell you about that." The detective went into another desk drawer and produced a selection of official-looking ID cards, which he waved before Eddie's eyes, a magician performing a trick. "We conduct inspections for various city and county agencies."

Eddie laughed at the subterfuge.

"In this particular case, it was easy," Sal said, dumping the fake documents back in the drawer. "I had Bink hang around the dock, and he buddied up to a guy who told him that the whole plant knows about it. The girl is on break the better part of the day. She's sporting some expensive gifts, jewelry and so forth. And she can't keep her yap shut about it." He shook his head in wonder. "The guy's a fucking cretin. A family company, and he makes everyone call him 'Mr. Stollman.' You believe that shit?" His face twisted up in disgust. "Well, *Mr.* Stollman is going to lose it all for a piece of nineteen-year-old tail." He waved a dismissive hand. "It's not the first time I've seen it, and it won't be the last."

Sal told him the trick in these cases was to let it go just long enough to get the goods. "Because one fine day, this bird is going to fly," he said. "And you know what day that is?"

Eddie thought for a moment. "The day he goes to all three banks right in a row."

"Well, goddamn," Sal said, nodding judiciously. "Not bad, Cero."

Eddie shrugged; it just made sense.

Another time he looked around the office and expressed surprise that Sal kept busy. The detective treated him to a narrow glance. "Why, 'cause this place is a rathole? Because I ain't Humphrey Bogart?" He shifted to his lecture tone. "Forget that shit. You know what I mean. That Sam Spade crap, with the tough guys in—whaddyacallem—fedoras, calling blond dames 'dollface' and whatnot. You see what investigation work is.

Ninety percent of the time, all you're doing is watching. Sometimes you get a little action, but this ain't the movies, okay?"

Eddie said, "Okay."

"Most of my clients are very comfortable," Sal went on more calmly. "They could afford PIs in those fancy-ass Center City offices. They don't care about that. They don't care that I don't have a suite with a view of the Mall. And they don't care that I don't look like a matinee idol. They want results. That's what I provide."

Eddie asked why he had never seen any of these clients in the office.

"I only see them off the premises." Sal snickered. "I mean, clients in this dump? C'mon."

At the risk of launching another rant about TV detectives, Eddie asked him if he ever carried a gun.

Sal gave him a long look. "I own one."

"You don't carry it?"

"I try not to. I might shoot somebody."

"Yeah, but what—"

"I know, I know, what about all the real detectives?" Sal's mouth crooked. "They carry, right? A rod. Or a heater. Or a *gat*. Well, you know what I say? I say if you got a cock, you don't need a gun." He raised a finger. "Unless you're a cop, of course. Though I've known a few of them who shouldn't be allowed anywhere near a loaded weapon."

Late on another afternoon, after a particularly long day, Sal took his bottle of Seagram's out of the drawer and poured a drink for Eddie and one for himself. After listening to Sal ramble on about his cases for a while, Eddie asked if it ever bothered him sticking his nose into people's business.

Sal straightened and poked a righteous finger into the air. "Listen, these clowns we investigate are fucking up in some serious way or I wouldn't be on them in the first place," he said.

"They're stealing, or they're breaking a vow, or they're taking advantage of somebody. We correct these situations."

Eddie gave him a dubious look. Sal lowered his hand and smiled. "Okay, then, look at it this way. Doctors get rich because people get sick. You going to hold it against them? The point is there's a place between legal and illegal, between doing the right thing and committing a breach of trust, where people try to get away with all kinds of shit. You see it on TV, or hear about it on the radio, or read about it in the paper every goddamn day. That's where we operate. The point being to give the police or the courts something they can sink their teeth into."

"But what if you're on the wrong side and if the guy's innocent?" Eddie said.

Sal frowned darkly. "We want to make sure they're not."

Though Eddie never asked, every now and again Sal would throw out additional information, some little detail or a quick anecdote, filling in chapters in his life story. It didn't take long for Eddie to suspect that some of the things he was hearing were exaggerated, the facts rearranged in some creative way, or complete fictions. It was okay with him. It didn't do any harm, and Sal seemed to enjoy himself.

A few times, after he had finished one of his little tales, Sal would pause for a few seconds and then say, "So, what about you, tough guy? What's your story?"

Eddie would shrug and say something like, "No story. I've been fighting for ten years. Working jobs on the side. That's all."

Sal's eyebrows would arch, but he'd let it drop. The truth was Eddie didn't like talking about himself. Who cared? You lived your life, you tried to stay out of trouble and not get yourself killed.

And what would he say? *I grew up in Allentown. My dad worked in a mill, and he died when I was a kid. I got two brothers and a sister I never see. I went to school and then I found the*

PAL gym and learned to box. Which is what I did until two weeks ago when T-Bone Mieux head-butted me. I live in a rooming house on Eleventh Street for which I pay fifteen dollars a week. Oh, yeah, I like music; I got a record player and about two hundred 45s. That's my story.

If Sal knew about what had happened in his fight with Willie Allred, he didn't let on, and Eddie wasn't about to bring it up.

"You're Italian, right?" the detective had asked him almost right away. "'Cause you look like a regular goombah."

Eddie told him, yeah, he was Italian, Abruzzese with the family name Ceronelli. Somehow, the end part got chopped off. That was all he knew. It was a touchy subject going back to the old country, so no one had ever figured it out. Whatever it was, the old man took it to his grave and his mother would never discuss it.

And, of course, more than a few times Sal tried to kid him about women. "You got yourself a girl?" he would ask. "My wife—ex-wife, I mean—she's got nieces, nice Italian girls; you want to meet one of them?"

Eddie just shook his head. Women came and went, and that was that.

One Monday he climbed the steps to the office and heard snarling voices echoing in the hall. He walked through the front office and stopped in Sal's doorway.

The punk with the pimples and the fat boy were at opposite ends of the desk, looming over the detective. Though Sal was boxed in, his mouth tilted in a bemused smile, and his eyes were merry. His visitors wore matching outfits: white shirts, pegged black pants, and Cuban stilettos. When the pimpled punk saw Eddie, he stopped poking his finger in Sal's chest.

Following his gaze, the fat boy turned around and said, "Whoa, fuckin' A. You."

"Yeah, me," Eddie said. "What's going on here?"

"We got business, that's what," the other punk said, sounding shrill.

"Go ahead and finish it." Eddie leaned against the jamb and crossed his arms. "I'll wait."

The punk was holding his finger in midair, as if he was ready to resume his harangue. Then he saw the way Eddie was looking at him. His Adam's apple bobbed in his scrawny neck and the finger went limp.

"We're finished," he croaked. He jerked his head. "C'mon, Tony."

They backed away from the desk to leave, only to find Eddie still blocking the door. The fat boy stumbled on his partner's heels.

Eddie nodded toward the window. "Go out that way," he said. They turned their heads in tandem. "It's only one floor down. G'head."

"Whaddya talkin' about?" The punk's voice went thin with panic.

"What, you need some help?" Eddie let the silence hang for a moment. The corners of his mouth turned up slightly. "Just kidding," he said, and moved aside. As they passed him, he dropped his voice down low and said, "Don't come here again."

The punk looked like he wanted to snap back with something. Instead, he sucked in a breath and led Tony through the front office and out into the hall. Their footsteps and their muttering voices echoed down the stairwell.

" 'It's only one floor down,' " Sal mimicked. "Jesus Christ, I might have to adopt you."

"What's the deal with those two?" Eddie said. "I'm getting tired of this."

"You and me both."

"So bust their fucking heads, why dontcha?"

"It ain't that simple." Sal motioned him to sit down. Instead, Eddie put his hands on the back of the chair and waited. "It's not exactly the way I explained," the detective said. "That night in the bar, I mean. The truth is . . . my wife sent them."

Eddie wasn't sure he'd heard it right. "Did you say your *wife*?"

"Ex-wife," Sal said. "I told you. We're separated." He sighed. "Anyway, she wants more money out of me, right? So she sends those two coconuts to see if they can get blood from a stone. They think they're hoods, but they're just a couple dumb punks."

Eddie felt a wild urge to laugh, but Sal looked so befuddled that he thought it would be disrespectful, so with an effort he kept quiet. "Who are they?" he asked.

"The one with the acne? Frankie? He's her sister's kid," Sal said. "And the other—"

"Wait a minute," Eddie broke in. "He's your fucking *nephew*?"

"Not by blood. By marriage. And the fat one, Tony, he's—"

Eddie let out a sudden shriek and lurched away like he'd been shot in the ass. Sal gaped in astonishment as the kid, the hard case who rarely ever cracked a smile, went staggering around the office, grabbing the walls for support, and letting out whooping laughs. Every time he tried to stop, a look at Sal's sad-sack face would set him off again.

After a few moments, Sal smiled and then he chuckled, too. "Hey, what can I say? *Amore*. It makes the world go 'round, am I right?"

"Jesus, Sal!" Eddie stopped to wipe his eyes. "She never heard of a lawyer?"

"She'd rather fuck with me this way. It's a long story. But she's a real work of art, no lie."

"And you want me to meet the nieces?" Eddie said. "I think I'll skip it. Sunday dinner must be something."

"It's the story of my life." Though Sal looked chagrined, Eddie's outburst had pleased him. The kid was too serious.

"You got anything else you want to tell me?" Eddie said.

Sal shook his head. "No, I think that's enough for now. Are you done enjoying yourself? Can we do some business?"

"Yeah, sure, go ahead." Eddie sat down. Then he let out another sudden laugh. He couldn't help himself. He saw Sal's eyes flash, and he put a hand over his mouth.

"All right, I got something for you if you want it," the detective said. "You know that joint we went to that night? The Blue Door?"

Eddie nodded, recalling the dim lights and the last fading echo of a smoky voice.

"Well, the guy owns it is a friend of mine," Sal said. "His name's Joe D'Amato. He thinks his bartender is dipping into the till. So here's the thing. You go down there, sit at the bar, have a nice meal and some drinks, anything you want on the house, and see if you can catch this *scungilli* in the act."

Sal told him it was an extra ten-spot plus his dinner would be covered. Eddie said that sounded fine.

"You own a sport coat?" Sal said.

Eddie had to think about it. "I . . . yeah."

"Wear it. Make a nice appearance, okay? Just a regular guy out for a bite and a drink, got it?"

"I got it," Eddie said, and headed for the door before he broke up again.

FIVE

The door was the only piece on the premises that was blue. Inside, a foyer and hostess station opened into a squarish room done up in sharp geometric panels of black and white and trimmed in cool coral. A small dance floor of checkerboard tile was bordered by a crescent of round tables. In the right front corner was a long bar that was curved at one end, and just beyond it the kitchen door swung open and closed as waiters passed in and out. On the far end of the room, a low stage was cast in dim red light. It was early, and smoke hadn't yet clouded the air.

Stepping up to the bar, Eddie recalled that the Blue Door had once held a reputation as a classy watering hole for the fast trade, with good meals and cocktails and the music to go along with all that. He remembered reading that Tony Bennett and Nina Simone had been guests, and that Dick Clark and some of the local hit-makers were spotted in the room now and then, along with certain featured actors in the local crime community. A place to be seen, in other words. Now most of the sheen was gone, replaced by a faintly seedy lounge, and not a celebrity in sight.

On this quiet Monday night, the crowd was small, a dozen

couples at tables and four or five guys sitting at the bar. Erroll Garner's piano trickled moodily from speakers near the stage.

Eddie took a stool at the bar that gave him a direct view of the cash register. The bartender came around, a guy about thirty, rail thin with a slick little mustache, a thin nose, and the kind of fake-friendly eyes that made Eddie distrust him on sight. He produced a quick, phony smile and said, "What'll it be, pal?"

Eddie asked for a draft beer. "What's good on the menu?"

The bartender, reeking of Aqua Velva, slid a coaster in front of him. "Can't go wrong with the steak and fries," he said. "The pork chops are decent. I'd leave the fish alone." He winked. "Unless, of course, you get lucky tonight."

He delivered the line in such a crude manner that it made Eddie dislike him even more.

"Steak and fries," he said.

A few minutes later, he saw a short, wiry guy in a green sharkskin suit making his way across the room, stopping at each table to chat with the customers. He was one sharp guinea and definitely a ladies' man. A cat on the prowl, he had an eye out for every female in the place.

He made his rounds and headed for the bar, greeting his customers with jovial good cheer, coming to a startled stop when he eyed Eddie.

"Hey, look who we got here!" Joe D'Amato said. His black eyes lit up. Eddie blinked and shook the proffered hand. This was not in the script.

"Hey, Jerry," Joe called to the bartender, still pumping away, "you know who we got here?" The other men at the bar turned to stare.

Jerry stepped over, peering at Eddie's face and smiling uncertainly. "I don't know, Frank Sinatra Jr.?" he said.

"Frank Sinatra Jr., my ass," Joe said. "This here's Eddie Cero." There was a puzzled pause and Joe plunged on. "Only one of the best welterweights on the East Coast! C'mon, ya kiddin' me?" He put up his dukes and did a little bob-and-weave.

Everyone at the bar was smiling the same blank smile. Who the hell was Eddie Cero? Joe started pumping his hand again, as if it was Rocky Marciano sitting there. "Anything this guy wants, it's on the house, all right?"

Jerry said, "Yeah, all right, Joe."

"All right," Joe said, and gave Eddie a light tap on the cheek before moving on.

Eddie sat back. It had been a good performance. Sal had called ahead and his cover was fixed.

It took him about an hour to figure it out. Between bites of his meal and sips of his beer, he watched Jerry at the cash register. Unless the guy was some kind of sleight-of-hand artist, there was nothing there. And it seemed he was ringing every sale. It all looked kosher, until Eddie noticed how often he went to make change out of the small brass bucket that held his tips.

He had spent time in bars—he'd been a busboy once when he was a kid, and he had worked a few nights as a bouncer (and discovered that little guys, even tough little guys, didn't impress big drunks), and he remembered that the bartenders usually traded out their tips for big bills at the end of the night. It was still early, and this character had already visited his tip bucket twice. Though he couldn't see the bills, he guessed that Jerry was trading up, taking five ones out of his tips and putting tens back. But that would seem obvious, especially if anyone kept track.

By nine o'clock, when the bar got busy and Jerry was running his ass off, he nailed the rest of it. The bartender had kept a count in his head, and with all the noise and activity, he now missed ringing every tenth transaction. Only someone watching and counting along would notice. And even then, the bartender could claim he had just forgotten; the money was just going into the till, right? Not a bad operation. He was taking home at least an extra twenty bucks a night. That was a hundred a week, a good salary all by itself.

Eddie drank another beer, then dropped a dollar tip of his own on the bar and waved a good-bye to Jerry. The bartender gave him another broad wink and a greasy smile.

Joe D'Amato intercepted him by the front door. Eddie told him what was going on.

"Sonofabitch, I knew it," Joe said, his face flushing darker. "Well, then, he's finished, the cocksucker. I oughta break his fucking arm, stealing from me like that." He gave Eddie a hopeful look, like maybe he'd be interested in that assignment, too.

"Thanks for dinner," Eddie said, and offered his hand.

"Hey, wait a minute," Joe said. "Where ya goin'? Stick around. I got a singer coming on."

"I gotta go," Eddie said.

"Well, listen, come back some night," Joe insisted. "Have some drinks on me, all right?" Eddie said he'd do that and headed for the blue door.

Outside a young woman stood alone at the corner of the building, smoking a cigarette and gazing at the passing traffic. He glanced at her and stopped, trying to act casual, looking around as if he was waiting on something.

With a small spike of surprise, he realized it was the same singer he had glimpsed that first night with Sal. Now, up close, her pretty, serious face struck him as even more familiar. He was just about to speak up when the blue door opened and the hostess stuck her head out.

"Joe says it's time, Valerie." The woman said something Eddie didn't catch, then flicked her cigarette into the gutter and disappeared inside.

It was then that he noticed the glass display case next to the door, and he stepped closer to find a menu and a sheet listing the talent that was "Appearing Nitely." The first line announced:

"The Piano Moods of Mr. Tony Kay," alongside the photograph of a Liberace copy. It was followed by "The Vocal Stylings of Patti Francis" and "The Jazz Generals," in smaller script. Finally, at the bottom, under the dates April 6th–21st, "Valerie Pope, Formerly of the Excels."

That was it: the Excels. They had once been the best group in the city, and all of them from right there in South Philly. Eddie had seen them a half-dozen times at theaters and once at Steel Pier four or five summers back, and among the six of their records in his boxes, one of them still had the picture sleeve.

He hadn't heard a thing about them in two or three years, ever since Johnny Pope, the lead singer and Valerie's brother, had gone missing. The group faded into thin air right behind him. Now Valerie Pope, formerly of the Excels, was singing at the Blue Door.

He walked down the street, got in the car, and went home.

As the door closed Valerie felt curious eyes fixing on her. She had seen his face before, and it took only a few moments to recall him from the late-night crowd a few weeks back. It was odd that she remembered after all this time. Maybe it was because he had such a way about him, like a cat, cool, watchful, and ready to pounce on something.

He was probably just another Italian guy in South Philly. She'd met more than a few of those types, guidos who all thought they were as bad as they came, on the one hand, and God's gift to the female gender, on the other.

She put him out of her mind; she had a show to do.

SIX

He worked William Stollman on Tuesday and Wednesday. On Wednesday night he went back to the Blue Door.

He walked in a little after nine and headed for the bar. No Jerry. It gave him a strange feeling. He had opened his mouth and the guy was a memory. Maybe even a memory with a broken arm. In his place was a man in his fifties who introduced himself as George. He had the air of an old-time saloon bartender, missing only a handlebar mustache.

Eddie ordered a beer and took the stool at the end of the bar that gave him a view of the stage, where four guys in matching powder blue jackets were running down an instrumental number for a room that was about a third full, mostly couples eating. He spotted Joe D'Amato making the rounds of the tables.

The houselights dimmed and the red spotlight glowed down on the stage. The band began a slow vamp, and the guitar player stepped up to the microphone. "Ladies and gentlemen," he intoned, "formerly of Philadelphia's own Excels, Miss Valerie Pope."

A few hands applauded as she walked slowly to center stage. She stood back from the mike, swaying slightly to the drummer's beat and gazing over the heads of the crowd. After a few bars, she stepped up and began a soft, smoky version of "Heartaches."

He had caught no more than a quick glance at her on the street. Now he got a good look. She was on the short side, maybe five three, and her red dress curved nicely about her chest and hips, her hair was straightened and puffed out with one wide peroxide blond streak, and she wore a lot of eye makeup. A lot of the girls were doing that, though only a couple years ago the look was a badge that read *slut*.

She was pretty, with high cheekbones, slanted eyes, and a nose that attested to Indian blood. In spite of the fine face and figure, she also looked like she might be a tough customer. He guessed she was a couple years younger than he was, which meant she would have been nineteen or twenty when she last sang with the Excels.

He remembered seeing them at the Regal, remembered Johnny tearing all over the stage, shrieking and whooping, throwing cascades of sweat into the first three rows. The two other guys clowned as they used their voices as a rhythm section. Valerie had been the solid center, and the men revolved around her in crazy, noisy orbits.

The same woman, four years later, looked at ease on the stage, not showy at all, standing still while her smoky vocal chords put on the show. She finished the song to scattered applause and went on to "Stormy Monday." When it came time for the instrumental break, she let her fingers drape the microphone as she leaned back, closed her eyes, and moved her head slowly from side to side while the guitar player bent the strings in a mellow twang. She stepped to the mike again, and the wounded echoes in her voice went a notch deeper. The song took a lonely road to the final chord, raising loud applause and whistles from the crowd. They played through a good set: a half-dozen R&B and pop hits and one more sweet, sad blues, which seemed to suit her, then she left the stage to a nice hand.

Eddie peeked out the door. She was standing in the same place, smoking as she watched the traffic. She glanced his way.

He didn't know what to say. *Hey, I got all of your records. I saw you at Steel Pier one summer night. I was out with Sherry Belaski, and you guys got her so crazy that she gave it up right under the boardwalk. By the way, did they ever find your brother?*

After fidgeting for a few seconds, he said, "I'm, uh . . . You sound good."

"Thank you." Her gaze rested on him for a moment, then went away.

"I got some of your records," he offered. "Excels' records, I mean."

She didn't say anything for a few seconds. Then: "Which ones?"

"Well . . . *Careless* and, uh, *Crazy Baby* and . . ." And what? He'd gone blank on the other one. It was getting strange, and he was about to slip away so she could finish her cigarette in peace when Joe came bustling out the door, saw the two of them, and stopped.

"Hey, hey, Eddie Cero!" He grinned happily. "Hey, you guys know each other?"

"I got, I got some of her, uh, records," Eddie stuttered. "I mean *their* records. The, the Ex—"

"Right, right." Joe held out his hands as if presenting a prize. "Valerie Pope! Am I lucky to have her?" Valerie gave Joe a smile that was wan but affectionate. He turned his grin on Eddie and started with the bob-and-weave again. "And what about this guy? Eddie Cero! One hell of a welterweight."

Valerie gazed at him steadily. "I was," Eddie said. "Not anymore."

"Guess what he does now?" Joe said.

She didn't look very interested but said, "I don't know, what?"

"PI," Joe said. "As in private investigator. Like one of those guys on TV. Peter Gunn or whoever."

"It's not like that," Eddie said.

"This guy"—Joe was beaming—"he's in my club two minutes, and he figures out how that bastard Jerry was stealing my money." He landed a fake punch on Eddie's jaw. "You come back inside, anything you want, it's on me." He gave him another happy grin, then glanced at his watch. "And I believe it's time, Miss Pope."

She dropped her cigarette on the sidewalk and treated Eddie to the briefest sidelong glance as she went inside. Joe was still grinning at him.

"What it is, is I got some of their records," Eddie said.

"Yeah, I heard ya." Joe reached for the door and pulled it open. "Come on in," he said. "Have a drink with me."

Joe took the barstool next to his and signaled George for drinks. They listened to Valerie work her first number, a sultry take of "You'll Lose a Good Thing." After two hypnotic verses, she stepped away to let the pianist and the guitar player wander through solos. Eddie watched her lose herself in the shadows.

"Hello, knock knock, anybody home?" Joe was giving him a quizzical look.

Eddie said, "Sorry, I was just thinking about the Excels. Her brother Johnny. They never found him, right? And it's been, what, three years?"

"Yeah, three years is right." Their drinks arrived. Joe took a sip of his and gave George a nod of approval.

"You'd think something would have turned up by now," Eddie said.

"Well, the cops were on it, and his record company had somebody look into it, too. They never found nothing. Zip. Zero." Joe shook his head. "It was some strange business, all right."

Eddie returned his attention to the stage as Valerie stepped back into the red spotlight. She laid a gentle hand on the top of the microphone to finish the song.

Joe gestured with his glass. "I'll tell you what: She was never the same after that. She and Johnny were real close. And then to lose him, it tore her up pretty good." He sipped his drink absently. "Yeah, it was really sad. He was here, he made this big splash, and then he was gone. Gone, and soon to be forgotten." He pondered for another somber moment, then lifted his glass. "So, hey, whaddya say? Here's to the late, great Johnny Pope."

SEVEN

Eddie woke up before the alarm went off. After a shower he dressed and crossed the street for scrapple and eggs, lingering over his coffee. It was early and he didn't have anything to do until it was time to drive out to Keystone. He paid his check, climbed in the Ford, and headed to Wharton Street.

The bolt slid back with a crack. Jimmy T jerked the door open, glared, and let out a snarl. "Cero! You got any idea what goddamn time it is?"

Eddie stood back from the cloud of rank breath. "It's ten o'clock."

Jimmy banged a knuckle on the door glass. "Sign says 'Open at noon.' What the fuck's wrong with you?"

"I'm going to be working at noon."

"So?"

"So I want to come in."

Jimmy growled as if he was ready to bite somebody, then huffed once and shuffled back a few steps. "All right, come on. Jesus!"

Eddie stepped inside. Jimmy kicked the door with his heel,

and it slammed shut with a mighty bang. He stalked off toward the back of the store, muttering something about coffee.

The deep, narrow room was divided in two by an aisle that was lined on both sides by racks and shelves, peach crates and stacked boxes, from the floor up to the low ceiling, so that almost every inch of available space was stuffed with black vinyl. A glass counter with an antique brass cash register sat near the back corner. The front windows were plastered with show bills that went back years, blocking the light so that it was dim even at the height of day. It was a dusty, cobwebbed hovel that smelled of rusty pipes, mildewed plaster, and cigarette smoke, and a lot of record fanatics believed it was the best store of its kind anywhere.

The proprietor, Jimmy Teischer, was a greasy Ichabod Crane, a tall, bony, hook-nosed beatnik or hoodlum, depending on his mood. He wore mostly blue jeans, engineer boots or sneakers, and a black or white T-shirt. His hair was long, dark, and slicked back, and he sported a scraggly goatee. He had tattoos on both arms, a permanent squint in one eye from his Lucky Strikes, and a crazy gleam in the other that made people who didn't know him think he was dangerous.

Eddie stepped past the counter and pushed through a curtain into the combination office and storage room in back to find Jimmy grumbling over a blackened saucepan and a hot plate. He noticed the mussed cot and the blue jeans and T-shirts tossed all over the place, evidence that Jimmy's girlfriend, Connie, had thrown him out of their apartment. It was not the first time and wouldn't be the last. Their battles were legends.

Eddie watched one-half of the legend spoon instant coffee into a mug and add some barely heated water from the pan. Jimmy glared at his visitor again. "Don't say a goddamn word till I drink this," he said, then sucked down half the cup in one gulp. Eddie leaned in the doorway.

The Maxwell House seemed to work right away, because Jimmy uncoiled, stretched his thin arms, and regarded Eddie with what passed for a pleasant smile. A Lucky and a Zippo appeared, and in one mighty breath he blew flame from the tip of the cigarette and smoke out of the corner of his mouth.

"Fast Eddie," he said, cocking one lazy eye. "How's the fight game these days?"

"Actually, I'm out of it," Eddie said.

"Yeah?"

"For a little while, yeah."

"So what are you doin'?"

"This and that."

Jimmy suddenly remembered his social graces. "You want a cup?" he asked, thrusting the dirty mug in the air.

Eddie shook his head. Jimmy shrugged and started smoking with great deliberation while Eddie gazed absently at the show posters that served as wallpaper in the cramped office.

"Hey, you know who I saw last night?" he said. "Valerie Pope."

Jimmy looked blank for a second. "From the Excels?"

"Yeah."

"Johnny's sister."

"That's the one. She's singing at the Blue Door."

"Oh, yeah?" Jimmy turned a puzzled eye in Eddie's direction. "What were you doing in that joint?"

"Listening to Valerie Pope sing. She's pretty good."

Jimmy shrugged. "She always was."

"Too bad about what happened to Johnny," Eddie said.

"Yeah, too bad. A South Philly guy, too."

They sat around shooting the shit, and Eddie lost track of the time. He didn't pull up at Keystone until eleven thirty and had just settled in when he saw the Chrysler roll out of the parking lot with Stollman at the wheel and Mary snuggled so close that they looked like Siamese twins. Another couple minutes and he would have lost them. He muttered a curse, swung the wheel, and gave chase.

The Chrysler came to a stop in the parking lot of a cozy little tavern a few blocks down Penrose. Eddie pulled up just in time to see what was going on in the front seat. He fumbled for the Leica and didn't stop snapping until he'd shot the whole roll.

After the lovebirds went inside, he caught a breath, realizing there would have been hell to pay if he'd missed the scene in the car. All because he'd wasted half the morning yakking with some crazy greaser.

At three o'clock he walked into the office and gave Sal his report. "They went to lunch."

"They who?"

"Stollman and the girlfriend. Together."

"You're kidding."

"Got in the Chrysler and off they went. Ate at some joint off Penrose." Eddie grinned. "They were making out in the car."

"They were what?"

"Necking, Sal. You remember. Kissing and stuff. In public. In broad daylight." He dropped the roll of film on the desk. "I got pictures."

Sal shook his head. "We better be ready. Something's going to pop."

"Because they're out in the open?"

"Because he's acting like a fucking teenager. I've seen it a hundred times. She's screwed his brains out. I mean literally. He doesn't have any sense anymore. All he can think about is those knockers and that thing between her legs. He doesn't care. He's liable to do anything."

Eddie was surprised. Mary McQueen was plain, just shy of homely. She did have the stunning body of the models in the magazines on the back rack at the corner store. If it wasn't for that, she probably wouldn't get a second look on the street.

He thought about the times he'd glanced into the ringside seats before a fight and seen guys with nothing going but money, hoodlums or rich straight guys like Stollman, and they often had knockouts on their arms, girls made-up with swaths of lipstick and mascara, with breasts as plump as melons and frosted hairdos piled halfway to the lights.

When he mentioned this to Sal, the detective said, "No, he's got a looker. His wife. A nice piece is the last thing he wants. Too scary. Remember, this is a guy who probably never had a date in high school that wasn't arranged by Mom and Dad. He's a, whaddyacallit, a *Clyde.*"

Eddie laughed. It was a beatnik word.

Sal frowned blankly. "What?"

"Nothing."

"Listen, Bink's busy, so you get back out there. Follow him home to Drexel Hill or wherever he goes next. Stay on him until he gets home. And then get back on him first thing in the morning." He wagged a sage finger. "I tell you, within a few days, a week tops, this one'll be over." Eddie stood up, his mouth half open, as if he was forming a question.

"What?" Sal said.

"Never mind." Eddie turned around and went out the door.

EIGHT

He spent most of Friday at Keystone. It was a quiet day. By afternoon the sun came out from behind the high clouds, the temperature climbed above sixty, and everyone was in shirt-sleeves. Neither Stollman nor Mary McQueen appeared, singly or together. The Chrysler sat in the parking lot.

Bink came around to follow Stollman home. Eddie watched the house on Saturday and Sal took Sunday.

The subject had been managing perfect attendance on weekends, playing the "fucking squire," as Sal put it, puttering in the yard, washing the car, taking his son to a Little League game. It was a picture right out of the Home section of the *Inquirer.* But when Eddie called to check in with Sal on Sunday night, he learned that the *squire* had escaped for two rendezvous with "McQueen Mary," as Sal called *her,* one on Saturday evening when Bink was on him and the second very early Sunday morning.

"Before church," Sal said, sounding disgusted.

Eddie was back at Keystone first thing on Monday morning, and it was a different story. At ten o'clock Stollman and Mary met in the parking lot, got in the Chrysler, drove into Center City, and went shopping at Wanamaker's. They took another long lunch. They didn't get back to the plant until the middle of the afternoon.

Eddie drove to the office to tell Sal about their day.

"Next weekend," Sal said.

"Next weekend what?"

"He's going to jump. After what happened Saturday and Sunday, it's clear as a fucking bell."

Eddie thought about it for a moment. "They were rehearsing."

"That's right."

"Jump to where?"

"That I don't know," Sal said. "Maybe New York. Or Atlantic City. If I was going to bet, I'd say he's got some kind of love nest in the Poconos in mind."

Eddie smiled crookedly. "Why, 'cause he's a Clyde?"

"That's right," Sal said. "Because he's a Clyde. Because his little girlfriend is a dumb mick from West Philly. One of those honeymoon suites would be her idea of heaven." He waved an emphatic finger in the air. "That's no guarantee, okay? So we can't let him out of our sight. We gotta stick on him from here on in. That means twenty-four hours a day. But there's a problem, 'cause Bink ain't going to be around. He's got personal business to take care of. And frankly, I wouldn't trust any of those other bums."

Eddie didn't ask what kind of "personal business" would occupy so much of the little gnome's time; he thought it would sound unkind.

"So you and me gotta cover the squire around the clock," Sal went on. "That means six hours on, six hours off. Starting right now. You wanna go?"

"You go," Eddie said. "I'll come out tonight."

"It's midnight till six."

"I know."

Sal shrugged. "All right, then."

Eddie said, "So, Sal, listen, what if he tries to run while I'm on him?"

"If that happens, you see which way he's going, then you stop at a phone and call me," Sal told him. "I've got everybody on alert. The cops, the lovely Mrs. Stollman, I even talked to someone at Immigration, in case they try to leave the country. I ain't too worried about that, though. You watch, they'll head for the Pocs like they're on their goddamn honeymoon."

The detective got his things together to leave and came through the outer office. Eddie said, "Hey, wait a minute, I want to ask you something." Sal stopped. "Where would I find old newspapers? If I wanted to read about something that happened a few years ago?"

"The main branch of the Free Library," Sal said. "Periodicals Department." He was putting on his sport coat. "Actually, it's a good thing for you to know. What are you looking for?"

"Just something I want to check on."

"Well, that's the place. It's on Vine, off Franklin Parkway. You can't miss it." He waved a hand and went out the door. "I'll see you tonight," he said.

The central branch of the Free Library of Philadelphia was a grand structure, as imposing as a courthouse, with sweeping staircases leading to the upper and lower floors, every inch of it Italian marble. The corridors echoed in sepulchral silence.

The Periodicals Department was on the fourth floor, just as Sal had described it. The librarian, however, was not what he'd expected. Instead of an old biddy with glasses and hair drawn into a severe bun, he was greeted by a pixie redhead, young and pretty, with a cute sparkle in her eyes. He told her what he was looking for, and she steered him to a seat at a table near a set of broad windows that looked out on the green of the parkway. As he waited he glanced around at the bent, busy heads, feeling a tinge of regret he had never been a part of this world of book learning. It seemed like a safe place.

Not one he'd ever had a shot at. Once he started fighting, the teachers in Allentown generally ignored him, assuming he'd end up a dumb pug until he went into a mill, a good-for-nothing stumblebum the rest of his days. It was a big school, an easy place to get lost in, and he did.

After ten minutes the librarian came back carrying two weeks' worth of *Inquirer*s, dated February 9–23, 1959. She gave him a sweet smile and bobbed away. He flipped open his notebook, opened the first copy, and started turning pages.

The Wednesday, February 11 edition had a page-three photograph of the Excels. Johnny Pope's face had been circled. The headline of the accompanying story was POLICE ASKING FOR ASSISTANCE IN LOCATING SINGER.

"Philadelphia police are asking the cooperation of the public in locating John R. 'Johnny' Pope, lead singer of the popular South Philadelphia vocal group the Excels," the story began. "Pope, 24, has not been seen since he left a Morris Street recording studio on Sunday night. He was reported missing by family members. Police are requesting that anyone with knowledge of Mr. Pope's whereabouts contact Missing Persons at GReenwood 4-3284." The story went on to close with a quick summary of the Excels' career successes.

The next mention was in the Metro section of the Sunday paper. There was a more in-depth article, noting that Pope's disappearance had the police stumped. They quoted a police detective named Don Hayner. "Generally in cases when there is no evidence of a crime, the missing person turns up within a few days," the detective had stated. "Mr. Pope remains unaccounted for. That usually points to foul play." Hayner noted that the subject's car, a 1959 Cadillac Eldorado, had been left in the parking lot of the recording studio.

A sidebar story, written by a reporter named Carl Beyer, went with quotes from Ray Pope and Tommy Gates from the Excels and George Roddy, president of StarLite, the Excels' record label, and owner of 45 Studios, the place where Johnny was last seen. Each expressed bafflement over Pope's disappearance, and each voiced confidence that he would soon reappear. Eddie thought the quotes sounded rehearsed. There was nothing from Valerie. The article closed with another, longer examination of the Excels' career, with a pronounced emphasis on Johnny Pope's central role. Everyone knew he was the star of the show.

The last mention, in the following Sunday's Metro section and written by the same Carl Beyer, noted that while the police were designating the disappearance an "open investigation," unnamed sources had hinted that the investigation had in fact been closed.

The story contained the usual capsule biography and concluded with a quote from Tommy Gates.

"We are praying for Johnny's safe return," Gates said. "He is a great talent, but more than that, a dear friend."

Eddie read between the lines and decided that whatever they said, no one had believed that Johnny Pope would ever return.

He reached Drexel Hill at 11:45 and parked on Woodland Avenue in a neighborhood of tree-lined streets with homes that had come out of a coffee-table book.

Sal had borrowed a two-year-old Buick for this job ("just like the rest of the MDs," as he explained), and Eddie saw the car sitting down a half block and on the opposite side of the street. He walked up and tapped on the window. Sal got out, stretching. Eddie thought he smelled booze.

"Stay here," the detective said. "I'm going to go piss on some rich man's lawn."

The Stollman house, an old Colonial with a broad lawn and a winding walk, was dark and quiet. The whole street was silent, not even a barking dog. Eddie had watched Stollman enough to understand that he wouldn't run in the middle of this night or any other.

As it turned out, Sal agreed. He came back, zipping his fly. "Get in," he said in a low voice. Sal cranked the engine and put it in drive.

"Where we going?" Eddie asked. No doubt about it, Sal had been hitting a bottle.

"Home. I'll take you back to your car."

"You don't want me to stay?"

Sal shook his head briskly. "I changed my mind. If he hasn't gone by now, he's not going. Not tonight. There'd be no way to explain it; he'd be drawing too much attention, et cetera, et cetera."

In the darkness Eddie allowed himself a small smile. "So he'll make his move when there's lots of other things going on."

Sal saw the Ford and pulled in behind it. "Yeah, at least he ain't that stupid. And there's something else missing."

Eddie allowed a few seconds to pass, as if he had to think about it. "He doesn't have the money."

"Right. So here's what we do. You go back to daytime. I'll follow him home and stay till he's tucked in." Sal gave him a bleary smile. "Mr. William Stollman don't know it, but his goose is already cooked and on a fucking platter."

They shared sitting on the subject through the week, watching as the behavior of the happy couple grew more reckless. Stollman and Mary didn't seem to care who knew that they were in serious heat. They had to tear themselves away from each other at the end of the day. Witnessing their abandon was like watching a fuse burn. Sal told Eddie that he made calls to Mrs. Stollman's lawyers and the cops, letting them know the rabbit was about to make his run.

On Thursday evening Eddie went out for something to eat and afterward a walk. It was a beautiful night. After wandering the blocks in aimless circles, he found himself standing on the corner of Tenth and Washington, right across the street from his gym. He leaned an arm on a parking meter and studied the brick building, its filthy windows now all steamy in the cool evening.

One of the windows had a piece of pane missing, and sometimes he would stop his workout to look out at the gray skyline of the city. He crossed the intersection and walked along the sidewalk until he located the broken window and peeked through the crooked frame. The brown, shadowless light reminded him of an old movie, and he heard feet sliding on canvas, the *tat-tat-tat-tat* of the speed bag, and the dull, thick *huff* when someone hit the heavy bag.

For ten years, starting when he was sixteen, it had been his life. The roadwork, the endless sit-ups and skipping rope, the bags, the sparring. At least three and sometimes four or five hours a day, and that was on top of working a job, every day except Sunday, unless he had a fight on. Now, observing the quiet routine, he realized that he missed it.

He missed the constant motion, working so hard that it shut off his brain. He missed the sweet rush of a hot shower and then going outside and never being cold, no matter what the thermometer read. He missed the calm that came after banging for six or eight rounds, and the peace when it was over and all he had to do was put one foot in front of the other and go home.

It was more than just the workouts. He missed the time he had spent sitting around talking with the other fighters as they shared a secret language of violence. Though it was true that Eddie kept to himself, for a while he had belonged in that musty old gym. It wasn't much, but something.

Stepping back from the window, he walked around to the front of the building to lay a hand on the tarnished brass bar that served as the door handle, wondering for that moment what would happen if he went inside. He saw Benny's round, grinning face, heard his raw laugh as he slapped his back and waved him to his locker to get dressed, telling him it had all been a mistake.

He opened the door, just enough to get a glimpse of a primitive dance under dusty lights, hear pounding fists, and catch the scents of steam, sweat, liniment, and old leather. It pulled on him, an old friend welcoming him home.

When his vision cleared, he saw that one of the fighters had stopped punishing the heavy bag and was gazing back at him with a blank face.

Eddie almost said, "I used to train here," but the guy was too far away to hear him. And why would he care?

Eddie who?

The fighter went on whacking the big bag. The *thunk-thunk-thunk* was a raw heartbeat, and the *clank* of the chain was a wheezing breath. A cold wind hurtled down the avenue, blowing dust and bits of paper as if whispered around the corner of the building.

Eddie who?

A young fighter stepped to the door, and Eddie moved aside to let him pass. The kid carried himself with the stalking gait of a predator. Eddie knew that walk, too, and found himself looking in a mirror turned back ten years. With a dancer's grace, the kid circled the old pug who went on pounding the heavy bag in the same endless beat: *thunk-thunk-thunk*.

Eddie let the door close, turned around, and stepped away. There was no invisible hand pulling him, no pang twisting his gut, and he wondered if it meant that it was all over.

Walking home, his hands jammed in his jacket pockets, he considered that maybe T-Bone Mieux's cheap shot had been a blessing, gift wrapped, with his name on it. He was lucky to be out, lucky that he wouldn't end up looking down a long road with a busted-up face and a body that didn't work anymore.

He thought about the pugs who lurked in the darkest corners of the gym. It wasn't that long ago that they had been something, as hard as pig iron and quick as light, or so they said. ("I had a right hook, kid; it was a thing of beauty.") But there had always been somebody harder and quicker. And so they labored on, away from the bright lights of the title fights, until their arms wouldn't flurry and their legs wouldn't bounce. They had to stand still, take the poundings, and hope a shot would get through. The one that would save them. The one that never came.

What did come was the moment when the story ended. Sometimes a bad beating did it; sometimes the flesh just gave out. Then they were broken machines, not worth fixing, and so they hung around the gym, carrying faded photographs of themselves when they were young and strong, before the war or the wrong opponent or time caught up with them.

"You remind me of me when I was a punk," they'd say with voices of crushed stone, and point to their broken noses, ripped ears, and half-blind eyes, counting the scars like beads. They'd grab his sleeve when he started to leave, begging him to listen to just one more story.

He stopped at the corner of Twentieth Street. Night had fallen and the traffic slipped by, headlights dancing through the darkness, sparks swirling from a fire.

In that moment, and for a reason he couldn't name, he wanted to talk to Sal and tell him how it had been. He wanted to tell him about his father, a tough dago who never took shit from anybody and smacked his wife and kids and the other neighborhood louts whenever the mood struck him, and how he had finally met his match when one of the heavy presses broke a gear and mangled his knotty body into a bloody scramble of meat and bone. He would describe how his mother had dived headfirst into a bottle the day the old man was buried, never once coming up for air, and how the tragedy sent him and his sister and brothers spinning away into their own angry orbits, with no one forgiving anyone for anything.

He watched the traffic as the night wrapped a cool, dark hand around the city. He knew he wouldn't be telling that tale to Sal or anybody else. He wouldn't know how to begin.

A bus stopped at the light, and he looked up to see two kids with bright faces pressed to the window. They looked like chipmunks and he smiled. The light turned green, the bus pulled out, and he crossed the street.

When he got to his room, he sat on his bed and stared out the dirty window. It was hard to imagine that he'd never tape his hands, pull on gloves, and step through the ropes again, but there it was. He lay back on the pillow. It was all too much, and he was tired. Anyway, he had a job to go to in the morning, and the thought that Sal was counting on him made him feel better.

He fell asleep in his clothes, as if the exhaustion from all the rounds had come on all at once.

Valerie Pope locked her car door and walked down the sidewalk to the Blue Door. Inside, she found Joe D'Amato in the midst of some kind of amorous overture to the new hostess. She looked to be just the type Joe could devour: young, cute, not overly smart, and so helpless in the glow of her boss's oily charm.

Valerie interrupted his advances with a roll of her eyes. Under her gimlet stare, he couldn't keep a straight face and pulled himself away. Though of course, he'd get back to the hostess later.

He walked her through the club to his office. She waited while he unlocked the safe and produced her paycheck. The band belonged to the house, and he paid them separately. She suspected that some of the guys' salaries came in the form of bags of a certain herb, but that was none of her business. She was no churchwoman; as long as they kept time and stayed tight, she didn't care what they did.

She thanked Joe for the check and turned for the door.

"Hey, wait a second," he said. She stopped, noticing that his voice and face had changed in an odd way. "Not to bring up touchy subjects," he said, "but no one ever found out anything more about what happened to Johnny, right?"

After a moment's pause, she said, "No, nothing. Why?"

"Well, I was talking to this guy, and it came up. And I was just wondering. It's been so long. What, three years?"

"That's right," Valerie said. "What guy?"

"It was . . . He was out front the other night? You remember? Cero. The boxer." Valerie nodded. "It was him. We were just talking. I guess he was a big fan of the Excels. I haven't thought about it in a while. So . . ." He shrugged. "That's all."

Valerie said, "Oh, okay," thanked him again, and let herself out.

She was halfway to the front door when it occurred to her that according to Joe, the Italian guy—Cero?—wasn't a boxer anymore, but a private detective. She stopped for a few seconds, then gathered herself and pushed out onto the street.

NINE

Sal didn't show up at the end of the day on Friday, so Eddie followed Stollman home. It was after six thirty when the detective strolled out of the shadows.

"I got held up with something," he explained. Jerking a thumb at the house, he said, "You think our bird is ready to fly?"

"Tomorrow morning," Eddie said. "The banks'll be open."

Sal chuckled. "Goddamn, Cero. You ain't half as dumb as you look." He waved Eddie away. "Go home, have dinner, get some sleep. Meet me at Louie's at five thirty, no later."

Eddie didn't sleep much; he was too keyed up. It felt like the night before a fight. He dozed until four and then got up, made coffee, and ate an apple.

He was waiting at Louie's when Sal stumbled in, looking worse for the wear. They ordered coffees and fried egg sandwiches to go.

"Write this down in your notebook." Sal recited a Pearl Street address. "That's for McQueen Mary. She lives with her mother and about six brothers and sisters across the river. Go sit on the house. I'll see you in a little while, either when Stollman picks her up or wherever they meet."

"You sure he's going to show?"

"Pretty damn sure," Sal said. "What do you think?"

"I think yeah."

"So, let's go," Sal said.

Eddie got in the Ford and drove west through the city and across the Walnut Street Bridge into a neighborhood of houses aflutter with hundreds of little flags, the confetti of laundry hanging on lines out windows and crisscrossing the backyards.

It was six fifteen when he found the address and parked. Pearl was a working-class street like the one where he had grown up, with gray shingled row houses crowded all against each other. As he ate his sandwich and drank his coffee, he saw shapes go by, ghosts in the gray morning light: Dad rolling out for a half-day's overtime or trudging home after boozing all night at the corner tavern. For a few moments, he was transported back in time and he half expected to see his father staggering to the door, drunk and angry at the whole world, his fists already clenching in—

The front door of the McQueen house banged open and a short, red-haired kid of sixteen came out and hurried down the street toward the bus stop. Another half hour, and a middle-aged woman with a heavy bosom—Mrs. McQueen, no doubt—stepped outside and walked off down the block, looking already weary to the bone. Forty-five minutes later, two boys ran out the door, bouncing a basketball between them. Their sneakers slapped on the sidewalk as they disappeared around the corner.

A few minutes after the boys left the house, the upstairs curtains began to open and close. Eddie watched the street behind him in his mirrors, waiting for the Chrysler to appear.

He got a surprise when a year-old Thunderbird convertible in gleaming midnight blue crept along the quiet street to stop in front of number 224. The front door of the house slapped open again, and Mary came rushing down the steps to the street, toting a suitcase. Her coat was open, revealing a tight, low-cut white top, capri slacks, and flats—traveling clothes. Eddie could see that her eyes were bright and happy, as if she had just won the big prize on a TV game show, and the delight that lit up her plain face made him feel sorry for her. She had to be thinking this was the day she would leave these sad, dirty streets for the kind of life that she had seen on TV.

The Thunderbird rolled away. Eddie was about to pull out when he heard the bleat of a horn.

Sal rolled down his window. "You stick with them," he said. "I'll hang back. If it looks like they're taking a powder, I'll stop at a pay phone. Then I'll catch up."

"You see that car?" Eddie said.

Sal shook his head in wonder. "You believe this fucking guy?"

When they got to the corner of Fifty-fourth and Chestnut, the T-Bird turned and started east, back toward town. Stollman had apparently bought the convertible on the sly and kept it garaged waiting for the big day when he could drive his new girlfriend into their new future.

The T-Bird turned off Chestnut Street near the Penn campus and pulled into the parking lot of the Delaware Bank & Trust. Stollman hurried inside. He reappeared ten minutes later, carrying a thick envelope. The couple kissed, and off they went. The scene was repeated almost to the second at the First National Bank, then the Merchants Bank of Philadelphia. Their kiss was longer after the last stop, and Eddie watched as Mary's head disappeared. Momentarily, she popped back up and they drove off again.

They now continued a few blocks on Chestnut and then got on the turnpike heading north, the Thunderbird picking up speed, though not enough to risk attention from Staties. At the exit for the Roosevelt Expressway northbound, a turn signal flashed. Eddie sat forward.

When they turned onto the expressway, he glanced in the mirror to see Sal pulling off at an Esso station. They moved at an easy pace onto Roosevelt Boulevard, past Fentonville and the exit for Cheltenham, heading toward Easton. That's where Sal caught up, passing Eddie to fall in a few hundred yards behind the T-Bird. Eddie saw a Statie pull up and go around. The road was busy with weekend traffic. Eddie thought that if Stollman had any brains at all, he would be checking his mirrors. But good sense was not this citizen's long suit. Apparently, it hadn't occurred to him that he would be tailed.

It happened fast. Eddie was watching up the road as Stollman exited at a rest stop. Sal pulled in and he followed, parking a hundred feet back, as the T-Bird swung into a parking space. A sudden rush of noise and motion interrupted the couple's first kiss. The state police car was followed by an unmarked sedan, then a county sheriff's car, finally a white Cadillac, crowding the rest stop with vehicles. Doors swung open and men in uniforms and gray suits swarmed. Travelers stopped to gawk, craning their necks and whispering.

Eddie and Sal got out of their cars and walked up to witness the melee.

"Look at this shit," Sal said. "It's a regular law-enforcement gang bang."

A couple of the detectives were buzzing around Stollman's convertible while another one stood at a picnic table, his hands on his hips, grilling Stollman. A cop came away from the T-Bird holding the three thick manila envelopes.

Mary had been escorted to another table, where a county sheriff's deputy guarded her. And standing back, watching all of it, were the two people who had arrived in the white Caddy, an attractive brunette woman and a thick man in a three-piece suit: Mrs. Stollman and her lawyer. Eddie caught the bitter light in the woman's eyes as she watched her errant husband being flushed down the toilet.

He returned his attention to the group surrounding Stollman. He couldn't hear what was being said, because they were talking in clipped, menacing voices. The suspect's lip was trembling, his Adam's apple was bobbing like a yo-yo, and it appeared that at any second he might start crying or lose his breakfast.

Eddie peered through the crowd of bodies and caught sight of Mary sitting two tables over. An officer stood behind her with his arms crossed. To Eddie's surprise, she didn't appear scared or even terribly upset. Disappointed, as if it had rained the day she wanted to go to the shore, and a little worried about getting into trouble. Studying her plain face and striking figure, he decided he had been wrong about her.

A girl from Pearl Street would know the score. She must have realized at some point that Stollman was a fool and how unlikely it was that they'd get away with the escapade.

Still, the prize was worth a shot, and all she had to do was lift her skirt for him. Now the adventure was over, and she would just want to go back home and spend the afternoon listening to the radio and playing with the pretty things her boyfriend had bought her. Eddie wondered if she'd have to return all the stuff.

There was nothing more to see. As he and Sal were leaving, a Dodge sedan roared up and slid to a halt. A guy jumped out holding a camera and said, "Hey, Sal! Where's the—"

Sal jerked a thumb. The photographer rushed past.

They stopped at the Triangle Tavern on Twelfth Street so Sal could have a couple cocktails to celebrate. It was still early and the place was almost empty. The detective perched on a stool and called for a 7&7. Eddie asked for a ginger ale.

When their drinks arrived, Sal took a quick slug and then gave Eddie a sly, satisfied wink. "We'll make a nice piece of change on this one. You'll be rewarded."

"It wasn't as hard as I thought it would be," Eddie said.

Sal nodded sagely and tapped a finger on the bar. "It's simple. Your basic human nature."

Eddie had heard this speech before, in one version or another.

Sal continued anyway. "You find what your subjects want and go from there. Stollman went for the money, right? Except that the dough was just a means to an end, a way for him to hang on to this young girl. He would have shacked up with her in a flophouse. That's what he really wanted. And not just to spread her legs or play a tune on his meat whistle whenever he felt lonely."

Though Eddie had jumped ahead to the point, he dutifully said, "What, then?"

"Time." Sal rattled the ice cubes in his glass. "Time he thought he had lost. I mean, look at this jerk-off. When he was a teenager, he was busy getting straight As and kissing the Melling family ass over at the country club. He should have been tearing up the backseat with some cheerleader. He missed all that. McQueen Mary gave it back. Or so he thought."

He waved his empty glass in the air and his features darkened. "The problem is, he's not some punk kid sitting in algebra class with a boner; he's a forty-four-year-old businessman with a wife and kids. Plus he's got a good job, which he didn't earn but was handed to him on a silver platter. He's fucking guilty, and what's more, he ought to be ashamed of himself."

Eddie smiled, as he always did at Sal's righteous rants. When he really got going, he sounded like one of the preachers on Sunday-morning radio.

"Well, you got him," he said.

"*We* got him," Sal said. "The only thing is that right now another William Stollman is out there pulling the same stupid shit and thinking he'll get away with it. Come Monday morning, there'll be a phone call and another case, and we'll do it all over again."

Eddie was quiet for a few moments while Sal tried to catch the bartender's eye. Then he said, "I want to ask you about something."

Sal cocked an eyebrow and Eddie shifted on his stool.

"A few years back, this singer disappeared. I mean, one minute he's there, the next minute he's gone. And nobody ever found anything."

"What was his name?"

"Johnny Pope. He was with a group called the Excels. They were rhythm and blues."

Sal glanced at him. "As in colored?"

"Yeah."

"And when did this happen?"

"A little over three years ago. Winter of '59."

Sal nodded. "Yeah, I think I remember. There was something in the paper about it. So?"

"Well, I was thinking"—Eddie shifted nervously—"that we could maybe take another look at it."

The detective gave him a puzzled frown. "What? You mean investigate? And who would be paying the tab?" When Eddie didn't answer, he said, "So I should chase around trying to find out what happened to some colored singer three years ago for what?"

"Well, he was big-time. He had rec—"

"He wasn't Mario-fucking-Lanza, was he?"

"No, he was—"

"Then I don't think so." Sal glared at the bartender, who had engaged one of the two other customers in a heated argument about the Eagles' past season.

"Well, then, how about if I do it?" Eddie said.

Sal's head came around and he squinted like he hadn't heard it right. "How about if you do what?"

"Look at what happened to Pope." Eddie felt his face flushing. "It would be, y'know, my case."

Sal came up with a short laugh. "Your case?"

"Yeah. I'll work on it by myself."

Sal laughed again, though he didn't seem at all amused. "You've been in this business for what, a little under four weeks? And now you're fucking Sam Spade? You want a case?"

"Okay, not a case," Eddie said. "I meant I'll just do some checking around. See if I can find anything out. It'd be good practice."

What was left of Sal's smile evaporated. "You still don't get it," he said. "We don't *practice,* Cero. This ain't a game and it ain't TV. It's people's lives."

Eddie said, "C'mon, Sal. I just want to have a look."

Sal frowned down into his empty glass, and Eddie felt as if he could read his mind. The detective didn't like it at all. A kid who had only been on the job a month wanted to pick up a case. Not just a case, a case involving a colored guy; no, worse, a colored *musician.* Nothing but trouble. On the other hand, he wouldn't want Eddie getting bored and leaving. And he probably figured that he couldn't do any damage; the whole thing was so old it had rust on it.

Finally, grudgingly, he said, "Not on my time."

"No, not on your time," Eddie said. "You don't have to lift a finger. I just might have to ask you a question if I get stuck."

"You mean when."

"Okay, when. You can do that, right?"

Sal frowned some more.

"Right?"

Sal sighed. "Right, right. Now tell the coach over there I want another goddamn drink."

TEN

The Sunday *Inquirer* came out with a page-three story with a photograph of William Stollman being hustled up the steps of city court by a gaggle of police, his face frozen with strain and blanched white by the glare of the photographer's flash. According to the article, he had broken down and confessed to even more voodoo with the company assets, the kind of shenanigans that could have run Keystone Valve into the ground in a matter of months.

Eddie read sitting propped up on his bed. It was a lesson about what some guys would do for a piece of ass.

Of course, he knew the lure of such sweet treasures; he'd enjoyed his share. And he never really had to go looking. In school the hard girls were easy after dark. Later, women went for him because he was a fighter, because they thought he was good-looking in a rough way, because they were entranced by his smoldering quiet. Eventually, all that would wear off, and then it would start: Maybe he didn't look so good with a banged-up face; or they wanted him to say something; or they wanted him to *be* something—as in something else. That's when he'd check out, leaving no forwarding address.

Sal liked to kid him about girls and regularly threatened to have one of his nieces show up at the office. The detective was of the opinion there was something wrong with any male under the age of fifty who didn't spend half his waking hours chasing tail.

He didn't know that Eddie had it covered. Not long after he moved to the city, he ran into a girl from his high school who had somehow ended up a high-dollar Philadelphia hooker connected to the Bufalino family. Her name was Susie Kelton, and she was a fair-haired, willowy, all-American girl. They had barely known each other when they were kids, and he'd never been around her at all in high school. But they had found each other in the city, and now, once or twice a week, in the wee hours, she came to his room.

Sometimes she stayed until morning; sometimes she left while he was still asleep. Sometimes she took the twenty-dollar bill he left on the night table, sometimes not. She didn't need it, and he really couldn't afford it. And yet it seemed to matter that it was there.

She never explained how she had graduated from cheerleader to call girl, and he never asked. Something told him that the subject was off-limits, and that if he started grilling her, he might never see her again. So he let it alone. She always came to him; he didn't know where she lived or anything else about her life. He figured everyone was entitled to their secrets; he had been letting her keep hers for almost four years.

She had come tapping at his door a little after two that morning. He got up to let her in. After sitting quietly on the edge of his sagging bed for a few minutes, she started to cry. She did that sometimes, and always with a kind of relief, as if letting out a breath she had been holding all night. She made Eddie think of an animal that had been chased through the dark before finally finding a place to hide.

She had dried her eyes and then undressed in a quiet, shy, unwhorelike way. She made love with him, her body rising and falling with no sound except her own hard breathing and, at the end, a tremulous moan. Afterward, as she lay watching his face, she ran a tentative finger over the scar and murmured a sound of hurt. A few minutes later she was asleep.

When he woke up, she was gone, though the bed still smelled of her as he sat reading the story about William Stollman's sins.

After he finished the article, he grabbed a towel and went down the hall to the bathroom. With the tepid water dribbling over his head, he replayed Saturday's melodrama, from the gray dawn street in West Philly, to the scene at the rest stop, with Stollman surrounded by suits and uniforms, a beached fish gasping for air, and Mary sitting at the table, calm but wary, her back straight and that tremendous chest jutting like the prow of a ship, etching a profile that gave every male on the scene cause to stare. Finally, he recalled the bar and the look on Sal's face when he brought up Johnny Pope. *You want a case?*

The water began to run cold. He turned it off, dried himself, climbed into his sweats, and went back down the hall. Carrying the cup of coffee he had fixed on his hot plate to the window, he thought about speaking up about it.

He had been surprised, too. It had come out of nowhere. Well, not exactly *nowhere;* it had started on Thursday night when he opened the gym door, saw that old pug, and caught a tiny glimpse of what he might have become in another ten years.

He looked down at the narrow alley. He'd had some decent fights. He wondered if anyone would remember.

If he was done with that, so be it. He had a job but didn't know if he would ever be a real investigator. He didn't know if he wanted to. The only way to find out was to dive in headfirst, like when he started boxing. He had gotten his head handed to him, but he stayed when the other kids quit and he learned his lessons. So maybe he could do that now.

He turned it over for a little while longer, then put it out of his mind. It was too late to back out anyway; he had already said his piece.

"Cero!" the landlord yelled up the stairwell. "Phone!" A door slammed, shaking the whole house.

Eddie went down to the foyer and picked up the receiver. It was Sal, sounding giddy. "You need to come over, have a drink with me. I got something for you."

"Got what?"

"Well, it's green. I can tell you that much."

"Come over where?"

"To my apartment, where else?"

"I've never been."

"I'll give you directions. It ain't far from you."

Eddie felt for the stub of pencil that was left on top of the phone. He jotted the address Sal dictated on the wall and the quickest route to get there. He said, "An hour, okay?"

Sal said, "Yeah, okay," in such a merry voice that Eddie wondered if he was already into the bottle.

But when he stepped into the apartment on the third floor of the brownstone off Mifflin Street, he found Sal sober, sitting at his kitchen table in a wrinkled rayon shirt, busily snipping the items about Stollman from copies of the Sunday editions of the *Inquirer* and the *Bulletin.* The noonday sun poured through the window, filling the room with dusty light.

As soon as Eddie walked in, the detective pushed the newspapers aside, got up, and went rooting into one of his cabinets.

Eddie looked around. It was a modest little dump, the kind of home he expected from a frumpy middle-aged bachelor. The furniture was all mismatched. There were magazines lying around everywhere, *Newsweek* and *Playboy, Sports Illustrated* and *Argosy.* An old hulk of a Zenith television set was shoved into a corner. Traffic buzzed by on the street below the open windows.

Eddie was surprised to find no dirty dishes in the sink. The kitchen was clean and tidy, in fact. The whole place smelled of Sal, which meant like day-old marinara sauce. And there was something else in the air, a trace of a sweet scent. Eddie could have sworn there had been a woman on the premises recently.

He sat down at the table and watched the older man putter around. Though Sal would stick his nose into Eddie's beeswax at the drop of a hat, he doled his own out carefully and in big, dramatic chunks, episodes from some guinea soap opera. There were always hints lurking around the edges of these tales, and Eddie had suspected right away that Sal and Marie didn't spend all their time fighting. Or maybe there was some other woman hidden away.

Probably the first. Whenever Sal talked about his ex-wife, he got an odd glint in his eyes and a husky note in his voice. Though it was pretty funny to imagine Sal chasing tail like some horny teenager, and funnier still to think of him humping away like some old dog, Eddie wouldn't put it past him. He wondered if he was ever going to meet the object of all this passion, the ex-wife, Marie. She had some kind of crazy magnetic pull to make Sal act so crazy. Why else would he put up with her sending her pimpled punk of a nephew and his fat friend to work him over? It made no sense. Sal could crack their oily heads like coconuts, and yet he seemed faintly amused by the abuse. Eddie couldn't figure it out.

Anyway, if Marie or any other female had been in that lair lately, the detective gave no hint as he came back to the table with a bottle of scotch and two glasses. He poured shots, straight up.

"Here's to sending Mr. William Stollman up Shit Creek without a paddle," he pronounced.

They clinked glasses and Sal reached into his shirt pocket to produce a hundred-dollar bill, which he presented to Eddie with a flourish. "On top of your day rate," he said. "This is what happens when we're good boys and clean our plates."

Eddie was stunned. He had expected maybe an extra twenty. He said, "Damn. Thanks, Sal."

"Better than getting hit in the face, eh?"

Eddie studied the crisp bill. "You know, I actually won some."

Sal laughed quietly. "I know you did. Eighteen and eight, right? Two draws." Eddie nodded, surprised and vaguely pleased. "I looked it up," Sal told him. He waved a hand over Sunday's newspapers. "So, you see all this?"

Eddie nodded. "I saw. So what's going to happen to him?"

"We got him nailed, so they'll make a plea bargain," Sal said. "He'll do time in Allenwood with the rest of the rich crooks. He'll have to give all the money back. He loses the wife and kids, of course. His house and the cars, et cetera, et cetera." He smiled grimly. "Don't worry, he'll be fine. Once you're in that club, you're in for life. Those guys take care of their own."

"What about Mary?"

Sal raised a sly eyebrow. "You tell me."

Eddie thought about it for a few moments. "Party's over, right? She and Stollman are done. She'll go somewhere else and get another shit job. She might end up banging her new boss. It won't be the same, though. She'll lay half the guys on Pearl Street and end up marrying the one that knocks her up. She'll have four or five kids, and she'll be an old lady by the time she's thirty-five."

Sal nodded. "I think you got it, kiddo." He took a sip of his drink. "But, hey, how'd you like to get your hands on those tits, huh? I mean before they're down at her knees."

"I'd settle for a look," Eddie said.

They drank in silence for a few moments. Then Sal said, "I wanted to ask you . . ." He rubbed a finger on the side of his glass. "This thing with the singer."

Eddie was alert, wondering if Sal had called him over to soften him up with whiskey and cash so he could pull the plug before he even got started. He was surprised when the detective said, "Go through it for me again."

"Yeah?"

"Yeah, g'head, let's hear it."

Eddie sat up. "Johnny Pope was the lead singer and songwriter for this group called the Excels. They got together sometime in 1956, and by the next year they were already on the charts. They were just about to make it in a big way when Pope disappeared." He flipped a hand. "I mean *gone*. It was investigated by the cops and also by some PIs, and they never found anything. And that's it."

"When did this happen?"

"Three years ago. February of '59."

"That's a long time," Sal said. "And what happened to the group after he was gone? What did you say the name was?"

"The Excels. I don't know about the other two guys. But his sister was in the group, too. And Joe's got her singing at the Blue Door."

The detective hiked an eyebrow. "Oh, yeah?"

"Yeah, I saw her over there. That's what got me thinking about it."

Sal leaned forward, unscrewed the cap on the bottle, and freshened his drink. When he tipped the bottle toward the other glass, Eddie shook his head. The detective screwed the cap back on and put the bottle aside.

"I gotta tell you what comes to mind here," he said. "First of all, I don't get why you want to fuck around with this thing, it's over and done. Three months, maybe. But three years? Why bother?"

Eddie tried to think of something that sounded right. "I have some of their records," he said. "I saw them onstage in Atlantic City one time, and they put on a great show. The guy was one hell of a talent. He would have been famous. But then he was gone. I mean without a trace."

"Yeah, well, these things happen."

"I think someone got away with murder."

"That happens, too." Sal regarded him narrowly, his elbow propped on the table and his chin in his hand. "So, what now, you think you're going to crack the case?" When Eddie didn't reply, Sal said, "You're just going to be wasting your time."

"Yeah, so what do you care?"

"I don't. But I'm going to tell you something right off the bat. There's certain parties in this city that are really good at making people disappear. You know who I'm talking about. If that's the case, I don't have to explain about nosing around in their business, do I?" The question didn't require an answer. "You want to go ahead with this? Fine. I don't give a shit. But first on your list is to make sure you're not stepping on the wrong people's toes."

Eddie frowned. "How am I going to do that?"

The detective sat back. "It's your case. So it's your problem. Figure it out." He gave Eddie a tight smile and then took a long sip of his drink.

Eddie sat in the kitchen for another half hour with a glass of whiskey he didn't want, hoping Sal would give in and tell him exactly how a citizen went about learning if any Philly mob guys had a hand in a particular murder. But Sal wouldn't say another word on the subject, no doubt hoping he would get the message and drop the whole thing. So he listened to war stories, then went home.

When he got back to his room, he turned on the radio and stretched out on the bed, paging idly through the newspaper. He read the sports and the city news. In the Entertainment section, he saw a little ad for the Blue Door noting that Valerie Pope, formerly of the Excels, was now the one "Appearing Nitely." He dozed off reading an article about Dave Brubeck.

It was early evening when he woke up to the sun turning orange over the tops of the buildings. He lay there, staring up at the ceiling, trying to figure a way around the problem Sal had presented him. After ten minutes of puzzling, he sat up, blinking with concentration, then hurried down the hall to wash his face.

A pretty blond was working the hostess station, and there was Joe D'Amato giving her a quick frisk as he whispered in her ear. When he saw Eddie, he smiled with delight. "Fast Eddie!" He went into his shadowbox routine.

Eddie shook his hand. "Can I talk to you for a minute?"

"Sure, sure, in my office," Joe said. He patted the blond's rear and led Eddie away with a look back over his shoulder. *"Madonn',"* he whispered, wringing a hand in the air. "I really gotta stop hiring girls I want to bang."

There was no one at the bar this early on a Sunday, and only a half-dozen tables in the dining room were occupied. Eddie followed Joe to the office, a little room stuck in the back corner.

Joe held the door for him to step inside. There wasn't much to it, a desk and a couple extra chairs, two file cabinets, some licenses in frames, and a dozen photos. He recognized the Orlons, Bobby Rydell, Dee Dee Sharp, and some of the other South Philly alumni. There was a window with blinds that Joe could open to see what was going on in the club. A speaker mounted over the door piped in the house PA, the performers onstage, or taped music that rolled off the reel-to-reel machine on the shelf in the corner. At that moment it was Chet Baker's moody trumpet.

Joe waved Eddie into one of the chairs and perched on the corner of his desk. He came up with a quick grin. "Hey, I called Sal and told him how it worked out with that fucking Jerry. How you helped with that situation."

"Thanks," Eddie said. He took the opening. "I was wondering if maybe you can help me with something."

"What kind of something?"

"You remember the other night I came by and we were talking about Johnny Pope?"

Joe nodded. "Uh-huh, yeah, at the bar."

"Right. Well, I might want to look into it."

"Look into what?"

"Johnny disappearing and all that."

Joe's brow furrowed. "You mean like an investigation?"

"Yeah. Like that."

Joe shifted and crossed his arms. "Well, you know . . . you know there was cops all over it back when it happened, right? They couldn't find nothing."

"I know. I just thought I'd have another look."

"Is Sal going to be in on this?"

"He knows about it. I'm doing it on my own."

Joe looked troubled. "Maybe that ain't such a good idea," he said. "You know you gotta be careful about where you're sticking your nose."

"Yeah, that's what I wanted to ask about." Eddie lowered his voice. "The way he disappeared, I understand that could mean certain people had a hand in it, right?"

"Yeah, that's right." Joe paused, staring at him. "What, you think I know something?"

"Well, with the club, I thought you might have some connections." Joe drew back a little and cocked his head warily. "I mean, if that's what happened," Eddie went on, "I'd like to know before I started anything."

"Yeah, I bet you would."

"Is there any way to find out?"

Joe scratched his chin thoughtfully. "Well, maybe . . . I'll tell you what, what I can do is make a phone call. All this time has passed; it's old news. Maybe somebody'll be willing to talk."

"That'd be great."

"I said maybe. No promises, okay?"

"Okay."

"You call me tomorrow, the next day, I'll let you know."

As he got up to leave, Eddie said, "So, what do you think, Joe?"

"About what?"

"About what happened to him?"

Joe pondered for a moment. "I want to show you something," he said, and went to one of the file cabinets, knelt down to open the bottom drawer. "Where is it?" he muttered. "Okay, yeah, here we go." He straightened up and handed over a framed eight-by-ten photograph of the four members of the Excels and himself, posing on the sidewalk in front of the club.

"They used to work here," Joe explained. "Right out on that stage. That's how I know Valerie. Of course, when they got big, I couldn't afford them anymore. Johnny still came around, though."

Eddie took a closer look. Johnny had one arm thrown over Valerie's shoulder, the other over Joe's. He wore a brash, beaming, top-of-the-world smile. Joe looked drunk. Valerie glowed, young and pretty and full of the moment. The other two, cousin Ray and Tommy Gates, were clowning in the wings. They looked like happy kids in the thrall of a crazy ride. Eddie handed the photo back. Joe regarded it fondly.

"You know, we used to have everybody down here," he said. "The Pastels, the Silhouettes, all of them. Dick Clark came by sometimes. It wasn't Palumbo's, but it was some jumping place for music. The whole city was that way. And Johnny was right at the top of the heap."

Joe took another moment to study the photo, his face falling. "Then that thing happened, and I had to take this off the wall. Couldn't stand to look at it." He dropped the photo to his side and raised one hand beseechingly. "How could it be? One minute he's here; the next minute he's gone. The lights went out." He shook his head slowly. "What happened? I got no fucking idea. I wish I did. It was such a goddamn shame." He put the photograph back in its place with tender hands.

"Call me tomorrow," he said.

ELEVEN

Eddie drove to Sansom Street through a Monday morning drizzle and found Sal at his desk, drinking a cup of coffee and reading the *Inquirer.* When the detective looked up from the paper, Eddie saw that he was sporting another nice shiner on his left eye. The guy was a regular punching bag.

"Liston's going to fight Patterson for the title," the punching bag said, tapping the page with his finger.

"He'll kill him," Eddie said.

"What about this kid—whatshisname, Clay—he's got some stuff, huh?"

"Uh-huh." Eddie pointed at Sal's eye. "Don't tell me your nephew and his fat pal came back."

Sal looked up. "What? Oh, this? Nah, they wouldn't dare." He continued reading. "It was her."

"Her who?"

"Marie. My wife. Ex-wife."

Eddie worked to keep a straight face. "What'd she give you, a smack?"

"Milk bottle," Sal said. "With milk in it."

It took more work for Eddie to stifle a laugh. He waited,

knowing there was a story lurking. One that the detective would relate, if he gave him a minute.

It was actually about half that. Still perusing his paper, Sal said, "She called me up yesterday after you left, asked me to come over for dinner. So we could talk."

"Talk."

"That's what she said. I should have known better. I get there and we go into the kitchen. I'm sitting at the table, my kitchen table, which I bought, and all of a sudden, *wham!* She belts me with this bottle. I think she was trying to bust it on the side of my head."

"Why'd she do that?"

"Why?" Now he laid his *Inquirer* flat on the desk. "Because we've been arguing about money, and things aren't going her way. Then she suddenly remembers that two weeks ago her Frankie had gone home crying that some guy at Uncle Sal's office had been mean to him."

"What?"

"Yeah. She decided to pay me back 'cause you scared her nephew. At least that was the excuse."

"This is the same nephew that jumped you in an alley. The same one came back up here to give you more shit."

"Exactly."

"That is one crazy woman you got there," Eddie said.

"That whole fucking family's mental cases."

"So why don't you just stay the hell away?"

"What would she do without me?"

Eddie had to smile at Sal sitting there with that big purple eye and yet all pleased with himself.

Sal caught the look and held his arms wide like an opera singer. "What can I say? The woman is still nuts about me." When Eddie started laughing, he dropped his outstretched arms and said, "Someday you'll understand that love is a many-fucking-splendored thing."

"I'll take your word for it." Eddie sat down. "You got something for me to work on?"

"Yeah, but before we get to that, you had a visitor."

Eddie cocked his head. "A what?"

"A visitor," Sal said. "Some colored girl. Valerie something. Is she—"

"She was here?" Eddie came out of his chair. "Why didn't you tell me?"

"I'm telling you now. Is she the—"

"Where'd she go?"

"—one with the—"

"Where'd she go, Sal?"

"I told her she could wait. She said she wanted coffee, so I sent her to Louie's. Does she have something to do with the singer or what?"

Eddie started for the door. "I'll be back in a little while."

He trotted three blocks through the rain to Louie's Diner and stepped inside, his hair dripping. She was sitting in the corner booth, a coffee cup before her and a cigarette burning in the ashtray. She was wearing a man's white dress shirt, black slacks, and a brown corduroy jacket. Hoop earrings the size of half-dollars hung from her ears. She stared at him from behind her one shock of blond hair, with mascaraed eyes that looked like the barrels of a shotgun pointed at his chest. He crossed to the booth.

"Why you messing in my family's business?" she demanded by way of greeting.

He stopped and his uncertain smile went south. "What? Why am I—"

"Who said you could do that?"

"I—"

"And who *are* you, anyway?"

"Just *wait* a minute!"

It came out louder than he'd intended, and the few customers who hadn't been glancing at the odd couple in the corner now turned to stare openly. Eddie and Valerie looked away from each other for the thirty seconds it took the last of them to go back to minding his or her own business.

She stabbed her cigarette into the ashtray like she was driving a nail. "I want to know right now what you think you're doing."

Eddie turned away to give himself a few seconds, catching the eye of the waitress and mouthing the word *coffee*. The girl nodded.

He slid into the booth uninvited, only to find Valerie's gaze locked on him. "I asked you a question."

"Okay." He tried to catch his breath. "That one night I was at the Blue Door, I was talking to Joe. About what happened to your brother." He shrugged. "So I started asking about it. And that's all."

She shook her head. "Uh-uh, Joe said you were *investigating*." She mouthed the word as though it was something dirty.

She was getting on his nerves. "All I did was ask him about it. Did I break some kind of law?"

Her eyes flashed, and he thought she was going to come at him again. Then, abruptly, she drew back and looked away, and in that moment he was startled by how pretty she was, even angry, with that caramel skin and those high cheekbones and dark, dark almond eyes. It took a few seconds for him to realize that she was talking to him.

". . . and it needs to be let alone," she said with a forced calm.

He returned to the present and considered for a moment, getting his words straight. "All this time has passed; I thought it might be worth another look."

"Oh, yeah? Is that what you thought?" She jammed another cigarette into the corner of her mouth and lit it, the match flaring. She leaned over, pushing a cloud of smoke and jabbing a finger into his face. "I'm going to say this as nice as I can. It's over. It was over three years ago—and even if it wasn't, it's none of your damn business. So you just leave it be." She dropped her voice very deliberately. "You hear me? You leave it be." She drilled him one more time with her black eyes, then stood up and walked out, leaving her cigarette smoldering in the ashtray.

The front door banged. She stalked past the window and down the rain-slicked sidewalk.

Eddie let out a long breath and reached over to stub out her cigarette. Glancing up, he saw the waitress standing a few feet away, a cup in one hand and the coffeepot in the other, frozen in place and holding her breath. Behind her, another half-dozen faces were staring at him.

"I'll take that to go," he said.

Valerie stalked away from the diner, fuming.

She had told herself to keep cool and then had lost her temper. Something had risen from inside her, and the next thing she knew, she was yelling in the face of some fighter from South Philly she barely knew.

After a block she slowed her angry pace and spent some time trying to make sense of it. From what Joe told her, Eddie Cero had been a boxer but now worked for some private detective and had suddenly appeared with the idea in his head to poke into Johnny's disappearance.

It was supposed to be all over. Just the thought of bringing it back to life sent her into a dizzy whirl.

She stopped on the corner of Franklin Street. It was only four short blocks to Lombard, and she spent the walk and then the ride on the 40 bus to Grays Ferry calming herself. There was nothing Eddie Cero or anyone else would ever find out about the death of Johnny Pope. It was too late for that.

When he walked into the office, Sal looked up and said, "That was quick." Eddie made a vague gesture. Sal said, "So?"

"So nothing. We talked."

The detective was watching his face. "And?"

"And nothing."

Sal studied him for another moment. "Okay, then. So can we go over this new thing? Or do you got other business to attend to?"

Eddie sat down. "Yeah, sure, go ahead."

Sal moved some papers around. "What we got is a situation with the concerned parents of a seventeen-year-old girl. A high school senior. Mom and Dad think their little brat is acting odd. Like there's something going on. She won't talk and they won't give her a slap in the kisser and make her."

Eddie smiled absently. "How did you land this one?"

"Friend of mine. Another ex-cop. Says the parents want someone small to handle it."

"And the girl's doing what?"

"Nothing, as far as anyone can tell. She's a regular kid, good grades in school, she's going to a good college next fall, but the parents still swear there's something wrong. They want us to tail her, make sure she isn't getting into trouble."

Eddie gazed blankly at Sal's face.

"As the father of daughters, I can tell you exactly what they're thinking," the detective went on. "They have this beautiful kid, they got her all this way, and they want her to graduate and get into college without getting knocked up or caught stealing cars or some such shit." He smiled dimly. "Anyone else would just let it pass. But they're rich, so they're going to throw money at it."

Eddie nodded.

"So we're going to keep an eye on her between the time she gets out of school and gets home. She usually goes out Friday and Saturday nights, so we'll trade—you take one; I'll take the other." He waited. Eddie continued to stare at him with glassy eyes. "Hey!" he yelled.

Eddie jumped. "What? I'm listening."

"No, you're not. What's wrong with you?"

"Nothing."

"What? That colored girl? What happened with her?"

"Nothing. I told you. We talked." Their gazes locked until Eddie looked away and sighed. "Actually, she . . . uh, just about took my head off." Sal was watching him, so he repeated the scene at Louie's and Valerie's tirade.

The detective thought it was funny. "You let her slap you around in public, tough guy?"

"She said it's none of my business."

"Oh, yeah?" Sal said. "Didn't you tell me this guy was a star? That means he was a public figure, and that makes him anybody's business."

"She was pretty pissed off."

"So?" Now Sal gave him a look of annoyance. "What's wrong with you? You spent the last ten years fighting guys who wanted to knock you into the cheap seats, and you let some girl rough you up? What's the matter, you scared of her?"

"I'm not scared of her."

"You got a funny way of showing it." A moment passed, and Sal's expression softened. "It's all right, kiddo. You just gotta be on your toes. Some people will try and run right over you." He tapped a finger on his desk blotter. "Listen, you don't need her permission. You just need mine. And I gave it to you. All right?"

"Okay."

"That's for the moment, and when it don't keep you from real work," he added pointedly. "Such as this girl. Marianne Gibson. Did you hear anything I said about that?"

"I got the part about the parents wanting us to watch her. But she's not actually doing anything."

"Not that anyone can tell."

"Sounds like babysitting."

"It is babysitting, my friend. We do that now and then when

the parents want to pay." He laid a finger alongside his bruised eye. "We have her through the end of May, and then she graduates and she's somebody else's problem. In the meantime, Mr. and Mrs. Gibson are willing to fork over a nice sum to have us watch her." The detective handed over a manila envelope. "There's a picture in there, the address of her school, friends' names, the places she frequents, et cetera, et cetera. Start this afternoon and stay on her the rest of the week. I'll take Saturday night. Then you'll be back Monday. By the way, I've alerted the local cops and they know you'll be out there. But you should stop in, pay a courtesy visit. The chief's name is Jack McKay; he used to be on the Philadelphia force."

Eddie stood up with the file in his hand.

"One other thing," Sal said. "I'm going to pay you for the week on Friday."

"Okay."

The detective made an odd sound in his throat. "And I'm going to pay you every Friday."

Eddie sat back down. "You mean—"

"Yeah, yeah, I'm giving you a job," Sal said quickly. "Which you have already, more or less, so what's the big deal? I mean, I ain't going to write you a check or do taxes. You won't be on the payroll or anything." He was getting flustered. "So is that okay with you, or are you still thinking about going back to the fight game?"

"It's okay with me."

"Good. You can spend some of the money on a telephone."

Eddie said that would be fine. He could use one anyway.

"And you can move, too."

"Do what?"

"Move. You said you want out of that dump, right? Well, there's this nice apartment house right over on Nineteenth Street and—"

"—and you know a guy."

"That's right," Sal said. He produced a business card with CALVIN JOHANNSEN—HOMESIDE REALTY printed on it. "Cal would appreciate some security on the premises. For which he would be willing to knock off half the rent."

"Security meaning what?"

"Security meaning making it known to the local hoodlums that this particular building is off-limits."

"Sal, I told you—"

"Right, right, you ain't going to beat nobody up. I understand. Though I don't get the point of spending half your life learning to fight and then not putting it to use."

Eddie stood up. "I'll see you tomorrow," he said.

He stopped for gas and, while the guy was pumping, he tore open the manila envelope and pulled out two photographs and a sheet of paper.

In her high school yearbook photo, Marianne Gibson was the kid off a cereal box, with light bouncing off her honey-blond hair, a sprinkle of brown freckles, and a precious turned-up nose—an all-American beauty. Eddie knew that for a lot of kids, a yearbook photo was a last pose before fading away. Hoods turned into choirboys and sluts appeared as angels. Eddie Cero had looked like . . . like Eddie Cero, with hard eyes in a face that was full of shadows.

In the other photo, Marianne had been caught staring directly into the lens, and Eddie caught a sharp, carnal look, as if she was about to devour whatever caught her fancy. The sexual power that radiated from her would fade soon enough, but what he saw from this angle was black magic.

He didn't think the Gibsons needed to worry about their daughter getting knocked up. The calculating glint in those eyes told him she was too smart for such a dumbass mistake.

She'd probably sit on it at least until she reached college, where the boys could offer something more than a sweaty tussle in the backseat.

Laying the photo aside, he read over the single sheet of paper. Miss Gibson was a month shy of eighteen, five six, and 120. She lived in an exclusive section of Havertown with Dad, an executive at DuPont; Mom the happy homemaker; and a younger brother, who was in the ninth grade. As a senior, she was involved in the usual stuff the snotty popular kids did, and on Saturdays she worked in a gift shop downtown. She kept an A average and had been accepted to Bucknell in the fall.

A list of her friends was included, and the parents reported that she was dating a boy named Steven Jamison. Two of the local hangouts were noted, along with a final note that she drove a 1956 MG TD painted British racing green. It would be easy to tail.

The gas jockey directed him to the police station. Chief McKay—a short, solid man with a red Irish face and a cop's gray brush cut—stepped out of his office to shake Eddie's hand.

"You know I was on the force with Sal," he said. "He was in plainclothes and I walked a beat, but I got to know him pretty well." He clasped his hands behind his back and rocked on his heels. "So Marianne Gibson's parents think she's hiding something? She's a teenage girl, of *course* she's hiding something. That's what kids do. I know; I've got one of my own." He shrugged. "So what's your plan?"

Eddie told him he would do a basic surveillance on Miss Gibson from the time she got out of school until she went home and stayed. Though McKay's expression broadcast his opinion that the intrusion wasn't welcome, he said he would notify his officers. If the cop had any doubts about Eddie's skills, he didn't say anything.

Eddie drove around until he located Buzzy's, one of the joints noted on the sheet. He cruised past the other hangout, a place on the four-lane called the Shack. Then he crossed town and located Franklin High School. Pulling around to the parking lot in back, he easily picked out the green MG from the small sea of cars. He found a place in an alleyway that abutted the school property and slouched down in the seat to wait.

At 3:20 the bell clanged and the students broke free, first a trickle, then in rushing waves. He couldn't find Marianne in the crowd but saw the MG putter through the parking lot and fall in with the line heading for the street.

She drove directly to the Shack. The parking lot was crowded, with a couple dozen kids hanging around in front, sitting in and on their cars, smoking and drinking Cokes. Marianne made the rounds, then went inside. It all seemed pretty normal, what a million kids were doing at that moment all over America. She stayed at the spot until six, then left and drove to her home on Edgewood Road. Two minutes after she closed the door, a light went on in an upstairs bedroom and Eddie saw a shadow moving about.

It was a long evening. At ten o'clock the bedroom went dark, and he decided to call it a day. The street was so quiet that he released the hand brake and drifted the car to the bottom of the next corner before starting the engine for the drive back to the city.

When he walked into the Blue Door a little before eleven, he heard Valerie's voice, swooning through a heartfelt version of "All in My Mind." He asked the hostess to find Joe and headed for the bar.

George had just slipped his glass onto a coaster when Joe came up, waving an apologetic hand. "I got you in trouble, eh?" He spoke in a tense whisper, as if Valerie could hear him from the stage. "She came by the other night to pick up her check. I let it slip out about what you were doing. You should have seen the look on her face."

"I'll bet," Eddie said. "She showed up at the office this morning. She was not happy."

"Jesus!" Joe whispered. "I thought you'd tell her."

"I guess I should have."

Joe jerked his head. "C'mon with me. Bring your beer."

He led Eddie into his office and closed the door. Pointing to one of the chairs, he took a seat behind his desk.

"I got something for you," he said. "You know who Winky Ragusa is, right?"

"He's that mob guy who fixes fights," Eddie said.

Joe's eyes flicked nervously. "Let's stay on the subject here, okay? I made his acquaintance a few years back. He and some of his associates used to come into the club. So I called him, mentioned someone was interested in the disappearance of Johnny Pope. I told him that this party was concerned he might be putting his nose in where it don't belong."

Eddie settled in the chair, smiling at the delicate footwork.

"The Wink appreciated the gesture," Joe went on. "He said him and his associates get blamed for everything goes on down here. He said it was nice someone had the courtesy to ask first. So he told me he'd check around and get back." He paused for a second. "He called me a little while ago."

Eddie came to attention. "And?"

"And what he told me is some strange business." He lowered his voice another notch. "It turns out there was noise back then about a contract on a colored singer. It had to be Johnny."

Eddie was stunned. "A contract? As in . . ."

Joe hiked his eyebrows. "As in *sayonara,* pal."

"Why? He was just a singer."

"I guess he got on the wrong side of the wrong person," Joe said. "Winky said he personally didn't have nothing to do with any of it, you understand. This is what he heard."

"Shit," Eddie said. "That's it, then."

"No, it's not," Joe said. "It gets strange. Winky says this particular contract wasn't ever carried out. Because Johnny disappeared before the ticket got punched. Winky said the only reason he remembered was because the guy that got hired to do the job had to give the money back. That never happened before, and everybody thought it was pretty funny. A refund on a hit."

Eddie was puzzled. "So . . . what, there was a whole other contract on him?"

"That wouldn't make sense," Joe said. "A contract is kind of, uh . . ."

"Exclusive?"

"That's the word. Once someone picks it up, it's done." He tugged one ear thoughtfully. "Something else happened to Johnny Pope."

Eddie sat back. "Is that it?"

"Yeah, except Winky did say it wouldn't cause him any problem if someone was to poke around. So I guess you don't have to worry about crossing the wiseguys." With a dry smile, he tilted his head in the direction of the door and the floor of the club beyond. "You only have to worry about her."

Valerie was on her way into Joe's office as he was stepping out. She stopped cold and glared at him for a second that seemed to stop the clock.

Sucking in a breath, she said, "Could I speak to you outside?" It wasn't a request.

As soon as they hit the sidewalk, she turned, hands on her hips. "What are you doing here?"

"Talking to Joe," he said.

"About Johnny?" She didn't give him a chance to answer. "I told you it wasn't none of your business. I told you to let it be."

Annoyed, Eddie said, "I don't need your permission, okay?"

He was surprised. Not only did it draw her up short, but as tough-guy lines went, it didn't sound all that bad.

Valerie jammed a furious hand into her bag, jerked out a Winston, and jammed it into the corner of her mouth.

"You know those are bad for your voice," he said.

Her dark eyes flared. "Shut up."

He drew back, startled, and bit down on a laugh. She snatched the cigarette off her lip and moved in. "Why are you doing this?"

"I want to look into it." He stretched his arms, palms up, in a gesture reminiscent of a certain rotund private detective. "Am I the only one who wants to know what happened?"

She shifted her posture like she was switching to southpaw. Cocking her head to one side, she said, "I'll tell you what happened. Three years ago my brother walked out of a studio, and no one ever saw him again."

"So that's the end of it?" Eddie said.

"You know something I don't?"

"Somebody does."

"Listen to me," she said in a tight voice. "What happened to Johnny tore my family apart. We're not going to go through it again." She drew back. "Do you understand? You're in the wrong place, mister. You need to just stay the hell away."

With that, she turned her back on him and went inside. The blue door slammed behind her.

TWELVE

When Eddie walked into the office the next morning, Sal was talking on the phone, so he waited by the window. He noticed that the detective's shiner was fading to a yellowish corona.

Sal finished his call. "So what's with Miss Gibson?" he inquired briskly.

"Nothing," Eddie said. "She goes to school, she hangs around with her friends, she goes home, she does her homework, she goes to bed. I don't get it."

"You get it when I pay you on Friday," Sal said. "Just don't go to sleep out there." He turned his attention to some papers on his desk.

"Hey, you know that question you wanted me to ask about Johnny Pope?" Eddie said. "I got an answer."

"From who?"

"Winky Ragusa."

Sal looked up, his eyes wide with surprise. "You talked to Winky Ragusa?"

"Joe talked to him," Eddie said. "And I talked to Joe."

Sal's astonished expression gave way to a smile and then a bemused laugh. "I'll be damned. The Wink, huh? That's decent work, Eddie."

Eddie felt his face glowing. It was the first time Sal had called him anything other than "kiddo" or "my friend" or "Cero." He felt like the teacher had just put a gold star next to his name. He related the rest of what Joe had told him. Sal listened, his eyes narrowing, and by the time Eddie finished, a pronounced frown had appeared.

"You don't know why whoever it was wanted Pope dead?" the detective said.

"No. I mean, not ye—"

"And him disappearing wasn't this contract? You sure about that?"

"That's the word. The guy had to give back the money."

"Sonofabitch," Sal said. "Anything else?" Eddie said no. Sal's grim frown stayed put. "I think it's time to drop it."

Eddie was stunned. "Drop it why?"

"Because now you're fucking around with Winky Ragusa, that's why. And because there's only one place you can go with this information." He waited.

Eddie thought it over. "Well, I guess I'd have to find the guy—"

"—the guy who took the contract in the first place," Sal said. "So now you're fucking around with hired killers. That's if you can find the guy, and if he'll talk. And who knows what else?" He leaned forward and tapped a finger on his desk. "This is not what we do, my friend."

"I know," Eddie said. "What we do is follow rich schoolgirls."

Sal's eyebrows shot up. "Hey, fuck you! Maybe you'd like to try making a living elsewhere."

Eddie threw up his hands. "You just gave me the job yesterday, and now you want to fire me?"

"What I want is for you to shut the fuck up about the working conditions around here."

"That's not the *point,* Sal."

"Yeah, what is the point, *Eddie*?"

"The point is I got something important, and you—"

"Important?" Sal let out a sarcastic laugh. "Some colored singer got himself knocked off three years ago. You call that breaking news?"

"He was murdered, Sal."

"Oh, and what? You're gonna bring the guilty party to justice?"

"Maybe."

"And maybe not." Sal leaned back in his chair, as stern as a judge. "Look, I don't need to make history here, and I definitely don't need my name in the paper. What I need to do is make a living. So just shut up about this shit."

Eddie's face was flushing with anger. Sal didn't flinch at all. They glared at each other for another five seconds. Then Eddie turned around and stomped out.

A half hour later, he walked back in and handed the detective his cup of coffee, fighting an urge to accidentally spill it in his lap. He was halfway to the front office when the phone rang.

Sal snatched it up. "SG Investigations." He listened for a moment. "Just a second." Keeping a straight face, he held the receiver out.

Eddie took it. "Hello?"

"This is Valerie Pope."

After a moment of surprise, Eddie braced himself. He wasn't in the mood for round three. Not that there was a case to discuss anymore.

She said, "I shouldn't have talked to you like that last night." Though her voice wasn't exactly dripping with honey, the ripsaw edge was gone. Eddie was aware of Sal slouching with his hands behind his head but with his ears perked.

Valerie said, "There's a place called Thelma's on South Street, corner of Twenty-third."

"I'm not—"

"I'll be there in a half hour," she said.

The phone went dead. Eddie dropped the receiver back in the cradle, picked up his coffee, and moved away.

"Who was that?" Sal asked casually.

"Valerie Pope," Eddie said over his shoulder. In the front offices, he stood by the desk, pushing an idle finger through yesterday's mail.

"What'd she want?" Sal called.

Eddie considered telling him it was none of his fucking business. "To tell me I could come talk to her."

"Where?"

"That fried-chicken place out South Street. Thelma's."

"When?"

"In a half hour."

There was a pause. "So maybe you should go."

Eddie stepped back into the doorway. "What?"

"I said maybe you should go." The detective was wearing a placid expression. "Who knows, something might come out of it. What I'm thinking is nobody makes that much noise over nothing."

Eddie could have sworn he heard a note of apology lurking in the detective's voice.

Sal began shuffling the papers on his desk. "Just make sure you get your reports done. And get out to Havertown in time for the bell." He watched Eddie scurry around to snatch up his keys and his jacket and said, "Jesus Christ, relax," he said. "It ain't a goddamn date."

She was approaching along the South Street sidewalk. In the morning light, and with only a touch of makeup, her face looked younger and softer, even with the cool mask firmly in place. Today she had donned blue jeans, saddle shoes, and a thin sweater, just a kid on her way home from school.

That image blew away when they came together under Thelma's neon sign. She treated him to a flat glance as she grabbed the door, jerked it open, and went in, letting it bang shut behind her. He was tempted to forget the whole thing right there. But he hadn't come all that way for nothing, so he followed her inside—where it was hopping, even at that midmorning hour, a swirl of noisy motion around the front counter and through the dining room in back. Waves of chatter rippled in waves, and the cooks and waitresses shouted back and forth, all to the beat of music from speakers on the wall. Meanwhile, tinny voices rasped out of a dozen transistor radios.

Family-owned and well into its second generation as a South Philly landmark, Thelma's was famous in its own way as the Melrose Diner, serving "Breakfast Anytime!" and specializing in fried chicken.

It wasn't just the food and the strong coffee that had the air crackling. As he trailed Valerie past the counter with its chrome stools and into the main dining area, Eddie picked up little bits here and there and realized that it was the news from Mississippi that had everyone excited—Martin Luther King, the sit-ins and Freedom Marches, and President Kennedy's well-publicized disgust with what was going on in Mississippi. The room fairly throbbed with the pulse of a ring before a title fight or a street when a parade was about to come into view, and Eddie liked it.

Valerie wasn't taking part, marching ahead without looking back to see if he was still there. Glances from the customers at the tables landed on her, shifted to him, and stuck there. The disjointed feeling of seeing nothing but faces in varying shades of brown came and went in an instant.

For her part, Valerie appeared irked by the calm way he took it all in. When they found a table, she treated him to a peeved look and said, "Have you been here before?"

"Oh, yeah," Eddie said. "They got the best cinnamon rolls in the city."

He saw the question mark in her eyes. She didn't know what to make of him. Within the space of a few quick seconds, her expression switched from amused to annoyed then back to puzzled, as she tried to make sense of what a boxer who collected 45s and now worked for a private snoop was doing in the middle of her family tragedy.

She was about to ask him when their waitress appeared, 250 pounds if she weighed an ounce, and with a stunningly beautiful face. Eddie gazed at her regal countenance, and she treated him to a dazzling smile, teeth glowing all pearly against her chocolate skin. It was as if some African queen had been transplanted to work the floor at a fried-chicken joint in South Philly, one who seemed delighted to have the only white face in the room at her station.

"We're just having coffee," Valerie told her.

"I'm ordering breakfast." Eddie ignored the glare from across the table.

"And I know just what you want," the waitress announced. "Two eggs scrambled wit' cheese, nice piece of pork sausage, biscuits and gravy."

Eddie smiled up at her. "Nix the sausage. Ham, if you got it."

The waitress raised an eyebrow at Valerie, who said, "Just coffee," in her tight voice. The waitress gave a nod and moved away across the crowded room, an ocean liner plowing into deep water.

Eddie turned to meet Valerie's frown of annoyance. "What?"

"Nothing. Enjoy your breakfast."

He got it. This was her turf, but he was making himself right at home, and she was not happy about it. Of course, he'd been there before; most of South Philly had eaten at Thelma's. And she didn't know about all the time he'd spent with black fighters (and Puerto Ricans and micks and Polacks, too), including hanging out in their bars, eating in their restaurants, and visiting their homes. And the fact was that skin tones and last names didn't matter near as much inside a boxing ring. The punches hurt about the same.

She wouldn't look at him, and the air around the table was cooling by the second. He was saved when the waitress swept back to the table to slide a brimming cup and saucer onto each place mat. Eddie smiled at her as she moved on, then began fiddling with the cream and sugar. Valerie didn't touch hers.

She said, "Is somebody paying you?" in that accusing voice of hers.

"Excuse me?"

"To do this investigation. Is someone paying you?"

"Nope. And it's not exact—"

"You just decided to do it."

"It's like I said. I'm interested. And nobody—"

"And why you?"

"Why me?"

"Yeah." She cupped a hand to the side of her mouth. "I think you're the wrong color."

"What difference does that make?"

"All the difference in the world," she snapped back. "White folks messing in black folks' business ain't ever been anything but trouble."

Eddie said, "But I'm not white, I'm Italian."

She glared sharply and he thought, *Uh-oh, here it comes.* Then one corner of her mouth tipped a fraction of an inch and she said, "Uh-huh."

He took the opening. "I just want to see what I can find out."

She frowned at him fixedly. "No one else could."

"I know."

She considered for another moment, pursing her soft lips. "Did you think I was going to help you?"

"I hoped, yeah."

"And why would I do that?"

"Because I'm your biggest fan," he blurted. She startled him and herself with a laugh, a warm breeze that came and went in the space of a couple seconds. She followed it with a sigh before hunching forward to look directly into his eyes. It was a sneaky punch, and he felt a tipsy jolt.

"It was three years ago," she said. "It's over and done. Nobody wants it all stirred up again."

"I do."

Her eyes flashed, and they were back on more familiar ground. "Fine, then. You go ahead. Just don't expect anyone to help you." She sat back, crossing her arms.

"That's it?" Eddie said.

"Yeah, that's it."

"Then what am I doing here?"

"I don't know," she said tartly. "What are you doing here?"

Eddie understood; she had been figuring him for an amateur or a crazy fan just playing around, one who would give up once she put him in a room full of her people and turned up the heat. Except it didn't work out that way.

He stirred his coffee. "Well, thanks for your time," he said.

She blinked in momentary confusion. She made a sideways turn in her chair. "So . . . I'm going now." She got to her feet. She sat back down. She peered at him, opened her mouth, closed it. He took a patient sip of his coffee. She fussed a little more, then began pushing her spoon around with an absent finger. "So what was it you were going to ask me?" she said. "I'm just curious."

Eddie gave silent thanks to Sal Giambroni. "Background, mainly," he said, keeping his voice offhand. "How Johnny's career got started, that kind of thing." He took another sip, reeling her in. "You were there all along, right?"

She hesitated, then poured a little sugar in her coffee and began to stir it in a slow swirl.

"Yeah, well, he was my brother and all . . ." She raised her head and looked at him frankly, as if searching for something. He was back swimming in that liquid gaze when he heard her say, "Go ahead, I guess."

Everybody out of the pool. "Do what?"

"Ask what you wanted to ask."

"Yeah?"

She bit her lip. "Just so it doesn't take all day."

He began patting the pockets of his sport coat, falling into a brief panic until he located his notebook. He clicked his pen as he flipped pages, hoping she wouldn't notice that most of them were blank.

She didn't, because she was still watching his face warily. "Maybe you could just start at the beginning," he said.

She looked as if she was about to change her mind again. Then she clasped her hands around her cup and started to talk.

For as long as she could remember, Johnny had been making music. He sang little lisping songs to her while she was still in her crib. When they were in grade school, he was always the star in the programs and plays. Later, when he was eleven and she was eight, he started staging his own shows in front of the radio. He was the lead (always), and she and her little brothers were the backup, though it was a struggle to get the boys to stand still and do their parts.

She loved music, too. Not the way Johnny did, with his jumping around and screaming all the time. She loved to sing, was thrilled by the sweet notes that came out of her throat, and Sunday morning found her in the choir at St. Anthony's.

Eddie stopped her there. "You're Catholic?"

"That's right."

"Me, too," he said. "Except I ain't been to Mass in a long time."

She was waving a remonstrative finger in front of his face

when their waitress chugged up, slid his plate onto the table, and chugged away. He picked up his fork and made a gesture for her to continue while he ate and wrote.

By the time he was fourteen, Johnny was in a group for real, a high school doo-wop outfit called the Flairs. Though she never understood how he had hooked up with them. "He would play hooky all the time and go over to my aunt's house and hang around with my uncle," she said. "He was a night watchman, so he was there during the day. He played piano. They had this big old upright in the front room."

Johnny learned to play from the old man. He learned some guitar, too, from a drunk who lived next door and would moan doleful blues from his Georgia home when he got a load on.

"And then he had all these records," she said. "He'd listen to anything. I mean anything. He even had a polka record once." She made a face, Eddie laughed, and for a few seconds the air lost a couple degrees of its chill.

She went on. When he was sixteen, Johnny wrote a ballad called "Every Night." The Flairs cut it, and it got some airplay around the Delaware Valley. Johnny didn't like the way the group worked the song, though, and he swore it would have broken out if they had done it the way he wanted.

"Broken out?"

"Got played outside of Philly."

"Right," Eddie said.

"Of course, he thought everything he wrote was a hit. Anyway, that's when he decided to put the Excels together. He quit school and collected my cousin Ray and Ray's friend Tommy Gates. And me." Eddie noticed the light coming up in her eyes as she fidgeted in her chair. "We rehearsed every night for six months, until we had a pretty good song list. Johnny found this man to be our manager. His name was Eugene White." She paused for a second. "And he was."

"He was what?"

"White."

She had an odd expression on her face, and it dawned on Eddie that it was a stab at a joke. The look went away as quickly as it had appeared, and she continued the story. "We went in and cut a demo record. Eugene sent Johnny to Fat Cat at WDEL, and Fat Cat sent him on to StarLite Records."

StarLite released "Uptown, Downtown." The record did good sales on the East Coast, making it to number fifty-one on the Billboard singles chart. The second release went nowhere.

"But the next one was 'Silly Girl,'" she said.

With that record, things started to pop. It did break out, and the Excels were suddenly in demand from Boston to Richmond. Shows every weekend turned into shows five nights a week. The New York papers did stories on them as an up-and-coming act.

The next release was "Ain't Got Time," and it shot up to number nine on the East Coast charts. Now their pictures appeared in *Song Hits* and *Teen Beat* and *Hit Music*. They were on the move, hot and getting hotter, on their way to the top.

"That's when I quit," Valerie said.

Eddie lifted his pen. "You quit?"

She nodded. "It got to be too much, and my mama said there was no way another one of her kids wasn't going to graduate. I liked school and I didn't want to miss it. So I quit."

Eddie was dumbfounded. He couldn't imagine any teenager giving up what only one in a million got to live. "But your picture is on the record sleeve," he said.

"Yes, and that's me on the recordings, too. I still worked with them when they did a show close by, as long as it wasn't on a school night. I didn't go on the road, except sometimes on a weekend and part of the summer. They just hired different girls along the way."

"That didn't bother you? Having someone take your place?"

She gave him a steady look and said, "I thought we were talking about Johnny."

The months flew by. The first batch of recordings included a dozen singles and an album of Johnny's songs with a few covers of other hits thrown in. Now the tours wound up and down the eastern seaboard and as far west as Chicago and St. Louis. The Excels did *Bandstand* and TV shows in almost every city east of the Mississippi. Most of which Valerie also missed. If it bothered her, she wasn't showing it. Eddie wondered why Johnny hadn't just replaced her permanently.

She talked about the places the group went, the crowds they drew, the celebrities they met. They hadn't hit number one yet, but with each release, they edged closer to gold.

In a tone of voice that was almost bragging, she talked about how the Excels matured from a bunch of eager kids to slick professionals who could tear up a room any night of the week. Looking back, she said, it felt as if it had happened overnight.

The roller coaster had run nonstop for almost two years, and they were all exhausted. Johnny decided he wanted to take the winter of 1958 off. The group had been out on a revue with Dee Dee Sharp, the Corsairs, Etta James, Brook Benton, and some lesser names. They came in before Thanksgiving and did three rave shows in Philly to close out the tour. Johnny spent the holidays working on new songs. He was making plans for the release of the singles and an album and then a tour to follow.

She stopped for a moment, took a sip of her coffee. "And, then, on February eighth, which was a Sunday, he left the studio, and that was the last anyone saw of him. He didn't come home that night. He didn't show up the next day. Or ever again. He was just gone." She held Eddie's gaze in hers for a brief instant, then looked away. "Your breakfast is getting cold," she said with a tremor in her voice.

He laid down his pen and picked up his fork. "So what do you think happened to him?"

"He was murdered," she said quietly.

"You sound sure."

"Pretty sure."

"Why?"

"What else could have happened?"

"Some kind of an accident?"

"They never found his body." She frowned. "His car was still there the next day. That's when I knew. He never would have left it. He loved that thing."

Eddie said, "New Cadillac Eldorado, right?"

Her face got hard again. "Yes, it was. But what else would a rich—"

"It was in one of the newspaper articles," he explained quickly.

"Oh. Well, that's when I knew he was gone."

"So he was murdered why?"

"I don't know. I guess he got into trouble with someone."

"Someone who knew him?"

"A lot of people knew him," she said. "And a lot more who knew who he was."

Eddie spent a few seconds on his breakfast, thinking about the kind of trails Sal would be following. Such as *first you look at the purse.* "He must have been making a lot of money," he said.

She nodded vaguely. "I guess so, but . . ."

"But what?"

"He was always going on about that. He used to say that Mr. Roddy missed his calling—he should have been a magician the way he could make money disappear."

Eddie said, "Mr. who?"

"Roddy. George Roddy. He runs StarLite Records. That was another reason why Johnny wanted off the road. To find out what was going on with his money."

"Did he?"

"If he did, he never told me."

Eddie wrote the word *money* followed by three question marks and went on.

"What about women?" he said.

Valerie blinked. "Excuse me?"

"Women. Did he have one? Or more? Was there trouble with one of them? Or someone's boyfriend? Or husband?"

She said, "I don't know about any of that."

"He must have had them crawling in the windows."

"I said I don't know. I wasn't around."

Eddie got the signal, backed up, and spent a little time on his eggs. "Any other trouble?" he asked presently.

"Like what?"

"Well, for one thing, that payola business was going on. It was in the papers. They were after Dick Clark and all those other guys."

She shook her head. "He wasn't involved in any of that. That was the record companies and the DJs. He was a singer and a songwriter. That's all."

Eddie changed the subject. "Did he have any bad habits? Did he gamble or drink too much or—"

"Okay, stop." She went for a cigarette, snapping the pack open and snapping her matches. "You said you wanted to hear how Johnny started out and all that. Now you're asking about his women and his money. Like he got into trouble because he was chasing skirts or doing something crooked." She struck a match and blew a plume of smoke. "Ain't none of that true, and even if it was, I wasn't around much then, so I wouldn't have seen it. So there's nothing I can tell you." She pulled her gaze off him. "I think we're done now."

There wasn't room for argument in her expression or tone of voice. Eddie pushed his notebook aside. He had finished eating, and the waitress came by to sweep up his plate and pour more coffee. "I know y'all gonna have some of Thelma's cinnamon rolls," she said.

Valerie glanced at him, then raised two fingers. The waitress let out with an emphatic "Yes, ma'am!" and charged off.

Eddie considered that Valerie had told him a good story, but he hadn't heard a thing that got him any closer to solving the puzzle. She had simply led him to a series of dead ends.

Her gaze drifted from his face and fixed on his permanently swollen knuckles. "So you were a fighter."

"I was, yeah."

"For how long?"

"Ten years. Six as a pro. I just recently stopped."

She gestured at the scar over his eye. "That where you got that?" He nodded. "Does it bother you?"

"It's fine."

"What'd they call you?"

"What?"

"Your nickname. For the fights. Y'all got one, right?"

"Oh. Well, a couple writers started calling me 'Fast Eddie.'" She raised an eyebrow and he blushed a bit. "From *The Hustler.* Before that it was just, y'know, Eddie . . ."

She peered at him gravely. "Why did you want to do it?"

He was slipping into her dark gaze again. "Do what?"

"Be a fighter."

"Oh." He snapped out of it. "I don't know. I started when I was a kid. It just happened."

Valerie was about to say something back when the waitress reappeared with the two rolls in hand. They were impressive pieces, tall swirls and dripping with melted brown sugar and butter. She said, "There ya go, babies!" and moved on to the next table.

Eddie started eating and felt the pounds piling on with the first bite. Valerie stubbed out her cigarette and nibbled at the edge of her roll.

"So, what's it like?" she asked him.

"What?"

"Being a fighter."

"It's hard to explain." He didn't want to talk about it.

She did. "You ever get hurt? I mean hurt bad?"

He put down his fork. "Yeah. Once."

"And did you ever hurt someone else bad?"

"Yeah, I did." He caught the look in her eyes and felt a chill of disappointment. He picked up his coffee cup to hide his annoyance. She just wanted to hear the gory stuff. *What's it like to get knocked out? Or to break someone's nose or jaw? Did you ever take a dive? Did you ever kill a guy in the ring?*

When she noticed he'd stopped eating, she said, "Something wrong?" He shook his head. "Maybe you'd rather have a cannoli."

He looked up. It was the third time she had almost smiled. "What do you know about cannoli?"

"There was a party when Johnny signed his record deal. They had everything you could think of. There was this ice cream . . . zaga . . . zabal . . ."

"Zabaglione."

"Yeah. And they had cannoli."

He picked up his fork again. "Agnelli's on Tenth Street. You come there sometime for cannoli. See how you do on the guinea side of the street."

The way it came out caught both of them by surprise. Eddie flushed and the trace of smile on Valerie's face evaporated and she looked away.

She led the way to the door, her chin up and the chip on her shoulder back in place, meeting the stares with sharp glances of her own. As soon as they stepped onto the sidewalk, she turned around and said, "So you're okay coming here?"

They were back to that again. "Sure, why?"

She moved on. "All right, I did this for you," she said. "So now you tell me something."

"Like what?"

"Like what you found out so far."

"Well, I went to the library and looked up all—"

"I don't mean that," she cut in impatiently.

Eddie said, "I can't tell you anything else."

She peered at him. "Why not?"

"It's an investigation, and . . ." He went looking for the word Sal used. ". . . and I can't divulge any of the—"

"Divulge?" She raised her voice. "I come here to help you and you can't *divulge*?"

He laughed shortly. "You didn't come here to help me."

"Well, I did, didn't I?"

"I could have read what you told me in a magazine."

"You're lucky I told you anything," she shot back. "You're lucky I'm even here, you . . ." She left it hanging out there, as if biting her tongue before she could add *guinea, wop,* or *dago.* It made him want to laugh some more.

There was nothing funny about the way she was glaring at him. He was losing her, and before he realized what he had done, he said, "I found out that someone was hired to kill Johnny."

Her hand came up to her mouth, and she took an appalled half step back, raising the other hand as if to deflect his words. "Was what?" It seemed to catch in her throat.

"Someone was hired to kill your brother," Eddie said. "You know, a contract? Only the guy never got to do it. Because Johnny disappeared before the, uh, before it could be done."

With an effort, she pulled herself together. Now her eyes narrowed suspiciously. "How do you know about this?"

"I asked around. I found out."

She fell silent, shaking her head in disbelief. Twice she started to say something, then caught herself. Finally, she said, "Hired to kill him why?"

"I don't know that part. I didn't get that far."

She treated him to an even stare before turning around and meandering, as if trying to find her way. Eddie watched her until she disappeared around the corner at Twenty-sixth Street.

When he got to the office, he sat at the front desk for long minutes, looking at nothing at all. When he roused himself to wander into Sal's office, he found the detective at his desk, cursing over his checkbook. Sal hated paying bills. Since he could never get his accounts to balance, he swore that the banks were screwing with his money. Eddie leaned in the doorway to watch him.

"What?" the detective snapped crabbily.

"Nothing."

"I said, what?"

Eddie stepped to the desk, pulled back a chair, and sat down. "There's something going on with her."

Sal gave his checkbook a last dirty look and shoved it into the drawer. "With who, the colored girl? What's her name?"

"Valerie."

"Why, what happened?"

Eddie described her hard attitude when he arrived at Thelma's and her change of tune when he told her she could leave. Sal nodded his approval. Valerie hadn't given him much of value, but at least she had talked. It was pretty steady, Eddie explained, until the moment at the end when he mentioned the contract on her brother.

Sal frowned. "Why'd you tell her about that?"

"Because I fucked up," Eddie said.

Instead of barking, the detective said, "Yeah, you did. How'd she take it?"

"Almost knocked her on her ass."

"I can imagine."

"But she didn't ask me anything else," Eddie went on. "She

just walked away . . ." He considered for a few seconds. "I think she knows more than she told me."

Sal laughed lightly and said, "After all my years on this planet, I've learned that everyone's hiding something. And very few of them are as smart as they think. Which means they'll give it up if you work them the right way."

"What's the right way?"

"Your guess is as good as mine, Cero."

Eddie pondered that bit of wisdom while Sal arranged the pens and papers on his desk. "She's a looker," he commented momentarily.

Eddie blinked. "What?"

"Valerie. She's pretty for a colored girl."

He was about to say, *She's pretty for any girl,* when Sal spoke up again. "Just don't go getting ideas."

"What ideas?" Eddie felt himself blushing.

"What ideas." Sal was eyeing him. "We got a standing rule. You don't get personal with clients. Not to mention that other line that you definitely don't want to cross, Freedom March or no Freedom March."

Eddie wanted to ask who "we" was; he also thought to point out that Valerie wasn't a client. But he let it go. Anyway, he knew all about the color line. Having Sal bring it up bothered him, though. Not that it mattered, since she could barely stand to be in the same—

"I want to know what's going on with this," Sal said.

Eddie came back to the present. "You do?"

"You work here. So I want to know what you're up to."

"Okay." He got to his feet.

"You go see Cal Johannsen about the apartment?"

"I'll do it on my way out."

"Okay. You need to go down and see Dom, too. Get something a little nicer than that piece of shit to drive around Havertown.

And, listen, same deal out there. You stay out of the way and by no means step in unless something serious happens."

"Like what?"

"Like if this cupcake drives down to the piers to pick up sailors for a gang bang or tries to buy heroin or a submachine gun. Other than that, just keep an eye on her, write up your reports, and later on I'll pass the information on to the parents. Let them deal with it. Though if they were handling her, we wouldn't be out there in the first place. Anyway, we're not law enforcement, and we're sure as hell not in the birth-control business."

Eddie finished writing up his notes on Valerie and was getting ready to go when Sal called him back into his office. "Just so we got an understanding here, you can work on this thing with the singer. Though I think you already got to the end of the line. But go ahead, talk to some more people, see what you come up with. All right?"

"Okay."

"And listen, about this girl . . . ?"

"Valerie." Again, he felt his face getting warm.

Sal had something else on his mind. "Valerie, yeah. She's the guy's sister, right?"

"That's right."

"Then you can't expect a straight story from her."

"Why not?"

"Because blood's thicker than anything, my friend."

He stopped at Dom's and left in a clean DeSoto sedan with a good radio, which he drove to the far end of Market Street and the offices of Homeside Realty.

"Call me Cal," Calvin Johannsen told him three times in the first thirty seconds.

Call-me-Cal was a pudgy, fast-talking man who looked like Santa Claus without the beard and kept an unlit cigar planted in the corner of his grinning mouth as if it was glued there.

He waved Eddie into his office and to a chair. "Sit down," he said. "Sal explained the situation?"

"He said something about security, but I'm—"

"Right." Cal was all business. "I got a problem now and then with punks harassing my tenants over there. Especially the older folks. Also breaking into apartments and some vandalism of the property. I want someone on the premises to make them think twice."

"The cops can't do anything?"

"Sometimes they do, sometimes they don't. Mostly they don't. This is not one of your tonier neighborhoods. I need help."

Eddie said, "What I told Sal was if you want these guys roughed up, you need to find someone else."

Cal looked baffled. "Ain't you the one who was a fighter?"

"Yeah. *Was*."

"And now you're what, a Quaker?"

Eddie wanted to say, "I don't beat people up for money," but it didn't sound right. What had he been doing for the past six years? "I don't think I'm your guy," he said. "Thanks, anyway." He got up to leave.

Baffled, Call-me-Cal said, "That's it? You don't want the apartment?"

"You need to get somebody else to handle this for you."

The real estate agent flapped a hand at him. "Sit. Sit." Eddie sat. "Okay, you're not going to muscle these punks. I still think it would help to have you in the building. You don't mind these bastards being aware of your presence, right? You ain't Greta Garbo, right? You don't have a problem with them *looking* at you?" Though he didn't understand what Greta Garbo had to do with anything, Eddie smiled and shook his head.

"Then I got a unit," Calvin said. "It's at Nineteenth and Pemberton, that's three blocks off South. It's small, one bedroom. Clean and completely furnished. I'll give you a deal. The rent is usually a hundred twenty-five a month. You can have it for a hundred. We pay heat and the water; you get your own electric. We don't need to bother with the deposit, either."

Eddie almost said no on the spot. He was only paying sixty a month at the rooming house. "I don't know," he said. "My job with Sal, I don't know how long it's going to last."

Calvin sat back, the cigar jutting. "Yeah? What he tells me is as long as you want the work, he'll have something for you. He said he let all those other bums go. Except for Bink, of course. Bink he'll keep around. He said you were his main guy."

Sitting there, Eddie reflected that it had been a long time since any of Sal's help, other than Bink, had been seen or even mentioned. He hadn't thought about it. Now one of Sal's friends was telling him he was the guy.

"So you interested or not?"

Eddie considered for a moment. "You said I can see it first?"

Call-me-Cal swiveled in his chair, snatched a key off the board on the wall, and tossed it across the desk.

What he found was an old brick tenement of eight units, fairly tidy, as if somebody was trying to keep it nice for the tenants. He climbed stone steps and let himself inside.

The apartment was the first on the right. A small living room, a small kitchen with a linoleum floor, a hallway leading to the bathroom and bedroom. The furniture sat staunch and solid, good quality stuff and not all worn-out. None of it belonged to him, and yet there was something familiar about it. The rooms were on the shadow side of the building, the walls were thick—a place someone could hide. Though compact, it was a lot more space than he had on Eleventh Street (and a good ten blocks closer to the office), and he had to admit that the price was fair.

An old woman came in as he was leaving, an ancient, white-haired thing, tiny and bent-backed, working her halting way up the steps just as he stepped out the door. She saw him and her eyes went wide, swimming like startled fish behind her Coke-bottle glasses. It would have been funny except for the fear that had her frail bones shaking.

Eddie took a step back and smiled to put the woman at ease. She hobbled by as quickly as her stick legs could carry her, hunching her shoulders as if he was going to pounce on her. Her key rattled against the lock, and she got in and the door closed with a bang of relief. He lingered at the bottom of the steps for a few minutes, just in case some punk had followed her.

He parked and waited for the bell to ring, then followed Marianne, this time to Buzzy's. It was the same routine at the Gibsons' home: lights on, shadows moving behind curtains, lights off. Just another quiet evening in the suburbs. He walked down the alley that ran along the end of the backyard, smelling the hydrangeas in the gardens as he lurked in the blue shadows. It was pretty and pleasant and safe.

He waited around until after ten o'clock, watching the back of the quiet house, and when nothing stirred, headed back to the city.

As the skyline and the constellation of lights appeared, and the radio blared away, he tried to fix his mind on the facts Valerie had shared at Thelma's. It didn't work; he kept seeing the light in her eyes and hearing the sound of her voice as she related the rise and sudden and sad fall of her brother Johnny Pope. He rolled the window down, hoping the rushing night would blow the image and the echoes away, but that didn't work, either.

THIRTEEN

First thing in the morning, he went downstairs to pay his week's rent. The landlord, a pale, crabby little drunkard who was not on speaking terms with soap, snatched the bills without a word, not even looking at him, and shut the door, the same as always. This time Eddie smacked the jamb with his open palm.

The landlord jerked the door open and glared at him with eyes the color of dirty water. "Yeah, what? Whaddya want?"

"I'm moving out," Eddie said, and stalked away.

After he took a shower and dressed, he went back downstairs to call Cal Johannsen and tell him he wanted the apartment. The real estate agent was happy. Eddie also called the telephone company and inquired about service. The lady told him all he had to do was come down and pay a twenty-five-dollar deposit. He conducted all this business in a loud voice, so the landlord would hear him through the thin walls.

Though it was only a little after ten, the door was open and the raucous music of the Mississippi Sheiks was crackling from the speakers. He found Jimmy T in the back room, sorting through a box of dusty 78s.

Jimmy looked up with a giddy grin. "Cero! Look what I

got!" He began shuffling the records for Eddie's benefit. "Look at these! Blind Willie Johnson . . . Mamie Smith . . . Blind Blake." He plucked out a disc and held it up like it was made of fine china. "Tommy Johnson, 'Canned Heat Blues' on Vocalion." He looked wild, as though he'd been up all night.

"Where'd you get them?" Eddie asked.

"Some old lady's basement down on Packer," Jimmy explained. "I convinced her to share them with the world." Eddie smiled, imagining the old woman throwing the records at Jimmy just to get him off the premises. The new owner of the treasures held up another of the 78s. "Meade Lux Lewis. 'Yancey's Pride.' You want?"

"How much?"

"How much you got in your pocket?"

"Four bucks."

"I'll take two."

Eddie dug for the money and handed it over. Jimmy presented the record with the little wince that came every time he gave anything up. To ease the pain, he quickly bent to pull another of the 78s from the box at his feet.

Eddie leaned in the doorway, studying the faded red label. "What all do you know about Johnny Pope?" he asked.

Jimmy rubbed a careful finger over the pale print. "Such as?"

"I mean about him disappearing and all that."

"I know they never found a body or anything. What else is there?" Jimmy's narrow eyes slid toward Eddie. "Why are we talking about this?"

"Because what I'm doing now is working for a private investigator."

Jimmy cocked his head curiously. "You're doing what? You're kidding. You're a fucking detective now? A gumshoe?"

"I just work for a guy."

"That's pretty cool, Cero." Jimmy snickered as he went for his cigarettes.

"Anyway, I told you I was at the Blue Door and saw Valerie. And I started talking to some people about Johnny, and so now I'm going to see if—"

"—if you can find out what happened to him? Yeah?"

Eddie said, "I just want to see what I can dig up, that's all. So what about it?"

"What about what?"

"Pope."

"Oh, yeah." Jimmy laid the 78 aside and dropped into his sagging office chair. He made his magic with his Luckys and the Zippo and blew a thin tail of smoke. His brow stitched as he leaned his head back to watch the gray curl waft to the ceiling.

"He came out of nowhere. Some row house in Grays Ferry, right? And he climbed the ladder. Had all those records on the charts. Cat was a star, or this close to it. But he had a reputation. Big mouth. Always starting trouble. Different chick every night, and I'm sure he was messing with reefer and pills. But if it wasn't a jealous husband laying for him, I'd bet on a stickup that went wrong. Some guys jump him, he fights back, and it's over-and-out. Bye-bye, Johnny."

He puffed on his Lucky for a reflective few moments. Then one eyebrow hiked. "I just remembered . . . there was some talk going around right back then. That he was going to break up the Excels to go out as a solo act. And I heard something about him leaving StarLite, too."

Eddie was puzzled. Valerie hadn't mentioned any of this.

Jimmy took another drag on his Lucky, blew another thin gray cloud. Abruptly, his eyes widened and he sat up and snapped his fingers. "Hey . . . the *tape.*"

"What tape?"

"The tape of all the songs he had laid down. He was in the studio, dummy. That tape."

"What about it?"

"It went missing." Jimmy sat forward and crushed the butt of his cigarette into the ashtray. "As far as I know, they never found it. Or it would have been released."

"So it would have been . . ."

"His last songs." Jimmy nodded with slow drama.

"Damn," Eddie said. Valerie hadn't mentioned that, either.

"I wonder what happened to it," Eddie mused.

Jimmy said, "Well, if we knew that, it wouldn't be lost, motherfucker." Eddie snickered as Jimmy gave a doleful shrug of his bony shoulders. "It's probably lost forever. Into the trash can of history, just like Buddy Bolden's wax cylinder and the master from Robert Johnson's last session." After another brief silence, he popped his fingers again. "You want to find out about Pope? Go see Fat Cat."

"Fat Cat the DJ?"

"No, Cero, Fat Cat your fucking Friendly Dodge Dealer. Yeah, the DJ. He was the first one on to Pope way back when. He could probably tell you some more about all that."

"How do I find him?"

"Go down to the station."

"They'd let me in?"

"Yeah, sure. Tell him I sent you." Now the eye that wasn't in a squint brightened. "Hey, holy Christ, what if you *found* it?"

"Found what?"

"That tape, man!"

"Don't get your hopes up."

Jimmy wasn't listening. He dug his fingers into his goatee and began scratching away. "Man, you find that, you're talking a fucking out-of-the-park home run." His eyes glittered and he grinned wolfishly. "And of course you'd want to put it in the hands of someone who would appreciate its worth."

"Didn't you just say that it's probably lost forever?"

Jimmy stopped scratching and considered. "Yeah, I did," he said. "What's it been, three years? That's ancient history, dad."

When he got to the office, he told Sal about Havertown.

Sal listened, nodding, and when Eddie finished, said, "So she went in and never came out?"

"She stopped by this burger joint after school, then she went home and stayed put. I walked around the back, checked that, just in case she was sneaking off. Nothing."

Sal said, "Good enough. As long as we've got an eye on her. You go tonight and tomorrow. I'll take Friday and Saturday."

Eddie said that would be okay. He sat down and wrote out what little there was to report on Marianne and, on another page, what he remembered from his talk with Jimmy T. When he finished that, he took the phone book from the top of the file cabinet and thumbed through it.

His first call, to Premier Talent, was answered after ten rings by the weak and whiny voice of Eugene White himself. The agent listened to Eddie's request, then complained that he didn't have anything to say. Then he claimed he didn't have any time to say it. "I'm busy, all right? Call me later." The phone went dead.

Next was StarLite Records. The receptionist put him on hold, then kept on coming back with questions regarding the nature of the call. Eddie said the same thing every time: "Johnny Pope." After five minutes and a half-dozen go-rounds, she discovered that Mr. Roddy was not in the office.

Eddie wanted to say, *Then who the fuck you been talking to?* Instead, he left a message. Not that anyone would be calling back. He knew a dodge when he heard it.

He put in a second call to Premier Talent. "This is Eddie Cero, Mr. White."

"Who?"

"Eddie Cero."

"Yeah, and?" The man sounded irritated.

"You told me to call you later."

"This is later? This is ten minutes later. I meant *later* later. You—"

"I'm looking into the disappearance of Johnny Pope."

There was a pause while Eugene White let out a long breath. "Again with this?" he said. "You're wasting your time. You're wasting my time. Because what I know about that business is nothing."

"You were his agent."

"Thank you for reminding me."

"Valerie said it would be a good idea to talk to you." It was a lie, but he was tired of the sparring.

It worked. The agent hesitated. "Valerie said?" He made a small sound in his throat. "Well . . . when?"

"How about tomorrow morning?"

Another long sigh. "All right. Ten o'clock." He proceeded to give up an address on Locust Street and then hung up.

Sal was being quiet as an Italian mouse, and when Eddie dropped the phone in the cradle, the silence was replaced by the sudden shuffling of papers, like listening in was the last thing on his mind.

Eddie left early for Havertown. Instead of heading west out of the city, he took a detour down Broad Street and parked across from a six-story building of white stone that was topped by a pyramid of steel with the letters WDEL spelled out vertically. He went inside, rode the elevator to the top floor, and stepped into a lobby to the *chugga-chugga* strains of "The Loco-Motion." He told the girl at the desk that he wanted to talk to Fat Cat and mentioned that Jimmy Teischer had sent him. She looked up from her magazine to stare at him as if he was a moron. "He's not here. 'Cause he's on, y'know, at *night*."

"So I should come back." The girl nodded slowly. "When?"

"At *night*," she said, now sounding like she was addressing a child. "Any time . . . after . . . six."

Eddie turned around to leave and was confronted by a wall plastered with photographs and 45s mounted in frames, stretching from a few feet off the floor to high over his head, a galaxy of hundreds of rock-and-roll stars and samples of their best work.

"Hey, are the Excels up here?"

"Who?" the girl said, her nose buried in her *True Romance*.

It took him a minute to find them. Johnny was posed on the right and closest to the camera, looking all slick and handsome in a sharkskin suit. Ray Pope and Tommy Gates leaned back-to-back, their arms crossed, grinning as they clowned. And there was Valerie, made-up like a movie star, wearing an impossibly tight sequined dress that was slit halfway up her thigh and was so low-cut that she seemed just on the verge of spilling out of it. Her smile was dazzling and her eyes were bright. She looked beautiful.

Eddie returned his attention to Johnny.

The face was that of a man on top of the world. A brilliant energy radiated from the sparkling eyes, the freckled skin, and the gap-toothed smile, as if he was ready to jump right off the glossy paper and start gobbling up everything in sight. He didn't look like someone who could count his time in months and days. Johnny Pope looked like he was going to live forever.

Havertown was six more hours of nothing, and Eddie fidgeted as he waited for the time to pass. It was almost ten o'clock when he got back to the city and cruised down a now-empty Broad Street, listening to the *Fat Cat Show*. He generally listened to the Geator on WCAM, when he listened to Top 40 at all. The Geator was a wild man—or a wild kid. Eddie had read somewhere that he was only twenty-two and made $100,000 a year for being one of the top DJs on the East Coast.

Fat Cat wasn't in that league and worked a different style. He didn't shriek and whoop, he didn't do the staccato bit. His voice rolled down mellow valleys between the songs and commercials. Just as Eddie tuned in, the DJ was murmuring about "more platter chatter from the Fatter Catter," and he remembered seeing a picture of a pudgy, goateed hepcat in a beret and black turtleneck, a cigarette dangling from his lip, the very image of cool.

Eddie switched off the radio, got out, and crossed the street to find the lobby doors locked. He banged on the glass until an old bald-headed black man in a guard's uniform shuffled out to ask his business, then waved him in without listening to his answer. The guard crept back to his desk and his newspaper.

Eddie stepped off on the sixth floor to find the reception area empty. He waited a minute to see if anyone would appear. Now Dion was humping on the speakers: *And when she asks me which one I love the best, I tear open my shirt and show her Rosie on my chest.*

He walked around the receptionist's desk and down a long hallway. A bulb glowed red over the door at the far end, and he stopped to peer through the porthole in the door. Instead of a goateed hepcat jiving away as he paced the room, he saw a heavy man in a white shirt and dark glasses parked at a sound board. The man—it had to be Fat Cat—leaned his bulk over a few inches to mutter into the microphone. The voice came out of the speakers deep and cool. He dropped the needle on one of his turntables and sat back. The red light above Eddie's head went off.

Eddie pushed the door open a few inches. The man at the microphone looked up. "Whaddya want?" he said.

The hipster on the airwaves was replaced by a pissed-off middle-aged blob in a sweaty rayon shirt that was turning yellow, as if to match the sallow flesh, looking more used-car salesman than big-time radio personality. Though the voice and the shades stayed in place, Eddie could feel the glare of cold eyes from behind the dark lenses.

"I asked what the fuck do you want?" Fat Cat demanded.

"My name's Eddie Cero and I'm look—"

"Cero?" The DJ dropped his chins and peered at him over the top of his glasses. "Eddie Cero? The fighter?"

Eddie said, "Yeah, but I'm—"

"Well, come on, come in and sit down." Some of the mellow in the voice came back, along with a sneaky grin, as he waved Eddie toward a chair that was pushed into the corner of the little booth.

"Why didn't you say so? I know you. I saw you at the Auditorium about a year and a half ago. Some colored kid. You knocked him out. His name was . . . what was it . . . Alfred . . . ?"

Eddie pulled the chair closer to the sound board and sat down. "Willie Allred," he said.

"Right, Allred." The head bobbed like a greasy ball. "That was one hell of a fight. You guys went at each other for all seven rounds, and about fifteen seconds before the final bell, boom, down he goes. Didn't get up, either. They had to carry him out of there, right?" All the time he was talking, his hands performed a routine of their own, as they slipped records on and off the four turntables. "Slow Twistin'" started, and the hands came to rest for a moment.

Fat Cat swiveled around and said, "Yeah, I made money on you that night. So, you still fighting?"

"Not right now, no." Eddie settled in the chair. "What I'm doing is working for a private investigator."

The sweaty brow did a slow furrow. "Oh, yeah?"

"Yeah, and I wondered if you had a few minutes to talk to me."

"What about?"

Eddie noticed the voice crept back toward the icebox and the eyes were flickering behind the lenses. "Johnny Pope."

The hand that was reaching for another record stopped in

midair. "Pope? What the hell for? He's been dead, what, three years now?"

"Missing three years."

The hand resumed its motion. "Believe me, he's dead. That's yesterday's papers and then some. I mean, who cares?" He took off his dark glasses, revealing pale eyes that were bulbous, red-veined, and watery, as if they hadn't been treated to a good night's sleep in a while. Eddie thought that this guy and Sal would make half-decent bookends.

"So who are you working for?" this bookend asked him.

"It's confidential." Eddie half expected Fat Cat to laugh at the line.

Instead, the DJ gave him a long look, then made a quarter turn in his chair to cue another 45. He turned back to Eddie. "So why the fuck should I talk to you?"

"Jimmy T said you could help."

"Jimmy?" The frown dissolved back into a laconic smile. "How's he doing?"

"He's sleeping at the store."

The DJ snickered. "Again? Big surprise, huh? So he said what?"

"He said you could help me with some information. Because you were close to the Excels and especially Johnny."

Fat Cat heaved round shoulders. "Well, kinda, yeah. What happened was their manager, Eugene White, called and asked me to give this kid a listen. I remember I was thinking, 'Good god, no. Not another one of Eugene's hacks.' But he wouldn't leave me alone, and I said okay, and Johnny came over with a demo that sounded pretty good. Real good. And he was so, I don't know, charming and all. I thought he had something. So I sent him to George Roddy at StarLite. The next thing I know, George picked him up. Him and the Excels."

Eddie nodded and went digging into his pocket. "So you gave

him his start." The DJ stared with distaste at the notebook and pen, so Eddie said, "I got a bad memory and I have to write stuff down."

"Well, write this down," Fat Cat said. "I didn't give him his start. He was already on his way. I just happened to be there. I helped him, yeah, and it did me and the station some good. He was such a talent, I would have done it just to be a part of it. And I was, for a while." He shuffled through some 45s. "And then he was gone, and it was over."

"You got any thoughts about what might have happened to him?"

The DJ dropped a needle and Chuck Jackson let out with a heartbroken plea. *Any day now, I will hear you say: good-bye, my love . . . can see you're slipping away from me . . .* Fat Cat sat back and his chair groaned along with the singer. "I know exactly what happened to him," he said.

Eddie blinked. "You do?"

"Yeah, he got on somebody's wrong side and got himself killed."

Eddie shifted in his chair. The man had a loose definition of *exactly.*

Fat Cat swung around and leaned forward intently. "Listen, for all his talent, Johnny could be a goddamn asshole punk. He would smile in your face and stick a knife in your back. He'd borrow your last dime and never even think about paying it back. He'd screw your wife and wreck your car and walk away whistling. He helped himself to whatever he wanted, and if you called him on it, he'd throw a fit like a three-year-old. But he was a genius when it came to music and an amazing performer. So he got away with it."

"Until his luck ran out," Eddie said.

"Yeah, well, he was always this far from trouble," Fat Cat said. "He chased tail, and I mean black, white, and every shade in between. He could drink like a fish, and he didn't mind a little reefer. And on top of that, he had a big mouth. He went crazy all over the place. I think what happened was he finally fucked with the wrong party. And the genius became a dead genius."

He took a sober pause. "What I'm saying is whatever happened, it wasn't no big surprise."

Eddie sensed that this was a moment to nod dutifully and wait for more.

"You got a kid who's poor and colored," the DJ said. "So he's screwed from the start, right? Except this kid's got this gift and, more to the point, he's got ambition. He wants a shot at the brass ring. Now, there's other kids out there, thousands of them, in garages and in church basements and in the hallways of tenement buildings, and they all want it. The brass ring. And out of all of them, one guy has a little more on the ball, and so he works at it, and I mean kills himself and runs over anyone who gets in his way. He gets some breaks and it happens. Suddenly he's got it all. But it's too much. Too much of everything. Too much money, too much pussy, too much liquor and dope, and whatever else. The point is, who can resist?"

He stopped as if it was a question that demanded a reply and then answered it himself.

"Goddamn few, that's who." He raised a finger, turned to the microphone. Chuck Jackson's operatic crescendo ended in a wash of strings, and Fat Cat's voice changed as he crooned honey into the microphone and from there to waiting ears up and down the Delaware Valley. He reached over and dropped a tonearm on the Orlons' bubbly "Don't Hang Up." He turned to face Eddie with an absent nod. "And that's what happened to Johnny Pope. There ain't no mystery about it. Except whoever did it. And I doubt we'll ever know." He yawned.

Eddie thought for a few seconds, then said, "Still, it's strange the way he just disappeared."

The bloodshot eyes shifted. "Strange how?"

"They never found a body. Never found anything. I guess somebody really knew what they were doing." Eddie left it there, deciding to keep the talk about the contract on Johnny's life to himself.

The DJ watched him carefully for a moment before coming up with a shrug. "You know what I think?" he asked. "I think he got caught banging the wrong guy's old lady. Somebody who didn't give a shit how many records he had on the charts. But it doesn't matter, does it? He's dead either way." He turned back to the board and spent some seconds getting another 45 cued.

Eddie caught the dodge, let it pass. "Do you remember hearing any rumors about him breaking up the Excels? And leaving StarLite Records?"

It took Fat Cat so long to answer that Eddie thought he hadn't heard. Then he said, "The part about leaving the group, yeah, I did hear something about that. He wanted to go out as a solo act. But leave StarLite? I don't think so." He laughed bluntly. "Johnny and George Roddy hated each other, but they overlooked it long enough to make them both a shitload of money."

"They hated each other?"

"Figure of speech," the DJ said quickly. "It's an old story. You got the artist on one side and the businessman on the other, and they're at each other's throats. But they both know they couldn't make it without each other, so they live with it. That ain't news."

"Jimmy said something about a tape that was missing, too," Eddie said.

"Oh, yeah, yeah, I remember hearing about that. *The missing tape.*" He shook his head. "Well, there ain't no tape. And there ain't no more Johnny Pope." He slipped some cartridges into a machine.

The music dipped into a commercial for a carpet store in Cherry Hill. Fat Cat glanced at the big clock on the wall. "Anything else?"

Eddie said, "I guess not. Can you think of anybody who could fill in some more of the blanks?" he asked.

"What blanks?"

"Just details."

"Oh. Well, everybody's pretty much gone now."

"Eugene White's still around. I'm going to go see him."

Fat Cat settled in his chair and nodded.

"What about this Roddy guy at StarLite?"

The DJ's mouth stretched in a thin smile. "I don't know how much he could tell you. He and Johnny kept their distance. By mutual agreement."

"How about the other members of the Excels?"

"They all just dropped out of sight. Johnny was the whole group. They were nothing without him." Eddie was thinking he should speak up on Valerie's behalf when Fat Cat said, "The girl, I think, still sings in clubs. I heard Tommy Gates has a church now. And then there's Ray Pope. Johnny's cousin."

He had spoken the name with a note of disgust in his voice, and Eddie said, "What?"

"Well, Ray is, or at least was, a real talented guy. But he was lazy. He didn't give a shit. He was happy just to keep the party going and collect his paychecks. Then Johnny was gone, the party stopped, and so did the checks. Ray figured he could just pick up where Johnny left off. He was the next best thing, right? So for about a year, he tried to get somebody to give him a shot. It didn't happen."

"Why not?"

"Because he's a mess. He's either drunk or on something else, depending on when you catch him. He got hired by some groups who wanted to cash in on the name, and he blew it every time.

He'd show up loaded or miss shows, that sort of thing. So he got dumped. Nobody could work with him. He's been up here about twenty times, trying to get something going. Won't happen. There was only one Johnny Pope."

"You know where I can find him?"

"Find who?"

"Ray."

The DJ gave him another long look and said, "You want some advice? Don't fuck with this."

Eddie blinked in surprise. The words had broken through the smooth patter with a hard edge. The DJ's cold gaze stayed on him, and he was vaguely aware that the last rollicking strains of "Don't Hang Up" had faded away and now a sizable number of teenagers all over the metropolitan area were listening to the tick of a needle.

Click . . . Click . . . Click . . . Click . . .

Fat Cat caught himself, swung around, and dropped the tonearm. An organ warbled a faraway echo.

"You already played that one," Eddie said.

The DJ snatched up the tonearm and dropped the other one. A tense few seconds went by as the first bars of "Beechwood 4-5789" chirped from the speakers. Without turning, Fat Cat said, "You ever hear of the Domino Lounge?"

"Way out the end of South Street?"

"That's right. Used to be a place for musicians after hours. Now it's pretty much a dive. Anyway, I heard Ray was hanging around there." The DJ swiveled to face him. "Tell me something. Why are you doing this?"

"I'm just—" He stopped. "I don't know. I was a fan of his. And it just doesn't seem right that he was killed and nobody knows what happened." He gestured in dismissal. "I probably won't get anywhere. All this time has passed."

The DJ nodded slowly, then tried for a contrite face. "What I meant with that comment . . . Nothing against you, but you oughta not waste your time. When Johnny disappeared, the cops investigated. Then Roddy hired private detectives to look into it. They never came up with a damn thing."

"Yeah, I know," Eddie said, and he got up to leave.

Fat Cat ran a hand over his tired eyes, then put his dark glasses back on. "Y'know, it was really sad about Johnny," he said. "But the truth is, when it comes to music, sometimes success is the worst thing that can happen." He leaned back and the chair moaned again under his weight. "You can ask Ray about that."

The first phone call went out five minutes after Eddie stepped through the lobby doors onto the street. The last one went to the Blue Door and Joe D'Amato took it. When the break came, he called Valerie into his office and passed her the slip of paper. She stared at it for a second.

"He didn't say what he wanted?"

Joe shook his head. "No, just that it was important that you call tonight."

Valerie pursed her lips into a frown.

Joe said, "I got to check on something." He gestured to the telephone on his desk. "Go ahead, use this one." Then he made an exit.

Valerie waited until the door closed to pick up the phone and dial the numbers. When she heard the voice on the other end, she said, "What do you want?"

The voice muttered a few words. She bit her lip. "All right, go ahead," she said, and then sat down to listen.

FOURTEEN

On Thursday morning Eddie drove to the phone company office to pay his deposit, then directly to the apartment house.

He unlocked the door and wandered around, listening to noises from the other apartments. It all sounded normal; no one yelling in a drunken rage, throwing up in a bathroom, or blaring country-western music with the door open. The quiet would take some getting used to.

He pulled up the front-window curtains and watched the street until a cop car raced by, the siren wailing. He looked at his watch. Early as it was, he decided to go ahead and leave for Premier Talent, sensing that if he was even a minute late, Eugene White would use it as an excuse to run away.

The old brownstone was off Locust Street at Third, a structure so decrepit it looked like it might have been there when the Liberty Bell last tolled, hunkering in the permanent shadows of the newer, big-shouldered office towers that crowded around it. The windows were narrow, and the glass was gray with the grime of the streets.

Eddie climbed worn wooden stairs to the third floor, walked

down an empty hallway, and opened the door of the Premier Talent Agency. He found a single room with a single desk displaying a telephone, a tray for accessories, a few pieces of paper, and a gooseneck lamp. Two green metal file cabinets were tucked in a corner. A gray overcoat hung from a rack. Aside from the feeble clink of a cast-iron radiator, it was dead quiet.

On the wall behind him, he discovered another gallery of photographs, three dozen portraits in five-and-dime frames, arranged in rows—men, women, pairs, and groups. Each revealed low-rent nightclub acts, the men trying for Sinatra or Dean Martin suave, the women mimicking Julie London sultry. There were several comics dressed up in tiny derbies and suits that were too small, and a couple magicians replete with slick black mustaches, capes, and top hats. A man posed with three chimps, and all four members of the quartet sported tuxedos.

Eddie didn't see a single face he recognized, and there were no photographs of the Excels in the gallery.

"What a lovely bunch of coconuts."

The man who stood in the doorway fit right in with the group on the wall. Eddie figured him for sixty and some change. He was short and thin and his shoulders were stooped, as if he was laboring under some unseen weight. Except for some stray white wisps, he was bald, and his heavy-lidded eyes peeped out through the thick lenses of gold-rimmed glasses. He did not look well; in fact, he carried himself like a man suffering from an ailment for which there was no relief, good material for a comedy routine.

Eugene White gestured at the wall. "I gotta do something about this. Half of them have retired from the business." He took another bleak look. "Others have retired from living."

Eddie held out his hand. "Eddie Cero."

White's handshake was like a piece of paper. "So what can I do for you?" he asked in a thin rasp of a voice that made it clear he wasn't much interested in doing anything for Eddie or anyone else. He didn't offer a seat, so Eddie stood and stated his business under the gazes of the two dozen never-would-be stars.

"I'm looking into the Johnny Pope case," he said.

Eugene White stared at nothing. "Why?"

"Because I want to know what happened to him."

"Is that right?" The agent didn't buy it. He probably didn't buy much of anything.

"So I want to ask you some questions," Eddie went on.

White closed his eyes. Seconds passed. The radiator clanked for no good reason. Eddie wondered if the agent had fallen asleep on his feet.

Then the older man blinked like an old turtle and said, "I don't know anything that would help you. The police and those private detectives never found a thing. It's been three years now. Johnny is dead. The Excels are part of music history. End of story." He crossed his thin arms and rocked on his heels. "Things don't always come wrapped up in nice packages. That's life. What are you going to do?"

Apparently Eugene White was an amateur philosopher. Now, having delivered his verdict, he seemed to be waiting for Eddie to bow to the truth and head for the door. He glanced at him once or twice and let out several little sighs.

"Okay, what?" he said at last.

"I want to hear about you and Johnny and the Excels."

White let out another weary breath. "All right. I'll give you the whole thing in a nutshell." With some effort he settled on a corner of the desk and perched there, a forlorn buzzard.

"Johnny came to me when he was just a kid," he began. "Sixteen years old. This would have been, what, '51 or '52? He was in that doo-wop outfit. Anyway, he was just a backup voice, not the lead. No one took him seriously. I listened. I heard him sing one of the songs he wrote, I saw the look in his eye, and just like that I said, *This is it, this is the one.* After thirty years in the business, this is where I hitch my wagon."

The agent allowed a dramatic pause. "To everyone else, he was just another colored kid who wanted to be a star. But I knew, I *knew* he was going to make it. Sixteen years old he was! So I worked with him. I took care of him. I bought him clothes so he would look decent. I took him to my house and fed him. My wife, she thought of him like a son. She loved that kid. I loved him. And when his career took off, it was Christmas. Except we're Jewish, of course. Anyway, we were all going to get rich and live happily ever after." He stopped, letting his words hang in the air. "And then just as we were about to climb on the gravy train, he was gone." He jerked a thumb at the photographs on the wall. "And what I got left is them."

Eddie nodded, wondering how much of this he was supposed to swallow. The Johnny Pope the agent described was an angel from heaven, the complete opposite of the spoiled brat in Fat Cat's memory.

"Tell me about February of 1959," he said.

"That plane crashed and killed Buddy Holly, Ritchie Valens, and the Big Bopper. A terrible tragedy."

"I meant what happened with Johnny."

Eugene White looked exasperated. "I told you. I don't know anything. He was holed up in the studio. I hardly saw him at all. And then he disappeared."

"All right, then, what about before that?"

White began touching the fingertips of one crabbed hand to the fingertips of the other, a hypnotic little pantomime. "Things were going well. The shows were drawing and the records were selling. They were on a tear. But in the middle of that summer, Johnny started calling me from the road. He said he wanted the winter off. He wanted the time to work. And he was complaining about money and wanted to get that straightened out." The agent flexed his arms slightly. "They got back to town around the second week of November. He got off the bus and came right in to see me."

"Why?"

"To talk about money. And his plans. He was going to write enough songs for a couple singles and an album. Which we would release in the spring. Then follow it with a tour."

"With the Excels?"

White paused for a few seconds. "No."

"So he was done with the group?"

"Isn't that what I just said?"

"Why?"

"He wanted to do something different." White paused, frowning. "And they were having some problems. Johnny and Ray especially." He glanced at Eddie. "You know about Ray?"

"I've heard."

"Anyway, Johnny wanted to move on."

"And leave everyone behind."

White shrugged vacantly.

"That would have made some people unhappy," Eddie said.

"I suppose so."

"What about StarLite?"

Now White tried a poker face that didn't work. "He—I mean we—hadn't made a decision."

"But he was thinking about it?"

The older man's gaze came to rest on a spot somewhere over Eddie's head. "The contract was coming up for renewal. Johnny wanted to do something, because there was a clause that if we didn't negotiate by March first, it automatically renewed for another year. It was a good time to make a break. New career, a new label. Maybe even his own label. And the con—"

"Wait a minute," Eddie said. "His own label? He could do that?"

White flipped a bony hand. "Why not? You pay some money for some studio time and then pay some more to get some records pressed and, bingo, you've got a label. You could do it out of your toilet. Then you get to keep the money you make, for the records and the publishing, too. The prob—"

"The what?"

The agent frowned at being interrupted again. "The publishing. You don't know about this? What kind of detective are you?"

"I'm new at it," Eddie said.

White sighed impatiently. "You can own the song on paper, you can own the record you make of the song, or you can own both. Anyway, what I was saying was that the problem is how do you compete against the big guys? The answer is you can't. Unless you have a name."

"Like Johnny Pope."

"Like Johnny Pope. But he was just thinking about it. Nothing was decided." The agent produced a dim smile. "And if the word about that happened to get out, it never hurts to let people think you might make a move."

"Was Johnny being cheated?"

The smile went away. Eugene White looked surprised by the question and a little more unnerved. "Who said anything about that?"

"Was he?"

"The fact is everybody fudges a little. It goes with the business. It's just a matter of how much." The agent shifted fretfully. "Johnny wanted to make a change because of the way George Roddy ran StarLite."

"Which was how?"

"Which was always pushing for more product. It was always *We need to get something out.* Johnny didn't want to work that way. And . . ."

"And what, Mr. White?"

The agent waited a few seconds before saying, "People were talking about George and his gambling. The word was that he was in trouble with some bookmakers."

Eddie was stunned. "What?"

"Bookmakers. Bookies."

"I know what they are."

"Then you know it's no joke. Anyway, that's what I heard. So I told Johnny, and we decided that we didn't want to support George's bad habits."

Eddie sat back, sensing that his investigation had just turned another corner. He wanted to rush to Sansom Street and tell Sal. He knew the detective would be expecting him to finish the interview.

"But before you could make any change . . ."

"Johnny was gone." White was dejected. "That's right. One night he was there, the next morning he was gone, and that was the end of it. Over and done."

Eddie tapped his pencil lightly on his pad and said, "What do you think happened to him?"

"What happened? What happened, he says." The agent shook his head tragically. "Johnny was a good boy and a genius at music, but this business can be a curse. People tell you you're wonderful, you're a star, you can do no wrong, and these kids believe it. I wasn't out there on the road to look after him, or maybe things would have been different." He stopped, swallowed, and studied the floor. "What happened? He made someone angry enough to kill him. Or somebody came along to rob him and it got out of hand." He gave his head a slight shake, as if he was chasing away a notion. "So if you're looking for something else, I think you'll be disappointed."

There was sadness in the old eyes, and the bloodless Eugene White appeared to be having a moment of grief. When, out of respect, Eddie didn't speak, the agent took it as a signal. He drew himself up and started to clamber from his perch on the desk. "If that's all, Mr. Ce—"

"Where did all the money go?"

White blinked from his half crouch. "What money?"

"Johnny's money. From his records. After he disappeared, I mean."

White straightened. "Oh. Well, his contract ended a month after he disappeared. He didn't have any kind of will or anything. That wouldn't occur to him. So most of it went to StarLite." He grimaced. "To George Roddy."

Eddie made a note, finishing just in time to catch White pushing himself away from the desk.

"What about women?"

The agent stopped again. "What about what?"

"Women," Eddie said. "Or a woman. Anyone special around?"

"That I don't remember."

"He's like family and you don't know if he had a woman?"

White straightened and rubbed his hipbone. "What are you, a cop? I said I don't remember. It's been three years. You've got everything. Now I have work to do."

Eddie's stare kept the agent from stepping away. Eugene White gave him a nervous glance. "What?" he said.

"No women?"

White began shuffling sideways, trying to nudge Eddie toward the door. "I said I don't remember."

"He wasn't by chance, uh . . ."

Eugene White stopped and let out a shaky laugh. His pale face went pink. "Oh, no. Johnny was a ladies' man all the way. He just didn't have a girlfriend at the time. I guess he just wanted to work." The agent resumed his slow slide toward the door.

Eddie said, "Did you keep track of his schedule?"

"Of course, that was part of my job."

"Would it include when he got back into Philly up till the time he disappeared?"

"Well, yes . . ."

"Could I see it?" Eugene White stopped and stared at him, his mouth half open. "Could I see it?" Eddie repeated.

"What for?"

"It might help."

The agent let out a short, dry laugh. "Help what?" When Eddie didn't answer, he waved a vague hand and said, "It's in a file somewhere. I'd have to look for it."

Eddie sat down in the chair. "I can wait," he said.

It took the better part of an hour for Eugene White to locate the schedule and then for Eddie to copy it down. Still, it was only eleven thirty when he finished, and he found himself with nothing to do until school was out. He decided to head to Havertown early, grab some lunch, and poke around for a decent record store before the 3:20 bell.

As he came up on Darby Road, a car zoomed through his line of sight. A second passed and he slowed down. He could have sworn Marianne Gibson had been behind the wheel. Except the car was a '59 Chevy four-door, and she was supposed to be in school. The driver behind him tooted his horn and he swung the car in a U-turn.

He caught up with the Chevy two blocks down as it turned onto Township Line and tailed it to North Drexel Avenue, where it cut directly into a narrow driveway of white stone that ran alongside one of the newer houses. Drifting by, he could just make out the Chevy creeping to the rear of the property, and coming to a stop in front of a two-car garage that had been built and painted to match the house.

Eddie swung to the curb a few doors down, jumped out, and hurried to the driveway in time to see the driver of the Chevy stride beneath a trellis and hurry across the backyard.

It was Marianne; except this Marianne had done something with her hair and had painted her lips a cherry red. With her tight short-sleeved sweater, she didn't look so much like a schoolgirl anymore.

Eddie slipped along the line of shrubs and watched as she stepped onto the flagstone patio on the far side of the house. The back door opened, and a male voice greeted her as she passed inside.

Eddie saw a two-year-old Corvette hardtop and a new Mercury Park Lane convertible parked in the garage at the back end of the property. In his rush, he had forgotten his notebook, so he jotted the plate numbers on his hand.

Before any of the neighbors noticed him skulking around, he took a roundabout path back to the DeSoto. Twenty-five tense minutes went by before he heard the quiet cough of an engine. The Chevy came into view, the tires crunching on pebbles. Marianne looked both ways, and for an instant her eyes seemed to linger on the DeSoto. Eddie froze. She pulled into the street and drove away.

He gave her a block lead. She moved out of the neighborhood at a sedate pace, then picked up speed until she was flying. Eddie stopped next to the school lot in time to catch her stepping from the car. She had pulled a sensible blouse over her tight top and wiped the lipstick away.

She'll be sweet sixteen, he thought, *and back in class again.*

The whole episode was so bizarre that he had to convince himself that it had actually happened. He wanted to call Sal but was afraid he'd miss chapter two, so he stayed put. As it turned out, he didn't miss anything. When the bell rang, Marianne followed her good-girl, after-school routine down to the second. She was back home and settled in by six thirty.

Eddie found a pay phone and called Sal at his apartment.

"She did *what*?"

Eddie described the scene at the house and then at the school. "What do you want me to do?"

"Stay until you're sure she's tucked in," Sal said. "We'll figure it out in the morning."

Eddie picked up something to eat, drove back to the house, parked, and waited. A borough police car drifted by at one point, and the officer behind the wheel waved at him. At nine thirty, when Marianne's bedroom light went out, he left Havertown and drove back to the city.

He almost made it. Driving down South Street, he heard music fluttering from the open doorway of a bar, and after spending the better part of an afternoon and evening with his mind elsewhere, he greeted Johnny, Valerie, and the rest of the cast once again.

FIFTEEN

Sal was standing by the window, holding a carton of coffee and watching the Friday-morning traffic. He turned around when Eddie walked in and gestured to a second carton and the paper bag on his desk.

"There's Danish in there," he said. "Help yourself and tell me about Miss Gibson."

Eddie took the coffee and left the pastry. He didn't need any more help getting out of shape. He joined Sal at the window to discuss his adventure at Havertown. In the morning light, it came out sounding bizarre and he felt a little silly repeating it.

Sal didn't find it at all foolish. "Goddamn!" he said. "So she sneaks off to visit some guy in a house?"

"Maybe she's got a good reason."

"Yeah, what would that be?" Before Eddie could respond, Sal said, "What if this rich, pretty teenager is getting dolled up to go bang this guy? You realize what kind of story it would make? The prom queen from Havertown screwing a grown man after school?"

"It's during school, Sal."

"That's right! Holy shit!"

"I could have it wrong."

"Well, it sure doesn't sound that way." Sal thought it over for another few seconds. "Okay, go ahead and write it up. Then get back out there and see if she pulls the same number. Get pictures. If it happens again, we'll both go back on Monday."

Eddie went to his desk, dropped his empty coffee carton in the trash can, and sat down. Then he stood up and stepped into the doorway. "You wanted me to let you know what was going on with the Johnny Pope thing." He had almost said "case."

Sal nodded absently. "Yeah, right. Go ahead."

"I talked to my friend Jimmy who has a record store. He said when Pope disappeared, a tape recording was missing, too."

"Tape recording of what?"

"The new songs he had written."

"And?"

"And it'd be worth some money if it ever turned up."

"Big 'if.' What else?"

"I went to see Fat Cat, the DJ at W—"

"Did you say 'Fat Cat'?" Sal looked amused.

"Yeah. You don't listen to the radio?"

"I listen to the radio. I listen to that station that plays records by Mr. Frank Sinatra. Tony Bennett. Rosemary Clooney. Good music."

Eddie let that one go. "Anyway, he knew Pope really well, so I went and talked to him."

The detective was gazing toward the window, and Eddie couldn't tell if he was paying attention. Glancing at his notebook, he went over the conversation with Fat Cat point by point. When he got to the *don't fuck with this* comment, it turned out that Sal had been listening after all.

"Seems a lot of people feel that way," the detective said with a sidelong glance. "First the girl, now this guy."

"I asked about the two other members of the group," Eddie went on. "One's a preacher now. The other one hangs out at a place down the end of South Street called the Domino Lounge. I'm going there tonight to see if I can find him."

Sal frowned and said, "You know there's people down there that'll cut you for pocket change, right?"

"It's fine," Eddie said.

"Yeah?" Sal said. "I hope so, because you ain't going to be no good to me with a razor stuck in your throat."

"I can handle it," Eddie said.

"If you say so," Sal said.

Eddie turned him back to the subject at hand. "I also talked to Pope's agent. Ex-agent. His name's Eugene White." He gave it a beat. "And he is."

"He is what?"

"White."

Sal didn't get it, either. He picked up a pen and started doodling on a legal pad. "And what did Mr. White have to offer?"

"He told me it was true that Pope was finished with the Excels."

"Oh? I thought they were doing good."

"They were. But Johnny wanted to be on his own." Sal frowned again, as if what he was hearing didn't make sense. "He was talking about leaving his record label, too."

The detective kept doodling. "Because why?"

"Money, for one thing. He thought maybe he was being cheated."

Sal stopped his scribbling and raised his head. "By who?"

"The guy who owned StarLite Records," Eddie said. "George Roddy. And listen to this. White says he had a gambling problem."

Now Sal swiveled in his chair. "What kind of gambling problem?"

"He owed."

Sal said, "Huh." He tapped out an absent rhythm with his pen. "And Pope was leaving the record company to go where?"

"He was talking about starting his own label. Then he would have owned it all. All the songs, the recordings, everything."

Sal said, "And who would lose that income?"

"Roddy."

"Hard to pay your bookie if you lose your number-one meal ticket," Sal mused. "I'd take a look at that character. Anything else?"

"I got Pope's schedule, right up to the day he disappeared." Sal nodded his approval. "I also asked White if he had any women around at the time."

"And he didn't," the detective said automatically.

"How did you know?"

Sal smiled. "The guy's stonewalling, right?"

"Everybody's stonewalling."

"Welcome to the exciting world of private investigation." The detective tossed his pen aside. "You ready to give it up?"

Eddie said, "Not yet."

Sal laughed and said, "Okay, then, in that case, you're on the clock." He picked up a stack of files. "Get these put away."

Eddie looked at the files. "Where's Bink been, Sal?"

"He's around."

"I ain't seen him."

"Bink comes and goes. That's all I know. When he's here, I give him some work to do. When he's not, he's got something else. And that means you get to do stuff. Put up those files, for example."

When Eddie finished with the files, he picked up the phone and tried StarLite again. It seemed Mr. Roddy got farther away with each passing day. Now the girl said she didn't know when he would be back in the office. Eddie sat for a moment, then dialed another number.

Jimmy T picked up on the eighth or ninth ring and yelled something. Eddie could hear the Jive Bombers wailing away in the background. "It's Cero, Jimmy."

"Fast Eddie! You find that tape yet?"

"It's only been two days," Eddie said.

"Remember our deal. I get first shot."

Eddie didn't remember anything of the kind. "What do you know about George Roddy?" he said.

Jimmy's voice came down a few notches. "Not that much. Why?"

"Tell me what you do know, then."

Eddie heard a rustle, a click, and a long, smoky breath. "Well, his brother Arthur was the one who started the company," Jimmy began. "That would have been 1948, around there. He was doing R&B, and they had some good acts. The Continentals and the Sparrows and Big Jimmy King. But Arthur got sick, y'know, and he died. George took over. He got rid of the acts Arthur had brought on and started doing garbage, novelty records, and that kind of shit. That was it, until he lucked into the Excels. They were the only decent act he had."

"What's his reputation?"

"Well, he's a businessman." Jimmy's tone curled on the last word.

"Meaning what?"

"Meaning he don't give a flying fuck about the music."

"What's—"

"He got rich, and most of his artists never had a pot to piss in." Jimmy was winding up. "You ever hear of Lee Jaxon? Or the Jaybirds?"

"Who?"

"*Who* is right. Just some artists that he screwed and left in a ditch. There were others. He took every goddamn thing they had and then dropped them."

"You ever hear anything about him having money problems?" Eddie said. "Or a gambling problem?"

A moment passed and Jimmy said, "Why you ask that?"

"Because I did hear some talk."

"It wouldn't be a surprise," Jimmy said. "And it would sure explain some things."

"What's that mean?"

"That means I don't want to talk about this anymore," Jimmy muttered before clicking off.

After Eddie hung up, he went in to talk to Sal and found the detective working on the second Danish. He sat down and recounted his chat with Jimmy T.

When he finished, Sal said, "It'll be interesting to hear what Mr. Roddy has to say."

"If I ever talk to him," Eddie said.

"You've got to," Sal said. "And by the way, have you gone by where the victim disappeared?"

Eddie said, "Not yet."

"You gotta do that, too."

Eddie smiled. "The scene of the crime?"

"Just like in the movies," Sal said.

Eddie stood up to leave.

"Wait a minute," Sal said. He grabbed a manila envelope that was lying on his desk and held it out. "This is for you."

"What is it?"

"It's a copy of the police report on the Pope investigation. I was down at City Hall, and so I just went ahead and picked it up."

Eddie was surprised. He said, "Thanks, Sal," and opened the flap to peer at the top of the first page, an official form of some kind.

"No big deal," Sal told him. "I was down there. Hey, don't be getting into it now."

Eddie folded the flap closed and tied the little strings. "Well, I appreciate it."

Before he left, he tried StarLite Records one more time. When the receptionist said that Mr. Roddy was not in and asked if he wanted to leave a message, he said, "Yeah, tell him Johnny Pope called." The receptionist noted it dutifully; the name didn't ring any bells.

Turning off Vandalia onto Morris, Eddie found himself staring at the monstrous black hull of a freighter. He dug out his notebook, flipped to the address, then drove up the street past blocks of warehouses and pulled to the curb.

The air smelled of brine and oil, and seagulls flapped and squawked overhead. Along the row of shipping companies, import-export offices, and storefront photography shops, he found the building with a glass door painted in bright brush strokes: 45 STUDIOS, HOME OF THE HITS! Through the glass he could see a set of steel stairs leading to the upper floors. Another sign read, OFFICES—FIRST FLOOR and below it STUDIO—SECOND FLOOR. He tried the door and found it locked, so he pushed the buzzer.

When no one appeared, he walked into the narrow entrance way and around to the brick courtyard. One long loading dock was attached to the rear of the building and two sets of steel stairs ascended to a second-floor landing.

Eddie climbed the stairs to the landing and made his way to the heavy steel door. An ashtray filled with old butts adorned a rusting metal table at which were placed three rusting chairs. Eddie pounded on the door.

While he waited, he stood at the railing to survey the parking area below, the scene of Johnny Pope's last moments. He pictured a dark and cold February night and Pope appearing from the studio after a long day's work.

Only to meet someone—someone he had known? a stranger?—stepping out of the shadows. From that point, it wouldn't have taken long for Johnny Pope's shooting star of a life to end. The body was most probably resting on the bottom of the thick green waters of the Delaware River, a short stone's throw away.

When no one appeared at the door, Eddie descended the steps and crossed the brick courtyard where Johnny Pope had most likely died.

The 12:05 bell shrilled and two minutes later, a green hunk of a Pontiac, complete with fake chrome exhaust ports, slipped out of the parking lot with Marianne at the wheel.

So she was clever enough to cover her tracks by borrowing a different friend's car for her escapades. That wouldn't be hard; she could probably get pretty much anything she wanted anytime she wanted it.

She was also taking a slightly different route this time, though the destination was the same. When she reached North Drexel Avenue and cut around the side of the house, Eddie drove by and parked at the next corner. Grabbing his clipboard and the Leica, he got out and started wandering, eyeing the homes and then scribbling on the paper, looking to all the world like a man engaged in official business, as he edged closer to the house.

For the next twenty minutes, nothing stirred except the breeze through the apple blossoms. Eddie kept an eye on his watch; she'd have to come out of the door no later than 12:40 to make it back to school in time.

She was right on the money. He was peeking from the corner of the garage when she appeared, and he got off two quick shots of her stretching to kiss the man who stood in the doorway. Eddie kept clicking as the man's hand swept down her back, and he brushed her bottom with familiar fingertips. He snapped two more before ducking away to scurry back to the DeSoto. His last shot was the car pulling out with Marianne behind the wheel.

He had just arrived at his car as she drove off. She had a good head start, and by the time he made it back to the school, the green Pontiac was tucked in as though it had never left.

He was creeping around the edge of the lot when she suddenly appeared between two parked cars to step directly into his path. He hit the brakes and the tires chirped.

She strolled around to the window, as languid as a willow in the breeze. It was the first time Eddie had seen her so close, and for a few seconds he was mesmerized by her youthful beauty, the skin a smooth freckled tan, her eyes a deep sea green, and a few strands of her corn-silk hair just touching her brow. Her nose was near perfect and her full lips arched in a fetching smile. She could have been on a magazine cover, the very image of young American innocence.

"You've been following me," she said softly. He stared at her, his brain stuck in neutral. "Did my parents hire you?" When he didn't speak up, she said, "You know that whatever you tell them, it will be your word against mine."

Eddie didn't know what to say to that, either, so he lifted the camera off the seat and said, "I took pictures."

She paused, considering, and then said, "Oh." She bit her lip fetchingly. Her eyes, glinting gemstones, found his. "All right, then what do you want not to tell them? Do you want to get under my skirt?"

Nothing in Sal's book had prepared Eddie for this one. "I can't, I'm . . . I'm working." It sounded ridiculous, and he almost laughed at the whole crazy moment. He still could not quite believe what had come out of this angel's mouth.

She stared at him, the angel face now pinching in annoyance. "Well, what do you want, then? Money?" The bell rang and she glanced over her shoulder. "I'm going to be *late,*" she said, and backed away from the car. "Whatever you want. Just don't tell my parents, okay? Don't!" She turned around and disappeared in the sea of cars.

Eddie found a pay phone and called in.

Sal listened, then said, "Jesus-fucking-Christ! She offered to lay you?"

"Or pay me. Maybe both, if I play my cards right."

The detective gave out a dry laugh. "Well, I'll be damned. I've heard some crazy shit, but this takes the cake. And she's just a kid."

"Not so much," Eddie commented. "What am I supposed to do now?"

Sal was quiet for a few seconds. "I don't know. Stick with her, I guess. See what happens. That's all you can do." He grunted his amazement. "Just when I thought I'd heard it all," he said, and hung up.

At the 3:20 bell, the MG pulled out of the lot. Eddie followed her around town and then back home. There didn't seem to be any point in trying to be devious, so he parked out in the open. Marianne, for her part, ignored him.

A little before eight, a car pulled into the driveway, and Steven Jamison got out and knocked on the door. There was a glow of warm light when he was ushered inside, and for a couple brief seconds Eddie was peering into the lives of the Gibsons, of 1199 Edgewood Road, Havertown, Pennsylvania, and took in the cheery warm amber of a dream. Then the door closed.

Marianne and her date drove into town with Eddie following behind, a dutiful hound. They parked on Landsdowne Avenue and strolled to the Strand Theater, where *Cape Fear* was playing. Eddie walked to a lunch counter down the street for a cheeseburger and French fries, then wandered Landsdowne Avenue up and down, keeping an eye on the theater doors. Though the whole exercise now seemed foolish.

They came out with the crowd at ten thirty. Eddie expected they would head for Buzzy's. Instead, he followed them back to Edgewood Road. Steven walked Marianne to the front door. The poor kid didn't even get a kiss good night before ambling back to his car.

Eddie started the DeSoto and had just put it in gear when he looked up to see the door open and Marianne step outside. She drew closer, her hands entwined behind her back with her hips swaying in an alluring dance. Eddie watched for another few seconds, then swung the wheel and hit the gas. He stole a glance as he pulled away and saw her standing at the end of the drive, a lonely white statue, watching him drive off.

It was a good night. The crowd was small but fervent, one of those rare instances when everyone in the house is there for music. There wasn't one drunken chatterbox to ruin the atmosphere; the band stayed together, giving Valerie just enough for a launch pad; and she was in a mood to let herself be carried away.

It wasn't her voice—it was everyone's, belonging to all the brokenhearted, lost, and lonely souls of the night. They knew it and remained hypnotically silent as she worked through two blues numbers and a ballad that no one had ever heard before, "All Your Tomorrows." It was one of those that Johnny had written but never performed, because he had died too soon. She had told the bass player where to go, and it was just her crooning against those low notes. It was the last song in the set, and when it was over and she let the final round, sad tone fade out, there was a moment of echoing silence. Then they began to clap. Not wildly but with feeling, every one of them. For three minutes she had carried them away, and they were grateful.

She bowed and stepped off the stage and into the dark wings.

As Eddie cruised past the Blue Door, he slowed to a crawl. There was a couple standing on the sidewalk, but no Valerie, and he pictured her up onstage, singing melancholy songs to a crowd of strangers.

He drove on to the far end of South Street, almost to the river, and located the Domino Lounge. It was a concrete block building that had seen better days. All the windows were blacked out, though the paint was peeling and a couple panes sported holes that looked suspiciously bullet-sized. Eddie could see that it might have once been a decent joint, but someone had let it fall apart and now it looked like a bunker. There were bulbs missing from the sign over the door so that it read: DOMIN LOU GE.

When he walked in the front door, the chatter in the room faded as if someone had thrown a switch. Except for a couple drunks who were too far gone to notice him and just kept babbling on, every tongue in the room went still. He walked to the horseshoe-shaped bar and ordered a beer as whispers lapped in his wake. The bartender, a tall woman with a high bouffant and a sharply planed face adorned with artful makeup, looked him up and down, then went to the cooler for an F&S.

"You're not one of our regulars," she said as she placed a bottle on a coaster.

"I just moved into the neighborhood," Eddie said, and the big man in a tight suit and porkpie hat who was sitting on the next stool let out a low chuckle. A wave of chatter rippled in the immediate vicinity, and he heard some laughs from the closest tables.

Within a few minutes, the novelty of his presence wore off and the buzz of conversation wound up again. The bartender went to serve another customer, then came back around. "You didn't walk in here by mistake, did you?" She was smiling slightly.

"I was looking for a good jukebox," Eddie said.

"It's in the corner, and it's five plays for a quarter." She moved away again.

He leaned on the bar and took in the room. Spread out around the room were twenty-odd mismatched metal tables, a tiny dance floor, and in the corner next to the door, a low stage. The room was cast in pale blue light except for the jukebox glowing red and gold as it throbbed the likes of James Brown, Clyde McPhatter, the Persuasions, and Big Maybelle.

Eddie listened to the music and watched the crowd. Two couples were slow-dancing, a sweet grind. The handful of customers who had been staring at him gave up, and the guy in the porkpie hat nodded his head once or twice, casually friendly.

Eddie looked over the small crowd, wondering if he would

recognize Ray Pope if he saw him. No one seemed to fit the bill. It didn't matter: He was fine just sitting there. After Havertown, the Domino was bedrock normal.

When his bottle was almost empty, the bartender came back around and leaned over as if to ask if he was ready for another one.

Instead she whispered, "All right, I give up, white boy. What the hell you doin' in here?"

"Looking for somebody," Eddie murmured.

Her eyes got hard. "Who?"

"Ray Pope."

She drew back. "Good lord! What you want that fool for?"

"I want to talk to him."

Now she gave him a speculative look. "Talk to him, huh? What'd he do?"

"Nothing I know of," Eddie said. "Really. I just want to talk to him."

"You're going to have to do better than that," she said.

"First things first," he countered.

The woman considered for a few seconds. "All right. You can find him in here three, four times a week, leastwise until I have to throw his sorry ass out on the street."

"Tonight?"

"Not yet. He probably ain't comin'. Try tomorrow. He's always here Saturday."

"I will."

"Anything you want me to tell him?" the barmaid said. "When I see him, I mean."

"You can tell him Eddie Cero wants to talk to him."

Out of the corner of his eye, he caught the porkpie hat turning slowly in his direction. In a deep rumble of a voice, the man said, "Eddie Cero. You a fighter?"

He looked at the man. "Was. Not anymore."

Porkpie nodded to the bartender. "Thas right," he rumbled.

"Fast Eddie Cero. Welterweight. Uh-huh. I seen this boy fight a couple times." He looked at Eddie. "You was good in there."

Eddie nodded a thank-you. The woman behind the bar watched curiously as he drained his beer and laid a dollar bill on the bar. "Keep it," he said.

"My name's Leona," she told him, and picked up the bill. "You be careful goin' home, Fast Eddie. This here's a rough neighborhood at night."

He moved across the floor and got his second surprise of the day. He was ten feet from the door when it opened and T-Bone Mieux walked in. The Creole came to a halt and stared at him through his slit eyes. Then his face cracked into a mean grin. "Well, damn, looky what we got here," he said. "Fast Eddie Cero! Damn, boy, what the hell you doin' round here?"

"I'm leaving," Eddie said.

The fighter looked between Eddie and the room around him, wearing a baffled expression, as if he had gotten lost going from A to B. Then the gears of his brain seemed to engage.

"Leavin' is right," he said. "'Cause you in the wrong part of town, unless you lookin' for another whuppin'."

Eddie had started to slide around him. Now he stopped. "Two out of three." He flicked a finger at his scarred eyebrow. "And right there's how you got the last one."

Mieux's mouth folded back, and he raked Eddie up and down with his dirty brown eyes. "Motherfucker, I beat your ass," he said.

Eddie brought his face close to the Creole's. "Fuck you, you fucking cheap-shot pussy," he said, and then brushed past him.

Mieux spun around. "What'd you call me?" He made a motion to grab Eddie's arm, but Eddie jerked it out of his reach.

"You're too slow, Mieux," he said. "Always were. You need to work on that."

Mieux's lips were flapping as Eddie went out the door. He had gone only a few steps down the sidewalk when he heard the

Creole yelling from the doorway. "What'd you say? Too slow, my fuckin' ass! I muh'fuckin' beat you, man! I retired you! I put you out of bidness, you dago fuck! So don't be bringin' your greasy guinea ass down here no—"

Eddie kept walking. He didn't think Mieux would come after him, but he cocked an ear anyway, hoping he was wrong. Out there on the street, without a crowd around and no rules, he could uncork his stuff. Even out of shape, he knew he could tattoo the Creole.

He did turn around when he reached the corner. The bar door was closed and Mieux was not in sight. It took him a moment to realize that he had turned on the balls of his feet with a dip of his shoulders and his pulse rising the way it did when he was in the ring.

He got in the car and sat for a minute, calming himself. It had been some shock seeing Mieux; a shock, followed by a rush of anger. He was glad he had managed to stay cool. A room full of black people was no place to start swinging; otherwise, he might have clocked him right there in the bar.

As he started the car, he pondered on what T-Bone Mieux, of all people, was doing in that place. Then he decided that it wasn't so strange. Mieux was a low-rent hustler, and a joint like the Domino would be one of his regular stops. South Philly really was that small of a world.

At the corner of Pemberton, he let the DeSoto drift to the curb. He recognized the profile immediately, the outline of her hair and the curve of her bust and hips, and the cigarette with the glow at its tip. He spent a half minute debating whether or not to get out to approach her, see her face and hear her voice, and discover which Valerie was on tonight.

Instead, he made a U-turn in the street and headed home. He wouldn't know what to say to her. And it had been a long day.

SIXTEEN

He woke to the sound of crashing garbage cans in the alley below his window and lay there, imagining banging the landlord's head between two of the lids. It was his last morning in that box, the last time his drunken landlord would rouse him to that particular music.

Rolling off the lumpy gray mattress, he pulled on sweatpants and a T-shirt, grabbed a towel, and walked out in the hall and down to the bathroom for his final chance to enjoy the cranky pipes and the rusty, lukewarm water.

After he dressed, he dumped the contents of the chest of drawers into his suitcase, dragged his boxes of records from under the bed, and hoisted his seabag from the closet. Piled up in the middle of the floor, his possessions didn't amount to much. He decided to leave the hot plate for the next poor sap.

As he was loading the car, he saw the curtains move. The creepy little fuck of a landlord was watching. Good. The last things out were his phonograph and his radio. He left the door standing open.

Moving in at Nineteenth Street took all of twenty minutes. He dropped his suitcase on the bed and stored his boxing gear in the closet. His records and phonograph were stashed near the door until he could decide where to put them. He placed his radio on the little night table. It was then that he realized that he was missing a few things.

At the Kresge's on Broad Street, he picked out plates, cups and saucers, some silverware, four water glasses, a shower curtain, two towels, sheets, and a pillow. The saleslady kindly wrapped the breakable items in newspaper and arranged them in a box for him. As he carried the box to the car, it occurred to him that his life was getting complicated.

Sal was standing on the sidewalk, gazing idly up at the brickwork, his hands jammed in his pockets and a newspaper under one arm.

Eddie pulled to the curb and rolled down the window. "What are you doing here, Sal?"

"I was in the neighborhood, and I thought I'd come see the place. You just moving in?"

Eddie said, "Yeah, I was."

The detective said, "So I'll help you with your stuff, and you can give me a tour of your new domicile." Eddie nodded vacantly. "Whenever you're ready," Sal said.

Sal wandered around from room to room. "Not bad, not bad," he said. "Not your best neighborhood, but what the hell, Cal gave you a good deal, huh?" When Eddie didn't say anything, he frowned. "What?"

"Nothing."

"You going to make me stand here all day?" Sal said. "I could use a drink of water, if it ain't too much trouble."

Eddie put one of the new glasses he had purchased at Kresge's in front of Sal and sat down across the table. Sal took a sip and said, "So Miss Gibson offered to put you on her dance card."

"I told her I'd think it over."

They batted the subject around for a few minutes more. Sal seemed saddened by the whole sorry business. Then discussion wound down and he said, "I see you got back from Grays Ferry in one piece."

"Yeah."

"How'd it go?"

"The guy I was looking for, Ray Pope? He wasn't there," Eddie said. "But something strange happened when I was leaving." He described the encounter with Mieux.

Sal didn't seem surprised. "Another bee in the hive," he said, and pushed back from the table. "Okay, kiddo." He stood up and, with a snap of his fingers, started going through his pockets until he located a slip of paper, which he handed to Eddie. "This is really what I came by for."

"What is it?"

"A housewarming gift."

Eddie saw the name "Gene" was scrawled on the paper, along with a phone number. "Who's Gene?"

"That contract on the singer?" Sal made a pistol of his right hand. "Bang, bang, you're dead."

Eddie stared at him. "You're kidding. How'd you get it?"

"Joe D'Amato ain't the only one who knows people," Sal said. "The point is I got it, and it's the real McCoy. Call that number and ask for Gene. Except that's not his actual name." He grinned slyly. "I also asked around, and I got something for you on this Roddy guy. He gambled, all right, the sports book, mostly. Horses, fights, college football, whatever. But he wasn't very good at it. The kind of dope who always thinks he's going to hit on the next one, so he never stops. He was into one of Winky Ragusa's books for a ton."

"But not anymore?"

"The word is that he's been right for maybe two years."

"Maybe two?"

"Could be closer to three," Sal said in an offhand way, then ambled out of the kitchen. Eddie studied the name and phone number on the paper for a few seconds before following him into the front room. He found the detective standing by the door, looking down at the boxes full of records.

"That's some collection," Sal commented. "How many you got?"

"Couple hundred."

"Rock and roll?"

"Rock and roll, rhythm and blues, some jazz, and some folk music, all—"

"Any Julius LaRosa in there?"

"No Julius LaRosa. Sorry."

Eddie waited for the snide comment that was sure to follow, but Sal just shrugged and said, "I'll see you Monday. Don't forget to make that call."

"You can, y'know, hang around if you want," Eddie offered.

Sal gave him a bemused look. "Tell you what, you get the place fixed up, put some beer in the fridge, and I'll come back." He went out and closed the door behind him.

Eddie felt bad. He hadn't been very polite. As grateful as he was for all Sal's help, it annoyed him the way he kept rearranging his life, first with the job, then a car, then an apartment. And the business about Eddie going out with one of the nieces in that nutty family was no joke.

And now he had arrived on his doorstep carrying the phone number for the guy who had been hired to murder Johnny Pope, along with the news that the rumors about George Roddy's gambling problems were true. This from the guy who hadn't wanted him anywhere near the case.

Eddie understood that Sal's feelings were hurt over him going to Joe D'Amato to get to Winky Ragusa. So he was doing his bit and then some. The piece of paper that Eddie held in his hand and the information about Roddy were signs of a grudging respect.

As he went about unpacking his things, he tried to picture Sal as one of those lonely guys looking for someone to tuck under his wing. There were plenty of them around the fight game, and they all had the same look, old stray dogs with no place to go.

That wasn't Sal, though; he had Marie, he had his kids, he had old friends from the police force. He mostly seemed to be a happy man, and that was something.

At four thirty he took a stroll around the neighborhood. Five blocks over on Rosewood, he found a diner with a phone booth stuck off in a quiet corner. He took the last stool at the counter, drank a Coke, and thought about what he was going to say. Right at five o'clock, he stepped into the booth, closed the door, dropped his nickel, and dialed. The phone rang six times before someone picked up.

"Yeah?"

"Can I speak to Gene?"

There was a pause, followed by a knocking sound as the phone dangled and banged against something. In the background he heard a quiet murmur of voices, a clink of glass, what sounded like the slap of cards. A social club, probably, somewhere not far from where he—

"This is Gene." Eddie was surprised at how ordinary the voice sounded. A regular Philly guy. Eddie stated his name. "Oh, yeah, the fighter," Gene said. "Tough racket, eh?"

"It can be, yeah."

"So you wanted to talk to me about this colored singer?" He was obviously a no-nonsense sort.

"Yeah. Do you remember it?"

"Oh, yeah, I remember."

"I want to find out who was behind it."

"I don't know that," Gene said without a second's pause.

Eddie said, "Okay, so how did you get . . . I mean, how did you hear about it?"

"What happened is I got a call from a friend of mine," Gene said. "He asked was I interested. He told me the price, and I said I'd take it."

"What friend?"

"I ain't tellin' you that." Now he sounded mildly amused.

"I don't care about the person," Eddie said quickly. "I'm just trying to figure out who wanted him, uh . . ."

"Gone?"

"Yeah."

"Sorry, can't help you." The voice was clipped, a little impatient. "Look, it don't matter; he was just a guy. He wouldn't tell you nothin', neither. He's not around anyway."

Eddie didn't ask whether "not around" meant left town or something else. "So, what can—"

"Hang on a second." Gene cupped his hand over the phone and spoke to someone. He was back in a few seconds. "What now?"

"What else can you tell me about it?" When Gene didn't respond, he said, "I need some help here."

There was another brief pause. Then: "What I remember is it needed to be done quick. I was working on it, but then the guy was gone. I thought maybe he heard what was cooking and beat it out of town. Except he didn't ever come back."

"So maybe someone else decided to jump in?"

"That would not have been a smart move," Gene said flatly. "And I already had half the money in my pocket. Half on the front end, half when it's done, that's the way I work. Of course, some people ain't got no sense. But I know nobody tried to claim it. Anyway, like I said, the guy never showed up again, and I had to give back the front end. It was a fucking joke, a big ha-ha, for a while. Anything else?"

"You were told it had to be done quick?"

"That was the instructions, yeah."

"Did anyone say why?"

"Nope. Just get it done in a hurry. Bing, bang, boom."

Eddie thought about asking how much money it took to hire out a murder, then decided it didn't matter. "How were you going to do it?"

"How was I . . ." He stopped. "Whaddya want to know that for?"

"I'm just filling in blanks here."

Gene hesitated again. "Well, that was tough, because everywhere he went, people came up and talked to him, asked for autographs, and all that. I spent a little time tailing him, seeing how he comes and goes. He was working at this building, down the end of, um . . ."

"Morris," Eddie said.

"Morris, right. He parked in back. He worked late and it was real dark out there. Catching him alone would have been the hard part, but then it would be one shot, he's down and in the trunk, and it's all over. Then I—" He stopped abruptly, as if realizing he had talked too much. "Listen, that's all I can tell you. And I gotta see somebody. We're done here." The phone clicked dead.

Walking home, Eddie started feeling a twist in his stomach at the casual way that Gene had discussed eliminating another human being. There was nothing to it, the voice said, you just kill the guy; just another job. All in a good day's work.

At nine o'clock he splashed some water on his face and changed into a white shirt and his sport coat.

South Street was hopping, with swarms of people parading up and down in the warm spring night, more crowding the doorways of the open stores, bars, and record shops, while others gathered in circles under the streetlights. Spirals of smoke from a hundred cigarettes curled upward into the night sky, while the mixed aromas of food wafted over the asphalt. Music blared, the jazz, blues, and R&B creating strange stews.

Eddie found a place to park a block away on Bainbridge and walked through the throngs to the Domino. The music pounding from the jukebox washed over the room, and while the chatter around the door dipped when he walked in, it wasn't the stone silence of the night before. The place was so busy that only a few of those crammed inside noticed him. Still, he didn't escape the glances that turned into cool stares, but he was used to those.

When he reached the bar, he found Leona hovering, the news a dago was in the room having gone ahead of him. When she noticed him, she turned and muttered something to the man sitting on the last stool, who rose unsteadily and swayed into the crowd. Leona pointed a finger and Eddie took the stool. She put a bottle of F&S in front of him and moved away.

He could feel the stares from the customers nearby who witnessed this pantomime. But when nothing further transpired, they lost interest and, one by one, forgot about him. Though the other bartender—a tall, thin, middle-aged man—gave him a long look and then went back to work, he kept frowning at him over his shoulder.

Eddie drank his beer and cast an eye about. The joint was jumping, the crowd all loud and happy, and it made him feel a little strange, a fly in the soup. Not that this congregation wasn't about to let him ruin their good time. He imagined the situation in reverse, with some Negro wandering into a bar on his side of the street. Not a pretty picture. On the other hand, why would anyone want to go into some deadbeat white joint when they could have the Domino on a Saturday night?

The bar customers were covered, and Leona stepped over, leaned on an elbow, and regarded him casually. "So you're looking to talk to Ray."

Eddie nodded. "Is he here?"

"Yeah, he's here," Leona said. "Getting an early start." Her gaze wandered. "You're going to need an introduction."

"That would help," Eddie said.

"Yeah, you don't want to go wandering around in here, asking questions. These folk won't care for that at *all*."

Eddie caught her drift. "And you would want what?"

Leona tilted her head appreciatively. "I just want to know what's going on in here. Especially when some Italian boy I ain't never seen before come lookin' for the likes of Ray Pope."

Quickly, and in a quiet voice, Eddie told her what he was doing.

When he finished, she said, "I thought you was a fighter."

"Was, yeah. Now I'm doing this. So I need to talk to Ray."

"I can tell you exactly what he's going to say." She took a pause and her eyes widened. "Why, it was all the *white* man's fault. What happened to Johnny, what happened to the Excels, what happened to him, is all 'cause of the white man. If I heard it once, I swear I heard it a hundred times."

Eddie said, "I still want to talk to him."

"All right, then." She stepped out from behind the bar and hooked one of her long, manicured fingernails. He stood up and pulled his notebook and a pen out of the pocket of his sport coat. Leona glared at him as if he had brandished a gun.

"Put that shit away!" she hissed.

"I have to write stuff down," he said.

"You want these people thinkin' you the law?" She grimaced. "The fool won't say nothin' worth a damn anyhow."

Eddie slipped the notebook and pen back into his pocket. As he followed her through the crowd, he leaned in to her ear and said, "So what's with the seating here?"

"What?"

"You chased that guy off the stool so I could sit down."

"Oh." She stopped. "I keep that one for our extra-special customers," she said with a straight face. "I call it the back of the bus."

When they reached the far side of the room, the crowd parted, and Eddie looked down on a blurred copy of the man on the Excels' record sleeve. It was Ray Pope, all right, but the portrait had been rendered by a shaky hand. He was short and slender, and his freckled face was twisted up as if he was in pain. His process looked months old, the shiny waves all brittle. A thin woman with wild hair that hung in strands and bulging, drunken eyes had an arm slung across his shoulders as he hunched over a cocktail glass.

Leona said, "Ray?"

Ray looked up. His red eyes flickered and his mouth moved wordlessly. The woman gazed at Eddie in astonishment.

"This here's Mr. Cero," Leona was saying. "He'd appreciate a few minutes of your time."

When Eddie sat down in the empty chair, the customers at the nearby tables stopped talking. Ray and his woman stared at him, baffled twins.

Ray found his voice. "Whatchu want, man?"

"I want to talk to you about your cousin Johnny," Eddie said. "And the Excels."

Now Ray came up with an uncertain frown. "Whatchu with, the newspaper?" Eddie shook his head. Ray said, "Well, what, then?"

"I'm conducting an investigation." It sounded like a line from a TV show, and he spoke it badly.

Ray missed that part. "A cop?" His voice went up, and heads started turning. "You're a *cop*?"

"Not a cop," Eddie said. "Private."

Ray looked at his woman, then back at Eddie. "And you want what?" He was breathing through his nose, as if catching the scent of something.

"I just want to talk to you. About Johnny. And the Excels."

Ray's bloodshot eyes widened in mock revelation. "Oh, I see! You wanna talk about Mr. Johnny Pope. And the Excels. You mean the *ex*-Excels. Why didn't ya say so?" He let out a dirty laugh that ended in a snarl. "Well, fuck that. And fuck you." He drained what was left of his drink and slammed the glass down on the table, popping the ice cubes. "You know whatchu need to do? You need to get out my fuckin' face right now." When Eddie didn't move, Pope snarled, "Hey, fuck, man. What I got to say on that subject is *nothin'*. Y'understand?"

"Maybe now's not a good time," Eddie said.

"What the hell are you doin' in here anyway?" His voice started going up again. "Who the fuck are you, comin' in here with this shit?" His eyes bugged out and he jerked forward. "You wanna know 'bout the Excels? The Excels was a *black* group, man, I mean as in *colored*. You know, niggers, working in the white man's kitchen. Fuckin' right, we was. We was workin' in the motherfuckin' white man's *yard*. And you know what happened when we decided we wasn't going to kiss his ass no more? He done got rid of us. Got rid of Johnny for good. Shut him up." His voice broke a little. "That boy . . . he could sing like a goddamn angel. He was a goddamn genius. But they shut him up for good."

Eddie said, "Do you have any ideas about what happened to him?" In the face of Ray's rage, it was a squeak.

"I told you, get the fuck away from me!" Ray was half spitting the words as his hands gripped the edge of the table. Eddie tensed. He didn't want to get into something with the guy, not in this place. It would be suicide.

He didn't get a chance to decide, because Ray suddenly came halfway out of his chair, screeched, "Motherfucker!" and threw a clumsy punch. Eddie picked it off as if he was swatting a bee. Ray lurched to his feet, his fists balled, yelling, "Don't you put your goddamn motherfuckin' ha—"

He suddenly jerked away as if he'd been snapped by a wire, almost tumbling backward over his chair. He righted himself and looked around wildly for someone to hit.

"Don't do it, Ray!" Leona's voice shrilled. "I'll put you right through that damn wall!" She was standing there, her dark eyes blazing, one long finger on him. "Sit your ass down!" The chatter in the room stopped in what seemed a single sucked-in breath, leaving only Slim Harpo's guitar slinking off the rafters.

Ray wavered for a few seconds, then abruptly deflated. He sat, hanging his head and looking so broken that Eddie almost felt sorry for him. His woman gazed hypnotically at Leona's bright red fingernail, hanging over their heads, a bloody sword.

"The gentleman wants to have a word with you," Leona said.

"I ain't got nothin' to say," Ray croaked.

"Shit. You always got somethin' to say. That's your damn problem."

Ray stared at the floor, refusing to look up. After a few seconds' deep pause, the noise in the room began a slow swell. The show was over. It got loud again.

Leona withdrew the finger and squared her shoulders. "Maybe you two can make some other arrangements." She tilted her head slightly, and Eddie stood up. Stares followed them to the bar, where the back-of-the-bus seat was still vacant.

"You want another beer?" she said.

"Make it a rum and Coke." He let out a long breath.

She fixed the drink, using the good stuff. "Didn't I tell you?" she said.

"You did," Eddie said.

Leona smiled as she placed the drink in front of him. "This one's on the house."

"I still need to talk to him," Eddie said.

"Come back, and maybe you'll catch him in a better mood."

"That won't be hard."

She hiked her eyebrows in agreement. Eddie sipped his drink. "You know Tommy Gates?"

Leona said, "Tommy? He's a preacher now."

"You happen to know where I can find him?"

"He's got him a church, six, seven blocks over here on

Twenty-sixth Street," she said, tilting her head. "The Holy . . . Holy Spirit something. I believe that's right." She reached under the bar for a glass and took a sip. Eyeing him, she said, "What's with you and that boy, whatshisname, Mieux?"

Eddie's eyes narrowed. "What about him?"

"He was asking me about you," Leona said. "Wanted to know what you were doin' in here."

"What did you tell him?"

"Didn't tell him nothin'. 'Cause I don't know nothin'."

"He come around a lot?" he said.

"Oh, yeah. We get all the fools at one time or another."

She went off to serve her other customers. Eddie looked across the room and saw Ray had fixed a drunk's bleary glare on him. He finished his drink, laid three ones on the bar, and nodded good night to Leona. He started picking his way carefully through the noisy crowd. He was a few steps from the door when he felt a hand clamp on his arm. He turned around and met Ray's eyes, gone all black and crazy again.

"Listen," the little man growled. "You want to know the truth? Ask Valerie. Ask *her.*"

Eddie, startled, said, "What?" But just as suddenly as he had appeared, Ray sank back into the crowd. Eddie thought about going after him. Then he saw the wall of bodies blocking his path and the line of dark, still faces watching him. He guessed he had pushed his luck enough for one night and turned around and went out the door.

He leaned on a parking meter to watch the sidewalk parade and listen to the music from the record shop across the street—Solomon Burke, at the moment. He was hoping Ray would come stumbling out the door after him so he could ask what he had meant in the bar. *You want to know the truth? Ask Valerie. Ask her.*

He was gazing idly at the facade of the record shop and pondering the outburst when something caught his eye. He took a step to the left and stared. A face had jumped out of the crowd of shoppers behind the window. T-Bone Mieux was staring back out at him; or at least he thought so. He let a line of cars go by, then stepped into the street, peering into the crowded, noisy store. The fighter was nowhere in sight. He hung around for a few minutes more, then walked back across the street.

He took a final look as he drove past the store. That made two nights in a row that he had encountered Mieux. Once was a coincidence. This was something else, and it put the Creole asking about him in a different light. As he crossed the intersection at Twenty-fourth Street, he rolled down his window to get some air and spend some time thinking over what he knew about Thibodeaux Mieux.

He had shown up a couple years earlier, out of "uptown N'awlins," as he put it, and, with light copper skin, straight hair, pale brown eyes, and a long, thin nose on a hatchet face, could almost pass for white. There had been talk that he was running from the police back home, though no one knew whether or not to believe it, since Mieux was the type to start that kind of rumor just to make himself look like bad news. He was an okay fighter, though around the clubs and gyms he had quickly become known more for his mouth than his fists.

The Creole hated him and Eddie knew why. Before their first fight, a six-rounder, Mieux had spent weeks telling everyone at the gyms that Fast Eddie Cero was nothing, a guinea punk, and that he was going to take him out early. Of course Eddie heard it, too. That was the point.

Mieux's prediction was off just a bit. Eddie let him have his way for the first three rounds, then came on when he started to fade. He spent the next two banging him in the gut, until Mieux finally had to take a knee. He couldn't answer the bell for the final round. Later he claimed the shots were low, and he also said he'd had the flu.

Their second fight, eleven months later, was an eight-rounder at the Municipal Auditorium. That time Eddie caught the Creole posing in the third and hit him with a shot below the ribs that lifted him about a foot off the canvas, then cracked him on the chin with a right hook that put him down. Mieux could have gotten up; his eyes were clear. He stayed on the canvas.

In the last one, Eddie was on his way to a hat trick when Mieux came in with his head. Just like that, the fight was finished, taking Eddie's career right along with it. He couldn't believe it had only been a month since that night. And now Mieux had appeared in his sights two nights in a row.

He turned down Nineteenth Street and pulled up in front of his building. He was thinking he'd go inside, turn on the radio, and run over the whole thing again while he waited for Susie to show up, when it dawned on him then that she didn't know his new address. If she went to Eleventh Street, she'd find his room vacated. Or maybe she'd knock and some creep of a stranger would open the door. She'd think that he'd deserted her.

He pulled back out, drove east through town, and found a parking spot. He slouched down in the seat and tuned the radio in to the Geator on WCAM. Ray's face suddenly jumped back into his mind, a photograph coming into focus.

You want to know the truth? Ask Valerie. Ask her.

What did it mean? Had Valerie talked to Ray at some point and warned him that there was someone asking about Johnny? Maybe somebody had seen them together at Thelma's. If that was true, she would have alerted Tommy Gates, too. And who else? George Roddy at StarLite? Fat Cat, the guy who had warned him not to fuck with the case, might have taken it upon himself to tell Ray and the others. Though why would he care? Maybe Eugene White called Valerie, who then called Tommy or

Ray, who then called someone else. He went around and around with it and still couldn't come up with anything that made sense.

The cab pulled up a little after two o'clock. She got out and looked up at the dark windows. He crossed the street, came up behind her, and said, "Hey." She turned to him with the wounded, weary smile that always stopped him short.

They never talked much, and after motioning the cabbie to leave, he waved her to the DeSoto. He held the door open and she got in. As they drove back down Catherine Street, she slid across the seat, laid her head on his shoulder, and closed her eyes.

He ushered her into his apartment. She stood in the middle of the living-room floor. "Yours?" she said, and walked slowly through the rooms. She stepped into the bathroom and closed the door. Then she went to the bedroom and turned on the bedside lamp.

Eddie stood in the doorway, watching her undress, a slow, silent dance that was cast in soft golden lamplight. Her clothes fell to the floor, one piece at a time, as if they were layers of skin she was shedding. She looked at him from behind a shock of hair, and he blinked, startled, realizing that all the time he had been watching her, he had been thinking about Valerie.

SEVENTEEN

Susie was gone when he got up Sunday morning. He hadn't left any money on the night table for her. He hadn't even thought about it.

Once he saw the sun peek over the rooftops, he pulled on his blue jeans, a T-shirt, and his jacket and walked five blocks through the quiet streets to the diner he had visited the afternoon before. He found the phone book at the end of the counter. There were a dozen listings under the name "Pope, V." He asked the waitress for change and started calling. She answered on his fourth try.

"This is Eddie Cero," he said.

"How'd you get this number?" She sounded startled.

"It's in the book."

Her surprise gave way to annoyance. "What do you want?" she said. "We're getting ready for Mass. And I told you—" She stopped in midsentence as what sounded like a cartoon character began jabbering in the background. Valerie said something away from the phone, and the little voice squeaked off.

"I asked you not—"

"You have a kid?"

She stopped again. "Yes, I do." It came out in a clipped voice that told him it was none of his business. "And where do you get off, telling Eugene White I sent you to him?"

"Did he say that?" Eddie said innocently. "He must have misunderstood."

"Yeah, I'll bet."

"Look, there's something I need to tell you. It's important."

She sighed impatiently. "All right, go ahead."

He told her about the Domino, about Leona, his encounter with Ray, and the muttered mention of her name afterward. It took him a little more than a minute to get it out.

When he finished, he heard her suck in a breath. "I told you to leave it *alone*!" She spat the words out with so much venom that he drew away from the phone. He heard a rude rattle and then a dial tone.

He put the receiver back into the cradle and looked at the clock on the wall. It wasn't even nine o'clock. There was an empty stool at the counter, and he ordered breakfast, then nibbled at his eggs and scrapple and drank a cup of coffee.

When he got to the apartment, he tuned in to the gospel show and spent a few minutes listening to the groaning, growling pleas for mercy, the multitudes of voices raised in happy praise, and the pounding piano, then turned it off, unable to get through more than a stanza or two before his thoughts veered away.

After an hour's fidgeting about, he went out and found a phone booth. Inside, he leaned against the glass and opened the white pages. This time he looked up her address.

The residents of Twenty-third Street had made an effort to keep their street of brick row houses tidy. Though a war zone where gangs roamed lay just a few blocks on the other side of Lombard, around this neighborhood, they'd be out scrubbing the steps religiously every Saturday morning, just as they did in the Italian, Irish, and every other section of South Philly.

The weather was clear and warming, and residents chatted, as kids played dervish games on the sidewalks and families strolled back from church in their Sunday finest. Not a few stopped what they were doing to stare at the DeSoto with the guy behind the wheel. More stares followed him when he parked, got out, and mounted the steps to number 2120.

He knocked. A few seconds passed before the door opened. Valerie glared, her mouth in a tight angry line. "What are you *doing* here?"

"I need to talk to you," he said.

"I told you no."

Eddie crossed his arms and settled against the railing.

She put one hand on her hip in a posture he already knew well, while the other hand gripped the doorknob so tight her knuckles went white. When she realized he was ready to stand there all day, sticking out like a sore thumb for everyone to see, she took a step back and directed him inside with a snap of her head, then quickly closed the door.

Beyond the small living room were the dining room and kitchen. A handsome woman, an older version of Valerie, appeared in the kitchen doorway. Dressed for church, she regarded him with friendly curiosity.

"Mama, this is Mr. Cero," Valerie murmured. "My mother, Ann Kate Pope."

Mrs. Pope nodded her head. "Good morning, Mr. Cero."

Eddie, flustered under those watchful eyes, said, "Yes, ma'am. I'm . . . it's . . ."

"Have a seat," Valerie said, saving him.

He sat on the couch. Mrs. Pope retreated into the kitchen. He heard her singing as she moved around and understood where Valerie got her talent.

Valerie said, "My daughter's upstairs changing. We were just going out."

The next moment rapid footsteps drummed above the ceiling, and a little girl came flying down the steps and into the front room, her two pigtails streaking out behind her. She came to a startled stop when she saw the strange man perched on the couch, and her black eyes went wide.

Valerie said, "This is my daughter, Janelle. Janelle, this is Mr. Cero."

Eddie stood up. He never knew what to do with small children—wave, say hello, offer to shake hands, what? He produced a fractured combination of all three and came off looking like a clown, causing the child's elfin face to twist up in puzzlement. Valerie said something about finding her shoes, and after one more baffled glance at the visitor, she scampered off into the kitchen.

"What I wanted to say—," Eddie began, but Valerie shook her head once, very quickly, cutting him off.

"I'm taking Janelle to the park for a little bit," she said, too loudly. "You can walk along with us if you want."

Eddie followed dutifully behind mother and daughter as they made their way along the sidewalk toward Montrose Street. Janelle kept peeking over her shoulder. He tried making some funny faces, which brought only a puzzled frown. The little procession drew more stares from people on the street. He was used to it; Valerie either didn't notice or didn't care.

As soon as they reached the park on Carpenter Street, Janelle streaked away to the jungle gym. Two dozen children raced about, and their happy shrieks echoed in the spring sunlight. Each child stopped once to gaze at him, then forgot he was there.

Valerie found a spot at the end of one of the two benches. Eddie sat at the end of the one next to it. Keeping her eyes fixed on the children, she said, "It was wrong for me to yell at you like that and then hang up and all." If it was meant as an apology, she didn't sound sorry. "But you shouldn't have gone and done that. Chasing after Ray."

"How did he know you'd been talking to me?" Eddie said.

"I got no idea," she said. "Maybe somebody saw us at Thelma's and said something. Or at the Blue Door. You've been spending a lot of time there. People talk. Things get around."

"Do you know what he meant?" he said. "That business about asking you for the truth?"

Her chin took a set. "No, I don't. It doesn't make any sense. But you are talking about Ray Pope, you know."

Eddie glanced at her as she watched the children run in their crazy circles. She was keeping her face carefully composed, and he decided to shake her up. "You remember that business about a contract on Johnny? Well, I talked to the guy who was supposed to take care of him."

It worked; she recoiled, then turned her head slowly and said, "You did what?"

Now it was Eddie's turn to keep his eyes averted. "He told me that what I heard was true. That he didn't do it, because someone else got there first."

She was quiet for a few seconds. "Did he tell you who sent him?"

"Some in-between guy called him. He wouldn't tell me who it was."

She took a moment, then stood abruptly and walked across the grass to speak to her daughter, though the child hadn't beckoned her and was now fussing at the interruption. Janelle broke free and raced away, and Valerie walked back to stand by the bench.

"What you're doing isn't right," she said. "Trying to get something out of Ray. Coming out here. And whatever you find out, it doesn't matter. It won't bring Johnny back, will it?" When she looked at him this time, her eyes were clouded. "I don't want to talk to you anymore. Do you understand? This is our home, and you've got no business here. Leave us alone. Don't come back again."

"And what if I find out what happened to him?"

"You won't ever—," she began, then stopped. "You won't."

She walked off to stand at the edge of the playground, keeping her back to him. He stood up and made his way out of the park, passing through dappled sunlight into the shadows of the clouds.

Later that afternoon he drove to Twenty-sixth Street and found the church, a narrow storefront with peeling white paint on the window glass. The front door was propped open to welcome the spring air and any lost souls who might happen by.

Eddie stepped inside to find a tiny chapel with twelve rows of folding chairs on either side of the aisle. The floors were old hardwood and the trim a dull white. A low stage in front held a pulpit, an upright piano, and a riser for the choir. The windows framed simple panes of colored glass that cast rainbows of squares into the dim room.

He stared up at a cross bearing a black Jesus. He had never seen one before, but then it had been a long time since he'd been in a church.

When his eyes adjusted to the light, he noticed the man in a dark suit making his way along one of the rows, picking up hymnals and stacking them on the end chair. The man had yet to realize that he had a visitor.

"Reverend Gates?" Eddie said.

Thomas Gates stopped and turned. He laid the stack of books aside.

"Good afternoon, sir," he said, and stepped into the aisle to greet his visitor. He was tall and broad and ebony-skinned, with a thin mustache, kind eyes, and a gentle smile. Wrapping Eddie's hand in both of his he said, "How can I be of service?" There was no mistaking the mellow thunder of the Excels' former bass voice.

Eddie said, "I want to ask you some questions about Johnny Pope."

Reverend Gates released Eddie's hand and gestured to the closest chair. Eddie started to reach for his notebook, then decided to leave it in his pocket.

The reverend took a seat, leaving a chair between them. "I don't think I can be of much help with that," he said. "It's been a long time. What, three years now?"

It sounded tidy and prepared, and Eddie figured that Gates had been warned about him.

"I'd still like to hear what you do remember about the last few months," Eddie said.

Reverend Gates ran a thoughtful finger over his mustache. "Well, all right, then." He crossed one long leg over the other, then gazed in the direction of the black-skinned Jesus. "That was the fall of 1958," he began. "We'd been out all summer and fall, and we came back to town the week before Thanksgiving to do those holiday shows. We were going to take a break while Johnny worked on new material. Everyone went their own way. I took my wife and children to a church retreat in Virginia. Ray made the rounds in the neighborhood, the bars and nightclubs and all those places. He loved playing the star for the home folks." He smiled laconically. "Especially the women."

"What about Valerie?"

"Valerie?" Eddie detected the slightest hesitant pause. "Valerie hadn't gone out with us. She would have been in the city with her family . . . She did sing with us those last few dates . . ." The words faded off, then came back. "Anyway, we were all busy getting ready for Christmas. It was the first holiday in two years that we weren't working straight through. We'd had offers, but Johnny wanted the time in the studio, so he turned them down. I didn't see him from just after Thanksgiving until the week before Christmas. We had a little party and exchanged gifts. After that I didn't see him again until January, when I went by the studio to check on how things were going."

"And how were they going?"

The preacher shrugged. "Fine, from what I could tell."

"So he was in the studio, writing songs?"

"That's correct."

"By himself?"

"Beg your pardon?"

"You and Ray and Valerie weren't there at all?"

"Well . . . we worked that way sometimes."

"It wasn't because he'd decided that the Excels were finished?"

Gates produced a pronounced frown. "Who told you that?"

"Couple people," Eddie said.

"Well, they're wrong." The reverend's tone was firm. "Oh, there were always rumors floating around. There'd be a spat, and the next thing you know, the word was out that the group was breaking up. I'm sure if you heard anything, that's how it started."

"Was there?"

"Was there what?"

"A spat. A fight. Any kind of problem."

Gates seemed to be conducting a troubling debate inside his head. He shifted in his seat, then hunched forward and folded his big hands on his crossed knee, as if on the verge of a prayer.

"We were leaving StarLite Records," he said.

Eddie let out a silent breath; finally, someone had said it. "I heard some talk about that."

"Well, this wasn't just talk," the preacher said. "Johnny wanted to start his own label, the way Sam Cooke did." Reverend Gates nodded once for emphasis. "That's right. He wasn't just working on new material. He had been talking to some people about what it would take to do it. The way he explained it, it was simple."

"Who knew?"

"About us leaving StarLite? Well, Valerie and I did."

"What about Ray?"

The preacher paused. "Johnny was going to bring Valerie and me along. But Ray . . . with his drinking and the women and all of that, Johnny didn't want to carry him anymore. So . . ." He gave a regretful shake of his head.

"Things sure turned out different for the two of you." The preacher produced a curious look, and Eddie said, "I saw him last night. At the Domino. He's not a happy man."

"Ain't that the truth?" Gates sighed, dropping the preacher's robes. "The truth is, Ray never got over it. All he ever had was the Excels. He knew Johnny wanted him out, but he thought if he straightened up, he'd change his mind. But then he was gone. Ray never got to fix what was wrong, and it tore him apart. I told him to look to God. He just said something I won't repeat. He went on down in the gutter, and that's where he stayed. It's a lesson."

Eddie said, "Did Eugene White know what was happening?"

Gates winced a little.

"What?"

"Well, near the end there, Johnny said he wasn't going to do the bidding of no white man no more. 'Including that *White* man,' that's how he said it. He thought it was funny, but I felt bad, because I liked Eugene. He had done a lot for us. But there was no changing Johnny's mind once he got fixed on something."

"Do you remember anyone around who wanted to do Johnny harm?"

Gates considered. "The police asked us about that. All I can tell you is that there were people jealous of the success, starting all the way back in high school. So there was that. And in the case of Johnny and Ray, there were women. Always."

"Just Johnny and Ray?" Eddie said.

The black man closed his eyes prayerfully. "Who knows the

wages of sin better than the sinner?" His voice rumbled. "Who sees Satan's handiwork better than the man who walks in his footsteps?" Eddie was wondering if he was supposed to answer when the reverend said, "God has blessed me with a beautiful wife and two children, whom I adore."

He opened grim eyes, the cut of his body went a little slack, and his voice dropped. "But I had my time," he said, almost whispering now. "Back at the beginning. More women than I can remember. Too many, that's for sure. Thank God, I got over it." Now the nod was grim. "That was me. With Johnny and Ray, there was always some young thing crying 'cause one of them had done her wrong. Or some man raising sand because one or the other had stole his girl."

He shifted his position. "But it wasn't that way during those last few months. Things had changed, at least with Johnny. He was working hard, getting ready to make his move, and he didn't have time to mess with no women. Leastways, not that I could see. No, he was working in the studio and with that other business, both."

"So there was nobody?"

A small cloud passed over Gates's features. "No one I could name."

Eddie didn't miss the fact that the response wasn't the same as "no."

"Like I said, he was wrapped up in the work," the reverend went on with an odd timbre in his voice. This pious fellow was a poor liar.

"Did you tell all of this to the police?"

Gates said, "I did, yes. But they didn't care much. The one Negro detective came around the day after he disappeared and asked if any of us knew anything. He said if Johnny didn't turn up, he'd be back to talk to us some more. He didn't, though, and that was the end of it."

Gates was now leaning away from him, gazing pointedly at the far wall, and looking ill at ease.

"I wish I could help you more," he said. "I remember so much. It all happened so fast. Johnny was there one day and gone the next. Sometimes God works that way. Now it's just memories."

The Reverend Thomas Gates unfolded from his chair, and Eddie did the same. The preacher walked him to the door and raised a hand in farewell as his visitor stepped onto the sunny afternoon street. Eddie hadn't spent all that much time in churches, but he had never been to one where they hadn't invited or even begged him to come back. Reverend Gates did neither.

He wandered around the apartment for a while. The little station at Penn was coming through, and he tuned in to a jazz show. With what he'd heard from Tommy Gates still buzzing in his head, he went to the closet to fish out the police report, found the schedule he had copied at Eugene White's office, and carried the documents to the porch. He sat down on the top step and stared at the papers, seeing lines and words in small type and blank spaces. None of it made sense, a puzzle with pieces that wouldn't fit—that, or a map to nowhere.

He took a moment to glance at the garbage can that was waiting at the curb.

It was too late to get out of it now. He laid the pages from the folder on his lap and started to read.

There wasn't much to it: ten sheets, half of them forms with boxes filled in, some precisely, some with a sloppy, hurried hand. One of the cops—the name was Detective Nash—had put some work into it, while the other—Detective Hayner—hadn't.

The report was summarized on the last page. The subject, John Robert Pope, had been reported missing on Tuesday, February 10, 1959. He was last seen on Sunday, February 8, at approximately 6:30 P.M. at 45 Studios on Morris Street. No witnesses had come forward as having seen him after that time. There were no records of airline, train, or bus tickets in his name. No one had known of any travel plans.

Detective Nash had questioned Valerie Pope, Raymond Pope, and Thomas Gates, as well as the subject's mother, Ann Kate Pope. Hayner questioned Earl Pettis and Robert Kosik, both of whom had worked at 45 Studios. He had also spoken to Eugene White, the subject's manager and agent, and George Roddy, president of StarLite Records and the owner of the studio.

No one offered anything helpful. Johnny Pope had walked out of the building and disappeared, utterly and completely, never to be seen or heard from again. The final entry on the report was "suspicion, but no direct evidence of foul play." That was it.

Eddie put the papers aside and watched the traffic, thinking about the report. He'd missed something, and after a few minutes, it dawned on him that there was no mention of any tape. He picked up the pages and took another look: nothing.

He next perused the group's schedule, following them through the summer and fall and to their Philadelphia engagements the week of Thanksgiving. Eddie hoped they were good shows, because Johnny never set foot on a stage again.

That was it. He carried the papers back into the apartment and tossed them into one of his dresser drawers, then went to the closet, to dig out his sweats and sneakers.

Just as he stepped outdoors, the old woman he had seen on his first visit hobbled up the steps. He nodded and smiled, waiting for her to pass. She stopped and leaned on her cane, examining him up and down, her bird eyes blinking behind those thick lenses.

"You the new boy?" she croaked.

"Yes, ma'am. My name's Eddie."

She glared at him. "You look like a wop."

Eddie let out a laugh of surprise.

"What's so goddamn funny?" Her dentures flapped.

"Nothing, I'm jus—"

"You in the Mafia, Pasquale?"

"The what?"

"You heard me!"

She poked her cane, turning on a turret as Eddie ducked around her.

"Get outta my sight, ya goddamn dago sonofabitch!" This was the little old lady who needed a prizefighter's protection.

Eddie hit the sidewalk running. He was still laughing when he crossed Seventeenth Street.

Though it had been a good while since he'd left the gym, he was pleased to discover that he could maintain a steady pace, and after a few blocks Valerie, Ray, Tommy Gates, T-Bone Mieux, and the invisible George Roddy fell away, one by one, as if unable to keep up.

He was surprised by how good it felt, and by the time he turned onto Spruce Street heading toward Center City, all he could think about was the next step, the next street, the next block. He felt the soak of sweat on his scalp and down his back, the burn in his lungs, the hard thump of his heart, the ache in his legs. It was all right.

His mind drifted into a familiar place, and he was crossing Sixth Street when he realized he was snapping jabs and hooks into the air, and quickly pulled his hands back where they belonged. His brain shut down completely as his legs took over. More sidewalk rolled by, and he was on Carlisle Street and hearing someone calling his name.

He looked around to see his ex-trainer Benny coming through the traffic, holding a cue stick in his hand. Eddie stopped, reclaiming his breath and heartbeat.

The trainer was wearing a broad grin. "Hey, hey, what's this?" he said. "I'm standing over there in the pool hall, lookin' out the window, and what do I see, Fast Eddie Cero doin' roadwork on a Sunday afternoon. I said, what's this, eh?" He looked Eddie up and down. "So, hey, hey, kid, what's the news?"

Eddie leaned against the facade of the building. His breath slowed to long draws as the air cooled his brow.

Benny leaned in, peering critically. "That eye, it healed up good, eh?"

Eddie gave him a hard glance. "No thanks to you."

The trainer drew back. "Hey, c'mon, what's with that shit? I did you a fuckin' favor."

"Well, thanks for nothing." Eddie tried to sound pissed, but his heart wasn't in it.

Benny said, "So, what, you going to hold a grudge forever?"

Eddie raised his hands and then dropped them. "Naw . . . never mind." He looked off down the street. As much as he really wanted to get mad and let the little man have it, it wouldn't come.

"I heard you're doin' okay," Benny was saying. "I heard you're what, working for some private dick now?"

"Yeah, that's right," Eddie said. It seemed the word had finally gotten around. He took a step away, then stopped. "Hey, I want to ask you something. What do you know about T-Bone Mieux?"

"Mieux?" Benny blinked. "I don't know, same as you, I guess. He's a cheap-shot artist. If he could crack as good as he talks, he'd be fighting in the Garden." He pointed to Eddie's brow. "Is this about—"

"You know anything else about him?"

Now Benny came up with an odd look. "Why?"

"C'mon, Benny."

"Well, you know he comes from someplace down around New Orleans. Now I believe he stays up on Addison somewhere. He's a fucking dumbass loudmouth, and he—"

"Yeah, yeah, what else?"

Benny glanced around, all furtive. "I can only tell you what I heard," he said quietly.

"Go ahead."

"I don't know if it's true."

"G'head, what?"

Benny dropped his voice. "What I heard was he's one of them available to anyone wants a beating put on another party. He'll break your face or your arm or your leg for the right price. That's just what I heard." He frowned with disgust. "I'll tell you what I know. He's a disgrace to the sport of boxing, is what." He looked grim for a moment, then brightened. "Hey, who cares, huh? You don't have to deal with that lousy fuck no more. Am I right?"

"Yeah, right," Eddie said. "So how are things at the gym?"

Benny made a rude gesture. "Same old shit. A couple decent prospects and a lot of bums."

Eddie wondered idly which category he'd fall into.

"Hey, hey, you oughta come in sometime, get a workout." The trainer was smiling again, like they were old pals.

Eddie said, "See you, Benny," and jogged away.

"Keep it up, kid!" Benny called after him. "You look good. You could be back in there in no time!"

EIGHTEEN

The windowpanes shimmered and gleamed in the morning sun. Eddie rolled over and turned on his radio in time to hear the announcer say it would be clear with temperatures in the sixties by midafternoon. Outside the window, a sugar maple was showing tiny green buds at the end of dark branches. It was the last day of April. Winter was gone.

He felt the soreness in his legs from his run, and for a moment he idly wished for his life as a fighter. It was simple: work and fight, win or lose; and, he had to admit, not a bad life.

Good or bad, it didn't matter one way or the other, because it wasn't his life anymore. Seeing Benny had been like meeting a guy he had known a long time ago. He was thinking about that, and the trainer's whispers about T-Bone Mieux, when he heard a knock on the door—his first. He pulled on his sweatpants and went out to find a man standing there in work clothes holding a black telephone in his hand. He got the guy started, then headed for the bathroom.

When he stepped into the office, he found Sal hovering behind his desk, wearing a strange expression, and he stopped cold. He had seen that look before and the first thought that came to his mind was *Somebody's dead.*

"Ray Pope," Sal said. He was holding a morning newspaper. "Isn't he that guy you went to talk to?"

"What about him?" Eddie said.

"Did you?"

"Yeah, I did, for a minute. What's go—"

"He's dead."

"What?"

Sal waved his *Inquirer* in the air. "They found his body in an alley down there near where Grays Ferry comes into South Street."

"Jesus Christ!" Eddie felt as if his legs had been clipped. His eyes lost focus, and he had to put a hand on the edge of the desk to steady himself. "When?"

"Sometime Saturday night. They didn't find him till noon yesterday."

"How did he die?"

Sal poked a finger into his sternum. "Two in the chest." He came up with a grim smile. "Rules out suicide." He handed Eddie the newspaper, folded to the Metro page. Eddie stared dully at the bold type: FORMER SINGER APPARENT VICTIM OF HOMICIDE.

As Sal reached for his coffee cup, the phone rang. He answered it, then handed the receiver to Eddie without a word.

"He's dead!" Valerie shrieked at him. "Oh, my god!" She choked back a sob, and her voice broke. "What did you do? He's *dead*! I told you to leave it alone! Look what you've done!"

"I didn't do anything." Eddie felt the words catch in his throat. "I just went—"

"Well, why do you think this happened?" Now she sounded caustic, almost hateful. A heartbeat passed, and she abruptly sobbed again. "Poor Ray! He never hurt anyone." Her voice shot back up to a thin wail. "I told you! Goddamnit! I told you to *stop*! Why wouldn't you listen to me?" The phone clattered and went dead.

He placed the receiver in the cradle as if he was afraid it would break. Sal averted his gaze, though he'd surely overheard.

Eddie carried the newspaper to the window and read the article through. At first his hands shook, rattling the pages, and he had to force them still. The piece was short, and he soon finished it, then folded the paper away.

Staring down at the street, he pictured Ray coming out of his chair like a dog on a chain, then Leona popping him hard and his face going from blustering rage to cowering shame in a matter of seconds. He was a sullen, beaten man and yet got up the energy to slip through the crowd and mutter a hint of a secret. And a few hours after he did that, someone pumped two bullets into his heart.

"Y'know, it could be a coincidence," Sal said.

Eddie gazed blankly at the traffic. "I thought you didn't believe in that."

"Usually I don't. Maybe he just started something with the wrong guy. You know how those people are."

Eddie looked at him, and Sal flushed a little. "What I'm saying is the guy gets drunk and starts something. Next thing you know, he's dead in an alley." He didn't sound all that convinced, either.

"It happened the night I talked to him," Eddie said.

"Well, I told you to stay the hell away from there."

"Yeah, you did," he said. "And you were right." Neither one of them mentioned Valerie's warnings.

Sal sighed. "C'mon, sit," he said. Eddie turned away from the window. When he got settled, the detective said, "Okay, tell me what happened from when you walked in until you left."

Eddie went through it in detail, working his way to the final encounter. "I'm heading for the door, and he comes up and grabs hold of my arm and says, 'You want to know the truth? Ask Valerie. Ask her.'"

Sal looked pensive as Eddie told him about catching a

glimpse of Mieux in the store window afterward. Then he went through Sunday and his talks with Valerie and Gates the preacher and finally seeing Benny while he was running. He left out the parts with Susie and the crazy old woman in his building.

Sal cocked an eyebrow. "You were running? As in roadwork?"

"As in running."

"You going back to the fight game?"

"Maybe I should."

"Yeah, maybe," the detective said as he fiddled with a pencil. "Okay, so what do you got to this point? Put it in a nutshell."

"Now?"

"Yeah, I want to hear."

Eddie knew that a lot of people wouldn't be able to concentrate, but he had experience. You let your mind wander in the ring and you end up on your ass. He also understood that Sal was trying to take his mind off the murder. So he went ahead and laid it out for him.

"Johnny Pope was leaving StarLite to start his own record label. Maybe he was going to keep the Excels going, maybe not. He was done with Ray for sure. The people in the group knew this and his agent did, too. As far as I know, the guy at the record company, George Roddy, was in the dark about it."

"Okay," Sal said. "That's the setup. What happened to the singer?"

"Everyone says he must have crossed somebody over a woman, or over money, or it was a stickup that went bad. But then I find out someone paid to have him murdered. Except it didn't happen."

"Because he disappeared before."

"That's right." Eddie made a vague gesture. "That's what I have so far."

"Tell me about the players in this little show."

Eddie shifted in his chair. "Well, there's Valerie. She wanted me off it right from the start. Eugene White wasn't much help. Tommy Gates talked some, but I could still tell he was holding back, too. This character George Roddy is nowhere to be found. When I tried to talk to Ray, he went crazy. Then he said that Valerie knows the truth, whatever that meant. And that's it."

"Valerie," Sal murmured.

Eddie shifted again. "What about her?"

"Well, Ray mentions her name, says she knows something, and the next thing he's dead."

It took Eddie a second to get it. He opened his mouth and then closed it. Sal looked thoughtful for a moment, then got up and went down the hall to the men's room, leaving him alone with his thoughts. Eddie picked up the paper and stared at the headline, feeling his stomach sink again as the reality of what had happened took hold. He had been playing detective and a man was dead. Maybe because of him. Definitely because of him, according to Valerie.

The door creaked and Sal reappeared. "Hey," he said softly. Eddie looked up. "There's nothing you can do right now. And we've got other business. We're going to go check out our schoolgirl, remember? We'll leave in a half hour." He caught the look on Eddie's face and said, "Go out and get coffees, okay?"

Eddie stared out the window as the streets of West Philadelphia passed by. Sal asked him for a report on his last visit to Havertown as they drove along. Eddie pulled out his notebook, glad for another excuse to busy his mind.

After he related what he had witnessed, Sal said, "You caught this after what, a week? Those cops out there should have nailed it. There's something wrong."

"Like what?"

"Like I don't know. That's what I want to find out."

They didn't talk anymore as they wound their way out of the

city and west through the Lansdownes. Finally, Sal looked over at him and said, "You think it's your fault what happened to that guy?"

"I think so, yeah."

"Well, it's not," Sal said. "Not unless you pulled the trigger or paid someone else to do it. These things happen. People die. Especially down in that part of town. It's a fucking jungle."

"People saw me talking to him."

"Yeah, so? What's the connection?"

"I don't have one." Eddie sighed glumly. "I don't have anything."

"That's the way it looks right now," Sal said. "But sometimes the pieces all of a sudden make sense. Tomorrow or the next day or next week, boom, it'll come to you." He paused for a moment. "On the other hand . . ."

"On the other hand, what?"

"It might end up all pieces. That happens, too."

"Thanks, Sal. I feel better now."

Sal smiled. Eddie brooded for another half minute. "She said, 'Why do you think this happened?' "

"What's that?"

"Valerie," he said. "I was trying to tell her that it wasn't my fault, and she said, 'Well, why do you think this happened?' " He looked at Sal. "She knows something."

Sal nodded judiciously. "Sounds that way."

"But she's not going to talk."

"You want me to make a run at her?" Sal said.

Eddie shook his head. "No. Not yet."

They rode in silence for another half block. "Don't miss the funeral," he said.

"What?"

"The guy's funeral. You gotta go."

Eddie was aghast. "I'm not going to his funeral."

"Oh, yes, you are," Sal said. "You got to. You're up to your ass in this thing. You can't jump ship now. It's against company policy. So you go." He gave Eddie a sidelong glance. "And don't forget to wear a tie."

While they waited for Marianne, Sal regaled him with some tales from his rookie cop days. Eddie half listened, feeling foolish chasing after a schoolgirl hussy even as Ray Pope was laid out on a cooling board in the city morgue.

When the bell rang at last, he directed Sal's attention to the double doors on the end of the building. As if cued, Marianne appeared, once again running for the Chevy. Sal had brought his field glasses, and he trained them on her as she zigzagged through the lot.

"That's not her car," Eddie said in a hushed voice. "She borrows from her friends."

"Why are you whispering?" Sal said. "She's a mile away."

"Oh, yeah," Eddie said. "Anyway it's part of her cover."

"Smart. I wonder why nobody at the school notices."

"She's a senior," Eddie said. "It's almost graduation. She can pretty much do what she wants. Or maybe she's entertaining the principal, too."

Sal didn't laugh. "I hope you're wrong," he said. "I hope you're wrong about all of it." He laid the glasses on the seat, put the car in gear, and pulled out.

They trailed Marianne to North Drexel. Eddie pointed the way around the block and down the crossing alley behind the house. Sal caught her pulling to a quick stop and hurrying to the back door.

"I'll be damned," he said. "The little wench."

"You get a look at the guy?"

"No, he's in the shadows there."

"She could be meeting some kid from school."

"Somehow I don't think so," Sal said softly. "Go have a look at those vehicles. I'll meet you around front."

Eddie crept to the garage as Sal drove off. This time the Mercury was joined by a Lincoln Continental. He jotted down the plate number and strolled back out to the street, where he and Sal sat in silence for most of the next twenty-five minutes. Then a door banged closed, and within a few seconds the Chevy tore off down the street.

They reached the school in time to see her running for the doors, her pretty hair flying behind her.

Eddie said, "Now what?" Sal was staring out the windshield. "Sal?"

"Yeah, yeah." The detective was frowning blankly. "Now we go to the courthouse and find the records room. Find out who lives in that house. See who's the upstanding citizen banging this schoolgirl."

It was another quiet drive down Route 1. When they arrived in Media and located the Delaware County Courthouse, Sal led him down a set of stairs to the basement and along a hallway lined with doors each marked with a little shingle: BUSINESS LICENSES, BIRTH AND DEATH CERTIFICATES, PROPERTY, and so on.

"Is there anything they don't got a record of?" Eddie asked him.

"Not much," Sal said. "And it's all open to the public. If it wasn't for these places, there wouldn't be a PI in business."

Sal found the plat book with the North Drexel address. The owner was identified as Richard G. Barnes.

They emerged from the basement and into the spring afternoon. Sal looked around and spotted a tavern on the next corner. Inside, they sat at the bar. Sal started on a scotch while Eddie drank a 7UP. The detective was quiet, brooding.

"What are you going to do?" Eddie said.

"I guess I could talk to the girl," Sal said. "You know, try to get her straightened out. But after that number she pulled with you, I think I'd be wasting my time. I could have a chat with this

Barnes character. Y'know, lean on him. Tell them it's over as of right now, or his goddamn name and deeds are going to be front-page news. And if he tried to tough it out, I'd break his fucking head."

He sipped his drink. "You know, there's more to this. McKay's no dummy. I'd lay money that he knows. Shit, there could be a half dozen of these cupcakes running in and out of school, screwing grown men all over town." His gaze fixed on something in the distance. "Sometimes I hate this business. These people and the shit they do. It makes me want to jump in the river." He drained his glass, rattled the ice cubes, and looked over at the bar.

Eddie said, "Whaddya say, Sal, let's go back to Philly."

Sal nodded absently. "Yeah, let's go home," he said.

When they arrived at the office, Eddie realized that he had only delayed the inevitable. Sal headed for his desk, pulled out his bottle and a glass, and prepared to drink and ponder the sordid case of Marianne Gibson, along with a selection of the world's other tribulations. Eddie begged off the invitation to join him, explaining that he wanted to go over his notes some more.

"That's good," Sal said. "You do that. You know where to find me if you need any help."

Eddie sat at the desk in the front for a long time, replaying Saturday night and mulling what could have brought poor Ray to his last grim moment in a cold and dark alley. That went nowhere, and so he snatched up the phone and put in yet another call to StarLite, then sat fuming as the receptionist went through the script. *No, Mr. Roddy wasn't in the office. No, she didn't know if or when he would be back. Yes, she would give him the message.* He dropped the phone in the cradle.

They had picked up the afternoon *Bulletin* on the way in, and on page three of the Metro section, he found a small item about Ray's murder and read that the police had no suspects in the crime. The piece had a tired, already-forgotten tone to it.

There was a rustle of movement from Sal's office, and he heard the detective murmuring into the telephone. After a few seconds, the murmur shifted to a growl.

Eddie read on. The victim, it noted, had once been part of the popular vocal group the Excels.

"Raymond Pope is the second of the group's members to meet an untimely death. Johnny Pope, the group's lead singer, disappeared over three years ago and is presumed dead." At the end of the story, it announced a memorial service for Raymond Pope "on Tuesday at 1:30 p.m. at the Holy Spirit Tabernacle, 1012 26th St. Friends of the Deceased are welcome."

He wandered in to find the detective gazing out the window. The afternoon had turned cloudy, the sky was a somber gray over the rooftops.

"How's things?" Sal said.

"Okay, I guess." Eddie sat down. "How's things with you?"

"Mezza mezz'."

Eddie waited. Sal wasn't one to suffer in silence. It usually took less than a minute for him to start spilling his guts. But he was quiet for so long that Eddie finally said, "What's the matter, Sal?"

"I just got off the phone with McKay out there in wonderland. I laid out what we had on the girl. I told him about Barnes. I passed on those tag numbers. And the little fuck said he'd look into it. He'll *look into it.*" He shook his head grimly. "I ain't been doing this twenty-five years for nothing. I can smell a bullshit story a mile away. He's on to it. And he's sweeping it under the fucking carpet."

"So what?" Eddie said. "We did our part, right?"

"He was a good cop," Sal said. "A solid guy. Now he's looking the other way while at least one schoolgirl is getting banged by a man who's probably old enough to be her father."

Eddie waited a few seconds, then said, "So what are you going to do?"

"I don't know."

Another silence followed, this one a half minute. "What do you want me to do?" Eddie said.

"You spend your time on the singer."

Though Eddie's first thought was to jump up and run for the door before Sal could change his mind, he had to ask, "Why now?"

"Because there's definitely something going on. Because you started it, and you got to see it through to the end. Because a man's dead. And," he finished, "because you got somebody tailing you."

Eddie came out of his chair. "What?"

Sal tilted his head toward the window. "He followed us to Havertown and Media and back. When we turned down the alley, he pulled in across the street. Sat watching us walk into the building. He's still there." Eddie stepped to the window to have a look. "Don't do that!" Sal snapped. "Haven't you learned anything from me? Go out and take the fire escape. Cut up the alley and cross over at the corner. Maybe you can grab him."

"How do you know he's not tailing you?"

"I'm assuming. Go find out."

"What kind of car?"

"It's a '60 Pontiac. Two tone, yellow and white." Sal turned around and reached for his bottle.

It took Eddie three minutes to get down the fire escape, trot up the alley in back of the building, and cover the half block to Sansom Street. The shoe store on the corner was faced with windows on the front and side, and he could see that the car was still there, in a space down a few doors and across the street from the office, the driver silhouetted in the rear window.

He waited until a truck rumbled by to cross the street and start up the sidewalk at a fast clip, thinking he was finally going to get his hands on somebody. In his excitement, he forgot about the mirrors, and when he was still fifty feet away, the Pontiac suddenly peeled rubber and shot into traffic. He raised his hands in frustration as he watched the car disappear around the corner at Twenty-first Street. He looked up to the office window to see Sal holding his glass and shaking his head.

Eddie walked in to find only two customers in the Domino. Leona glanced up from wiping down the bar and then stared at him, her face all tragic. She wasn't wearing much makeup, and grief had drawn stark lines on her dark skin.

"You want something to drink?" she said.

He shook his head. "What happened?"

She leaned on the bar, looking weary. "He got in a fight with Theresa. That woman he was with. He was out of his mind. I had to shut him up again. He still wouldn't behave, so I tossed him outdoors. That was about one o'clock. He went off down the street and . . ." She put a despairing hand to her forehead. "Lord have mercy! Someone shot him dead."

Eddie gave her a moment to recover, then said, "No one knows anything?"

She shook her head slowly. "No. The cops came in and questioned me. I don't believe they had anything at all."

"Did you tell them I was here?"

"They didn't ask. Maybe someone else said something. I don't think they cared. One nigger more or less ain't nothin' to them."

"Is there any talk about what happened?"

"There's lots of talk. Nobody knows nothin', though." She regarded him evenly. "Unless you do."

"I wish I did," Eddie said.

Leona studied his face for a moment longer, then went back to wiping the bar. "You know, it wouldn't be no surprise to me if Ray's number just come up," she said. "You saw how he was. I can see him leaving out of here and going down the street and getting into a fight with somebody who wouldn't take his shit."

"This was the same night I talked to him."

They were both quiet, thinking their own thoughts. Eddie's wound to a certain Creole. "Was Mieux in here Saturday night?"

Leona said, "I didn't see him but probably so. He's pretty much a regular. Just like Ray." She stopped. "Like Ray was, I mean. Why you asking about him?"

"It's nothing," he said. "I changed my mind. I'll have the drink."

She started pouring. "You goin' to the service?"

"Guess so."

"Come around after. We're going to have a little wake here." She placed the glass in front of him. "I think Ray'd appreciate it." One of her other customers called her name, and she moved away.

The drink helped. Elmore James on the jukebox helped some more. He settled on the stool and ran through it one more time. He had tried to talk to Ray Pope, and now Ray was dead. Though he had talked to other people—Valerie, Fat Cat, Eugene White, Jimmy T, and Tommy Gates—and they were all in good health. So far.

So why Ray? Because he knew something none of the others did? Or because he couldn't be trusted to keep his mouth shut? Or was it the way Leona saw it, that the visit from the Italian guy got him so upset that he went raging onto the street and into the path of some other angry person?

Eddie didn't think so.

He finished the drink and asked for a refill, which he nursed through rush hour. Before he had finished it, Leona poured herself a shot of brandy and they drank a sad toast to Ray Pope's poor departed soul.

NINETEEN

Eddie got into the office at nine, just as Sal was heading out to get the lowdown on Richard Barnes, the hawk who was preying on their chick. Sal told him his work in Havertown was finished, and so he needed to take the DeSoto back and start driving the Ford again. With that happy news to start his morning, Eddie tried to do some paperwork and found he couldn't keep his mind on it. He opened his notebook a half-dozen times, stared at the pages, then closed it. By eleven o'clock, it felt as if the walls were closing in, so he locked up, drove to Dom's lot, and left with the Ford trailing the familiar cloud of blue smoke.

Cruising back north, he rolled down the window, turned on the radio and pushed the volume until the speaker under the dash rattled. He took a meandering route, driving down one cross street, up the next, all to the noisy beat of the city.

As he crossed Broad Street and rounded Penn Square, he glanced at the sober facade of City Hall. Franklin Parkway led to a loop at Logan Circle, and he realized that if he kept driving, he'd be in Allentown in less than an hour. And then what? A visit to the old homestead? A reunion with his mother? He pictured her peering out of her drunken fog.

Eddie? Issat you?

It's me, Ma. Guess what? I got a guy killed. You proud of me or what?

He pulled to the curb on Fifteenth Street and stared at the heavy brass-plated doors of City Hall for a long minute before getting out. Inside, he asked the guard at the stand where they kept the public records.

An hour later he turned onto Twenty-sixth Street and parked around the corner from the church. The hand-lettered sign next to the door announced the memorial service for Raymond Pope. Tacked just above it was a framed photo of the deceased in better days.

Two elderly black men in identical dark suits were posted as ushers. Both nodded in solemn greeting, and one of them handed him a folded program, a bad mimeograph splotched with blue. Poor Ray didn't even get a decent piece of paper for his final testament.

Eddie slipped into the last row on the right side, moved to the middle, and sat down. Organ music, reedy and off-key, swelled and faded as a silver-haired woman bent over a keyboard that had been placed in the corner beyond the choir riser.

At the moment only the front row of chairs was occupied. He ducked his head when he recognized Valerie with her mother and another older woman, the three of them dressed in somber black. He slouched a little more, hoping to God that Valerie wouldn't turn around, see him, and start screaming as she chased him out the door. But the women were too engrossed in their sad whispers to notice him or anyone else. The open coffin was arrayed on the floor before the altar. Eddie could barely discern Ray's profile.

It was quiet, save for the plaintive organ and the murmurings of the mourners as they trickled in, and Eddie felt another sad spike of pity for Ray. The guy had been on top of the world with the Excels, until in a sudden moment, it all came tumbling down, and he spent what was left of his life wallowing in drink and dope and the heartbreak of watching a dream die.

Ray had been a harmless, pain-in-the-ass, loudmouthed drunk until Eddie came around asking questions. Then his loud mouth became a problem for someone, who decided to shut it for good.

What had started out as curiosity ended in bloody murder, and it made Eddie feel sick and ashamed. He wondered darkly how long Sal had been on the job before he had caused a death. Thinking about it that way made him want to jump up and run away, so he fixed his thoughts on the congregation, as Sal had instructed.

The detective had spent a minute before he left for Havertown dispensing advice on casing the service. He swore he had broken cases by what he had picked up at funerals.

"Get there early," he said. "Sit in the back. Take a good look at everybody who walks in the door."

"What am I looking for?" Eddie asked him.

"Anything that strikes you as off. Somebody who might be a little too interested, or someone who doesn't belong there, like that. See if you can figure out who's grieving and who's not."

Eddie understood; still, Sal felt it important to tell him not to expect someone hanging around looking sneaky, with a hat pulled down over his eyes, or collapsing on Ray's corpse with wails of woe. The tip-offs would be smaller cues.

Peering through the assembled heads, Eddie saw Ray's woman Theresa sitting by herself, looking scared and miserable. No one approached or spoke to her. Leona had entered on the arm of a sturdily built black man and was greeted by a half-dozen people. There was no one else he recognized. He saw only two other white people in attendance. One was a tweedy guy around thirty who looked like a professor, the other a lanky man in his forties who appeared uncomfortable in his dark suit. They were sitting together about halfway to the front. The rest of the mourners appeared to be neighborhood folks, family, or friends of the family. No one came off as suspicious.

Joe D'Amato appeared and went immediately to Valerie. Eddie watched her rise to her feet and accept his embrace. There was no mistaking the affection, so natural that no one could take exception. They were friends. She resumed her seat, and Joe moved away.

He spotted Eddie and took the chair next to his. A wink and a handshake were followed by a reflective silence.

By two o'clock the tiny chapel was two-thirds full, maybe forty people in all. A few quiet minutes went by, and the door in the back corner opened. Reverend Gates stepped out and made a slow trek to the pulpit, stopping to gaze at the deceased. To Eddie's eye, the reverend appeared to have aged a few years.

He stepped up to the pulpit and raised his eyes to look over the congregation, slowly regarding each face in turn. His gaze lingered on Valerie. When he got to Eddie, he hesitated, then continued until he reached the last man in the farthest corner. He steadied himself and was just about to begin speaking when a rustle of movement at the door stopped him short.

Joe jabbed an elbow into Eddie's ribs and whispered something. Eddie glanced around to see a tall, thick white man standing in the doorway with a woman at his side. The man's flesh held a deep tan, and his hair, a shiny blue black, had not been shaped and oiled by any South Philly barber. Except for a sharp spike of a nose, his face was round and flat. His suit was dark gray, double-breasted, and perfectly cut. The features of the woman at his side were obscured by the veil draping from the large hat; still Eddie could tell that her hair was a platinum blond that came from a bottle. Her black dress showed off a curvy figure.

Eddie watched as the man, satisfied that everyone had marked their entrance, made a small gesture in the direction of the last row of chairs on the left side. The woman sidled in, and he followed in a silent glide. Once they were settled, he crossed his arms and looked up at Reverend Gates, raising his chin imperiously. Eddie knew without asking that the late arrival was George Roddy.

The preacher cleared his throat, took another moment's respite, and started again.

"Raymond, my brother," he intoned, his voice low with melancholy. "Were we ever so young? Were we ever so innocent?" He let the question hang in the air, and a few people murmured in response. His gaze settled on the casket. "Oh, my dear friend," he preached sonorously. "You were once so full of joy! What devils visited their curses on you? What demons laid claim to your soul?" He spread his arms in helpless supplication. "If only I could have reached out my hand to you. If only I could have delivered you into God's saving grace before it was too late."

All over the chapel voices rose up. Eddie peered around the people in front of him to see Valerie, her head bent and shoulders heaving.

The reverend's eyes seemed to search the heavens. "But it is *not* too late for God!" The voice rumbled over the congregation. "You have come to the end of this journey and now lie in his loving embrace. You leave your broken body and broken heart behind. Your spirit has crossed the wide river to a kinder shore. You walk with the angels. Now, now, at last, you are at peace."

A tear glistened against the preacher's deep black cheek. "Good-bye, Raymond, my friend, my brother." The mellow voice broke with emotion. "May God rest your weary soul." More calls echoed off the walls as bodies swayed and gentle hands were raised in the air. The reverend stepped back and folded his hands. "Let us pray," he said.

Eddie looked over at the late couple. The woman had bowed her head, but the man's face was stony as he stared straight ahead. He did not join in the prayer.

Reverend Gates had departed the chapel, and the organ droned for the slow procession that filed past the casket. Valerie, her mother, and the other woman—Eddie guessed she was Ray's mother—sat quietly, accepting condolences. Congregants drifted outside, shaking mournful heads and talking in whispers. Eddie decided against joining the line viewing the body and continued to study the crowd, including several glimpses at the white couple across the aisle.

The last of the stragglers were filing to the door, and Eddie watched with interest as George Roddy and his companion stood up to take a somber walk down the aisle. They drew near the casket, and Valerie's head came up as if she had sensed something. She uncoiled, rising to her feet, her eyes black stones. Eddie knew that look and shifted his position to see what would happen next.

Roddy stopped when he caught the force of Valerie's frigid mask. For the first time, he lost his cool, the color draining from his face. His woman was a helpless bystander as the freeze dragged on. Joe D'Amato, witnessing the encounter from Eddie's flank, made a sound in his throat. Eddie looked at him, and he shook his head.

Recovering, Roddy grasped the woman's elbow in his palm, and without giving Ray's body as much as a glance, turned her around and steered her back down the aisle. It had all transpired within a few sudden seconds, and the tension was taut as a wire.

Though by the time the couple reached the door, Roddy was back in his game. His hawkish gaze took in the remaining mourners, including Eddie, as he ushered his companion through the doorway.

Eddie turned to see Valerie staring at their retreating backs. Then she shifted her gaze and saw him. He was ready for a dose of the same treatment and was relieved when she simply let her wounded eyes light on him for a still moment before moving away. He slipped out of the pew and made his exit.

Outside, the mourners grouped around in the hazy sunshine. Joe wandered off to greet some people he knew.

Eddie saw George Roddy standing next to a cream-colored Chrysler Imperial convertible that was sitting in a No Parking zone across the street. Roddy's arms were crossed, and he grimaced with impatience as he waited for the old man who had buttonholed him to finish. The blond lounged in the passenger seat, looking bored.

Eddie crossed the street and came to a stop in front of the Chrysler just as the old man was walking off. Roddy stared for a second, then jerked his head and said, "You want to move?" He grabbed the handle and opened the door.

"My name's Eddie Cero."

Roddy stopped, and Eddie sensed the eyes narrowing behind the shades.

"Yeah, so? Do I know you?"

"Yeah, you do," Eddie said. "From the messages I've been leaving at your office three or four times a day." Roddy shrugged a rude dismissal and put one foot in the car. "Okay, never mind that. We can talk right now."

"I don't think so. Now move."

Roddy slid into the leather seat and slammed the door. Eddie stayed where he was. Roddy cranked the engine, and when Eddie didn't budge, he opened the door, put a shoe on the street, and stretched to his full height, his arm draped over the window frame.

"I said move it." Eddie stayed put. "I mean it. Get the fuck out of my way." He sounded like a man who gave lots of orders.

"Couple questions," Eddie said. "It'll only take a minute."

Roddy stood there, half out of the car, as if he couldn't decide whether or not to get tough. Something about the way Eddie was watching him made up his mind, and he got back behind the wheel and slammed the door again. The engine revved to a roar, and the steamship of a car lurched backward, pitching one of the rear tires onto the curb at a crazy angle, then rocked down into the street and jerked away with a squeal of tires and a cloud of blue smoke. The woman in the passenger seat stole a look at Eddie as they drove off, her mouth a painted O.

Eddie turned to watch the Chrysler swing to the curb a little way down the street. He had just stepped back onto the curb when he heard a voice say, "Anyone who can piss off that asshole is okay by me."

Joe D'Amato, the professor, and his friend were standing in a circle watching him, as were a couple dozen of the other mourners.

Eddie said, "I think I caught him at a bad time."

Joe did the introductions. "Carl Beyer and Earl Pettis. Eddie Cero."

Eddie said, "Carl Beyer. I know that name."

"You read the *Inquirer?*" Joe said. "Carl's one of the music writers. And Earl is a recording engineer." He paused for a single beat. "For a while he was at 45 Studios."

Before Eddie could digest that bit of news, the reporter spoke up. "So how's your investigation going?"

Eddie was startled. "You know about it?"

"I heard someone was poking around, and I see you here. I figured it was you."

Eddie treated Joe to a sidelong glance, and Beyer said, "It wasn't Joe told me. News gets around." The reporter was about to form a question when one of the ushers came out the door and made a quiet request for everyone to please get in line for the procession.

Eddie and Joe started for their cars.

"So what was that business with Roddy all about?" Joe inquired.

"I wanted to ask him some questions about Johnny. But I don't think he was in the mood to talk."

"At least he didn't run you over," Joe said.

The line of cars crept to a small cemetery on Reed Street, twenty-odd blocks to the southeast. The graveside service was brief as Reverend Gates murmured prayers, a sad and quiet music.

George Roddy and his companion stood out from the somber congregation, the woman with her pale blond tresses and glamour-girl kisser, Roddy in his fine clothes wearing a haughty scowl. Eddie sensed drama in the way Roddy struck the pose of lording over the mourners while Valerie and Ray's people ignored him. At one point Roddy treated him to a hard-eyed stare before returning his sullen gaze to the casket.

Eddie felt a cold wind rising as they lowered Ray into his grave. He thought it was probably the loneliest thing he had ever seen, and he remembered that same bleak mood coming over him when they buried his dad. So that's all there is to it: a few prayers, you go down into the ground, and everyone walks away.

A woman began to sing "Amazing Grace" in a deep and vibrant voice, and most of the mourners joined in, for the warmth, if nothing else, or so Eddie imagined. George Roddy and Valerie Pope were too busy staring tight-lipped at each other across the open grave to join in on the hymn.

It was over. People began ambling off; as the crowd thinned, Eddie saw two old men in dusty coveralls, one white and one black, standing a hundred feet away, waiting patiently, death's footmen with their shovels at the ready.

Joe said he had to get back to the Blue Door, and Eddie watched him wind his way through the gravestones.

"Mr. Cero?" A hand touched his shoulder, and he turned around to encounter Reverend Gates's disconsolate face. "Thank you for coming to the service," he said.

Eddie waited; Gates had something on his mind. The preacher held out his hand and looked into his eyes.

"You're welcome at the chapel anytime," he said. "I mean that sincerely. I hope you'll come visit again soon."

"I'll do that," Eddie said.

The reverend released his grip and turned away. Eddie stared after him. He wasn't the only one. Valerie was watching as Gates moved through the crowd of mourners.

As Eddie joined the line heading for the front gate, he saw George Roddy leading the blond across the grass at a stalking pace, as if he couldn't get away fast enough.

Carl Beyer caught up with him on the street. Together they watched the cream-colored Chrysler screech away from the curb and hurl back toward Center City.

"So, you going to tell me how your investigation's going?" the reporter said.

Eddie took a closer look and noticed that Carl Beyer was pretty rough around the edges. His shirt was wrinkled, and there were grease spots on his tie. His glasses were so blotted with fingerprints, it was a wonder he could see through them. The smile he turned on Eddie was yellow with tobacco stains.

"What I want to know is how you heard about it," Eddie said.

"I hear things all the time. That's part of my job. So?"

"Slow," Eddie said. "It's going slow."

Beyer stopped to wait for Earl Pettis to catch up. Eddie felt it would be rude to keep going and stopped, too. He wanted to ask Pettis about the studio anyway.

"We should talk," the reporter was saying. "Maybe we can help each other out here."

Eddie said, "Oh, yeah?"

"Could be," Beyer said. "What are you doing right now?"

Eddie started unknotting his tie. "They're having a thing at the Domino Lounge. It's kind of a wake for Ray."

"A wake at the Domino?" The reporter smiled lazily. "Sounds like my kind of party."

From her post behind the bar, Leona gave Eddie a small smile and nodded a curious greeting to his two companions. It appeared that about half the people from the funeral had made it to the club, including Valerie, who sat in a corner booth with another young woman. The three white men received only a few stares from around the room. Hard feelings were on the shelf, quieted by grief. The jukebox was turned down low.

Beyer led the way to a table while Pettis went to the bar, returning with three bottles of F&S. Glass clinked and they settled back. The reporter reached into his jacket pocket for a pack of Pall Malls. He offered one to Eddie, who shook his head. He lit up, blew a jet of smoke, and said, "Don't blame you. We get all these reports now about how the doctors say they cause cancer. You know what I say? I say so fucking what. You read the paper? The end is near. We're all going to disappear in a mushroom cloud any day now."

They sipped their beers. Eddie glanced across the room and saw Valerie talking quietly with Leona, who had come out from behind the bar to stand next to the booth. He turned back to the reporter. "So you wrote about the Excels."

Beyer said, "Yeah, but I had to fight for it. To this day, my editor thinks rock and roll is all shit. He calls it 'greasy kids' stuff' and worse. Never mind that it's been around for ten, twelve years already. He swears it's the Commies trying to brainwash our innocent youth, and he keeps waiting for it to die, so he can go back to listening to Sinatra in peace. But now Jackie's doing the twist in the White House."

"What about Johnny Pope?" Eddie said.

"I interviewed him a half-dozen times," Beyer said. "He was as good as anyone who's ever come out of this city, and I wanted people to know about him." He frowned sourly and dragged on his cigarette. "But he disappeared, and I swear he took all the good music with him, because what we got now is a bunch of pretty boys, half of them can't carry a tune in a fucking bucket."

Eddie noted how he echoed Jimmy T on the subject. Tapping

an idle finger on the side of his bottle, he said, "What didn't you write about?"

The reporter came up with a sly smile. "You mean like his taste for Johnnie Walker, Mary Jane, and Miss Anne?"

Earl Pettis laughed quietly. Eddie said, "Miss Anne?"

Beyer's eyes flicked left and right, and he leaned closer. "If you're going to work this street, you better learn the lingo," he said in a low voice. "'Miss Anne' means a white girl. Yeah, the man had some vices, but he managed to keep them out of sight."

"That's all?"

"He had a reputation for acting wild. Making scenes when he didn't get his way, bullying people, picking fights, that kind of thing."

"*Especially* when he didn't get his way," Earl Pettis put in.

Eddie considered the information for a few seconds. "Do you think he was murdered?"

Beyer shrugged. "What else?"

Eddie glanced at Pettis, who said, "I think so, too."

"A random crime?" Eddie said.

The reporter nodded. "Well, sure, it could have been that. Someone puts a gun in his gut, demands his money, and Johnny says, 'Fuck you, I ain't givin' you a dime.' The other party says, 'Well, fuck you, too,' and bang, he's gone." Beyer puffed thoughtfully for a second. "But knowing Johnny, I think it was something personal, a jealous husband maybe. Some woman he banged and then brushed off. Someone from the old neighborhood he ignored, that kind of thing."

Eddie watched the reporter crush his cigarette in the ashtray and immediately light another one, and thought that this guy and Valerie would make a good team. He was gazing across the room at her when Earl Pettis said, "I'd vote for the jealous husband theory."

Eddie looked at him. "Oh yeah? Why's that?"

"Because there was something going on at the end there." Pettis spoke so softly that Eddie had to bend an ear to hear him. "Whenever he was in the studio, he'd spend a lot of time on the phone. I overheard a few times and I could tell it was a woman. He was sweet-talking her, but it also sounded serious, like they were cooking something up." He smiled ruefully. "Believe me, I know what I'm talking about."

Eddie cocked an eyebrow.

"My ex-wife slept around," Pettis explained. "A lot."

"Oh," Eddie said. "Sorry."

"Yeah, well . . ."

"You don't know who the woman was?"

"He never brought anyone around," Pettis said.

Eddie sat back. It wasn't much, but it wasn't nothing, either. Valerie had told him that she didn't know about any women. Tommy Gates had sworn that there were none. And yet both of them had been a lot closer to Johnny than Pettis, an employee of 45 Studios at the time. So how did they miss this mystery woman? The answer, of course, was that they hadn't missed her at all; they knew about her and had chosen to keep the information to themselves.

He took another sip of his beer. Carl Beyer, who had been fidgeting, hunched forward impatiently and said, "Okay, your turn."

Eddie made a dismissive gesture. "Everyone says the same thing you did. Either he crossed someone or it was a random crime."

Beyer looked momentarily annoyed. "C'mon, you can talk to me. I'm not going to put your name in the paper. You have my word."

"That's all I've got," Eddie told him. "Really."

Beyer shook his head slowly. "No, it's not."

Eddie considered for a few seconds. "Well, okay . . . the word is he was leaving the Excels. And he was leaving his record label to start his own."

"Yeah, I remember hearing talk about that," the reporter said. "He was really doing it?"

"He was working hard on it the last few weeks before he disappeared."

"You think one had something to do with the other?"

Eddie said, "You wouldn't think so. Except that his cousin, who was also a member of his group, just got murdered in an alleyway."

"And this was after you started your investigation."

Eddie picked up his beer bottle and took a sip. Beyer was watching him with narrowed eyes.

"So you think Ray's death is connected to Johnny's? After all this time?"

Eddie realized that he had gone too far and started backpedaling. "I don't see how that could be," he said quickly. "I mean, I don't know about Ray. I've been trying to find out what happened to Johnny." He saw the way Beyer was studying him, ready to pounce, and he backed up some more. "Look, everything I've heard has been talk. Three-year-old talk. Nobody knows anything. It's all just . . . talk," he finished weakly.

The reporter sensed the retreat and puffed on his cigarette, looking perturbed. To escape Beyer's probing eyes, Eddie turned to the third man at the table.

"Were you there the night Johnny disappeared?" Pettis nodded. "Do you remember what had been going on that day?"

"It was business as usual," Pettis said. "Johnny would work on something until he was ready to lay down his piano and vocal. It was just a scratch track, and he probably could have done it himself. Everybody knew how to start the deck. But he wanted somebody around. He always wanted an audience, even if it was just us. Anyway, there wasn't nothing much to do, so around four thirty I let Bobby go."

"Who's Bobby?"

"Bobby Kosik. The kid who helped out on the board. Johnny just kept working on that one particular tune. Real pretty ballad. It got late and he told me to go home. So I left."

"What time was that?"

"Around six thirty." Pettis's mouth made a tight line in his thin face. "I was one of the last people to see him alive, except for Ray and Tommy and whoever, y'know . . ."

"Did it," Beyer finished for him.

"Wait a minute," Eddie said, staring at the engineer. "Ray and Tommy were there?"

"Yeah."

"I thought he was working alone."

"Well, he was," Pettis said. "But they were in the building. Hanging around up front, I think. I guess just waiting in case he needed them for any of the other vocal parts."

"What about the tape?" he asked. "He was recording, right?"

"There was one on the machine," Pettis told him. "I put it there."

And that answers that, Eddie reflected.

"I don't know what happened to it," Pettis went on. "I guess Johnny took it with him."

Eddie spent a few moments going over the information. "You said Ray and Tommy were there," he said. "What about—"

"Gentlemen."

Eddie saw Beyer and Pettis look up and smile, and he glanced over his shoulder to find Valerie was standing just behind and to the right of his chair, so close that he could smell her perfume.

"Earl, it's been a long time," she said. Pettis mumbled shyly.

"Mr. Cero," she said evenly. He bobbed his head and kept his mouth shut. At least she wasn't yelling at him.

The reporter spoke up. "Valerie, you don't know me. My name's Carl Beyer."

"I do know you," she said. "You're from the paper. You interviewed Johnny."

"That's right." He gave her a thoughtful look. "Would you be willing to sit down with me sometime?"

"Do what?"

"Sit down for an interview. About your career. I mean, what you're doing now."

"Oh, well . . ." She looked abashed. "It's really not much of a career. Not anymore."

"You should do it," Eddie said quietly.

She glanced down at him, then returned her attention to the reporter. "I'll think about it," she said.

"You can call me at the *Inquirer*," Beyer said. "Which is where I'm supposed to be working." He drained his bottle, stubbed out his cigarette, and got to his feet.

Pettis said, "I'm going, too." Eddie stood to shake hands with them.

"We'll talk again," the reporter said.

Eddie got the jab. Beyer and Pettis said their good-byes to Valerie and ambled out into the afternoon sun.

They left a yawning silence in their wake. Valerie was watching the door with a faraway expression, and Eddie wondered if she was waiting for him to leave, too. He was about to create an excuse so he could make his exit when she said, "You know, it seems that lately I've spent a lot of time getting mad at you and then feeling bad about it."

Eddie waited.

"I know what happened to Ray wasn't your fault," she continued. "He was always doing crazy things. He couldn't stop." She stood there, looking crestfallen, as the silence resumed.

"Would you like to sit down?" Eddie said.

She regarded him with her lips pursed, as if he had posed a

troubling question. Then she said, "All right," and pulled out the opposite chair.

"Do you want a drink?"

"No, thanks."

She went digging into the pocket of her sweater for her cigarettes and a lighter, as he cast about for something to talk about. He saw Leona making the rounds of the tables and tilted his head in her direction. "Are you and Leona friends?" he asked.

"Yeah. Johnny used to come around here." Her gaze moved about the room. "It was a nice place then. Players from the Phillies and the Eagles were here a lot, and musicians would come by late. It went on all night long. I used to get so sleepy." She looked at him and her small smile faded. "You don't really want to hear about all that, do you?"

"Sure, if you—"

"No, you don't." She folded her hands before her. "Tell me what's on your mind, Mr. Cero."

"You should call me Eddie," he said.

"All right. What's on your mind, Eddie?"

He took a second to brace himself before saying, "Ray said I should ask you if I wanted to know the truth."

He half expected her to get up and walk away. But she sat still, regarding him with the same slight frown.

"Maybe he thought I knew more than I did because Johnny was my brother," she said. "There's something you should understand. At the end there, Ray was on the outs. He was drinking and taking dope and acting crazy all the time. He wasn't doing his job, and Johnny wanted to get rid of him."

"I know about that."

She looked surprised. "You do?"

"Tommy Gates told me."

"When?"

"I talked to him Sunday afternoon. After I saw you."

She drew a random design on the table with a fingertip. "What else did he say?"

"That's all. I think he was shaken up."

"Not just him."

Eddie said, "Is there anything else you can tell me?"

"About what?"

"Well, when you called the office on Monday . . ."

She smiled slightly. "You mean when I screamed at you?"

"Yeah, that time. You said, 'Why do you think this happened?' Do you remember that?"

"Not really. I was very upset. I guess I had this idea that the person who murdered Johnny was still around. And whoever it was would think Ray was talking."

"Talking about what?"

"I don't *know.*" She was starting to sound irritated again. "I don't know what Ray was doing. Or what he was thinking. I didn't stay in touch with him." Her face fell. "He was mad at me. I guess he died mad at me."

"Mad at you why?"

"He blamed me for what happened," she said. "Somehow he got it in his head it was me and Johnny against him and Tommy. It wasn't true, but that's what he thought. And then after Johnny was gone, I wouldn't help him keep the Excels going. He never forgave me for that."

"You think he forgave Johnny?"

"No."

"And he had a temper."

"Yes, he did. But if you're thinking he was the one, I can tell you he wasn't."

"You're sure?"

"Ray was all mouth. And no matter what, Johnny was family. He would not hurt him. As mad as he was about being fired and all."

"What about you?"

She gave him a sharp look. "What about me what?"

"How did you feel about that? The end of the Excels, I mean."

"Oh." She relaxed. "I understood. Johnny had to move on. He couldn't go any further with the group. And it was around that time that I found out I was pregnant, so . . ." She lifted a hand and dropped it. "We weren't kids anymore. I didn't want to sing for a bunch of fourteen-year-olds. Just like Johnny didn't want to keep writing songs for them, no matter how much money it made him. It was bound to happen sooner or later."

"Who outside the group knew?"

"That it was over? Eugene White."

"George Roddy?"

She hesitated for a short second. "Probably not. He never paid attention, as long as we were earning money." He saw the cold gleam in her eye return. "I didn't want him at the funeral. He didn't care about Ray. The only reason he was there was to put on a show."

"He and Johnny didn't get along, right?"

"Johnny didn't trust him. He used to say he found all the money for StarLite and George lost it."

"With his gambling."

She stared at him. "You know about that, too?"

"I heard. I also heard he got in deep with the bookmakers."

She seemed about to say something, then caught herself and shrugged. "Well, none of that matters anymore, does it?"

"It does if it had something to do with Johnny's death."

She studied him carefully. "Johnny sold a lot of records for that man," she said, and looked away again.

Eddie tried a different angle. "That guy Earl thinks it was a jealous husband."

She fixed her eyes on the burning ember of her cigarette. "I guess that wouldn't be a surprise." Another pause, then: "You asked me if Johnny had any women around. I think there was one. I don't know who it was. But he was strutting around like he had something going on."

Eddie bit his tongue, thinking, *Now she tells me.* "Pettis said the same thing."

She gazed at him through the curling cigarette smoke. "Johnny didn't let anything or anybody get in his way. He just took what he wanted. Some people got their feelings hurt and other people got mad. But because he was this great artist, he always got away with it."

"Not the one time."

"I guess not."

The Dinah Washington song on the jukebox ended, and some familiar chords came tinkling over the speakers. It was an Excels' song called "Maybe Never," and they sat listening to the interplay between Johnny and Valerie as they wound through the smoky ballad. When it finally faded out, Valerie gave a slight shake of her head. Eddie saw that her eyes were wet. Thankfully, the next song was "A Hundred Pounds of Clay," and her mood lightened.

"You ever think that maybe he's not dead?" he said. "That he just took off for some reason? And right now he's sitting on a beach in, I don't know, Tahiti or someplace?"

"No, I don't." Her mouth tilted back to the sad smile. "Johnny could not live one day without having a million people telling him he was wonderful. He loved his music and he loved his career. No, he's gone. Him, and now Ray, too."

Her cigarette had burned down to the filter, so she tossed it and lit another one. Clearing her throat, she said, "Were you asking that reporter about Johnny?"

"Yeah."

"What did he say?"

"The same thing everyone says. He crossed someone and got himself murdered."

She looked quietly thoughtful for a few seconds. "Do you think you're ever going to find out what really happened?"

"Not if I keep running into brick walls."

"Like me?" He didn't say anything. "I've been pretty hard on you, huh?"

"It's all right," he said. "I understand."

"I wish I did," she said. It was an odd rejoinder, but he let it pass.

Leona had propped the door open, and the pale light of the spring afternoon illuminated Valerie's face as though it had come looking for her. It was a stunning image, and he felt a small throb in his gut.

Without thinking, he said, "Do you want to get out of here?"

She looked startled, then confused. "Do what? Get out of where?"

Eddie felt himself blushing. "Here," he said. "We could, y'know, go out. Just take a walk or something."

"You mean now? Walk to where? Why?"

He shrugged. It was too late to take it back. "I just thought you might want to," he said. "It's just . . . I'm . . ."

He was suddenly feeling like a world-class dope. Valerie's face came out of the light, and she was frowning at him, all perplexed, but after a few seconds her expression changed, and she tilted her head as if something had just dawned on her.

"Do you think we can talk about something besides Johnny Pope?" she said.

"Yeah," he said, relieved. "I'm tired of it, too."

They strolled along South Street with the golden orange sun of late afternoon at their backs. Traffic rumbled through the intersections, and horns blatted and tootled random jazz. The street smelled of acrid exhaust, rusty pipes, and food cooked in grease. Every fifth or sixth doorway gave up music from a radio or record player, so they walked in and out of little clouds of rock and roll, rhythm and blues, and gospel. Soon would come doo-wop, Italian crooners, then Irish tenors. A typical South Philly selection; it was the world's biggest jukebox.

At first they were careful to keep some distance as they sauntered along, lest some passerby get the notion they were together. Eddie had his hands in his pockets, and Valerie kept her arms crossed, like two kids forced out on a first date. She had exchanged her dress shoes for flats and was wearing a black sweater over her black dress with her pocketbook slung from her shoulder. He had his sport coat on; he'd left his tie in the car.

As the blocks went by, they gradually wended a little closer, and by the time they crossed Twentieth Street, they could exchange a few words. She asked about his work, and since Johnny Pope was off-limits, he told her about William Stollman and Mary McQueen.

She remembered the photograph and the story in the *Inquirer.* "That was you who caught him?"

"Not me. It was Sal's case. I just helped out a little."

Then he told her about Marianne Gibson and her offer in the school parking lot, and Valerie raised an eyebrow. "I didn't take her up on it," he said.

"I think you made the right choice," she said drily.

He described Sal: his stories, his deals with half the population of Philadelphia, the guerrilla warfare with his family. She smiled over his lurid depictions of life in Giambroni-land. He in turn asked her about her singing, and she said she wanted to keep performing, since it was the only thing she could do well, except for being a mother. The Blue Door wasn't the classiest room in town by a long shot, but as long as she took a request now and then, Joe let her sing whatever she wanted.

At the corner of Eighteenth Street, she asked if they could stop at the park that was two blocks down on Catherine. When they arrived, Eddie spied an ice-cream cart and went to get two cones. He came back to find her perched near the middle of a bench, and sat down before she had a chance to figure it out and move away.

The Center City skyline was a postcard, the spires painted with the amber brush of the waning day. They could hear the happy shouts of children on the playground on the south side of the park. Pigeons fluttered down and paraded back and forth before them, chests puffed with importance.

They were both quiet, attending to their cones. "Can I ask you about her?" he said presently.

She eyed him warily. "Who?"

"Your daughter."

She hesitated. "What about her?"

"Whatever you want to tell me."

"Oh." Her smile lit her eyes. "Well, she's why I get up in the morning." She paused to watch an old couple toddle by. "If you want to know what happened, I was a young stupid girl and one night things got out of hand and I ended up pregnant. Her daddy is long gone. That's probably for the best."

He nodded, and she worked on her cone for a moment.

"My turn," she said.

"Okay."

"How come you don't have a woman?"

He laughed, dribbling ice cream on his chin, then wiping it away with his finger. "Who says I don't?"

"You don't," she said. "Leastways not a steady one. You got that look, like some alley cat, out looking for trouble." He thought that her eyes actually twinkled. "Is that why you're so serious and all?"

"*I'm* serious? I think this is maybe the second time I've seen you smile."

"You just haven't been around at the correct moments," she said.

A gaggle of schoolgirls, all Italian, passed by in blue skirts and white blouses.

"So what about you?" Eddie said, trying to sound casual. "You got a boyfriend?"

"Not hardly," she said, with a little roll of her eyes. She looked at him and said, "Go ahead."

"Why didn't you and Janelle's father, you know . . . ?"

She shook her head. "Because it would have been a mistake. He didn't want to be anywhere near a baby. He would not have been a good daddy. It's better this way."

"He doesn't want to see her?"

"Some men are just that way," she said flatly. The veil came down again, and he understood that he had stepped on another line. She took a slow lick of her ice cream, then said, "How did you end up being a boxer?"

"I don't know," he said. "I just started messing around. And then I got good at it."

She kept working on her ice cream. Her oval eyes settled as she read him, so he gave in.

"Because my father used to pound on my mother," he said. "And me and my sister and my brothers, too. I wanted to learn how to fight so I could make him stop. He died before I got around to it. By that time I was pretty good, so . . ."

"So you kept going."

"It was either that or go into one of the mills."

"Do you like beating people up?"

He felt a small spike of anger. Why didn't people understand that it wasn't *beating people up*? Or maybe it was.

He tried to explain. "It's real. Nothing fake about it. You bring your stuff, the other guy brings his, you fight, and then it's over. It's simple."

"That's all?" she said.

"That's all."

"Why don't you want to talk about it?"

"I just don't."

"Did something happen to you?"

It was such a nice afternoon, and he didn't want to ruin it. But she was watching him as if it mattered.

"Actually, a couple things happened."

The first one had been a Mexican fighter named Angelito Perez. The word was he was nothing, a tomato can. So Eddie treated him like a punk, and Perez returned the favor by busting him apart, a piece at a time. The guy had bricks under his gloves. He was the one who cut Eddie over the brow for the first time, and bloodied his nose and split open his cheek, too.

"It went on that way for six rounds," Eddie said. "I couldn't get away from him. There was blood everywhere. I didn't know where I was. I kept waiting for someone to throw in a towel. That last round I was dead on my feet, and I felt like he was pounding me into the ground with a sledgehammer."

As he described it to her, he was back in there with Perez closing in and feeling the sour twist of fear in his gut, the monster that was never to be let out. He thought he was going to die, until Perez did him a favor by knocking him and the monster halfway to the moon.

"I made it to the bell, but I was in the hospital for two days." He stopped for a moment. "After that I thought I'd never get back in the ring again."

"But you did."

"Yeah." He shrugged. "I heal quick. At least I used to." He looked off across the park, hoping she would forget about part two.

No such luck. "What about the other one?"

He kept his gaze averted. "The other one was Willie Allred. That was year before last at the Blue Horizon. It was an eight-rounder, and we banged on each other for the first seven. I'd crack him, he'd crack me. He'd go down, I'd go down. And then in the eighth, I caught him. I hooked him really hard under the ribs, and he opened up and I landed one up on his cheekbone, and it hurt him."

He stopped, seeing Allred's eyes dim as his legs buckled and his gloves dropped.

"He was out on his feet, but I hit him anyway, an uppercut, flush on the jaw." He clenched his right fist to keep it from shaking. "I caught him so clean I almost took his head off. The best punch I ever threw in ten years as a fighter. I saw the lights go out in his eyes. I thought I fucking killed him." He glanced at her. "Sorry."

"Never mind. Was he all right?"

"No, he wasn't." Eddie felt a moment of dizziness. "They carried him out on a stretcher. It took him about a week to come around. And he was never right again. He was done as a fighter. I would see him around and it was like he was retarded. It was some kind of brain damage. And I did it to him."

A few seconds passed, and he felt her tap the back of his hand with her finger and looked down to see that it was still balled into a white-knuckle fist. He let it fall open and when he glanced up to meet her eyes, he had to look away. In that moment, he realized how much what happened had changed him, too, and that it wasn't Mieux who had finished him, but Willie Allred.

Valerie said, "It happens, doesn't it?"

He nodded. "Yeah, it does."

"Do you ever think about going back?" she said.

"Yeah, I do." He laughed shortly. "Even after all that. *I'm* not very good at anything else."

He shook his head, as if to clear it. They were quiet for a minute. Eddie noticed for the first time that some of the pedestrians who strolled by stared as if the two of them were committing some indecency in broad daylight. Except for the tap on his fist, they hadn't even touched.

Valerie hadn't missed the looks, either. "Why did you want to do this?" she asked abruptly. "Come out here? With me, I mean."

"I just wanted to get away for a little while," he said. "I thought maybe you did, too."

She studied him pensively. "We should start back. It's getting cold. And I'm working tonight."

They didn't talk for the next two blocks. When they turned onto South Street, she treated him to a cool smile. "So, Mr. Detective," she said. "You weren't trying to get something on me, were you?"

"Get what?"

"I figured you might be trying to catch me at something here."

"No. I just wanted to go for a walk."

"And is that all?"

"Don't worry," he murmured. "Your secrets are safe. Just for today, you get to keep them."

She nodded earnestly and said, "Well, thank you."

They were both smiling, and Eddie felt that a piece of the wall between them had abruptly fallen away. He moved closer and laid his palm on the small of her back. She didn't jump away or scream, but simply turned to regard him with dark, quizzical eyes.

"Uh-uh, don't you be doin' that!" someone yelled, and Eddie snatched his hand away as if he'd been caught stealing. He turned around to see T-Bone Mieux standing at the curb not twenty feet away, treating them to a haughty stare.

"Jesus *Christ*!" He threw up his hands in exasperation.

Valerie looked confused. "Who's—"

"Whatchu think you're doin'?" Mieux demanded loudly. A few people passing by slowed their steps, sensing that the odd tableau of a black girl and two men, one Creole and the other

Italian, might get interesting. Meanwhile, others started to scurry away before they got caught in the middle of something.

"What do you want, Mieux?" Eddie said.

"I believe I just ast you a question," the Creole said. "I believe I just ast you what you think you doin' puttin' your damn hands on a colored gal."

"*Colored* gal?" Valerie said.

Eddie said, "What's it to—"

"You don't touch no colored gal," Mieux repeated, injecting a threat into his tone. He looked at Valerie. "And you, girl, you oughta know better."

Valerie started toward him. "Did you say *col*—"

Eddie moved in front of her. "Hey, if you want something, come on."

The Creole wouldn't take the bait. "I'll come on when I'm good and damn ready," he said. "Then it's lights-out."

The line was so overdone and the scene so ridiculous that Eddie let out an abrupt laugh. It caught Mieux off guard, and he had to settle for a stare that was meant to radiate danger. He pointed a warning finger, backed up, and stepped into the street.

Eddie watched him stalk off through the traffic, then turned a hard glance on the two high school punks who were standing by, hungry for blood. They hitched their shoulders and walked away.

"Who was that?" Valerie said.

"His name's Mieux," Eddie said. "He's a fighter. The last guy I fought, as a matter of fact. And he keeps following me."

"Why?"

"I got no idea. Nothing else to do, I guess."

She glared after the Creole, angry about being called down on the street.

"He's just a screwed-up guy," Eddie told her. "I beat him two out of three. The last time he won. He had to butt me to do it, though." He pointed to his brow. "He's the one who gave me this."

She stared at the scar.

"Hey, it's all right," he told her.

She nodded pensively, folded her arms, and started walking again.

She stayed in a funk over the encounter with Mieux, so he kept quiet as they walked on. Though by the time they got to Twenty-fifth Street, a block away from the Domino, she had relaxed again, so with a crooked smile, he said, "I'm going to damn make sure I never call you 'colored.' "

She stopped and gave him a sharp stare that took him back to the first time they met. The next second her eyes brightened. "And I won't call you 'dago,' " she said.

"That's—"

"Or 'guinea.' "

"Okay, I—"

"Or 'wop.' "

"Okay!" He raised his hands in surrender.

They reached the Domino, and she put her hand on the door.

"You don't have to worry about Mieux," he said.

She gave him a bemused look. "Oh, is that right? Are you my white knight now?"

He was about to tell her he didn't mean it like that and that he wasn't actually *white* when she caught him cold by reaching up to brush the tips of her fingers on the scar over his eye.

She drew her hand away, peered into his startled eyes, and said, "Good night, Eddie."

Pushing the door open, she stepped inside.

He kept glancing in his mirror as he drove away. He turned on the radio, listened to Gene Chandler for a few bars, then turned it off. The touch on his brow had confused him. That was nothing new. Every time he saw her or talked to her or even thought about her, he got mixed-up feelings. As he turned onto Nineteenth Street, he began to understand why that was.

He wasn't supposed to be thinking about her in any sort of personal way. He wasn't supposed to want to be around her. He wasn't supposed to want her to smile at him, or to hear her laugh at something he said, or to take off her armor and talk to him the way she would to someone she liked. He couldn't remember feeling that way about anyone before. For sure, he had shocked himself by blurting the business about Willie Allred. It had just come out.

He watched the streets—her streets—recede into the night and thought about her some more. He knew he wasn't supposed to find her beautiful. He wasn't supposed to think about the light in her dark eyes, or how she always smelled so good, or how smooth and soft her skin had felt the few times they had touched. He knew for sure he wasn't supposed to imagine the brown curves of her body, framed in a doorway and bathed in lamplight. But he did.

Valerie went to the Blue Door early and found it nearly empty, with only the usual barflies bent over their lonely drinks. Something about it was comforting, more than the Domino with all those people—her people—consoling her. She didn't need that right now. She was already too confused.

Joe was sitting alone at one of the tables working on some papers. He looked up when he heard her footsteps on the tile floor. She sat down across from him and he laid his pen aside.

"You sure you want to work tonight?" he said.

"I'm sure."

Joe noticed the strange expression she was wearing.

"What?" he said.

She dropped her gaze from his and said, "I want to ask you about Eddie Cero."

TWENTY

She was still on his mind when he woke up in the morning. He opened his eyes and closed them again, taking a drowsy walk with her down a city street that was awash in a deep red sun into a green park. He saw her smile and heard her laugh. She listened when he told her about Willie Allred, and seemed to understand. There was the raw patch when Mieux appeared, and then the story ended with a small, tender touch, just as the sun came over the rooftops and through his window.

The dopey grin was still in place when he walked into the office and saw Sal glaring at him from behind his desk. He stopped and came to attention.

The detective picked up a section of the morning *Inquirer* and tossed it across the room, hitting him in the chest. "Next-to-last page."

"What's—"

"Read it!"

Eddie flipped through the section until he saw the column called "On the Record," with a photograph of a younger, tidier Carl Beyer inserted in the upper corner, and felt his stomach sink. Below the newsy items about the local music scene, he came to the lines: "In the wake of the recent death of Ray Pope, formerly of the Excels, a new investigation of the disappearance of Johnny Pope, the group's former leader, is in progress. Sources report that new information on the unsolved three-year-old case may emerge."

Sal's glower burned through the page. "What the hell is that?" he said. "Where do you get off blabbing to a reporter?"

"I didn't know he was going to write about it. He said he wouldn't . . ."

"Said he wouldn't what?"

"Use my name," Eddie mumbled.

"Well, I guess he kept his word," Sal said. "I gotta tell you everything? You never talk to a reporter unless you want some thing on the street. They don't use you; you use them." He pointed an irate finger. "Don't do that again."

"Don't worry, I won't." Eddie thanked his stars that Beyer hadn't repeated more of what he'd said. Sal was still giving him the hairy eyeball. "I got it, Sal."

"Good." The detective pushed the rest of the paper aside and went about opening the carton of coffee on his desk. Eddie noted that there wasn't one for him. After a lip-smacking sip, Sal said, "All right, tell me about the funeral."

Eddie recounted the previous day, leaving out the details of his walk with Valerie, but including the run-in with T-Bone Mieux.

"That fucking guy is something, huh?" Sal said.

"Lately I see him everywhere I go."

"Sounds like he's out to fuck with you any way he can."

"You know he didn't start showing up until I got into this."

"You're the one that showed up," Sal said. "You're hanging around, uh . . . on South Street. You're in his yard. And now he's got a hard-on for you. Did he see you with Pope? Or with the girl?"

"I guess he could have," Eddie said carefully.

"Well, there you go," Sal said. "Why don't you just clock him and get it over with?"

"I might have to," Eddie said, and sat down.

After another sip of his coffee, Sal said, "So now the preacher wants to talk to you?"

"Yeah. I'll go see him next."

Sal rocked back in his chair. "What else?"

"Nothing else," Eddie said. "Except that two of the four Excels are dead. There's that."

The detective made a small show out of musing on this. "That leaves two, right? And one of them's a man of the cloth."

It took Eddie a few seconds to catch his drift. "C'mon," he said. "She's—"

"She's what?" Sal cut in deliberately. "Too pretty to be a suspect?" Eddie felt himself reddening, and Sal gave him a long look. "You want to tell me what's going on?"

"Nothing's going on." Eddie shifted in his chair.

"You went out with her."

"We weren't out. We just . . ."

"Just what?"

"We were just talking."

Sal was studying him as if he could see right through his skull and into his brain. "I want to tell you a story," he said.

Eddie rolled his eyes at the ceiling. He wasn't in the mood, but he knew there was no stopping him.

Sal took a moment to open his drawer and produce a second cup of coffee, which he passed across the desk without comment. Eddie managed to keep a straight face.

"Back when I first got my shield, I caught a case," Sal began. "This young girl lived down off Wolf Street was being bothered by this goombah she dumped after one date. Some corner guy, you know? She didn't care for him, didn't want to go out with him no more. But the guy wouldn't take no for an answer. He tried to call her, hung around her house, followed her home from work, all that. She toughed it out for a while, thinking he'd give up and go away. He just got nastier, started making threats, and she got the idea that this piece of shit was going to hurt her if she didn't give in. She was putting up a front, but I could see she was scared.

"So I checked around and found out he was a petty criminal and also a sick fuck, a disgrace to the Italians. He'd pulled the same number with some other girls and the one he beat up pretty bad. So I went to have a talk with him. I let him know the score." He took a sip of coffee. "It didn't do any good. He wasn't going to listen to reason. He was going to make her sorry she gave him the boot and even sorrier that she'd talked to a cop. What I had there was a mental case. I could see that look in his eyes. You got any idea what I'm talking about?"

Eddie nodded. He'd seen it a few times in the ring. And just about every day of his life when he was a kid.

"Anyway, I knew it was just a matter of time and I'd be watching them pull a sheet over her face. Or if not her, some other girl. And then maybe this citizen would spend some time in the pen or maybe some slick shyster bastard would get him off. Either way, somebody was going to end up six feet under. So . . ." He sat back and folded his arms.

Eddie gave him an uncertain look. "What?" Sal held his gaze. "You telling me you got rid of him?"

"Me?" The detective let out a short laugh. "Not me. Though as it turned out, he did get in harm's way not too long after. The word got around that he had been skimming bag money from one of your friend Winky Ragusa's boys. A week later his body turned up in the trunk of his car. Shot behind the ear. Too bad for him. Lucky for her."

Eddie waited to see if there was more, but Sal just sat there, looking complacent.

"You're telling me this why?" he asked.

"Because that young girl's name was—I mean is—Marie."

"Marie."

Sal nodded slowly. "My wife. My ex-wife. The mother of my

children." He watched Eddie for another moment. "There's a point there, Cero."

"Which is?"

"Be careful who you rescue."

"Sal—"

"All right, forget that she's colored. With all this shit going on, you'd think she'd be scared, right?" He stopped. "She have any kids?"

"A little girl," Eddie said.

"So why hasn't she left town? Two people dead and she hasn't left town. You gotta wonder. Anyway, she's a suspect. This preacher, too. Same deal. And whatshisname, Roddy. Anyone else who's in the picture. Right now, the only ones you can clear are the dead guys."

Eddie knew there was no point in arguing. Sal didn't know her. He started to get up.

"Aren't you going to ask me about my day?" the detective sniffed.

Eddie sat back down. "Oh, yeah. What happened?"

"I did some checking on Mr. Richard Barnes." He made a face. "I had to spend the better part of my afternoon in saloons."

Eddie laughed. "That must have been rough."

"The guy's a local Romeo. Havertown's peewee Hugh Hefner. There's been rumors about his activities for a long time. The word is he runs a regular pussy parlor in that house. You know, the hi-fi, the bar, the whole deal."

Eddie shook his head in amazement.

"He's basically a pimp," Sal went on. "I ain't sure if he does it for money or because it makes him feel like a big shot to get his friends laid."

"Maybe he wants to get something on the guys."

"Blackmail?" Sal poked an eyebrow. "Maybe, but that's scary stuff."

"Did Marianne show up there again?"

"Yep, same routine." He paused. "That's her third strike. It's time we go talk to the parents."

Eddie cocked his head. "Who's we?"

Sal said, "Delivering bad news is part of the job, Cero. What, you think you were going to spend your days with newspaper guys and pretty dames?" Eddie didn't bother to respond to the gibe. "Get your reports and the eight-by-tens together," Sal said. "We'll leave in an hour."

Eddie was halfway to his desk when the phone rang. Sal put the receiver to his ear and said, "SG Investigations." He listened for a moment. "Who's calling?" He listened some more, then cupped his hands around the mouthpiece. "It's for you," he whispered to Eddie. "Some lawyer, says he's representing George Roddy." Sal held the phone away, and his voice was urgent as he leaned across the desk. "Don't give him a thing, y'understand?"

"Yeah, yeah, okay." Eddie took the receiver from Sal's hand.

The voice on the other end of the line was clipped and direct, advertising a man who expected to get his way at all times and without question.

"This is Roger Beckley. Beckley and Kane. I represent George Roddy of StarLite Records." He waited. "Mr. Cero?"

"I heard you," Eddie said.

"Are you represented by counsel, Mr. Cero?"

"No," Eddie said. "I really don't like lawyers."

He heard Sal laugh. Beckley the lawyer lost his bullying way for a moment. "Well, then . . . I'll speak to you directly. I understand you've tried to contact Mr. Roddy a number of times by telephone and once in person, to speak to him about the late John Pope." It wasn't a question, so Eddie kept quiet. "Mr. Cero?"

"I'm here."

"And there was mention of an investigation in the newspaper this morning." Now Beckley sounded disgusted.

"I saw that, too," Eddie said.

Again the lawyer seemed to stumble. "Well, then . . . In any case, Mr. Roddy has nothing to say to you in regard to Mr. Pope. At the time of that unfortunate incident, he was interviewed by the police. His statement is a matter of public record. He also took it upon himself at no small expense to hire private investigators to look into the matter. It failed to produce any information of value. Mr. Roddy has nothing further to say on the subject and will not be available to speak to you." Beckley politely allowed one second for comment, then came back with a harsher tone. "Your actions, including this incident at the memorial service, constitute harassment. Consider yourself warned."

Eddie decided that he'd heard enough. Keeping his voice casual, he said, "Hey, do me a favor and tell Mr. Roddy to go fuck himself. You're his attorney, so you can do that, right?" He could feel the shock echoing on the line, and before Beckley could recover, he said, "But, listen, since we're talking, I want to ask a question. Say two guys have an agreement. Or a contract. A recording contract, even. And one of the parties dies. Is it still good?"

Beckley said, "You . . . I don't . . . I'm not—" His tongue finally found some traction. "I don't dispense legal advice gratis, Mr. Cero. And certainly not to you."

"Oh." Eddie thought for a few seconds. "Well, then, you know when I asked you to tell Roddy to go fuck himself?"

"I'm not about to—"

"That goes for you, too," he said, and dropped the receiver in the cradle.

His pulse was doing a jitterbug. Sal let out a happy bark of a laugh. "Beautiful!" He was beaming. "You know that prick thought you'd roll over the minute he said 'boo.' I'll bet he didn't know whether to shit or go blind." Eddie was confused, but pleased. He thought he'd let his temper get the best of him. But Sal was delighted.

"All right," the detective said. "What'll happen now is he'll call the client and repeat the conversation, and in about ten minutes, the phone is going to ring again. They'll have a change of heart, and you'll be invited to go see him."

"How do you know?"

"I know because I know. Because people are predictable. Because I've been in this business a long time." He leaned back complacently. Eight minutes passed and when the phone jangled, he came up with a self-satisfied smirk. He held up his hand, and Eddie waited for his signal to pick up. He dropped the hand after the sixth ring, and Eddie lifted the receiver.

"SG Investigations," he said crisply. "Cero speaking."

He was expecting another dose of Beckley's thin, snotty whine. Instead, the voice on the other end was all west Jersey. "It's George Roddy, Cero."

Eddie gazed dumbly at Sal, who mouthed, *What?*

"Mr. Roddy," Eddie said. Sal brought his hands together in silent applause.

"Fucking lawyers," George Roddy was saying. "They complicate everything, then charge you for it. Well, what the hell. Look, no offense about that business yesterday, all right? With the service and all that, I just didn't want to go into it."

"It's all right."

"You want to come talk to me?"

"Yeah, I do."

"Two o'clock suit you?"

"That'll be fine."

"You know where my office is, right?"

"Yeah."

Roddy let out a hoarse chuckle. "See how simple that was? Goddamn lawyers," he said, and hung up.

Eddie handed the receiver back. "What time?" Sal said.

"Two o'clock."

Sal nodded, looking all pleased with himself. He began shoving his papers aside. "Okay, good, that's taken care of. Now go do your reports. We leave at eleven."

They cruised along Chestnut Street to the end when it switched onto Route 3. Along the way they passed a string of car dealerships, and Eddie looked out his window and saw new Mercurys, Plymouths, Studebakers, and Cadillacs, shimmering from the showrooms and front lots in ruby reds, sea blues, pearl whites, and inky blacks. Eddie and Sal talked about cars a little bit, what they'd drive if they had all the money in the world. Sal chose a foreign car, a big Mercedes sedan. Eddie said he'd pick something really quick off the line, like a Vette or a Cobra.

Sal said, "And loud?"

"Just barely."

"Figures," Sal said.

Eddie saw the detective watching the mirror and swung around to have a look. As far as he could tell, no two-toned Pontiac or any other car was on their tail.

They turned off Route 3 and wound along a series of two-lanes. To Eddie, the landscape was something dreamed up for a color spread in a magazine, so far removed from anything he had known that he didn't feel envy, just an odd curiosity, like a tourist in a foreign land.

They passed a peaceful and pristine little park, the stunted trees adorned with spring blossoms. George Roddy and his snotty lawyer and the death of Ray Pope and all the rest of the headaches were back in the city. Which suited Eddie fine. Not that there was a picnic waiting.

Sal pulled into the Gibsons' driveway, turned off the ignition, and laid a hand on Eddie's arm.

"There's something about this situation I didn't tell you," he said. "See if you can catch it."

Eddie raised an eyebrow. "You're giving me a test?"

"Call it a game, all right? Just keep your eyes open." He looked up at the front of the house and tapped the steering wheel for a moment, preparing himself for the encounter inside. "Okay," he said. "Let's get it over with."

Gerald Gibson opened the door for his visitors. He was a tall, narrow-framed, starched-looking man in his late forties, an executive at DuPont. Mr. Gibson led them into the dining room, where his wife, Margaret, was waiting. The small, slim woman was attractive in a pale way though she looked as though she might blow away in a stiff breeze. Of course, her hair was coiffed carefully in a Jackie Kennedy style.

The house was gorgeous, and Eddie imagined he and Sal in that setting were akin to a couple of water rats that had wandered out of the local dump. The Gibsons would probably fumigate after they left.

A black girl in a maid's uniform appeared in the doorway that led to the back of the house, and Mr. Gibson asked if they would care for some refreshments. Sal looked as if he would love to be refreshed by a double scotch, but he shook his head and said, "No thanks."

Gibson turned flat eyes on Eddie. "Mr., uh . . . ?"

"Cero," Eddie said. "I'm fine."

The maid went away as silently as she had appeared. Mr. Gibson waved them to seats at a long, highly polished maple table, where his wife was waiting. The house was hushed, with not even the sound of a clock ticking.

Sal gave it to them, short and sweet: Marianne sneaking out of school and using her friends' cars in order to pay visits to a house on North Drexel Road. He told them about the various cars at the house, which pointed to different visitors at the same time their daughter showed up. As Eddie arranged the photos on the table, Sal opined that there was no other reason for these rendezvous, other than trysts of some kind.

In a patient voice, he shared the results of his interviews with various people around town in regard to the ongoing activities in the house. He concluded quietly with an offer to take the parents along on surveillance so they could see for themselves. Marianne's proposition to Eddie in exchange for his silence was left mercifully unmentioned.

The Gibsons kept sober expressions in place throughout Sal's presentation and reviewed the photos without comment. The father kept nodding his head mechanically, as if listening to something that didn't interest him, while his wife sat at the end of the table with her face rigidly composed, a china statue. There were no sighs, no tears, not even a glance between them.

When neither one spoke up to inquire about the occupant of the house, Sal went ahead and provided Barnes's name and related some of the rumors about him.

The mention of the name was the giveaway. Eddie saw a bit of color rise to Margaret Gibson's pale cheeks and heard her release a tiny anxious breath. He shifted his gaze to her husband and noticed his teeth were now clamped behind tight lips.

Sal finished his spiel and sat back. Mrs. Gibson cleared her throat. "Do I understand that you haven't actually witnessed Marianne inside that house?"

Sal raised his head as if he'd caught a whiff of something unpleasant. "That's correct."

"So you don't actually know what she's doing in there."

"We only know what we observed, ma'am." Sal tapped one of the prints. "And photographed."

The woman said, "So any conclusions you draw would be . . . inference." Her voice was dry.

Sal nodded. The Gibsons regarded him stoically, a pair of mannequins.

"Is that all?" Mr. Gibson said after the silence.

"That's all," Sal said. "If you want us to continue, we can work on getting inside."

"That won't be necessary," Margaret Gibson said in a whisper. Eddie now noticed the miffed and haughty poses the Gibsons had assumed, as if they were trying to retreat from the bad odor that the two visitors had carried into their home.

"My wife and I will discuss this information," Mr. Gibson announced. "And decide on a course of action."

He pushed back from the table and stood up. Sal and Eddie followed suit. Gibson thanked them for their time and led them to the front door. His wife remained seated, immobile, another piece of the dinette set.

The door closed, and Sal and Eddie walked down the slope to the car. At the curb Sal tossed the keys and said, "You drive." Eddie cranked the engine, and the two of them spent a moment gazing out the windshield at the house. "Some fucking show, huh?" Sal said. Eddie agreed that it was. "You catch it?"

"Barnes," Eddie said. Sal smiled crookedly. "They know about him." His smile got broader and Eddie said, "What, she knows him?" Now Sal chuckled. "Jesus, she's screwing him, too?"

The detective, delighted by the stunned look on Eddie's face, said, "She was. About six months ago, or so the grapevine has it."

"And what about Daddy?" Eddie said.

"What about him, is right. Guy's made out of fucking glass. We just told him his daughter is getting banged and pimped out by the same guy who banged his wife, and he just sits there." He shook his head in numb wonder. "Jesus and Mary, you know what I'd do if I ever caught one of my girls mixed up in something like this? Forget about my wife." His round face pinched in disgust. "I can't fucking believe it. And this is supposed to be class out here."

"What do you think they'll do?"

"I don't know. Get her the hell out of here. Maybe send her to Europe for the summer."

"That's all?"

"That'd be my guess. As long as they can keep it quiet." The detective gave a shrug that was just short of angry. "Who gives a shit? Just so he pays his bill. Which I guarantee he will, in full and on time, just to get rid of us." He made a rude gesture. "Let's go back to Philly. This place gives me the creeps."

Eddie backed the car into the street and pointed it for the city. He wanted to hear more about the weird little drama at the Gibson home, and Sal was happy to oblige.

"What you got there is your classic example of keeping up the front, whatever the cost," he proffered. "I could see it in their faces. They want to bury it. They'll keep the Ozzie and Harriet act going if it kills them."

"But there's all that talk going around."

"I guess it's not enough to make a difference." Sal peered grimly out the windshield. "If it was my kid, I swear to God she'd be in a convent by sundown." He fell silent for a while. "Some people will do almost anything for their money and status. And they'll do even more to hang on to it."

They didn't talk at all the rest of the way into the city. When they got to Sansom Street, Sal called him into his office. "You're going to go see this Roddy guy later on, right?"

"Two o'clock."

"Then I want you to meet me at the Eighth Precinct on Bainbridge at three."

"What for?"

"I might have a piece of your puzzle."

"I was going to go see Tommy Gates after Roddy."

"Change your plan. You'll want to hear this."

Sal was enjoying being devious, so Eddie let him have his fun.

"You said Bainbridge?"

"Yeah, right near Fifth."

"Okay," Eddie said, and leaned in the doorway. "What about Marianne?"

"What about her?" Sal said. "We're done with it. We're not cops. I can't arrest Barnes. I could try to push McKay, but he ain't going to do nothing."

"Why don't you feed it to a reporter?"

The detective rolled his eyes. "Very funny. Actually, I might do that, except for the girl. I feel sorry for her. Somebody should have straightened her out a long time ago. It's too late now. Be interesting to see how she turns out, but . . ." He smiled without humor. "The case is closed."

With that he pulled open the drawer where he kept his bottle.

StarLite Records maintained a suite of offices in the Keystone Trust Building, a thirty-six-story monolith located on Market Street, halfway between the train station and the Mall.

As he stepped out of the elevator to the thirty-third floor, Eddie was greeted by the sight of a desk shaped and painted to resemble a 45-rpm record, with the receptionist sitting in the middle. He stopped and stared.

"May I help you?" she said in a tone that was as blank as her expression. Apparently, she didn't think there was anything odd about spending her day sitting directly atop what would have been a phonograph spindle.

As soon as he stated his name, she raised a cool eyebrow, then deliberately punched a button on her telephone console and murmured into the mouthpiece of her headset. The exchange was brief. She told Eddie to have a seat.

He had barely settled when the office doors opened and the blond woman from the funeral hurried out to greet him. When he stood up, her blue eyes swept over him from head to toe and back, as if she was evaluating a piece of merchandise. A smile curved her mouth in an arc, and she extended a hand. "Mr. Cero, I'm Candy Ralston. Mr. Roddy's assistant. Can I take you inside?" Her voice rode a musical scale.

She walked ahead of him as they passed through a double

door into the offices and crossed a large room that held eight desks, each attended by a busy young woman, every one of them a looker.

When they arrived at the double doors, Eddie got an up-close glimpse of Candy Ralston. She appeared to be in her midthirties and was pretty in a showy, Hollywood way—a glamour-puss. Though her expertly applied makeup provided a glossy sheen, something loose and a little vulgar lurked just beneath her skin, and the whole package seemed to be just a little hard around the edges.

She had spared no effort to make herself look good, however, with a sleeveless blouse that plunged to a provocative V in front and black capri pants that appeared to have been painted on. She wore black sandals with heels, and her toenails were as pink as bubble gum.

She pushed one side of the double doors open and called out in a sprightly voice, "Mr. Roddy, Mr. Cero to see you." There was something deliciously phony about the delivery, a line from a play badly spoken.

From inside Roddy called back, "Thank you, Candy," doing his own fake-hearty part.

Miss Ralston gestured for Eddie to enter. As he stepped through the door, he glanced back in time to catch her watching him with tight eyes that were webbed with lines that hadn't been there before. She went into a blushing flutter as she hurriedly replaced the mask.

At that moment Eddie felt a hand on his shoulder.

"Mr. Cero." His host offered the other hand. "George Roddy. Welcome to StarLite." Both hands went away, and Roddy waved Eddie to an oddly sculpted modern chair while he moved around to sit behind his desk, a rakish affair with a mahogany top that swept this way and that in a French curve.

Eddie surveyed an office that was about half the size of his entire apartment. The furnishings looked expensive, down to the sleek pen set on Roddy's desk. Album covers and 45-rpm records in frames covered the walls. A wide window provided a view of Center City all the way to the river.

He came around to the lord of the little kingdom. With his tanned skin and jet-black hair, George Roddy might at a quick glance pass for Mediterranean, except that his eyes looked too close-set and his probe of a nose too thin. The dusky flesh on his face was dry from too many sunlamps, and his hair was sooty chemical black. Though he was well above average height, his shoulders were round and hunched, making him appear shorter. As before he was decked out, the tan suit a rich Italian silk, and the dark brown tie and cream-colored shirt had come from the finest haberdashers in the city. All this perfect tailoring couldn't hide a thick middle, and Eddie guessed that he'd be some blimp under those pricey clothes.

Roddy's eyes were the main thing, an odd shade of green, close to olive drab, with heavy lids that made Eddie think of a reptile sunning on a rock.

"So," the reptile began with a small smile, "did you really tell Roger Beckley to go fuck himself?" Eddie nodded. "And me, too, huh?"

"It was the heat of the moment," Eddie said.

Roddy chuckled. "Hey, it's fine. I respect people who speak their minds." The lizard eyes drooped a little as he studied his visitor. "You were a fighter?"

"That's right," Eddie said, wondering if every person he met for the rest of his life was going to ask him that.

"So how did you get into the investigation racket?" It was delivered with feigned curiosity; Eddie was sure the guy already knew all about him.

"Just happened that way," he said, hoping he would drop it.

"Sounds like me," Roddy said. "My background is in import-export. My brother was the real music lover. Crazy kid. He started the company. It was a small thing, local artists for the local market. Jazz and rhythm and blues, mostly. When he passed away, it was either keep it going or let it fold. I decided to keep it going. And that's what I did. Ended up falling in love with it. Not that it wasn't hard, learning the business, but it has its rewards. We've managed to make a few dollars along the way. I've been lucky . . ."

After a half minute, Eddie was already tired of the happy horseshit. He thought of Sal's admonitions about never letting a subject control an interview and realized that if it went on, Miss Ralston would be poking her pert nose through the door to tell her boss it was time for his next appointment. Of course, that had been the point of the exercise, to let him see what a regular, good-hearted guy George Roddy was so he would go away.

"I came to talk to you about Johnny Pope," he broke in.

Roddy's smile hung out in the air as his last word hit the floor. His mouth re-formed into a line and the green eyes went cool. "Oh, yeah? Why?"

"Why?" Eddie fumbled for a second. "Because . . . because I'm trying to find out what happened to him."

"Did somebody hire you for this?" The voice was turning brittle in a hurry.

Eddie said, "No, not exact—"

"So let me get this straight," Roddy said, shifting tersely. "You were a fighter, and then, what, you got a job running errands for some private snoop? And right away you decide to start sniffing around a crime from three years ago? Do I got it right?"

Put that way, Eddie had to agree that it did sound strange. He was trying to think of a response when Roddy said, "Okay, listen, I don't know why you're doing this, and I don't give a shit." What little was left of the phony cordiality was gone. "Johnny disappearing, it was a goddamn shock. This company was like a family. StarLite was the only label he'd ever had. I made sure the police were all over it right away. When they couldn't come up with anything, I paid out of my pocket to hire a private firm to investigate. And they didn't find anything, either."

Eddie said, "That was three years ago."

"Right, exactly," Roddy snapped. "So what's the point in fucking around with it now?"

"Some time has passed. Things change."

"And?"

"And maybe now we can find out how Johnny Pope died."

A crimson hue invaded the tan. "We already know how he died, goddamnit. He was the victim of a crime. He was murdered and his body was dumped somewhere. Probably in the river."

"Nobody knows any of that for a fact," Eddie said.

George Roddy's dark eyebrows peaked. "Oh? And you're the one's going to figure it all out, huh? What, are you kidding me?"

"I'm working on it," Eddie said. It wasn't much, but it was something.

"Yeah?" Roddy sat back and stared at him. "So who else have you talked to? In addition to Fat Cat and Eugene White." He took a moment to enjoy Eddie's look of surprise. "Oh, yeah, I know all about that." He laughed sourly. "Jesus H. Christ! Eugene? You're kidding me, right? What a waste of time." Roddy shook his head in derision. "That fucking antique should have stayed in vaudeville. You know who he managed besides the Excels? I'll tell you: nobody. It was nothing but dumb luck. I think Johnny closed his eyes and picked him out of the yellow pages. Good god! That schnook couldn't get a dog to bark—you think he could handle Johnny Pope?"

Now Roddy flicked a hand in the air. "I know, I know, he did this, he did that, he dressed him, he fed him, he treated him like a son. If I heard that spiel once, I heard it a hundred times. The truth is, he had Johnny in zoot suits, singing songs out of some damn minstrel show. He looked like an idiot and he sounded worse. He would have been working for dimes if I hadn't given him a break. I brought him back to the twentieth century. I did that. Me. And because of me, he got famous and he got rich." He glowered and his voice got loud again. "So, how come, after all of that, I got some dumb fucking guinea pug sticking his nose into my business?"

Eddie ignored the insult and the question that had couched it.

"I asked, who else have you talked to?"

Eddie let that one go, too. "Why was Johnny leaving StarLite?"

Roddy stared for a second before giving up a harsh laugh. "Oh, yeah. He was *leaving*. Sure he was. I heard that, too, just about every goddamn day. Eugene's way of trying to chisel more money out of me. He really thought I'd fall for it."

"Some other people said it was true."

The green eyes flashed. "I don't give a fuck what some other people said. The Excels were doing great. They had three records on the Top 100. And Johnny was leaving? I don't think so. I can show you the contract he was about to sign when he disappeared. What you—"

"Okay," Eddie said.

Roddy slid to a stop, looking uncertain. "Okay, what?"

"The contract. I'd like to see it. Unless you'd prefer that I didn't."

Eddie could see the *no* in the green eyes, but Roddy said, "Yeah, fine, why not? We've got nothing to hide."

He knotted his hands before him once more, and Eddie saw the knuckles go white. "I'm going to tell you something," he said. "I'm the one who built this company. Not my brother, God rest his soul. He didn't have what it takes. This is not what you call your average business. It's nothing but kikes and guineas, and most of them are crooks. Well, I ain't a kike, I ain't a guinea, and I ain't a crook, but I made it anyway." His voice went up another notch. "I built this label from next to nothing. I earned every fucking penny, and I don't have to explain anything to you or anybody else. Especially something that happened three goddamn years ago! You keep this up and I'll make more trouble for you than you know what to do with. That's what lawyers are for."

Eddie nodded placidly. "Can you think of any reason why Ray's and Johnny's murders might be connected?"

Roddy's lidded eyes flashed again, and for a second Eddie thought he was going to lunge across the desk. He caught and calmed himself. The fierce light left his eyes. He sat back, laid his hands on the desktop, and rose to his stooped height.

"You just don't get it, do you?" he said. "Whoever killed Johnny got away with it. We're all going to have to live with that. And as far as Ray goes, anyone who knew him will tell you he was living on borrowed time. It's a goddamn wonder it didn't happen sooner. It's too bad, but that's the way it is. And that's all I have to say."

"You know that two of the four mem—"

"I said that's it!"

Eddie felt a breathless silence from the outside office. Roddy noticed it, too, because he glanced at the doorway and said, "We're done here. Candy will see you out."

Eddie caught a whiff of perfume as she appeared magically in the doorway. She'd been skulking around the whole time. He thought about trying to tough it out with Roddy, but he knew he wouldn't get anywhere. The man had that look in his eye, as he stood behind the big desk with his arms crossed in a posture of rude dismissal.

When he reached the doorway, Eddie greeted Candy. "Mr. Roddy says you can show me a copy of the Excels' contract."

It was a good thing he was looking right at her or he would have missed the twitch in her mouth and the sudden blank space in her gaze. She managed to hold herself together as Roddy said, "It's all right, Candy." He sounded like he was being strangled.

Candy produced a gay chuckle as she led him away. "Of course. I'll be happy to send you a copy."

"I'll just wait," he said, loud enough for Roddy to hear. "Save you the trouble."

"Of course," she said. Her smile was as bright as a new dime and just as thin. "Come to my office and I'll see if I can find it."

They walked down a corridor. Two women passed by, both knockouts. Eddie realized he had yet to encounter even an average-looking woman since he'd walked in and had seen only one other man, a stooped, bony, frazzled-looking guy wearing a white shirt with a pocketful of pencils. George Roddy had made sure he was cock of the walk in that particular barnyard.

Miss Ralston stepped into her office. Eddie followed, stopping just inside the door.

"Come in, I'm not going to bite you," she said. He didn't move. "What was it again?"

"A copy of the Excels' last contract."

"Oh, yes." She sashayed to a file cabinet in the corner. "Let's see, let's see . . ."

She wasn't much of an actress. Not that she wasn't trying. She fussed about for a minute, rustling folders and papers. "I can't seem to find it," she said.

Eddie leaned against the doorjamb.

"Did I hear correctly, you were a fighter, Mr. Cero?" she asked over her shoulder.

"You heard it wrong," he told her. "I was a *waiter.* Down at Palumbo's."

She gave him a baffled glance. "A what?"

"It was a joke. Yeah, I was a fighter."

"Oh. Well, you must be in good shape."

"Not so much anymore," he said.

She treated his physique to another review. "I don't think you have anything to worry about just yet."

"What about the contract?" he said.

She rifled the files for a few seconds more. "I'm sorry." She came up with a helpless little girl smile. "I can't seem to locate it."

He fixed his gaze on her and the smile went away. She shot a quick look at the doorway.

"I'll find it, all right?" she said. "I will. Where can I call you?"

He went into his coat pocket for one of Sal's business cards and held it out to her. She took the card between two manicured fingernails. "Thank you so much." She stepped back. "Sorry about the contract," she said in a loud, vexed voice. "But I'll keep looking."

"Let me know when you find it."

"I will," she said.

"I'll come back if I have to," he said. "I don't mind."

"It was a pleasure to meet you!" she chirped as he ducked out the door.

He walked into the Eighth Precinct station and waited until the desk sergeant finished with a man who was arguing loudly that if his neighbor didn't keep his "goddamn fucking mutt from pissing on my rosebushes," he was going to shoot the dog and the owner, too. The cop listened, nodding his head until the man wound down, gave up, and went away. He looked at Eddie.

"I'm supposed to meet Sal Giambroni here," Eddie said.

The desk sergeant said, "We went ahead and locked him up while we had him." Eddie laughed and the officer jerked a thumb. "Try Andy's. End of the block."

Eddie stepped into the cool darkness of the bar and found Sal sitting in a booth with a powerfully built black man who could have been a heavyweight, except that "cop" stuck out all over him, from his durable suit to the fedora that rested at his elbow. He had a moon face, like a smiling brown jack-o'-lantern, and a thin mustache showing a few gray hairs. The smile on Sal's face was another tip-off. Though his boss was basically a loner, Eddie knew he still enjoyed spending time with his old buddies from the force.

"I brought you a present," Sal said as he stepped up. Though Eddie had already guessed the stranger's identity, he let Sal enjoy himself and make the introduction. "This is Al Nash, Philadelphia PD. Eddie Cero."

"I saw you fight once or twice," Nash said.

Eddie shook the big man's hand. "Did I win?"

"The one, you did."

Eddie slid into the booth. He guessed this was no time for pleasantries and got right to it. "You worked on the Johnny Pope case."

The cop nodded. "Me and Don Hayner, yeah. Sal says you're looking at it again."

"That's right," Eddie said. "I read your report."

"That wasn't no report of mine," Nash said gruffly. "It was Hayner's."

"Not much there," Eddie said.

"That's right, there isn't." Nash shifted in his seat. "And there's not much more I can say about it. Case was clean as a whistle. At first I didn't think it was a homicide. I thought maybe the guy just up and left town for some reason. Because there was nothing in the way of evidence. No signs of a struggle. Nothing."

"You mean that's the way Hayner reported it."

Al Nash's eyes flicked, and he cocked his head, regarding Eddie more closely. "That's right," he said. "There were also no witnesses. Not one. Sal'll tell you, most murders just don't go down that way."

Nash rolled his glass between two fingers for a few seconds. "The thing is I wasn't lead investigator on that case. I was just there to, uh, add some color." He smiled again, this time tightly. "Hayner was the lead. It was his case. And his calls."

Eddie glanced between the two older men. "Detective Hayner's white?"

"Last time I looked, he was," Nash said in a dry voice. Sal laughed shortly.

"Then why did he get it?" Eddie said. "The victim was colored."

Nash's gaze met Sal's for a moment, then came back to Eddie. "He asked the captain to put him on it," he said.

Eddie mulled this for a moment, then said, "You did question some of those people, right?"

The cop said, "Some, yeah. The ones Hayner gave me. We had other cases."

"I guess you heard that his cousin Ray Pope was murdered."

"I heard." He cocked an eyebrow. "You think one's tied in with the other?"

"I don't know," Eddie said.

Nash glanced at Sal, who shrugged noncommittally.

"So what do you think happened to Johnny, Detective?" Eddie said.

"I ain't got no doubt it was a homicide," Nash said. "He didn't just wander off somewhere. He had fans, thousands of people who knew him on sight. A lot of people can disappear. Not Johnny Pope."

The three men spent a few seconds without speaking while the music played in the background.

"You think Hayner would talk to me?" Eddie said.

"Can't say," Nash said. "He left the force. I haven't seen him in a couple years." He sat back and moved his glass aside. "That's it. Sorry I couldn't be more helpful."

Eddie relaxed and studied the cop a few seconds. "You were in the ring, huh?"

Al Nash's face broke into a grin. "Golden Gloves. A long time ago." He laughed and patted his gut. "I was a *middle-weight.* You believe that?" He shook his head, sighed, and reached across the table to shake hands with each of the men.

"Sal, it's always good to see you again." He looked at Eddie.

"And it was good to meet you." He slid out of the booth and moved off, blocking the daylight when he stepped through the door.

Eddie turned to Sal. "So?"

"So?" Sal said. "Whaddya mean, 'so'?"

"What?"

Sal treated him to a look of dismay and then began to hum off-key to the Nat King Cole song that was playing on the jukebox. When the song ended, he drained his glass and said, "Whaddya say we take a walk around the neighborhood?"

A half block down Fifth Street, Sal glanced over his shoulder and then said, "Listen, kiddo, no cop is going to just come out and speak ill of another one. Especially one he used to partner with. It's a superstition."

"Yeah, so what's going on?" Eddie said.

"First tell me how it went with Mr. Roddy."

Eddie took him through his visit to StarLite. When he got to the part where Roddy started threatening him, Sal shook his head and said, "Well, that's just fucking great."

"Don't start. Please."

The detective stopped in the middle of the sidewalk. "You got any idea what the hell you're messing with? I asked around about your *record* business. There's mob guys all over the place. I had no idea. Christ, Cero!"

Eddie flinched, struck by how much Sal suddenly sounded like his old man crawling up his back about something.

The detective came after him. "And this Roddy asshole is just another egg in the basket. A lot of these guys are into loan sharks. Because the banks don't lend money to people who want to make records for punks. So they borrow from the sharks to get started and keep borrowing to stay in business."

"What—"

"Wait a minute. A lot of them gamble, but of course they're fucking losers, so they're into the books, too. Either way, they're on the hook with the goombahs. How you like them meatballs?" He wasn't finished. "You know what else I heard? I heard that Philly's a fucking playground compared to New York. They're throwing guys under buses up there. Cutting their nuts off. All over some fucking records! What the hell have you got me into here?"

Sal's eyes bugged so wide and his hands flapped so crazily that Eddie had to laugh.

"Oh, that's funny?"

"It is when you say it."

Sal gave it another second, and let out a blunt laugh. Then he got serious again. "Listen to me, Cero. I really don't want it on my conscience if you get hurt. Or worse."

Eddie shoved his hands in his pockets and stared down at the pavement. The detective sighed once and they started walking again. They went along for a little while without speaking. Then Sal said, "All right, let's have the rest of it."

Eddie related the end of his visit to StarLite and the scene with Candy Ralston. "You told me there wasn't going to be any of that," he said.

"Any of what?"

"Blond dames whispering in my ear."

Sal laughed a little. "Listen, I think you can play her," he said. "She probably knows a secret or two, and if she thinks it's coming apart, there's a good chance she'll roll."

They turned the corner onto Monroe Street. "All right, so what about Nash?" Eddie asked.

Sal wagged a finger, a sure sign that a lecture was coming. "There's two types of detectives," he pronounced. "The ones who investigate and deliver their actual findings and the ones who investigate and deliver what someone wants to hear."

"For instance?"

"A foregone conclusion. 'This wasn't a murder, it was a suicide.' That kind of thing."

"How do they get away with it?"

"Same old story." Sal rubbed his index finger and thumb together and snickered. "We used to say 'Where there's a bill, there's a way.' "

"Why are you telling me this?" Eddie said.

"I'm passing along what Al wouldn't."

"Which is what?"

"Which is where Don Hayner went to work after he left the force."

"Where?"

"One of them three-piece-suit agencies. Norwood Investigations."

"Yeah, and?"

Sal came up with his sneaky smile.

Eddie said, "And Norwood's the company Roddy hired to investigate."

Sal gave him a broad wink, and as they strolled on, he related the rest of it. Nash had explained that once Hayner got the lead on the Pope case, he was in a rush to put it down as unsolved, just another beef down in darktown. He got annoyed when Nash wanted to talk to more of the people around Pope. There was the race angle, of course—colored cases didn't rate with those in the white column. But Nash was used to that. The black cop's nose told him this was different, that there was something going on, something more than just a cranky detective who was not far from retirement and didn't want to be bothered with nigger business. It didn't matter that it involved a major recording artist. Hayner treated the investigation as a waste of the taxpayers' money.

As it turned out, Nash had it right. Ten months later Hayner left the force, and he was quietly named assistant vice president of investigations at Norwood, the very company that had been brought in to sweep up after the Philly PD on the Johnny Pope case.

"Hayner made himself a sweet deal, and all he had to do was nothing," Sal said. "Because somebody wanted this one buried."

"I'd pick Roddy," Eddie said.

"He'd be at the top of my hit parade, too," Sal said.

Eddie smiled at the reference. "Do you know Hayner at all?"

"I remember him," Sal said. "I wouldn't count him among Philadelphia's finest."

They had made their way around the block and were coming up on the space where Sal's Chevy was parked.

"So, what say tomorrow we go pay him a visit?" the detective said.

"Who, Hayner?"

"Yeah. Or we could talk to him right now. He's sitting back there in his car."

This time Eddie didn't turn around. "Yellow-and-white Pontiac?"

"No, you made him in the Pontiac. It's a blue Ford Galaxie," Sal said. "What the hell, let's do it tomorrow. We'll ambush him at his office."

"I'm going to see Tommy Gates first thing," Eddie said.

"We'll go after." Sal winked. "It'll be a nice surprise. I know he'll appreciate it."

They went back to the office to finish the day's business. When Sal opened the door, there was an envelope from a messenger service lying on the floor. He opened it to find a check from Mr. Gibson, the amount paid in full, just as he had predicted.

It put him in a mood, and he went for his bottle. Eddie knew he would now sit and drink and brood until the traffic died down. He didn't want to hang around, in case Sal tried to corral him for a boozing partner, so he slipped out before Sal noticed he was gone.

It had been twenty-four hours since he had seen her, and the pang in his gut was back. He didn't want to think about that, so he cruised for a while, then went home, changed into his sweats, and ran a couple miles. When he got back, he took a shower, got dressed, and walked over to Chancellor Street to buy a slice, which he didn't finish. He wasn't very hungry.

It was nine o'clock when he walked into the Blue Door, feeling only a slight case of butterflies. Joe wasn't around to greet him and he didn't see Valerie, so he stood in the darkness just inside the archway that opened into the main room. The stage—her stage—was bathed in deep red light. He was thinking that showing up was a bad idea and that he should get out before she saw him, when she appeared at his side, wearing a puzzled smile. "Eddie?" He saw the light in her eyes and felt that he had lost his balance. "What are you doing here?" she said.

"Waiting for you," he blurted.

She looked surprised. Then she laughed. In Eddie's mind, everything around her disappeared into darkness, and the room went dead silent. He now saw something in her eyes that—

"Hey, hey! Look who's here!" It was Joe D'Amato, coming out of the shadows, waving happy hands before him. "Fast Eddie, what's the good word?"

Eddie said, "Uh . . ."

Joe stood there waiting for the good word. He looked between the two of them, noticed their odd expressions. "So, what's . . ." He stopped and took a step back, the baffled expression on his face slowly giving way to comprehension. He said, "Valerie, you need a drink?"

"I'm fine," she said.

"Eddie?"

"I'm good, Joe."

"Well, then . . . I'll see you later on, okay?"

"Okay," Eddie said.

"Okay," Valerie said.

Joe moved away.

"Uh-oh," Eddie said.

"Don't worry about him. Of all people." She proceeded to feed him some gossip about Joe and the various hostesses and waitresses, how he hired them, bedded them, and then broke their hearts when he moved on to his next victim. "They just keep falling for him," she said.

"Some guys just got it," Eddie said.

"That's right," she said wisely. "Some guys do."

The band came onto the low stage and began working through their short instrumental set. Eddie knew it was time for her to go on. He didn't know what to say or do, and neither did she. There were customers around, some of whom had already treated them to cool stares.

"Okay, I have to go on now." She stepped away, then came back and squeezed his arm. "Don't leave yet," she said, and gave him a mysterious smile.

Ten minutes into the set, he found out why. The band finished a shuffling rendition of "Fever," and while the applause was still going on, she stepped away from the mike to whisper to each of the guys in the group. The piano player began an intro that Eddie recognized right away. The mournful sax was gone, but the melody was unmistakable. Valerie stepped to the mike, shielding her eyes from the lights. She saw him, dropped her hand, and began to sing.

Eddie, my love, I love you so
How I've waited for you, you'll never know
Please, Eddie, don't make me wait too long

She crooned it with a broad flair, almost clowning her way through the drippy lyrics.

Eddie, please, write me one line
Tell me your love is still only mine
Please, Eddie, don't make me wait too long

Joe sidled out of the darkness to stand by his side. Apparently, he got the joke, too, because he was grinning. "I guess you two made up, huh?" he said.

Eddie nodded. "Yeah, I guess so." It was a good thing it was dark; his face had turned tomato red by the time the band reached the bridge.

You left me last September
To return to me before long
But all I do is cry myself to sleep
Eddie, since you've been gone

The music swelled and she wailed the final verse.

Eddie, my love, I'm sick in bed,
The very next day may be my last
Please, Eddie, don't make me wait too long
Please, Eddie, don't make me wait too long

The diners at the tables and the men at the bar applauded. Eddie and Joe joined in. Valerie bowed her head in his direction as the band launched into the opening bars of "Heartaches."

Eddie leaned against the wall, trying to wipe the smile off his face. After a moment he felt Joe's searching gaze on him. "What?" he said.

Joe raised his hands. "It's none of my business, okay? Except that I know the both of you and . . ."

"And what?"

Joe held Eddie's eyes, suddenly serious. "And I think you better be careful, that's all."

TWENTY-ONE

Eddie came awake in the dead of night with the echo of a song playing in his head. The moon had cast a silver oblong through the window and across the bed.

In the dream they were standing on the sidewalk outside the Blue Door and she was trying to tell him something, but she was speaking in a language he couldn't understand. Frustrated that she couldn't get through, her face tightened up in anger and her eyes blazed. She raised a furious hand, then turned and hurried off, disappearing into the darkness of the lonely street.

He closed his eyes in the hope that he could summon her back. It was no use; the dark tableau was gone, and she with it. He wondered if she was now going to be haunting his nights, too, and decided that he wouldn't mind. A cloud passed across the moon, the shadows returned, and he let sleep pull him down once more.

He turned onto Twenty-sixth Street and pulled around the corner to park on Alter Avenue. The Ford belched and rattled ominously.

The door of the church stood open on this bright morning,

and he stepped inside to find Reverend Gates seated in the front row of chairs, his head bent meditatively.

He took a couple steps down the aisle. "Reverend Gates?" The preacher didn't turn around. Eddie moved up beside him. "Reverend Gates?"

With a shocked shout, he took a stumbling step to the side and grabbed the back of one of the folding chairs for balance.

The preacher was sitting there with his eyes open, staring down at nothing. Blossoms of dried blood had spread from the two black holes in the front of his white shirt. Eddie had no doubt that the man before him was dead; he could feel the same strange absence around the body that he felt when they brought his father's corpse out of the mill, the empty vacuum of a house long vacant.

As much as he needed to run for help, he stood staring with horrible fascination at the reverend's still-gentle visage. Some moments passed and he crossed himself, something he hadn't done in years. Then he backed away and made a hurried exit for the street.

He dialed the pay phone on the next corner with a shaking finger. After Sal listened to him stutter it out, he said, "Sonofabitch! You sure he's dead?"

"I'm sure," Eddie said. His head got light as he conjured Gates's dead eyes again. "Oh, man . . . now someone got him, too!"

"All right, take it easy," Sal said. "Just wait there. I'll call it in."

The first car slid to the curb and the siren wound down. Two black patrolmen swung out, and one of them stepped up purposefully to ask Eddie if he was the one who found the body. The cop jotted down his name and stood by while his partner went inside to secure the scene. Within a minute, a second patrol car raced around the corner and pulled up, tires screeching. Right behind it came an unmarked sedan. The doors opened and Detective Al Nash and another detective—this one tall, thin, and white—stepped out.

"Didn't expect to be seeing you so soon," Nash said. He took Eddie by the arm and steered him inside the church doorway.

"This happened because of Johnny Pope," Eddie blurted.

Nash, watching his face, said, "You sure about that?"

"This one was in the group, too. That's two in a week." He was assailed by a sickening flush of shame. "This is my fault," he murmured.

They took chairs in the last row so that Eddie could tell the cop what little he knew. It didn't matter; he was in a daze and barely heard the detective's questions.

Meanwhile, Nash's partner went about examining the body. Eddie dreaded being in the room with Reverend Gates and was relieved when, after ten minutes, Nash let him go. The cop said he'd catch up with him at the office if he had anything else.

Eddie had just reached the sidewalk and fresh air when he heard a scream and turned to see a woman lurching along the sidewalk.

"Thomas!" she wailed. She let out a heartbroken sob. "Oh, God, no!"

She weaved toward the doors of the church. One of the patrolmen stepped up, and she collapsed in his arms.

Sal was waiting for him. "Sit," he said. Eddie sat. "You want a drink?" Eddie nodded, and Sal pulled out his bottle and a glass and poured a good inch of Seagram's. Eddie snatched it up and drank it down in one swallow. "Take it easy," Sal said, and poured another inch.

Eddie took a smaller swallow. He was starting to feel sick again. "He was just sitting there *dead.* Jesus!"

"I know, it's a hell of a thing the first time." Sal leaned on the edge of his desk. "Tell me about it. The door was open?"

"He left it open."

"Then it could have been a random thing. Some street—"

"It wasn't random, Sal. None of this is."

"Yeah, well, you gotta consider the possibilities." Fixing an envious eye on the glass in Eddie's hand, he said, "Who knew you were talking to him?"

Eddie took another short sip and forced himself to think, casting his memory back step by step to the scene at Ray's grave site.

"Anybody at the cemetery could have seen when he came up to me. But . . ."

"But what?"

Eddie stared down into the amber swirling in the glass, entertaining the chilling thought that only one person knew for a fact he was going to talk to the preacher.

"What's wrong with you?" Sal was watching him closely.

Eddie downed the whiskey. "I talk to Ray, and he's murdered. I talk to Gates, and he's murdered. That's what's wrong." Eddie saw the look on Sal's face and said, "What?"

"All the members of that group are dead. Except for one."

Eddie sat, his thoughts in a spin. What if her sweet kindness, her smiles and her eyes, her "Eddie My Love," were all part of a ruse to throw him off her trail?

He didn't buy it; or maybe it was *wouldn't.*

"She couldn't do it, Sal."

"Okay, maybe not alone. There any chance she could be in cahoots with someone?"

"No. No chance. I'm sure."

"Well, I'm not." The detective straightened and went around the desk. "I'll call the precinct and see what I can find out. You going to be all right?"

Eddie gave a brief nod, and Sal went into the front office. Momentarily, he heard the detective muttering into the phone.

He sat there, feeling numb as he recalled Tommy Gates's body in detail as if he was viewing a photograph. The preacher had been sitting stiffly, his head tilted forward and to one side, his arms draped down and his hands resting on the chairs on either side. His eyes had been half closed, as though he was dozing through some other preacher's sermon. His deep black skin was taking on an ashen tinge.

Eddie pushed the picture away, trying to keep his brain from reeling off its rails. Two lives had been snuffed out in a matter of days, and he had played a part in both. No, it was worse: They were his fault. Ray Pope and Tommy Gates were murdered to keep them from telling him something.

What was it? A secret? The *truth*, as Ray had whispered?

He wanted to call Valerie to tell her about Gates and warn her to be careful. So then she could tell him she was not involved, no matter how suspicious it looked, that she hadn't lured him into a wicked game, and that the innocence in her dark eyes was real.

There was no way he could do that; Sal would go through the roof. And truth be told, if he sat there and walked through it calmly, she would make a good suspect. Maybe she was bewitching him to cover her crimes. As far as he knew, there was no law against lying to Eddie Cero.

And yet it didn't feel right. He had seen her face soften when she talked about her little girl. She had laid gentle fingers on his damaged brow. She had played a sweet, private joke on him at the Blue Door. He could not in his wildest imagination picture her pumping bullets into her cousin Ray or her dear friend Tommy Gates. Or doing any other evil, for that matter.

Sal, on the other hand, would tell him that anyone was capable of anything. Even Valerie Pope.

The call ended and the detective stepped into the doorway. "Right now they don't have a whole lot more," he reported. "They're checking to see if it was the same weapon used on Ray Pope. They were both .22s. Probably the same one."

"It was," Eddie said.

"No witnesses so far. It looks like whoever did it got away clean." He watched Eddie for a few seconds. "You remember we were going to see Hayner?"

"Yeah, right." Eddie got to his feet.

"Why don't we forget about that for now."

"No, I want to do it," Eddie said.

"You sure? 'Cause I can go alone."

"I'm sure," Eddie said. "We need to ring his bell. Especially after this."

"Okay, fine," Sal said. "But why don't you take a few more minutes? Catch your breath."

Eddie shook his head. The last thing he wanted was to sit around replaying the scene at the church in his head another dozen times. "No, I'm ready now."

The building was on the corner of Sixth and Walnut, near the heart of Center City. Sal stopped in the middle of the sidewalk, leaned his head back to take in all thirty-six granite stories, and said, "It's a fucking tombstone."

They rode the elevator to the twenty-fifth floor. Sal saw Eddie's glazed expression and put a hand on his shoulder. "I can do this myself," he said.

Eddie said, "I'll be all right."

"Okay, then." Sal released his grip. The doors opened, and they stepped into the lobby of Norwood Investigations.

The furnishings were blandly conservative, heavy, austere grays and browns. Men and women passed by, well dressed in business attire and speaking in hushed tones. The broad window behind the receptionist's desk looked out on Independence Mall.

It reminded Eddie of a bank, so elegant that it made the office on Sansom Street look like the toilet at the bus station by comparison.

Sal announced his name and asked for Donald Hayner. The stiff-backed woman at the desk asked if they had an appointment.

"We don't," Sal told her. "But he'll see us, if he's got any brains."

The receptionist nodded her head mechanically, as if she hadn't caught a word he'd said or the rough tone. Eddie saw the ripple of a smile pass across Sal's face and knew the detective was considering asking the woman if there was any place in the neighborhood where a fellow might get laid, just to see if he could crack her porcelain cover.

Whatever the urge, Sal let it pass. He jammed his hands in his trouser pockets and waited. The woman spoke on the telephone for a few seconds, then told them to have a seat.

They waited twenty minutes. Sal whispered that Hayner was no doubt using some of the time to call Roddy.

"Mr. Hayner will see you now." The receptionist nodded in the direction of the corridor. "Down the hall. Second door on the right."

They walked in. Sal stopped, looked around, and whistled appreciatively. It was some office.

Don Hayner looked up from behind a heavy walnut desk. He was in his midfifties, thin, and a little bent, his silver hair slicked back. He had small, mean eyes and a thin-lipped mouth. The skin of his face was the mottled pink of a man who spent too much time indoors. He was holding a cigarette in the fingers of one hand and a bottle of 7UP in the other.

"Well, well," he sneered by way of greeting. "Sal Giambroni. What a nice surprise."

Sal gave him a pleasant smile and settled into one of the plush chairs with a grunt of pleasure.

Eddie snapped out of his daze. He stared at Hayner for a second, then stepped directly to the end of the desk.

Hayner drew away, blew an angry little plume of smoke, and said, "Back it up, sonny." Eddie didn't move. "I said, back it up, jerk-off."

"Now, now, be nice," Sal said gently. "A man in your position don't need to be cracking wise."

"Oh, yeah?" Hayner's eyes slid sideways and his thin lips stretched. "What position is that?"

"Tommy Gates is dead," Eddie told him. "He was murdered. This morning. Or maybe last night."

Hayner jerked around. It took him a half second to recover. "Who?"

"Who?" Sal snickered. "You're a cute one, Donny," he said. "You always were."

Hayner's face flushed. "Fuck you." He shot a look at Eddie. "And I told you to get away from the desk." Eddie stayed where he was. "Sal, tell this punk to get the fuck away from my damn *desk*."

Sal held up his hands. "I'm not telling him nothing. He's having a bad day."

Eddie started inching closer. "What happened to him?" he said.

Hayner frowned in annoyance. "To who, Gates?"

"To Johnny Pope."

"Pope?" The mottled brow stitched. "I don't remember nothin' about that."

"Sure, you do," Sal said easily. "I bet you remember everything about it. Now, my associate just asked you a question, and we'd both appreciate an answer."

Hayner stubbed out his cigarette and slouched down in his chair.

"All right, yeah, I know what happened to him," he said, putting his sneer back in place. "He was the victim of a crime. Some niggers jumped him for his cash and his watch and then dumped his body in the goddamn river. That's all. It only happens every fucking day. That one was three years ago. So what the hell is this?"

Eddie leaned over confidentially. "That's not a very polite word," he said.

"What isn't?" Hayner huffed and puffed for a few tortured seconds. "What word?" Eddie kept staring at him. "All right, *Negroes*. Jesus!" He let out an angry breath. "Now you want to tell me what the fuck you guys want?"

"Let's hear it, Don." Sal sounded patient.

Hayner did not look happy. He muttered, "Okay, goddamnit. What I remember is that he disappeared, and nobody saw nothing, nobody knew nothing, so we dropped it. It wasn't like we let somebody walk on it."

"We?" Sal said.

"All right, me," Hayner said. "I was the lead. Nash wanted to work it, but I told him to let it be. There was no body, no evidence, nothing. The goddamn thing was cold ten minutes after it happened. We had other cases."

Sal stood up and sidled over to the front of the desk. Hayner was cornered, and he crossed his arms to hide his discomfort.

"What did Roddy offer you to drop it?" Eddie asked him.

Hayner turned his head slowly. "I ain't even going to fucking answer that. You heard what I said. It would have come out the same way. The guy was dead and gone. Period."

"We need something on him, Don," Sal said.

Hayner's head turned the other way. "He's my client."

Sal's face got red. "He's going to be your fucking cellmate if you don't start helping us out here!"

Hayner tried snorting in derision. It didn't quite work, and Sal tilted his head thoughtfully.

"You drop a case for some citizen," he said. "Then you retire and end up working a sweet job in a new office for the same guy's PI agency. Three years go by, and he needs your help again—on the exact same case that got you here in the first place. And the next thing you know, there's two bodies on the street."

Hayner shrugged. "So who says there's a connection?"

"Anybody with half a fucking brain, that's who!" Sal was yelling again. "Of course they're connected, you moron!"

"Well, who—"

"Your fucking client, that's who!"

Eddie came at him from the other side. "Why does he have you tailing me?"

Hayner glanced over his shoulder. "None of your goddamn business. I mean it's confiden—"

"You know he hired someone to murder Pope."

"He what?"

"Only it didn't happen."

"It didn't?" Now Hayner looked confused.

"Never mind that," Sal said. "The point is, he hired someone to do the job."

"Who says it was him?"

"Who else would it be?" Sal snapped. "Pope was going to leave his record label. There goes the money tree."

The gears were grinding behind Hayner's small eyes. Eddie couldn't tell if he was buying what he'd thrown out about Roddy or not, and he didn't want to give him time to think about it.

"What about Mieux?" he said.

"What about him?" Hayner said.

"You hired him to follow me?"

Now Hayner's mouth curved into a surly smile. "I got news for you, pal. There are places in this city a white man don't go." He paused to let it sink in. "I saw you and him in front of that nig—" This time he caught himself. "That colored joint."

"The Domino."

"Yeah. So I talked to him. Since you were hanging around down on South Street, I needed someone who fit in. And he wanted the job." He looked at Sal, his jaw stiffening with impatience. "Are we done now?"

"No, we're not done," Sal said. "We ain't even getting started. And I wouldn't be so fucking smug if I was you, Don. You hired him and he looks pretty good for these two homicides."

Hayner said, "I didn't have—"

"Shut the fuck up and listen," Sal said. "He's your guy. Which means we got you by the balls here." He stopped to shake his head in wonder. "What the hell were you thinking? He's a fucking mental case."

"Well, how was I to know that?" Hayner crabbed. "These dumb fucking"—he glanced at Eddie—"*Negroes*. All he was supposed to do was get the word around that nobody talks."

"Well, I guess he's ambitious," Sal said. "He made sure the two of them ain't ever going to talk. And we can make a case for you as an accessory."

Hayner's eyes got hard. "Shit. Prove it."

"We won't need to *prove* it," Sal said with a rough laugh. "I'll tell you right now, this fucker's starting to leak all over the place. You think Mieux wouldn't flip on you? Or this Roddy character?" He put an impish hand to the side of his face. "Oops. I'd say you're going to eat it, pal."

Hayner shifted in his chair, cleared his throat, blinked nervously a few times.

Sal said, "Going once, going twice, go—"

"Hey, fuck you, all right?" He tried blustering again. "I said I didn't have nothing to do with it." He drew himself up haughtily. "And as far as this job goes, forgive the hell out of me for taking advantage, so that maybe I could be something besides a tired old cop on a lousy pension." One eyebrow hiked. "Or some run-down, piece-of-shit gumshoe."

Sal grunted something, and his hand shot out to grab Hayner by the front of his shirt and drag him up out of his chair. Hayner gritted his teeth and tried to struggle as Sal held him hanging halfway over the desk. His face went dark pink as the detective pulled him closer.

Sal jerked his head at Eddie and said, "This guy right here never spent one day on the force, for chrissakes, he got most of the damn case put together just by staying on it. You, you worthless prick, you were a police officer. A detective. You could have closed it. Now it's three years later, and there's two more people dead."

Eddie saw the crazy glitter in Sal's eyes and stepped closer to wrap a hand around the thick wrist.

"Sal," he said. Sal still held on tight. "C'mon, let it go."

Sal released his grip and dropped Hayner back into his chair. He made a rude sound, turned around abruptly, and stalked out of the office.

Hayner stared at the doorway. "Fucking asshole. If he—"

Eddie slapped him, a hard backhand across the mouth. It knocked him sideways in his chair, and his little eyes bulged with rage. He started to come around. Then he saw the look on Eddie's face and stayed put.

"Sorry," Eddie said. "It's just that you haven't been very helpful."

Hayner touched a finger to his swelling lip and said, "Shit."

"Do you know anything about the girl?" Eddie said.

"What girl?"

"The singer from the group. Johnny's sister. Valerie Pope."

"No, I don't know nothin' about her," Hayner muttered. "Why?"

"Never mind. Is there anything else you want to tell me about Roddy?"

"I can tell you he's not somebody you want to fuck with."

"Is that right?" Eddie said. "What do you think he'd do? Send Mieux after me?"

Sal was waiting down the hall. They walked through the lobby and waited for the elevator in silence. As soon as the doors closed, Sal grinned and said, "Well? Now what? Does he call Roddy again?"

"He's calling him right now," Eddie said. "And he'll tell him what I said about the contract on Pope."

"That's what a good detective would do. See what he'll say. Play him, you know?" The detective snickered. "If Roddy's guilty, he'll be shitting his britches, wondering what you got on him. No telling what he'll do next." He eyed Eddie. "So, listen: As long as that fucking Mieux's on the loose, you watch your back."

"I can handle him."

Sal jabbed a finger. "Hey. Johnny Pope was murdered. Ray Pope and the preacher were murdered. You want to be next in line?"

"It's all right, Sal."

They didn't exchange a word the rest of the way down to the lobby. When the elevator stopped and the doors opened, Sal noticed the look Eddie was giving him and said, "What?"

"That was some show you put on up there."

Sal shrugged. "Yeah, well, I've had a lot of practice." He treated Eddie to a judicious glance in return. "Actually, you didn't do too bad yourself."

When they got back to the office, Sal cut a direct path to his desk. Eddie heard the drawer open and the familiar sounds of glass tinkling and liquid pouring. The detective was still pouring when the phone rang.

"Gee, I wonder who that is?" he called out.

Eddie picked up the receiver, expecting to be greeted by George Roddy's angry growl. What he heard instead was an urgent, whispery breath. "Eddie? It's Candy Ralston. I just heard about Tommy Gates. That's awful!"

"Yeah, it is."

"I need to see you. Can you meet me?" She sounded a little desperate.

"When?"

"Tonight at . . . at seven thirty."

"Where?"

"At 45 Studios. It's on Morris Street, down near the—"

"I know where it is."

"Don't come to the street door," she said. "Go around back and up to the rear entrance."

"I've been there."

"Oh. Well, then you go up to the first landing. It's the back door to the studio. I'll leave it open. Just come inside. I'll be waiting for you."

"Do you have the contract?"

"There isn't any contract," she said, losing the whisper. "Don't worry, I'll have something even better for you."

"We can't just meet at a bar?"

"No, that won't work."

"Won't work why?"

She had an answer ready. "Because I can't be seen with you. And there's a reason it has to be the studio. You'll understand when you get there." She allowed a dramatic pause and her voice got kittenish. "I think I can give you what you need, Eddie."

"And what do you want out of this?"

"I want a promise that I won't get into any trouble," she said, sounding panicked again.

"All right." He was lying; he couldn't keep anyone out of anything.

"Seven thirty," she said. "Don't worry, it'll be worth your while."

He put the phone down and went in to repeat the conversation to Sal.

"It sounds like a setup," the detective said. "Hayner calls

Roddy; Roddy tells his piece to dangle something under your nose. It's bait."

"I figured that when she said it had to be at the studio."

Sal sipped his drink. "*Me dispiac'.*"

"But if they were going to try something, wouldn't they pick another place?"

"You mean a dump over in Jersey?"

"Yeah, like that." Eddie started talking faster. "She was straight with me about the contract, right? Maybe she's figured out that we're getting close. Maybe she knows it's coming apart and wants to deal. You said she might roll on him. You said that."

"All right, settle down."

"That's right, isn't it?"

"Yeah, I said that."

"So I'm going."

"And I'm coming with you."

"You can't," Eddie said. "It'll spook her." Sal was giving him one of his looks, so he said, "I'll be careful, all right? It's my deal. I'll handle it."

Sal mulled it over as he finished his drink. He put down his glass and said, "Hey, really, I'll come with you. Whaddya say?"

"No, this one's mine," Eddie said. He turned to the window. The sun was going down.

Eddie drove along Columbus Boulevard and parked the car near the corner of Tasker. Except for the streetlights and the window of a corner grocery two blocks farther on, the street was dark. The hulls of tugboats groaned against pilings, heavy chains clanked hollowly, and he could hear the forlorn, faraway fog-horns of the freighters, like the mournful cries of lovers out on the waters of that lonely river.

Heeding Sal's last-minute instructions, he ducked into a doorway a block up from the building to watch the street. Other than the odd passing car, nothing was moving. He waited a long five minutes, then came out of the doorway, walked past the building, and stepped into another doorway on the diagonal corner. He watched from the shadows there until he heard the bells of Old Swedes' Church toll seven thirty.

A quick shot across the street, and he made his way up the entranceway, alert for any strange sound, ready in case someone was waiting for him in the darkness. As someone likely had for Johnny Pope.

It was so still and silent that he was imagining noises and seeing shadows flit about. He skirted the perimeter of the cobblestone lot and made a quick climb up creaking metal stairs. When he reached the landing, he stopped to look down into the courtyard. Nothing moved.

The steel door was unlocked, just as Candy had promised, and he stepped through it and into a dim storeroom with only the light of the city night behind him and the glow that outlined a door that led into the studio to illuminate it. Boxes were stacked against the walls on both ends of the room and an unused desk had been shoved into a corner.

Eddie stopped again to listen. Music was playing softly on the other side of the door.

Just as he grabbed the doorknob and tugged, he heard a metallic squeak, and with it came the thought that he'd been too eager for the prize and slipped up. The door was locked and he was cornered. Sal would have his head.

"Well, look who's here. Yes'suh. And right on time."

Eddie was barely surprised to turn and find T-Bone Mieux blocking the outside doorway. The Creole was wearing blue jeans and sneakers, a black T-shirt, and a thin cotton jacket. He was smiling.

"Guess I caught you trespassin' on private property," he said. He flexed his corded arms one time across his chest and took a prowling step inside the room, shifting into his fighter's stance, though his hands had dropped to his sides. Just as automatically, Eddie settled, getting ready. He'd only done it a thousand times.

Mieux, as usual, went on talking. "You been causin' trouble, boy," he said. "Uh-huh. Well, that's gon' stop. We gon' finish all o' that right now."

Eddie lifted his hands and waved him in. "Come on, then, you fucking punk cocksucker."

Mieux's eyes flashed and his right hand snaked around his back. It was supposed to be one smooth move: the step forward, the snapping of the pistol, and the shot to the chest. But Eddie saw it and was ready and stepped in to hook a fast pinpoint right into Mieux's wristbone.

The gun flipped out of the Creole's grasp and went clattering against the wall. Mieux stopped to blink at it in momentary surprise. Then he grinned, cool and lazy, and said, "Well, yeah, we can do it another way." He was still grinning when Eddie let one go, a left that landed flush on his mouth.

Mieux jerked back, blood spurting from his split lip. "Motherfucker!" He wiped the blood with the back of his hand and charged in swinging.

For the next thirty seconds, the only sounds in the room were the dull splats of flesh smacking flesh, raw curses, and animal grunts. Eddie had him going; he split the Creole's lip open in another place, bloodied his nose, and caught him with a hard jab that started his right eye puffing. Though his hands were throbbing, he thought that he could put him down with one clean shot.

But then the Creole tucked his head and waded in close, throwing overhand rights that banged the side of Eddie's skull, doing little damage but moving him back a step at a time. Eddie felt his heel touch the inside door as Mieux used his shoulders and elbows to keep him pinned. A left uppercut came through and whacked his jaw, and he saw flashes of light as the room took a crazy tilt. He knew if he took another one he'd be in trouble, so he bent down and pulled his arms in to cover. Denied the head, Mieux switched to rabbit punching, planting his feet and laying heavy shots on the back of his rib cage. One caught him clean over the liver, and he had to straighten up to ease the cramping pain.

It was then he saw that the Creole's eyes had turned to black glass, and he understood that Mieux wasn't going to stop until he was dead. The spike of fear brought a sour, burning taste to his mouth and froze him where he stood.

Mieux sent another hook to the ribs and then came in with a shot over Eddie's eye, and the brown knuckles turned suddenly slick with blood. A second shot opened the old cut and produced a burst of red and a shock of pain, and Eddie felt like he was being pushed over the edge of a cliff and into a bottomless well.

The moment seemed to last for a few minutes. And then something snapped, and the harsh rage he had buried so long ago came roaring out, a sudden, racing ball of fire that blew everything out of its path.

Mieux had just taken a step back to get the leverage to finish the job when a furious flurry caught him looking and slapped his head back. Eddie's brain unlocked, and he slid a half step to the side, threw out his right, and caught Mieux a glancing blow to the cheek. The Creole was still grappling with the fact that his opponent wasn't done when he ate a machine-gun combination, three lefts in a row, all on the side of the jaw. He tried to duck inside just as Eddie brought a right hook that came from Jersey.

It banged flush on the cheekbone, and Mieux's head jerked and wobbled. When the Creole pulled up his forearm to cover, Eddie threw a straight left right down the pipe that flattened his nose and sent out a red mist. The left that came behind it bashed his jaw, and his eyes rolled and legs buckled. When he backed up, trying to find the door, Eddie went with him, the punches now coming a wink slower but much harder. A wave of furious blood went washing through his brain, and he was ready to commit murder.

Then he caught Mieux a hard uppercut, the same punch that had knocked Willie Allred cold. The lights went out, the Creole dropped, and as suddenly as it had come on, Eddie's dark, sick rage was gone. He staggered around the bloody, broken body on the floor to crumple against the doorjamb, choking for breath.

Mieux was spewing blood and the contents of his stomach, moaning between the spasms. Eddie staggered and almost toppled over as the smell of blood and vomit churned his stomach. He pushed the door open and leaned there for a few seconds, drinking in the night air.

The nausea passed and he shuffled across the room like some crippled old man. Blood was dripping in his eye, and he held the palm of one hand on his slashed brow to stanch it. He crept around until he found Mieux's pistol. From what little he knew about guns, it looked about right for a .22. He pushed open the chamber, dumped the bullets into his palm, and pitched them and the pistol through the doorway and over the steel railing.

The Creole was out, breathing with strangled, gurgling groans. Standing over him, Eddie tasted adrenaline in his throat, strangely bitter. With it came a tingle of exhilaration that he was still on his feet.

Though barely so. He limped out the door and down the metal steps, holding the railing for support. Making his way across the courtyard and along the alleyway was easier, though he still winced with every step.

At the end of the driveway, he stopped and poked his head around the corner of the building to see the red taillights of a car that hadn't been there before, an ivory Plymouth Fury. He caught a glimpse of the driver's profile and cursed under his breath. There was no cover, so he hobbled across the street as quickly as he could, gritting his teeth against the pain, hoping the driver wouldn't see him and burn rubber. He made it, jerking open the passenger door and dropping into the seat with a noisy breath.

At the sound of the door opening, Candy's head snapped around. When she realized it was Eddie, her red mouth went up and down mutely. She spent a few seconds in an almost comical shock and confusion before she managed to recover.

"What do you think you're doing?" Her voice took a shrill swoop.

"We had a date, remember?" He had to gasp out the words.

She didn't think it was funny. "You get out of the car right—"

"Shut up."

Her eyes went wide, all but glowing in the dark. "I'm going to go call a cop if you don't get out right now!" She grabbed her door handle. Her wild gaze went bouncing around the street for someone to save her.

"Go ahead," Eddie said. "Do that."

Their stares locked for a few seconds. She blinked first. "Okay, look, it wasn't my idea," she said in a blurted rush. "I just did what I was told." Her tone changed to a whine. "Please. I don't want to get into trouble."

"You're already in trouble."

"But I didn't *do* anything!" Now she sounded like she was going to start wailing.

"Okay, calm down," Eddie said, and settled back. Candy grabbed the steering wheel to steady her hands. "You all right?"

She nodded and whispered, "I think so."

"How about we get out of here? Can we do that?"

"Yes, okay . . ."

He waved a hand. "Get over on Front Street."

"Okay." Her fingers fumbled with the keys. Before she pulled out, she took a glance back at the 45 Studios building. "What about . . . ?"

"Don't worry about him," Eddie said. "Just go."

She steered into the street, and he let out a gasp at the first bump. She said, "Sorry," and slowed down.

Once they got under the streetlights, he saw that she was wearing a pretty off-white cotton dress. Her makeup was perfect, as if she had gotten dolled up for a night out. At the same time, her face seemed to be cracking into jagged pieces. She kept licking her painted lips, and her shadowed eyes blinked furiously as she maneuvered the sedan around the corner.

"Okay, what's your part?" he said.

She hesitated, trying to decide how much or how little to give him. "I was told to come down and unlock the outside door," she said. "Then I was supposed to wait in the car. That colored boy would show up, and when it was over, I had some money to give him."

"How much money?"

"A hundred dollars."

Eddie was stunned. "That's what my life's worth? A hundred goddamn dollars?"

"It wasn't like that," she said. "I mean, it wasn't supposed to be. He was just going to talk to you. And make you stop what you were doing."

"Yeah, well, Mr. Mieux doesn't follow instructions very well. What's he hiding?"

"Who?"

"Your boss," Eddie said. "The one who set this up. Him."

"I don't know," she said too quickly. "I was just doing—"

"—doing what you were told. Right." She turned onto Second Street, heading west. "Find a police station," he said.

"Do what?"

"You can take your chances with the cops."

She swerved suddenly to the curb and hit the brakes, bouncing him off the dashboard. He let out a yelp of pain. She opened the door as if she was going to jump, and for a second he thought he had blown it.

Then she pulled the door closed and placed her hands back on the steering wheel. "I don't know very much about it. Really."

Though it was poor soap-opera agony, he sensed that she was telling the truth. "Okay, forget it. Let's get moving." She put the car in gear and pulled back into the street. "Will you tell me what you do know?" he said, keeping his tone steady.

She was quiet, considering, and held out until they reached Christian Street, where he told her to take a left. As they turned the corner, her eyes flicked slyly in his direction, and he knew he had her.

It had started about two weeks before, she began, when Roddy threw a raging fit over the news that some stranger was nosing around and asking questions about Johnny Pope's disappearance.

"He heard from who?" Eddie said.

"It was getting around. Then Ron called and he—"

"Who's Ron?"

"Fat Cat. That's his real name."

"Oh," Eddie said. It had never occurred to him to collect that bit of information.

"He and George used to, you know . . ."

"Do business?"

"That's right." This didn't surprise him; the DJ would no doubt be happy to play for whoever paid. It also explained the *don't fuck with this* comment. Fat Cat wouldn't want the payola coming back to haunt him, so he had probably picked up the phone the minute Eddie had walked out of the booth.

Candy said that once Roddy learned Eddie's name, he gave instructions that he was never in when he called. Meanwhile, he got in touch with Don Hayner, who owed him favors, and the ex-cop reported back that Eddie had talked to both Valerie and Eugene White, and had been looking for Ray Pope at the Domino Lounge.

"And the next thing we know, Ray's dead."

"George said it was just one of those things. It was bound to happen."

"And you believed it."

She didn't answer.

"It was probably your friend Mieux back there who did it," Eddie said. "And after that, it was Tommy Gates's turn. Because he talked to me, too."

She stopped at the red light at Tenth Street and stared ahead, looking genuinely saddened. "I really liked Tommy," she murmured.

"Yeah, well, your boss felt otherwise," Eddie said.

He let her chew on that while he pieced together what she had told him so far.

Mieux must have seen him coming out of the Domino that Saturday night and went inside to ask around. Of course, he heard about the loud scene with Ray Pope. On Hayner's orders, he warned Ray to keep his mouth shut. But Ray wasn't the type to listen. Once Leona threw him out, Mieux could have easily followed him. Another confrontation in the alley and another threat. Eddie could imagine Ray telling Mieux to go fuck himself and Mieux responding with two angry shots from his pistol. Or maybe the Creole had orders to get Ray to shut up, whatever it took. How Mieux had gotten mixed up in it in the first place was a puzzle that would have to wait.

Ray's death caused Gates to have a change of heart, evidence of which was witnessed by George Roddy at the cemetery. Yes, and Valerie, too, he reminded himself. In any case, Mieux must have gone to see the preacher. And so two men had been killed to keep them from revealing something.

The light turned green and Candy drove on. "What's the big secret?" he said.

She frowned. "The what?"

"Ray and Tommy are dead because they both knew something," he said. "What was it?"

"I told you everything I know."

They came up on the lights of Broad Street at City Park and, in the light of the streetlamp, she saw the cool way he was looking at her. Her gaze shifted away.

He decided to make it easier for her. "Johnny wanted to leave StarLite because Roddy was stealing from him, right?"

"Not just him," she said after a moment. "From all of them. It had been going on a long time. Johnny was just the first one to find out. So he decided to leave. And that was bad news."

"Because Johnny was his star act."

"No. I mean, yes. That was only part of it." They came to a stop at the next light. "George gambled and he owed a lot of money. But he couldn't pay, so he went to loan sharks to get the money. Then he got in too deep with them. He gave almost everything he had away. The only thing he had left that was worth anything was Johnny's contract. So he, uh, gave them that, too."

Eddie cocked an ear. "He did what?"

"He signed over Johnny's contract to those men he owed," Candy said. "As a guarantee that he would pay them. If he didn't give back the money, then Johnny would end up belonging to them. So they were, y'know . . ."

"Partners." Eddie stared out the window, hearing the click of one large piece of the puzzle falling into place. "Cannoli," he said. "And zabaglione."

"What?"

"Never mind." They continued west. So Roddy had been using Pope's contract as a marker. Which meant that if Johnny didn't renew, that marker would be pretty much worthless, and Roddy could easily end up very dead. "Found out how?"

"What?"

"How did Johnny find out Roddy was cheating him?" Eddie

said, and immediately noticed a strange tension on her face. "Did you tell him?"

"It just wasn't fair," she said. "Johnny was everything to StarLite. And George just stole from him. He would print records and not tell Johnny and sell them to try and pay off his gambling debts. It wasn't *fair.*"

The repeated word quivered out of her mouth, and Eddie stared at her. "You and Pope." Another piece dropped onto the table. "You had something going with him." Her eyes settled dazedly on the street ahead. "You were screwing him."

She winced. "I wasn't *screwing* him. He and I were . . . we were . . ."

"Were what?" Eddie said. "What? In love?"

She either missed or ignored the sarcastic edge in his voice. "George told me to be nice to him," she said. "So I could find out what he was up to."

"And were you nice to him?"

"It wasn't like that," she said. "It started out that way, but . . ." She swallowed. "My feelings changed."

Eddie studied her for a moment, mulling this over. "Who else knew about you two?"

"Ray and Tommy. That's all. We kept it secret. My god, there are people out there who would kill a colored man for just looking at a white woman." She glanced at him and smiled tightly. "You should understand that."

The comment caught him off guard, and he was glad it was too dark for her to see his face. He pushed it aside and said, "How did you manage to keep Roddy from finding out?"

Her pretty mouth took a downward curve, and he saw a tear glisten at the corner of her eye.

He said, "Christ, you were fucking *both* of them?"

The look she gave him could have cut steel. The moment passed, and her expression turned dull. "It doesn't matter what I was doing or who I was doing it with," she said. "Not anymore."

"But he was your boss," Eddie said. "You didn't tell him what Johnny was up to?"

"I told him some things," she said quietly. "Just not everything."

Just like you're not telling me everything, Eddie reflected. Who knew how much of it was true? How much had Pope lied to her and how much was she now lying to him? She had tried to play the angles all along.

He watched the passing street, forgetting for the moment about his aching rib cage and pondering the mystery of women. It was clear to him that Candy Ralston was one of those clever females who went stupid when it came to the men in her life.

He turned back to regard her with more kindness and more respect. "When was the last time you saw Johnny?" he said.

"That Saturday night. The one just before."

"And you don't have any idea what happened that Sunday?"

"I don't."

He took some painful breaths and thought over what she had told him.

Roddy had discovered that Pope wasn't going to renew his contract. Candy might have told him, or maybe he just put two and two together. Either way, Johnny had to go, so that his songs and the Excels' records would continue to earn. It was the only way Roddy could hope to pay the bad guys and stay healthy. So he found "Gene," probably through his gambling contacts.

Then came the twist. Some other party stepped in and Johnny disappeared. When it was over and Roddy realized his problem had been solved, he went right back to stealing from his musicians and banging his sexy assistant. Eddie puzzled over how Candy could have kept servicing him, knowing what she did.

That question would have to wait. He directed her around the block at Eighteenth Street. Though he had a lot more information, there was still nothing he could pin on Roddy; and Candy hadn't shed a bit of light on what had happened on that final Sunday night.

"What about the tape?"

"What tape?" She gave him a blank look.

"Forget it." They turned onto Nineteenth Street and approached his building. "It's there on the left."

She pulled to the curb. He reached for the door handle. "Can I come in with you?" she said in a muted voice.

He produced a pained frown. "Do what?"

"Please," she said. "I'm scared."

"I don't think so."

Her face fell. "But I did what you wanted," she said.

"And I appreciate it." He clambered out to make his shuffling way through the glow of the headlights to the sidewalk.

She dropped a beseeching hand out her window. "What am I going to do now?" she said.

He stopped. "Get to a phone, call the cops, and tell them where to find Mieux. Then, I don't know, go somewhere. But stay away from Roddy."

She held his gaze with such a frightened look that he had to turn and hobble away before he changed his mind. He wondered if she would come after him, but as he reached the bottom of the steps, he heard the car pull away from the curb with a creak of tires.

It took him a long minute to make his way up the steps, across the porch, and into his apartment. He locked the door behind him. It occurred to him that Candy now knew where he lived, and he had just chased her away. She might decide to take her hurt feelings back to her boss. She had tried to hedge her bets, first with Johnny, then with Roddy, and with who knew who else along the way. She would hedge them now. If Roddy was going down, she wouldn't want to join him.

It didn't matter; if Hayner was any kind of detective, they already knew his address. And what would they do now, with Mieux out of commission? Did either one of them have the guts to do his own dirty work?

In the bathroom he used a washcloth to wipe the dried blood from his face, cleaned the cut as best he could, and slapped three Band-Aids on it. He stood over the toilet bowl, groaning with the pain. At least there was no blood.

He hobbled into the living room, stretched out on the couch, and lay still for ten minutes, letting the aches have their way. He had done it so many times before, and he could always tell if there was anything seriously wrong. Over all the years and all the rounds, his body had learned how to take a beating. This time he was just battered; and underneath the rough pain, he felt the giddy narcotic of having survived. No, not survived; he'd won. And not in a ring, where they rang a bell. This time it meant he would greet another day.

He lay still a few minutes more, then got up and went to the phone. She picked up on the third ring.

"It's Eddie," he said.

"Eddie . . ." Her voice sounded faint and distant. "Did you hear about Tommy?"

"I'm the one who found his body."

"Oh, my god! It's so horrible! It just can't be—"

"I need to talk to you."

She caught a breath. "Why, what's wrong?"

"Can you come over here?"

"Over where?"

"To my place."

"Are you all right? You sound awful."

"Can you come or not?"

"You mean now?"

"Yeah. It's not that far."

She was quiet for a few seconds. Then she said, "What's the address?"

When he opened the door, she gave a start and drew back. "My god, what happened to you?"

He tried to smile. "I got into a little scuffle."

She pointed at his brow. "You're bleeding."

He touched his forehead and felt the wetness seeping through the Band-Aids. Waving her inside, he closed the door. "I'll be right back," he said, and retreated into the bathroom.

She followed him and stood in the doorway. "You should let me do that," she said.

He almost told her, *No, don't bother,* but his forehead was throbbing and he was feeling a childish need to be tended. Obediently, he sat down on the edge of the bathtub. She placed the washcloth in the sink and began running warm water. Using gentle fingers, she peeled away the Band-Aids, now soaked pink.

"This is why you called me over here?" she said, trying for humor.

He wasn't in the mood. "I can do it," he said.

She paused for a second before pulling the last of the Band-Aids away. Peering at his brow with a mutter of disgust, she said, "Good lord." She used the washcloth to dab gently around the cut. "Who did this to you?"

"That guy Mieux? It was him. But he got the worst of it." He grimaced. "He was working for George Roddy."

She stopped what she was doing and drew back. "How do you know?"

"Candy Ralston told me."

"When?"

"She drove me home."

"Then it must be true what they say about her." It was another good line, but she wasn't smiling.

Neither was he. "Roddy set a trap," he said. "She called and said she had something for me. I went to meet her at the studio. When I got there, Mieux was waiting. He was supposed to shut me up. Just like he did Ray and Tommy."

Her expression remained composed as she laid the washcloth aside and used toilet paper to stanch the last trickle of blood. But her hand shook just a bit as she opened the first-aid kit.

Eddie said, "Candy was the woman he was hiding."

"She was?" She held a strip of tape in midair. He looked up to see her eyes had taken on a faraway cast, as if she had forgotten what she was doing.

"Hey," he said, and pointed to her still hand.

"Sorry." She went about placing a new bandage.

"She told me Roddy got in too deep with the mob guys and turned your recording contract over to them." He felt her fingers pressing the edges of the tape. "She's the one who told Johnny the Excels were being cheated, and that's when he decided to leave StarLite and start his own label. So Roddy had to stop him. And he was trying to. Only someone else fixed the problem first."

Valerie frowned distractedly. "But who told him Johnny was leaving?"

"Candy says it wasn't her. Maybe he did it." He glanced up at her. "He never talked about this?"

"No, never."

She took a step back to study her work. "That should be okay," she said. Closing the first-aid kit, she stepped out of the bathroom. He stood before the mirror. She'd done a nice job.

He found her in the living room. The streetlight through the front window had cleaved her face in two, and something stirred in the back of his mind and began to take shape, a muddled image coming into focus.

She turned to him. "Do you feel all right?"

The image blew away. "Yeah, I'm okay."

"Been through it before, huh?"

"Yeah, I have."

She was quiet for another moment. Then she said, "I better go."

He took a step toward her. "Don't go," he said. "Stay."

TWENTY-TWO

The sky had gone dark with clouds that had come down so low they threatened to swallow the tops of the tallest buildings. A curtain of rain was moving in from the southwest, turning the May dawn an eerie shade of electric green. Along the edge of the city, thunder rumbled and random lightning cracked.

Eddie felt a dull knob of pain and let out a groan. When he opened his eyes, he saw a swatch of milk-coffee skin entwined in white sheets, a shock of black hair and a shock of peroxide blond, a pink palm with the fingers curled slightly at the edge of the pillow. He smelled perfume and an earthier scent. Her body took a gentle rise with each deep breath.

He dozed, floating on a slow river. Time passed, and another rumble of thunder, this one closer, woke him again. He lay still a little while longer, then slipped from under the sheets and sat up, stiff and sore with a throbbing head. Standing gingerly, he made his way into the bathroom, where he washed down three aspirin with a palmful of tap water. A glance in the mirror showed that the bandage had held, stark white against the welts and bruises on his face and neck.

Back in the bedroom, he pulled the lone chair close to the

window and sat down to watch the storm move across the city while he retraced the night in small pieces.

Don't go, he had said. *Stay.*

She hadn't looked surprised. After regarding him for a pensive moment, she spoke his name, her voice soft and low, a note in another song sung just for him. With one hand on his biceps and the other arm around his waist, she guided him through the darkness and into the bedroom.

She stood by while he undressed down to his shorts and T-shirt, and helped him into bed. He was hurting too much to feel any shame. Once she got him settled, she went back into the front room. He'd heard her talking on the phone.

She was standing in the doorway. He couldn't make out the expression on her face. "I've got to go to work," she said.

"Come back after," he told her. "There's a key on a nail by the front door. Take it."

She stood there for a few seconds without speaking, then slipped away. He heard the door close and her footsteps in the hall. He hadn't been able to make himself get up to see if she had taken the key.

It had taken some time for him to fall into a fitful sleep, one that was visited by more odd images and words he couldn't understand. Now a stranger with veiled features muttered before drifting back into the darkness.

It was after midnight when he came awake to the sound of a scraping in the lock. In that brief second, he imagined her turning the key over to a goon who had come back to finish what Mieux had started. Then he heard the hushed sounds of her moving about and putting her things down: her coat, her keys, and a purse.

She was silhouetted in the doorway again, looking his way, as if searching for something. He could sense her indecision. It took some minutes for her to make up her mind and cross to his chest of drawers, where she rummaged about. Eddie realized what she was doing and smiled.

She stepped into the bathroom, and when she reemerged a few minutes later, he saw that she had donned a pair of his sweatpants and one of his old and worn soft sweatshirts, with the sleeves cut back.

In slow motion she stretched out next to him. She laid her head on the pillow and touched gentle fingers to his face. She whispered, "Poor baby," sighed, and closed her eyes.

Eddie drifted down the same gentle river, then woke a third time, this time by the sound of tapping at his front door. In his half-awake jumble of thoughts, he imagined someone coming to do him harm or the police sent by Candy Ralston, and his next thought was how he would explain Valerie in his bed. Another knock, this one fainter. Then he heard footsteps moving off and got up to stand by the window in time to see Susie climb into a taxi. The cab rolled away, carrying her off into the night.

He crawled into the bed and fell into a dreamless sleep, but before he went off, a sudden nagging thought had come to him: Valerie wasn't afraid. Johnny, Ray, and Tommy had been murdered, she was the only one of the Excels left, and she hadn't expressed any fear for her safety. As if she knew she wouldn't be a victim.

He shifted in the chair and looked over at the alarm clock. It was a little after six. Only the timpani of distant thunder and the occasional swish of tires on the wet street broke the silence.

He turned his head to regard her, thinking back to the moment when he first saw her stepping off the stage at the Blue Door. He jumped through their history like he was flipping pages in a book. She had gone from all but spitting in his face to lying in his bed, and it had happened so fast. Too fast.

As he gazed at her face, that odd elusive something came back nibbling at the edge of his consciousness. He slouched in the chair and put his feet up on the windowsill, watching the coming storm and walking his thoughts backward, slowly, as Sal always instructed him, waiting for an impression, a memory, or a shred that had been lost or forgotten to stir and take form.

It came to him just as the first hard raindrops rattled the windowpanes, and he was so startled by what he was thinking that he put his feet on the floor and sat upright. He spent long minutes turning it over in his mind as a steady drizzle fell. Quietly, so as not to wake her, he got up and went to the closet in the front room, bent down, and opened a box. At the top of the stack was his 45 of "Crazy, Baby" with the picture sleeve of the Excels intact. He carried it to the bedroom and sat down to study the cover in the dim light.

After another minute, he wanted to get up and shake her out of her sleep, so she could tell him that what he was thinking wasn't true. Instead, he sat there and worked through it one more time.

The rain drumming on the glass woke her. She shifted beneath the sheets, and Eddie heard her whisper something. She was still and quiet for a few moments, and he guessed she was taking stock of where this morning found her. Presently, she raised up on one elbow, blinking sleepily.

She saw him sitting in the chair and gave him a smile that all but cracked his heart.

Clearing her throat, she said, "How are you feeling?"

"I'm all right," he said.

She rubbed her face. A few seconds passed before she noticed the way he was watching her. The shine in her eyes dimmed. "What is it?" she said.

He caught himself and waited another moment. It was going to be a long drop. "Was Johnny Janelle's father?" he said.

She jerked away as if he'd slapped her.

"Was he?"

She didn't move or speak for several long seconds. Her face seemed to lose its light and fold inward as her mouth drew into a melancholy curve.

"He was," he said.

She pulled the sheet around her and fixed her gaze on the rain pelting the glass.

He waited another silent moment, then said, "How could—"

"He wasn't my brother." Her voice was flat. "He was my cousin. And not even by blood." She glanced at him with empty eyes, saw the look on his face. "Do you want to hear this? Or should I just go?"

Eddie said, "I want to hear."

She returned her empty stare to the rivulets on the window. "My aunt Mae had this man, called himself Memphis John," she said. "We never did know his real name. Johnny was his son by some other woman. Anyway, Memphis John took off one day when Johnny was five, and Aunt Mae went after him. She didn't come back. She left Johnny with my mama. So we just said he was my brother. It was easier." She took a quiet pause. "How did you know?"

"She was born the end of August, so that means you got pregnant in late November of '58," he said. "That matches up with just after he came home from being on the road. That's some timing." He held up the record sleeve that had been lying in his lap. "And she looks like him."

A tear welled and drew a slow line down her brown cheek. "Yes, she has his smile." She wiped the tear away and glanced at him. "And how do you know when she was born?"

"Public records," he said. "Something Sal taught me. I went to City Hall. It's all there."

She shook her head slightly and went back to watching the gray rain.

Eddie spent a moment before he took the next plunge.

"What I want to know is if it has something to do with his disappearance," he said.

He thought she hadn't heard him, and he was about to repeat it, when she said, "Yes."

He felt his heart begin to race. "Do you know what happened to him?"

She hesitated. "Yes."

"What was—"

"I was responsible for his death."

Eddie felt a stone sink through his chest.

"And for what happened to Ray and Tommy, too," she finished.

"You let me run around in circles," he said bitterly. "Mieux tried to kill me."

"That's too bad." Her face took a hard set. "I told you to let it be. More than once. But you wouldn't."

He glared right back at her. "You lied to me."

"Yes, I did. And now you know why."

"It's no excuse."

"It wasn't meant to be." She looked away from him. "I lied to you, and I'd do it again if I had to."

Neither one of them spoke as a minute went by. The rain fell harder.

"Are you going to tell me what happened?" he asked her.

Now she gave him a harsh look. "Well, that's what you want, isn't it? That's what you wanted all along."

"Yes. That's what I want."

"Is that all?" Her voice dripped a quiet venom. "Is there anything else I can do for you?"

Before he could respond, she unraveled herself from the sheets. When she stood up, the bed gave off an aroma that held him in a daze as she moved past. She marched away with such purpose that he thought she was about to get dressed and walk out.

She didn't go for her clothes; instead, she disappeared into the living room. He pushed himself out of the chair and trailed after to find her standing by the couch, digging into her handbag. For a crazy second, he imagined her pulling out a .22. End of story.

What she produced wasn't a weapon, but a square, thin box with the word SCOTCH emblazoned on the cover.

"The tape," he said.

"You have something to play it on?" she said.

He stared at the box. "Sal does," he said, and hobbled to the phone.

The detective walked in, saw Eddie's face, and stopped in his tracks, staring at the patched eyebrow and the purple and orange bruises that had flowered in a half-dozen places. *"Madonn'!"* he said. "What happened?" He watched Eddie turn and move toward the kitchen in a creeping shuffle, wincing with every step. "Jesus, look at you!" he said. "What the hell?"

"I made coffee," Eddie said. "You want some?"

Sal closed the door and set the tape machine on the floor and followed him into the kitchen, where the percolator was going. Eddie sat down at the table with a little grunt of pain. Sal gave him a once-over, his forehead stitched with concern, then went about fetching two cups from the sideboard and pouring the coffee. "Milk?" he said.

Eddie nodded toward the fridge. Sal found the milk carton and poured a little into each cup. He set one of the cups in front of Eddie and took the opposite chair. "So?"

Eddie tried for a smile. "I hit a guy."

Sal wasn't in the mood for humor. "Looks like he hit you back."

"He got a couple in."

"Who was it?"

"Mieux."

"Shit."

"Small world, huh?"

Sal's face flushed, and he rapped his fist down on the tabletop. "You knew it was a fucking trap," he said. "I knew. And I let you go anyway."

"It's all right. He and I were going to get to it sooner or later."

"What are you, a fucking cowboy?" Sal's face flushed. "You're lucky he didn't just pull out that piece and put one in the back of your head. What's wrong with you?"

"Sal—"

"Don't 'Sal' me! Are you out of your fucking mind?" He was furious.

Eddie glared right back at him. He didn't need a lecture. Sal fumed for another moment, then settled down. "Did you hurt him?"

"Yeah."

"Bad?"

"Yeah, pretty bad."

The detective took a sip of his coffee. "So what happened?"

Eddie recounted what had transpired and what he'd learned, from the time he drove down Columbus Boulevard until he got out of Candy Ralston's car.

"Where's she at?" Sal said.

"I told her to go hide somewhere."

"Good idea." Sal pondered for a few seconds. "So Roddy's in up to his nuts, but you still don't know for sure whether or not he killed Pope."

Eddie hesitated for a moment and then said, "Actually, I do know. He didn't."

"I did." Her voice came from the doorway.

Sal made a startled turn in his chair to see Valerie standing there, still wearing Eddie's old sweats. Though it was a grim moment, the look on Sal's face almost made Eddie smile. For once speechless, the detective shot baffled glances between the two of them, trying to catch up.

Valerie went to the counter and poured herself a cup of coffee. After ten tortured seconds, Sal pointed a finger at her and let out a long, "Uh . . ."

Eddie said, "Sal?" Sal was staring at Valerie. "Sal?" Sal pulled his eyes off her to look at him. "We need the tape machine."

The reels turned and the piano and a voice flowed out of the speaker, a ballad with a church feel, with lyrics that painted a picture of a man so deep in love he reached out in forgiveness of a terrible betrayal, asking only for his lover's tomorrows. It was a simple delivery, Johnny singing solo over a hypnotic tapestry of quiet minor-key chords.

As they sat listening, Valerie's eyes began welling. Even Sal was moved, tilting his head and gazing absently at the floor, sensing the honest emotion of the lyrics.

The song ended and the last notes faded out. Johnny played some random moody chords, until a muffled voice spoke from the background and the music stopped abruptly.

The voice, now closer, became George Roddy's Jersey bray. "I like that," he said. "What do you call it?"

"'All Your Tomorrows.'" Johnny coughed, a little hoarse.

"Very nice."

Papers shuffled, the keyboard cover closed, and the bench legs squeaked as Pope stood up. "I'm leaving," he said.

"Yeah, well, good night."

The singer chuckled. "No, man, I mean I'm *leaving*. As in over and out. Our contract's up and I ain't signing no new one. We're through."

After a short silence, Roddy said, "Is that right?" He sounded sour, though not surprised.

"Oh, yeah, and something else." Johnny's tone was breezy.

"By noon tomorrow, I'm going to have a couple downtown lawyers crawling up your funky ass."

After a pronounced silence, Roddy said, "Lawyers, huh? Lawyers for what?"

"To get what's mine, motherfucker!" Johnny yelled suddenly. He coughed again. "Tell you what," he said. "You can have the Excels' name. It's all yours. I'll take Valerie and Tommy. You can keep Ray. With my compliments." He laughed, cool and low. "I'm going to fuck you so bad, you're going to wish you never saw my face."

"I already do, you piece of shit."

Pope's voice went up a notch. "I *got* you, jack! I got it all. I know you been stealin' from me and from everybody else." He paused to enjoy the moment. "Now I'm going to get it back. With interest. I'm going to own every goddamn thing you got. What do you think your guinea pals will have to say about that?"

"You fuck, who do you think you are?" Roddy was sneering. "You'd be standing on some street corner singing for dimes if it wasn't for me. You want to leave, go ahead and leave. See how far you get."

Johnny laughed shortly. "Yeah, well, that's what I'm gonna do," he said, though now he sounded just a bit off, and not so sure of himself. As if to regain some ground, he said, "I'm taking Candy, too."

"Oh? Another surprise. Big man." Now there was derision in Roddy's voice, as if he was listening to the boasting of a spoiled child.

Johnny kept at it. "You didn't know I been banging that a couple dozen times a week?" he said, now full of glee. "You are one *dumbass,* man. I get to pump that thing anytime I want, and I ain't about to give it up. And by the way, she's the one—"

A door thumped in the background, and he stopped abruptly. He said, "Shit." Then, "Valerie? Valerie! Hey!"

A flurry of padded footsteps receded and the door closed with a muted thump.

After a quiet second, George Roddy growled, "You fuck!"

The tape rolled on with only the slightest hissing sound. Sal and Eddie sat back.

Valerie stood up, said, "Excuse me," and walked to the bedroom.

Sal was reaching to shut off the machine when the tape hiss was abruptly replaced by the sound of a woman's voice, shrieking in a hysterical rush. He snatched his hand back. They could barely make it out, something about Johnny falling down the stairs and lying out on the bricks, and that somebody needed to help him right away. It was followed by a hurried shuffle of feet, the sound of the door opening and closing. The faint tape hiss resumed.

Valerie emerged from the bedroom and took her seat at the table.

Sal switched off the machine. "What was all that?"

"It was that Sunday night at the studio. The night Johnny died."

Sal laid his hands flat on the table. "Why don't you just, y'know, go through the whole thing," he said quietly. "From the beginning."

She stared down into her coffee cup, composing her thoughts.

"What happened was I had missed my, uh . . . my period that December. I waited for a while, till the end of January. The first week of February, I went to the doctor and went back home and waited."

She took a small sip of her coffee.

"Johnny was in the studio that Friday, and he didn't come home. On Saturday morning they called back to tell me I was pregnant."

Sal was watching her, puzzled that she seemed to be wandering off the subject. He let her go on.

"I was scared when I got the news, but I was happy, too," she continued, her eyes brightening. "I couldn't wait to tell him. Then he didn't come home Saturday night, either. I waited all day Sunday, and I couldn't stand it anymore, so I went down to the studio."

She raised her cup, put it down again. "The front was always locked on the weekends, so I came around back. I walked in just in time to hear him and Mr. Roddy arguing. They did that all the time, so I didn't think anything about it. I stood at the door to wait until they were through. Then I heard what he said about him and Candy, and . . ." She took a sharp breath. "I was so mad that I pushed the door open all the way. I wanted him to see me, to know that I heard the whole thing. The two of them just stood there looking at me. I turned around and walked out."

"And Johnny came after you," Sal prompted her.

She nodded. "He caught up with me on the landing. I was crying and everything, and he started saying he didn't mean that about Candy, wasn't none of it true, that he was just trying to get back at Mr. Roddy." She swallowed. "But I knew he was lying. That's when I told him I was going to have a baby. His baby."

Sal's jaw almost hit the table. "Wait a minute. His baby? You got pregnant by your—"

"He wasn't her brother," Eddie said.

The detective's mouth was still open with another half-formed question. Eddie gave a shake of his head, and he dropped it.

Valerie clasped her hands tighter around her cup. "What happened was an accident. But there it was. We were going to have a baby. I mean, *I* was going to have a baby." Her face tightened. "And that's when he told me he couldn't have none of that. Said it could ruin his career. Said it wasn't the *right time.*" Her voice took on a bitter edge, and she clenched and opened her fists. "And then he said he could find someone who would take care of it right quick."

She paused to fight back tears. "I told him there wasn't any way I was going to do that. He stood there trying to tell me why I had to do it, and then he tried to put his hands on me, so he could get his way, the way he always did, and . . ." She raised her palms before her. "I pushed him away. And he fell. He went back and hit the railing, and then it was like I was dreaming, because he reached out for me, but I couldn't move fast enough, and he fell, I mean all the way down."

Eddie sat picturing Johnny's sick expression as he saw the future he had constructed falling apart. Thinking of himself only, how the news was going to wreck the grand plan; the return of that slick smile as he tried to talk Valerie into a solution; and the look of hurt and rage on her face when she realized what he wanted her to do. He saw her shove him away in her fury, and the body pitching over the steel railing and down to the hard macadam, lying there, a broken doll.

"I ran down and he was lying there, making these sounds," she went on. "He tried to get up, but he couldn't move. When I went to lift him, he screamed, he was hurt so bad. So I ran back inside and got Mr. Roddy."

Sal was watching her intently. "And what did he do?"

"He told me to stay there and he went out. It was probably only a couple minutes, but it seemed such a long time, so I went back out there and down the steps. George was standing there, and Johnny was . . . he was . . ."

"Dead," Sal said.

She broke down, sobbing with such grief that Eddie didn't know what to do or say. Sal watched her with a gentle pity, producing a clean handkerchief and handing it to her, murmuring softly. He had daughters.

A half minute went by, and she stopped weeping and sat staring at her clenched hands, breathing shakily.

"Why didn't you call the police?" Sal said.

She settled and cleared her throat. "Because he told me we couldn't do that. He said I'd get blamed for what happened. That I'd get arrested. I thought I would end up having my baby in prison. And what if they took her away from me? I couldn't think, so I did what he said. He told me to go get Tommy and Ray. They went outside. I went onto the landing, and they were standing around Johnny."

"What happened to the body?"

"They put it in the trunk of Johnny's Cadillac and took it away. Later on they put the car back where it was. George told us don't ever say anything about it." She shook her head slightly. "And nobody did. Ray and Tommy never told. They did that, to protect me and my baby."

"And that's why they had to die," Sal said.

"Did you kill them?" Eddie said, with such an edge to his voice that Sal looked at him in reproof.

Valerie glared spitefully. "No. I wouldn't. I couldn't."

He was about to say something else when Sal caught his eye, and he crossed his arms.

The detective pointed at the tape on the machine. "How the hell did you get this?" he asked.

"After they left with Johnny's body, I went back inside. I went through the booth, and I saw the reel going around. The Record light was on. I'd been around enough to know. The tape had been running the whole time. It was all there. Johnny's songs, and what he and Roddy said after. So I took it. And kept it."

Sal was looking at her, nodding appreciation at her guile. "When did you let him know you had it?"

"After."

"So you had a standoff," the detective said.

For a few moments, no one said anything. Valerie looked miserable, and Eddie crossed his arms. They kept their gazes averted.

Sal allowed himself a small smile as he began packing the tape machine. "Congratulations, Cero, you broke your first case," he said.

"I didn't break anything," Eddie muttered.

"Pretty damn close," Sal said, but Eddie wasn't having any of it.

The detective took the tape reel off the machine and put it back in the box. "Who gets this?" he said.

"It's hers," Eddie said. "She can keep it."

Sal laid the tape at Valerie's elbow. "I'll be at the office," he said to Eddie. "You come in whenever you're ready; we'll figure out what we're going to do."

He walked out of the kitchen. The apartment door opened and closed.

Valerie kept her gaze fixed on her coffee cup. Eddie sat there, thinking about how he had been drawn in and hooked so that he couldn't do anything to hurt her. He had been a volunteer, and she had let it happen, to save her child and herself. He wanted to say something, but he knew he couldn't trust what might come out of his mouth, so he kept quiet.

She pushed her chair back, got to her feet, stepped into the bathroom, and closed the door. Outside, the rain was slowing to a gray drizzle. Eddie picked up his cup, found the coffee cold, and put it down again. She reappeared in the clothes she had worn the night before and crossed to the table to pick up her handbag. Now he caught the odors of the Blue Door wafting from the red dress: cigarette smoke, whiskey, and the close air of a dark saloon. The scents took him back to the moment he'd first laid eyes on her. It had only been weeks, but it seemed they had lived a lifetime.

Their eyes met for a moment, and he pointed to his bandaged eyebrow.

"Thanks for this," he said.

She gave him an empty look. "It'll heal, right?"

"Yeah, it always does," he said.

She left the tape on the table when she walked out.

He took a taxi to Columbus Boulevard to pick up the Ford. The gray streets were a match for his mood. On the way back to the office, he managed to forget about Valerie long enough to consider his next step, and by the time he climbed the stairs, he knew what he wanted to do. He went inside, sat down, and laid it out for Sal. They batted it around for a while, and he picked up the phone to make the call as the detective swiveled his chair to watch the afternoon traffic.

He expected the bored receptionist to come back on and tell him that Mr. Roddy was not available to speak to—

"Cero." Roddy's voice was oddly muted, a bully deflated of all the hot air. "Are you a reasonable man?"

"Yeah, sure," Eddie said. "Ask anybody."

"Then maybe we can settle this, once and for all."

"Oh, yeah?"

"Come to the studio so we can talk."

"When?"

"Well, we can't do it now. How about tonight?"

Eddie let out a laugh. "You got to be fucking kidding."

"No, no problems. Just you and I."

"I should take your word?"

"What can I say? I've handled this badly." When Eddie remained silent, he said, "Think about it. You've got the upper hand now. So no more rough stuff. That was a mistake."

"Mieux would probably agree with that."

Roddy sighed. "Yes, well, that was not my doing."

Eddie said, "All right, what time?"

"Six thirty," Roddy said. "Come to the front door this time. I'll be waiting."

Eddie dropped the phone in the cradle and said, "Bingo."

Wearily, Valerie climbed the steps and let herself in. She found Janelle and her mother sitting at the kitchen table, playing old maid.

Ann Kate and the child watched in silence as she opened the door to the cabinet where they kept the brandy bottle. She stood there in her nightclub dress, gazing at nothing. After a few moments, she closed the door.

As she moved around the table, she laid a tender hand on Janelle's head. She sat down and regarded the two people who meant the most to her. Her mother, with her huge heart, had witnessed the tragedy and had been a rock.

Then Valerie looked at Janelle and saw in that small face a whole history unfold: growing up with Johnny in the house; a puppy love blossoming over the years into the real thing; giving up her virginity to him late one night; the secret romance that couldn't be a secret anymore, because she was carrying his child; and the final tragic scene on a cold February night. It was all so, so sad.

She began to weep inconsolably. Janelle slipped off her chair to wrap her arms around her neck, and Ann Kate enveloped her hands.

They remained that way, the three of them bound together in unspoken love, until the telephone rang.

TWENTY-THREE

The studio was a thickly carpeted twenty foot square with a ten-foot ceiling, and lights turned down to cast tones of warm amber. Microphones stood in a row along two walls, and a half-dozen stools, ten music stands, and as many baffles, hinged like dressing screens, were arranged about the floor. A baby grand piano resided against one wall—the one Johnny Pope had played on the tape—and an upright bass and two guitar cases leaned in the opposite corner. Eddie noticed how dead a space it was, though some of the music that had been made there must have shaken the whole building. Every sound lived and died in seconds.

George Roddy stood in the middle of the floor with his arms akimbo and his jaw clenched. Eddie had shown up a half hour late, and the man was fuming. It was something Sal suggested, as a way to get the proceedings started on the right note, and it had worked perfectly. Roddy kept looking at Eddie like he wanted to ask him who the fuck he thought he was. He settled for a cold glare of his muddy-green eyes. The reserved, almost polite pose that had couched the invitation to the meeting was nowhere in sight.

Roddy had bolstered his profile by dressing in a slate gray three-piece suit, black shirt, and sober gray and white tie. All in all, it was about a month's pay in haberdashery. Eddie thought that he resembled the sharply attired dagos who stepped out of Cadillacs on certain South Philadelphia street corners and wondered if he'd been getting fashion tips from his business partners.

Eddie, by contrast, appeared to have slept in his clothes before being dragged through the streets and dumped at the door. In fact, he had spent the afternoon nursing his various bruises and contusions. He was still aching from his waist to his brow and hobbled around the room, ignoring his glowering host.

The wide window of the control booth on the back wall was completely dark, save for the glow of a tiny red light. Next to it was the door that Valerie had thrown wide after hearing Johnny bragging to Roddy about his conquest of Candy Ralston.

Now on the scene, Eddie stopped to picture it flying open and Johnny and Roddy turning in surprise to see her standing there with accusation blazing from her eyes. Then the door had slammed, and Johnny had gone rushing across the room to chase her down. Roddy had stood there, fuming bitterly, wearing a pissed-off expression not unlike the one he was sporting at that very moment. Valerie had reappeared, bursting through the door, shaking and screaming . . . and then what?

It occurred to Eddie that the door also led into the storage room where he and Mieux had slugged it out the night before. He wondered if anyone had cleaned up the mess.

Roddy's angry stare was fastened to the back of his neck. Eddie ignored it as he took another appreciative survey of the studio and said, "So this is where it all happens."

Roddy glared icily. "All right, cut the shit," he said, and stalked to the piano, sat down on the bench, and crossed his arms. "Are we going to talk or not?"

"Go ahead," Eddie said. "Talk." He picked up one of the stools and dragged it close to the piano. Climbing on was only slightly painful, and he was now close enough to lean an elbow on the long sound box.

Roddy studied his face for a few seconds. "If I didn't know better, I'd think you got the worst of it. So what's with . . . whatshisname?"

"Mieux? He's at Graduate. There's cops watching him. But he can't talk right now. Because I broke his jaw. So you're okay for the moment."

Roddy said, "It was that dumb fuck Hayner who found him. So he's not my problem." One of his eyebrows arched in cold emphasis. "You are." He shook his head slightly and dropped his gaze to the keyboard. When he tapped a key with a tentative finger, a rich treble note rang out.

"I don't have a musical bone in my body," he mused. "I wonder how the hell I ended up here." He plunked some more keys. Then, in the same deliberate voice, he said, "I never could figure out what you thought you were doing. It was all over. And none of your damn business, anyway. You were a fighter. And not a very good one, from what I heard. Not after that Allred guy died."

"You heard wrong," Eddie said. "And he didn't die."

Roddy tapped out more notes that chimed and then faded. He closed the keyboard cover and looked at Eddie.

"Okay, no more bullshit," he said. "I want to settle this. If you've got anything on me, let's hear it. Otherwise, we can move on." Eddie kept quiet. "I didn't think so." He made a quarter turn on the bench. "I doubt you're ever going to get anywhere with this investigation or whatever the hell it is. I still want you to drop it. I mean now."

"And if I don't?"

"Then you're going to have a lot more trouble. You and your girlfriend both."

Eddie felt his face reddening. "She's not my girl—"

"Save it. I know all about you two." The lizard mouth curled in a rude smile. "I never knew she went for white meat. Johnny's probably spinning in his fucking grave. I'm sorry I never got a piece of her while I had the chance."

In the time it took him to blink, Eddie came off the stool and slapped him a hard forehand, flush on the cheek. Roddy grunted a curse as a shock of pain flashed through Eddie's wrist and arm while another shot across his rib cage. Roddy grabbed on to keep from tumbling off the bench. His eyes flared as he went about righting himself.

"Touchy, huh?" He tugged at his lapels. "Well, you oughta be."

He spent a moment straightening his suit and fussing his hair back into place, then rubbed the spot on his cheek where Eddie's palm had connected. He said, "Okay, sit down." When Eddie didn't move, he snapped, "You want to get this fixed or not? Sit."

Eddie clambered back onto the stool. Along with the pain in his arm and sides, his own cheeks had turned a chagrined red. He wasn't supposed to be hitting people anymore, and he'd smacked three different men in the space of some two days.

"She told you what happened, right?" Roddy said. "Did she play the tape for you?" Eddie nodded. "So you know it was her that pushed him."

"But the fall didn't kill him," Eddie said. "He was still alive."

Roddy shrugged. "Not for long. Anyway, she's the one on the spot. I talk and she goes to jail. And she loses her kid. So here's the deal. You walk away from this, and I will guarantee that she'll never be implicated in Johnny's death. In exchange, I want your silence, I want her silence, and I want that goddamn tape. It's my property. If you don't agree, then neither of you will live happily ever after. You get my drift?" Eddie kept staring at him. "So do we have a deal?"

"Not quite."

"Not quite?"

"I want something else. I want to know what went on that night."

"You heard the tape. It's all on there."

"No, I mean the rest of it," Eddie said. "I started this because I wanted to know what happened to Johnny Pope. So you tell me what's not on the tape. What happened out there, after the door closed. Before Valerie came outside again. That's what I want."

Roddy stared at him with a tight smile. "Speaking of tapes, you're not by chance hiding one of those recorders, are you?"

Eddie pulled up his shirt. Roddy stared at the bruises on his bare gut with a grimace. "Jesus. You get those from Mieux?"

"That's right. And I won. You want me to drop the pants, too?"

Roddy let out a curt laugh. Then he said, "All right, I'll tell you what happened. But then there's no going back. We'll have a deal."

"Go ahead," Eddie said. Roddy continued to watch him with narrowed eyes. "There's no one here, right? So what's the problem?"

Roddy's mirthless smile evaporated. "You think I'm stupid? I give you what you want, and you just walk out of here, and that's the end of it, huh?" He shook his head. "You do think I'm stupid. I wouldn't trust you as far as I could throw you. You know too fucking much already."

Eddie realized it was the moment for him to come off the stool and flatten him, but for some reason he kept still, even as Roddy reached into his pocket, pulled out a .22-caliber pistol, and pointed it at his chest.

"You're not a very good detective, are you?"

"I'm not a detective at all," Eddie said.

"You got that right, you dumb wop. You never should have come here." He sighed resignedly and gestured to the padded walls. "One nice thing about a studio is that it's soundproof. I could shoot off a fucking cannon in here and nobody'd hear it."

Eddie forced his mind off the pistol. "Then nobody will hear if you tell me what happened to Johnny," he said. "Unless there's nothing to tell. But then you wouldn't need the gun, would you?" He kept a poker face, hoping the bait would work and he could keep him talking.

It did. Roddy thought it over for a few seconds, then gestured expansively. "Yeah, what the hell? I'll tell you exactly what happened. It'll be a fucking pleasure. You won't be around to repeat it anyway, will you?" His eyes slid sideways. "Or maybe you don't think I've got the balls to use this thing. I've got news for you: I do. I already have. So don't try anything."

First Mieux, and now this character, had pointed a gun at him. It had never happened before, and it was his momentary luck that both men liked to hear themselves talk.

"That Sunday night Johnny was throwing that tantrum, threatening me with lawyers and all that shit," Roddy began, his voice simmering. "Then he started talking about how he had been screwing Candy. You heard all that." He grimaced. "Dumb cunt. Her job was to keep tabs on the sneaky fuck, and she goes and falls for him. A white woman going for that crazy nigger. Figures. She never was very bright. Believe me, if she didn't give such a great blow job, I probably would have put her ass out on the street years ago. I wish I had." He stopped for a second to glower. "Anyway, he's bragging about her, as if she wouldn't fuck anything in pants, right? He didn't know that Valerie had come in through the back door. She'd heard it all." He glanced coolly at Eddie. "You know about them? He knocked her up. His own sister."

"She wasn't his sister," Eddie said.

"So they say." Roddy shrugged. "Anyway, she overhears all that crap about Candy and takes off. He goes out the door after her. And the next thing I know, she's back, all hysterical. I went outside, and there he was on the ground. She had pushed him off the landing. And he was in bad shape."

"He wasn't dead, though."

Roddy shook his head. "No, he wasn't dead. He was lying there, trying to move and talk. I sent Valerie inside, and as soon as that damned door closed behind her, I leaned over him and said, 'Look at you, you no good prick. Now who's going to fuck who?'" His eyes glimmered harshly. "I made him lay there and think about it."

"You let him die," Eddie said.

Roddy got a strange look on his face. He let out a sudden, cracked chuckle and made a chopping motion with his free hand. "No, I didn't let him die, you dumb guinea punk. I put my hands around his throat and choked the life out of him myself."

For a stunned second, Eddie forgot about the pistol aimed dead at his chest. "*You* did it?"

"You're fucking right I did it!" The man was crowing.

"Because he was going to leave?"

Roddy got more agitated, waving the gun in the air. "He wasn't just going to leave! He was going to take it all away! I made him, goddamnit, and what did he do? He betrayed me! That motherfucking nigger prick was going to destroy my business and destroy my life. I owed serious people a lot of money. He goes away, and I'm a dead man. So it was him or me. That simple."

He fixed his wild eyes on Eddie for a few seconds, then raised his empty hand righteously. "Well, I put a stop to that, didn't I? And you know what? There's a lot of people who'll thank me someday. Forget about my trouble. Can you imagine what would happen if Johnny had gone off and made his own records? God knows who else would try it. It would be the end of the business. The monkeys would be running the zoo. Christ almighty!"

Eddie, feeling as if he had wandered into a fun house, said, "He wanted out because you cheated him. You cheated all of them."

"Oh, my god! Listen to this shit!" Now Roddy threw up both manicured hands. "What am I, a goddamn babysitter? These fucking jungle bunnies and guineas and spics come to me with a little talent and maybe one half-decent song, and I turn them into stars. If they can't keep track of their own affairs, well, then, too bad for them."

His rant came down a notch, his eyes narrowed, and he wagged his index finger. "But Johnny . . . Johnny wasn't just leaving. He was going to ruin me. I knew he'd been talking about it all along. I never thought he'd have the nerve to go through with it, though." He sighed deeply. "I was wrong. The bastard."

Eddie knew he needed to keep him talking. "How did you know he was going to leave?"

He snorted in disgust. "How do you think? Candy told me. As always, she was trying to play both ends. She probably spilled her guts to you, too. Did she offer to fuck you while she was at it?" He gave up another cold laugh. "Yeah, well, she's a decent piece of ass, but she's not smart enough for that kind of action. She was always falling for this guy or that one, making a fool of herself. And she doesn't know when to shut her damn mouth. Anyway, she told me Johnny was up to something."

He turned on his heel and wiggled the pistol, finishing his lecture. "And that Sunday night, that was it. I had him right there. I couldn't let that good of a chance go by, not after what he had said to me. And done to me. So I took care of him myself, looking him right in the eyes."

"What did you do with the body?"

Roddy jerked an impatient thumb. "There's a very deep river right across the street. Ray and Gates helped me." He smirked. "Too bad no one bothered to look in the trunk, or they would have noticed that his chains and the spare were both missing."

"Hayner probably did," Eddie said.

Roddy stopped to smile slightly. "You know, you're right. He probably did."

"But you had hired someone to get rid of Johnny before this happened," Eddie said.

"Damn, you do have your nose in things, don't you?" He

flipped the pistol idly. "Yeah, I did. One of your *paesanos.* Turned out I didn't require his services."

"And it wasn't Mieux who murdered Ray and Tommy, was it?"

"Mieux?" Roddy laughed again. "Jesus Christ. You think I'd trust some damn swamp coon to handle that? I took care of those two. It was too bad, but I had to. I tried to talk to Ray, and of course he was out of his mind. Sooner or later he was going to spill. And Tommy, I saw him corner you at the funeral. I knew what was going on. I couldn't chance it." He stopped, raised his empty hand, palm up. "I told him we needed to talk. He probably thought we were going to pray or something. Stupid. Stupid."

"You murdered three people over this," Eddie said.

"Yeah, yeah, three people. Actually, four, counting you." He grinned wolfishly and took a step closer, once again fixing the pistol on Eddie's heart. "You really are one dumb dago pug, aren't you? What'd they call you? Fast Eddie? You think you're faster than a fucking speeding bullet, Fast Ed—"

In a half-second blur, Roddy went from vertical to horizontal and slammed down onto the carpeted floor with a rough grunt. The pistol flew out of his hand and went bumping away to collide with the baseboard.

Sal had come out of the hallway where he'd been lurking to hit him dead on the run, a blind-side forearm to the side of the head. Now he bent down, grabbed Roddy by his silk lapels, jerked him to his knees, then to his feet. Roddy's eyes were rolling up in their sockets, his mouth was hanging open, and his legs were buckling. Sal was three inches shorter, but he held him up like a well-dressed scarecrow.

"You know, it's rude to point a gun," Sal admonished him. "Goddamn dangerous, too. Those things go off accidentally all the time. So say you're sorry." Roddy was gagging. "Say you're sorry!"

Roddy made a gargling word that started with an *S*.

Sal frowned peevishly. "I don't think you mean it," he said, and dropped him to the floor.

Within a half hour, the studio was swarming. Al Nash showed up with two other detectives and two uniformed officers. They took statements from Sal and Eddie. George Roddy was in no shape to answer their questions.

Sal had brought Valerie along, and she stood in a corner, watching the cops work, wearing a look of dull shock. She had heard everything from out in the hallway, too.

They spent the better part of an hour at the scene. Roger Beckley appeared, and the attorney went scurrying behind when the police took Roddy away. Al Nash, all business, gave Sal and Eddie a brief nod as he left. One of the uniformed officers was posted in the building.

Eddie drove Valerie to the Blue Door, where she had left her car. They didn't talk at all, and he could tell from her expression that she was deep in thought about her own problems. Sal had made some calls and worked out a quiet arrangement with his cop friends so that she wouldn't be prosecuted. Though the deal lifted a ton of weight from her back, she would still have to answer to herself. Eddie guessed that she would probably spend a few minutes of every day for the rest of her life wondering if she could have saved Johnny that night, or if in a moment of hurt and anger, she had paid him back for his selfish cruelties.

He found a parking space right across the street and went around to open her door. She got out slowly, looking exhausted. They crossed the street and stood in front of the club. It occurred to Eddie that they had arrived back at the same spot where the story had begun.

"What are you going to do?" he asked her.

"Go home and hold my baby," she said. "Ask her in my heart if she can ever forgive me for taking her daddy away."

"You didn't take him away," Eddie said. "And if it was up to him, she wouldn't be here in the first place." The minute the words were out, he regretted them.

Her eyes flashed at him. "It's none of your damn business. None of it was ever any of your business."

"You're welcome," he said.

Her face went cold, and just like that, they really were back to where they had begun. "What, did you think I was going to thank you?" she said. "That I was going to fall down on my knees in gratitude for all you did? I'm not."

"I can see that."

"Good. And so now it's all over. You got what you wanted, right? So we can say good bye."

It was his turn to stare. "Why?"

"Why?" She waved her hands in a mime of exasperation. "What did you think was going to happen? What? That we were going to keep on, you and I? That we were going to go out? Go to bed? Get married and have children? And live happily ever after?" Her voice had gone up to a shrill contralto, and some people passing on the sidewalk across the street looked their way. "Have you lost your damn mind?"

"I don't care about that," he said.

She drew back. "Well, I do," she said, her voice cutting. "I have to." She took a weary pause. "I went a little crazy with you, but that's over. I've had enough heartache to last a lifetime. I don't need to start that again. Okay?" He didn't answer. "Okay?"

"Yeah, okay," he said.

"Okay!" She turned around and stalked toward her car. As she reached it, her steps slowed as she was dragging some impossible burden. Wearily, she unlocked the door, got in, and drove away. She didn't look back, and he didn't try to go after her. Women came and went. She was gone, and that was that.

Sal slouched in his chair, his feet up on the desk. Eddie leaned at the window, watching silver clouds drift through the city night. The detective sipped a drink and studied his somber profile.

"So what's with the face?" he said. "You did good. Except for the part when you almost got yourself killed."

Eddie sighed. "I still don't understand all of it. Why didn't those mob guys just get rid of him and step in?"

"They probably didn't have all the details," Sal said. "That would have been the smart move. Just knock him off and take over. Maybe they'll do it now. Take over the business, I mean."

"They'll fit right in."

"Well, anyway, it's finished. And the good guys won."

"It doesn't feel that way."

"I told you, this ain't TV."

"I spent a lot of time on it."

"Yeah, you did."

"Didn't make you a dime."

"We'll call it on-the-job training." He pushed a hand through the mess on his desk. "Speaking of which"—he located an official-looking paper and held it up—"this is for you."

"What is it?"

"Application for a PI license."

Eddie looked at the paper. "I don't think I'm ready for that."

"Whenever, it's up to you." Sal laid the form aside. "It's there if you want it."

Eddie returned his attention to the night sky. After a minute's silence, he said, "I guess I won't be seeing her again."

"Oh?" Sal said. "Why's that?"

"Because she doesn't want me around. She said she doesn't need any more heartaches." He surprised himself. He wasn't the type to blurt something so personal, and he was embarrassed. It had been happening a lot lately.

Sal didn't seem to notice as he swirled the liquor in his glass. "Well, she's going to have them, whether she wants them or not. She knows that, too. She just needs a break. You both do."

Eddie stared out the window. He couldn't see the stars for the city lights, though the moon was peeking in and out of the clouds.

"Eddie?" Sal murmured quietly. Eddie turned his way. "Wait a little while, then you can go see her."

"She said she doesn't—," he began, but Sal waved him quiet.

"Do what I say, eh? Wait a little while, and then go see her." The detective came up with a kind smile. "Hey, don't worry, kiddo. It's going to be all right."

TWENTY-FOUR

Eddie saw her the following Monday at Tommy Gates's funeral. They didn't speak. She warned him off with her eyes, and once he saw the grieving faces of the reverend's wife and children, he wasn't much in the mood to talk anyway.

That Wednesday night he made an arrangement with Joe D'Amato and slipped into the Blue Door to hear her sing. Though Joe stuck him in a dark corner, she kept looking his way, and he couldn't shake the feeling that she knew he was there.

On Saturday afternoon he drove to Grays Ferry and knocked on her door. She was not pleased that he'd shown up like that and didn't invite him in. She also didn't chase him away, and after a few stubborn minutes, she came out onto the stoop. A few more minutes, and she agreed to go for a walk. Janelle skipped ahead of them as they made their way to the park.

He was back Saturday evening. This time she allowed him inside, and he stayed until it was time for her to go to work. She said it was okay if he wanted to come see the show, but she didn't want to find him waiting outside when she got off.

The next morning, Sunday, he reappeared in his suit to accompany the family to Mass. He was the subject of whispers, before, during, and after the service. Mrs. Pope invited him to stay for dinner.

The next day, Monday, May 14, the following item appeared on page four of the *Inquirer:* HAVERTOWN POLICE INVESTIGATING SHOOTING:

> Havertown police are investigating the death of Richard G. Barnes, 37, a sales executive. Barnes was found in the front seat of his car on Darby Road, north of the borough limits.
>
> Police Chief Jack McKay reported that Barnes apparently died of a single gunshot wound to the chest. A handgun was found in the car, and McKay said there was "evidence of foul play."
>
> Chief McKay added that the investigation into Barnes' death is continuing.

That afternoon, McKay called to discuss the case. Sal was out of the office, so he went ahead and talked to Eddie about it.

ACKNOWLEDGMENTS

Thanks are due my corner at Harcourt: Jenna Johnson, Sarah Melnyk, and Sara Branch.

A special thanks to Kelly Eismann, who created the cover art to this volume, and to Cathy Riggs, the designer for what appears inside. Also to Dan Janeck, Debbie Hardin, and Erin DeWitt for their diligence in making it all readable. The errors in the text are mine.

To the members of my writing classes, who keep reminding me of the passion of words on paper.

And to those friends, named and anonymous, who deliver kind sentiments when they're needed most.

I'm grateful to you all.